PASSION FRUIT

Also by Sue Limb

UP THE GARDEN PATH
LOVE'S LABOURS, OR FURTHER UP THE GARDEN PATH
LOVE FORTY
THE WORDSMITHS AT GORSEMERE
OUT ON A LIMB (COLLECTED PIECES)
SHEEP'S EYES AND HOGWASH

as Dulcie Domum

BAD HOUSEKEEPING

SUE LIMB

Passion Fruit

HEINEMANN : LONDON

First published in Great Britain 1995
by William Heinemann Ltd
an imprint of Reed International Books Ltd
Michelin House, 81 Fulham Road, London sw3 6rb
and Auckland, Melbourne, Singapore and Toronto

A CIP catalogue record for this title
is available from the British Library

Paperback ISBN 0 434 00278 x
Hardback ISBN 0 434 00360 3

Typeset by Deltatype Ltd, Ellesmere Port, Wirral
Printed and bound by Mackays of Chatham PLC, Chatham, Kent

For Sarah Huddlestone

ACKNOWLEDGEMENTS

Many people have helped me write this book. For assistance with background and research I am indebted to Joan Tucker, Margaret Tweedie, Richard Brown, Charles Trollope, Betty Carrillo-Shannon and Peter Campbell.

I would also like to acknowledge the invaluable historical and editorial advice of Rosemary Canter, Roy Porter, Louise Moore and Mark Harding.

Any historical, botanical or zoological absurdities are, of course, entirely my own responsibility.

1800: The Governor of Antigua had a pair of tongs made to receive objects from blacks.

Museum of Antigua and Barbuda,
Chronological History researched by D. V. Nicholson.

1

A Troubling Enigma

On 10 May 1775, a marriage was solemnised at St Mary's church, Hempshott, in the county of Derbyshire, between Frederick Wetherby and Miss Isabella Sullivan. They had met in the Assembly Rooms at Buxton, and an attachment had grown at a rate which surprised both families, and caused not a little misgiving.

For a start, there was a disparity of fortune. Isabella's father, Daniel Sullivan, had been a composer of music, a man of great promise, who died before his talents could provide much more than elementary comforts for his family. His widow and two daughters lived in some austerity in a neighbouring village. The Wetherbys, however, had made a vast deal of money out of sugar. They owned a handsome house, Hempshott Park, in the west of the county, and lived in some style.

There was a difference, too, in temper: the Wetherbys were reserved, the Sullivans ardent and outspoken. Indeed, the Wetherbys feared that in his courtship of Miss Sullivan, their son had abandoned his habitual prudence and acted with dangerous impetuosity. The Sullivans for their part felt that Isabella had abandoned her healthy impetuosity and acted with a mysterious prudence. The match was a troubling enigma.

Isabella's sister Sarah endured the deepest doubts, for since the start of Frederick Wetherby's courtship, the sisters' easy intimacy of a lifetime had been replaced by a sort of tender constraint. Isabella no longer shared the secrets of her heart: she feared Sarah's disapproval, not of Frederick Wetherby's person or character, but of his fortune, or rather, not so much the fortune itself, as the means by which it had been accumulated. In the event, Sarah's disapproval was more extensive than Isabella had feared, for she disliked not merely the fortune and its origins, but the hapless heir himself.

She held her tongue, however, and wrestled away all impulses to remonstrate with her sister, after her first few reservations had provoked a storm of tears. When the time came, she nerved herself up for the wedding with a kind of deadly calm.

'It must be his fortune,' she pondered aloud to a small wax doll with one eye – a relic of childhood and a patient confidante for almost two decades. 'For he is such a stolid, dull fellow – not to Isabella's taste, at all, I would have thought. Though she was quite bruised, I think, by Atkins.'

Isabella had endured a previous attachment which had ended badly. Tom Atkins had behaved capriciously. After a great deal of wit and compliment, dash and dazzle, he had disappeared at the very moment when Isabella had been convinced he would declare himself.

After such deceptions, the steadiness and courtesy of Frederick Wetherby had been reassuring. And Isabella was not so reckless a romantic as to consider his fortune a disadvantage. She had been content in the small house she shared with Sarah and her mother, but who can blame her if her heart stirred a little at the prospect of carriages and servants? The Sullivans had only a pony and trap, and Mollie to wait on them. Mollie was an amiable soul, but she had a laugh like a donkey. The Wetherbys in their great house at Hempshott never had to endure the inconvenience of hearing their servants laugh.

And there seemed to be so many servants at Hempshott. Isabella was dazzled by it, once she was engaged to Frederick and often invited there. But the labour of these servants, sustaining the Wetherbys' elegant life at Hempshott, was as nothing compared to the toil, far away on their West Indian estates, of the Wetherby family's slaves. The elegance of Mrs Wetherby's drawing-room, with its fine porcelain teacups and sugar bowls, depended on a world she had never seen, where women of her own age laboured, half-naked, under the whip. She never spoke of it: she never thought of it, but Sarah Sullivan had read and thought about it a great deal, and saw her sister's marriage with the Wetherbys not as a triumph, but a contamination.

The Wetherbys' sugar estates had been founded four generations earlier by Colonel James Wetherby, who had served in Cromwell's garrison in Barbados in the middle years of the previous century. The Colonel was a man whose unusual energy and ambition had made enemies as well as friends in his native land; the scars of civil war were in his soul and he resolved, upon his retirement from military service, to settle in the West Indies for good.

A legacy from an uncle enabled him to buy a small estate in the north of Barbados: by his own shrewdness and industry the project thrived, and he grew at first comfortable, then wealthy. He married a widow of Scottish decent and had a son. The Colonel's descendants proved worthy custodians of their ancestor's achievements, adding to the estate in Barbados a plantation on the neighbouring island of Sabato.

Here richer soil, and plentiful water running off the thickly forested mountain tops, greatly favoured the cultivation of sugar. Rushing rivers turned the mill-wheels that crushed the cane. The Wetherbys were able to increase their production. This was fortunate: the demand for sugar was growing, for tea and coffee drinking had become a passion in Europe. They also secured a highly profitable contract to supply the British Navy with rum – a by-product of the sugar-cane. So far the family fortunes had increased without mishap, the estates on Sabato and Barbados together amounting to more than 600 acres, and almost as many slaves.

The Colonel's great-grandson John, however, tired of the inconveniences of West Indian life. The climate did not suit him: none of the ladies attracted him. In 1748 he went to England to seek a bride, and having found one, settled in Derbyshire, buying Hempshott Park and amusing himself in improving it. He left his West Indian estates in the hands of managers, and his London agent relieved him of the fatigues of administration. He was happy.

On his son's wedding day, John Wetherby could afford to be generous in his sentiments as well as his hospitality. When his wife repeated her familiar disappointment that Miss Sullivan had scarce a farthing to her name, her husband assured her that it was of no consequence. The Wetherby fortune was more than enough to sustain their only son in comfort all his days. When Mrs Wetherby went on to lament the alarming fact that, a couple of generations back, the Sullivans had been really completely Irish, her husband only laughed.

'You are forever fretting, Sophie. Miss Sullivan will bring some fire and poetry with her, and that will be good for Fred. I like the match, and so will you, in a year or two, when they name their firstborn daughter after you.'

Frederick and Isabella duly married, and settled at Hempshott, not far from his parents, in a square new house, with large windows, high ceilings, good dry attics, a shrubbery, an orchard, a coachhouse, and stables. Isabella took great delight in the convenience of their own carriage, and especially loved the exhilaration of a ride on her own bay mare. But all too soon she had to abandon that luxurious novelty, for her physician informed her in August that she would have her first child the following spring.

Isabella was helped through the discomforts of pregnancy by her sister Sarah, who though the elder, was not yet married, nor even very much courted, despite her fine eyes. Sarah preferred to exercise her eyes with reading, rather than flashing them about in ballrooms. Indeed, Isabella feared that reading had given her sister such vehement opinions that she would quite frighten off all suitors and condemn herself to the dreaded destiny of old maid.

This idea held no terrors for Sarah. When Isabella was safely delivered of a healthy boy, her sister claimed the pleasing title of aunt, and having seen at first hand the agonies of childbirth, she felt it was an experience she was in no hurry to share, nor would it particularly disappoint her to escape it altogether.

The child was named George, after the king, and his father was delighted with him, though his Grandmamma Wetherby noticed, as he grew, that he had inherited his mother's black curls and large dark eyes, which was a pity. Still, he was Grandmamma's pet – always indulged, and very fond of sweetmeats, and knocking over furniture, and kicking the groom's old blind dog, Hector, who liked to doze by a sunny wall in the yard.

George's grandmother smiled at his boisterous ways, and his parents considered him the finest child in England, but his aunt, though she loved him dearly, found his energies more trying. Even in infancy George seemed to consider that a contempt for female

4

company, and a distaste for education, was the proper exercise of male energies. In vain did his aunt try to interest him in story-books. He would struggle off her knee and run away looking for a cupboard to ransack.

In any case, Sarah was not the sort of woman who prefers children when they are very small. Books and ideas were the engine of her existence, and she was impatient to share them fully. Since Isabella's marriage, though she had spent many weeks with her sister, there were many topics upon which she felt strongly, but dared not speak. The one to be most scrupulously avoided was slavery.

It was an abomination to her. She wept in shame sometimes at the thought that her own countrymen were engaged in a trade which involved the buying and selling of human beings. She had learnt, by reading many pamphlets on the subject, that the Africans were snatched from their native land, then transported across the ocean in the most vile conditions: on arrival in the West Indies they were auctioned like cattle, children ripped from their parents' sides without a moment for goodbyes: and all put to a life of toil, punishment and humiliation.

Of all the causes that burned in Sarah's sympathetic heart, slavery was the most painful. In 1776, the year of Isabella's first confinement, the American Colonies separated from the crown and established a society founded on the conviction that all men were created equal – though slavery persisted in America long after these noble ideas were articulated.

A storm of books and pamphlets followed, and Sarah read avidly, encouraged by a correspondence with an old schoolfellow, Elizabeth Morton, who was a Quaker and passionate advocate of the abolition of slavery. Since the previous decade there had been much debate as a result of Mr Granville Sharp's attempts to have slavery outlawed in England. Now the revolutionary sentiments coming out of America provoked increasing discussion in England, and a rebellious atmosphere on many West Indian plantations.

John Wetherby lost his happy state of oblivion with regard to business and became, for the first time, really concerned about his West Indian estates. He received disturbing news, rumours of riots and murders, though nothing, so far, touching his own plantations. Nevertheless, a journey to the West Indies seemed unavoidable. He must pluck his son Frederick from the bosom of his young wife and the smiles of little George. They must brave the Atlantic crossing and satisfy themselves that all was well with the Wetherby sugar estates on Barbados and Sabato.

They returned two years later convinced they had succeeded. Frederick was welcomed back with rapture by Isabella and George, who was by now enjoying all the tyrannies of boyhood. Grandmamma gave thanks for the safe return of her husband and only son, and permitted herself the hope that, now that Frederick was reunited with Isabella, another grandchild might soon be anticipated. Perhaps the next son would be a Wetherby in looks as well as name, with a satisfactory nose, smooth chestnut hair, and an elegant and restrained smile, not that sly Sullivan grin.

Within six months, Isabella was indeed pregnant again, but the issue was to disappoint her mother-in-law on both counts. She produced not a Wetherby boy, but a Sullivan girl. More dark eyes and unruly curls. Grandmamma sighed at this persistence of the gypsy blood. But the child was named Sophie after her, and the baby's sweetness of temper soon endeared her to everyone, most of all to her Aunt Sarah.

The baby Sophie, unlike her brother, seemed entranced by her aunt's readings, and her first word, after 'Mamma' and 'Papa' was her aunt's name, though it provided a considerable challenge to the infant tongue. 'Thawah' was the best she could manage, but this name was cherished so much by her aunt that she was rather sorry when her young niece conquered her quaint lisp and learned to talk more clearly.

Alas, Frederick Wetherby had scarce begun to contemplate the joys of a baby daughter when he had to return with his father to the West Indies. Disaster had struck the Wetherby estate in Barbados. It was not rebellious slaves, but a dishonest manager who by greed and cunning had contrived to bring the plantation to ruin. Once more Frederick and his father made their tender farewells, though with great reluctance. Isabella, deserted again so soon after her second confinement, felt she would absolutely sink beneath the weight of such solitary responsibility if Sarah were not by to comfort and assist.

The early return of Frederick Wetherby was made impossible by the sudden death of his father from typhoid, a mere two months after their arrival in Bridgetown. Frederick was master now, and it was his duty to sell all he had in Barbados to satisfy his creditors there, before establishing himself at Mount Grace, his smaller plantation on Sabato, where he began the formidable task of repairing his fortunes.

Meanwhile in Buxton, Sarah and Isabella's widowed mother had surprised her daughters by making an unexpected marriage to an elderly but hearty gentleman who could offer her comforts beyond anything she had so far enjoyed in her life. With her mother so happily established, and her sister so unhappily abandoned, Sarah naturally rejoiced in being able to settle at the New House in Hempshott for good. Eagerly she assisted in the care of the children, particularly in the guidance of her niece's mind.

George soon became too much for mother or aunt, and was sent away to school, to see if enlightenment and civilisation could be beaten into him. His sister enjoyed a much more congenial education at the hands of her aunt who, having no interest herself in fashion, gossip or other traditionally female preoccupations, did not burden her niece with them, but offered her instead wonderful stories, a love of natural history and a passion for justice. She never mentioned slavery, however. She could not trust herself on that subject.

In the holidays, Sophie wrestled, ran and jumped alongside her brother. Despite Grandmamma Wetherby's disapproval, Sophie could not be convinced that exercise was harmful, when she felt its irresistible appeal all over her body. Her mother occasionally roused herself to protest at some particularly muddy exertion, but Aunt Sarah could put a pretty persuasive case for a girl's right to a vigorous life in mind and body.

Isabella could see how her daughter bloomed, and sensibly contented herself with a plaintive demand that at least Sophie should behave with decorum whenever they visited Grandmamma Wetherby. Sophie always tried her best in this regard, though Grandmamma had become even more chilly and formal in her widowhood. But Sophie hated to upset Mamma, whom she loved passionately, so did her best not to fidget more than absolutely necessary.

Letters came regularly from Sabato, but Frederick's absence was not really keenly felt except by his wife. The years passed, and Sophie grew up knowing that she had a papa, but for her he was no more than a kind of vague idea. When George's school finally bade him a despairing adieu, he sailed out to join his father on Sabato, and was so favourably impressed with life in the West Indies that he laboured to produce a couple of letters to his mother, in which his enthusiasm shone out despite many blots and mis-spellings. A strange, intoxicating secret started to steal over Isabella: she began to dream of going out to Sabato herself.

Once the idea had taken root, she could not resist it, and only lacked the courage to reveal it to her sister and mother-in-law. A particularly awkward visit with Grandmamma Wetherby provided the occasion. The old lady found fault with her granddaughter's manners, and recommended that Sophie should be sent to school to acquire a little polish. This so wounded Isabella's heart, that she flared out:

'Why, to be sure, I shall send Sophie to school for a year or two – when I go to join Frederick in the West Indies.'

'You, my dear? Go to Sabato?' Her mother-in-law's teapot stopped in mid-air.

'Why yes, indeed!' cried Isabella, glad for once to provoke the disapproving old dame. 'If I don't go, I am sure I shall never see Fred again until I am quite an old woman, and what then is the point of my being married to him, I should like to know?'

Old Mrs Wetherby was speechless at this. But Isabella was resolved. Almost twenty years of marriage to a Wetherby had not diminished, only buried, her impetuosity, and now it blazed forth. She longed to see her husband again: it was natural.

Yet perhaps the long separation, though unnatural, had been a blessing. Isabella had been spared the discovery which must otherwise have followed, that her husband's sensibility was different from and perhaps even hostile to her own. She cherished sentimental memories of a romantic courtship and an ardent young bridegroom, and was spared the mortifying sight of a husband sliding into middle-aged indifference and irritation.

So it was with a young girl's heart that she longed to join him. Her looks and spirits had faded very little: she had escaped the ordeal of repeated pregnancies. But Sarah could not view Isabella's proposed trip to Sabato with the same enthusiasm. She feared disillusionment for her sister, and loneliness for herself, especially as Sophie, her pride and joy, was to be sent away to school.

Preparations were made, and shortly Isabella was bidding her daughter goodbye.

'Aunt Sarah will take care of you, my darling, till we meet again. I shall write to you every day, and as soon as I am settled in Sabato, if it is suitable, you shall come out and we will all be together again.'

Sophie clung to Isabella with the tenderest sobs, but was saved from absolute despair after her mother's departure by the clever and resourceful aunt, who proposed a visit to a poor family who lived by the canal, and whose spaniel had just had a litter of pups. Nothing could console Sophie for her mamma's absence so well as charity and puppies, and soon the great challenge of going away to school offered her a more prolonged and complete distraction.

After a year at school Sophie had had enough. She returned to find her aunt living in a small lodge on the edge of Hempshott Park. The New House, where Sophie and George had grown up, had been sold. It was one of her father's braver economies, encouraged by his wife's arrival on Sabato, and her delight in the island, which was communicated in rapturous letters to Sophie.

Eventually the letter arrived which the aunt was dreading, but which Sophie had been longing to receive. She read it with shaking fingers and a thudding heart.

'My darling, I miss you more than I can express, despite the comfort of being here with Papa. And now I have seen Sabato, and lived here for a while, I am confident there is no reason why you should not join us . . .' Sophie felt her skin prickle all over with joy. . . . 'Papa is sending George to England about some business, to see our agent Mr Gregory in London and order equipment, &c. George will be in London first, then travel up to Hempshott to escort you back to us. I am writing separately to Aunt Sarah about it all – I do hope she will consent to accompany you.

'George is waiting for me to finish this letter. Godspeed, my darling. I can hardly believe that in a few months I shall be welcoming you here at Mount Grace. My tame mot-mot (which is a kind of bird) is here on the verandah, at my elbow, waiting for a crust. His head is the most glorious colour – a sort of turquoise. Oh! How you will love it here! Soon we will all be together again.

'A thousand kisses – Your very loving Mamma.'

For almost the first time in her life Sophie was puzzled to find that Aunt Sarah did not share her excitement. Worse, she declined absolutely the invitation to accompany her nephew and niece on their journey.

'I can't go, Sophie – it would not suit me at all.'

'But mother says she has got used to the heat – and you are stronger than she is, I'm sure.'

'It's not the climate.'

'What then? I can't bear it if you won't come.'

Sarah paused in her packing, stared into her niece's indignant eyes, and sighed. 'My dear, you must excuse me if I just say that I don't think life on a plantation would be bearable for me.'

'Why not?'

Sarah knew that the moment she had been dreading for so many years had arrived. She could no longer avoid the subject: she must speak. Sophie's innocent bewilderment demanded an answer. With a mixture of relief and apprehension the aunt put aside the muslin gown she had been folding.

Not many words were needed to explain to Sophie the principles behind the Abolitionist cause, and to confess that her aunt had always found the idea of slavery abhorrent.

'But surely,' cried the confused girl, 'Papa would not be cruel to his slaves. I am sure he treats them kindly.'

'It is not a question, for me, of how they are treated,' explained Sarah patiently. 'It is the fact of slavery itself which is insupportable.'

Sophie was silent. She had heard the Abolitionists mentioned at Grandmamma's house, without really listening or understanding. She seemed to recall a bitter resentment towards them. And now here was her dearest aunt confessing she was of the Abolitionist party. Sophie did not know what to think. Her aunt saw her distress and gently took her hand.

'Remember, my dear, that you have an excellent opportunity, now, to observe it all at first hand. I have read much, but you are going to see everything with your own eyes. I depend on you to report to me. Tell me how things are. You may decide that I am mistaken. You must judge for yourself.'

Sophie nodded. There was relief in this idea. Her loyalty to her father's family had received a shocking jolt, but her heart was steadying again. A few hours later the delightful sense of anticipation had returned: within a few weeks she would be with her adorable mamma again, in a place where the rain was warm and the birds had turquoise heads. She could hardly wait.

All the same, the eventual separation from her aunt was most painful. The carriage was waiting; the luggage stowed; Aunt Sarah embraced her fiercely and uttered a strange gasp that was almost like a cry of pain.

'Go now – go, and God keep you safe, my darling girl!'

Sophie turned away. A freezing wind flew down off the High Peaks, straight into her face, and seemed to try to push her back into the house. She forced herself forward down the path to the waiting carriage. Once installed in her seat, she looked back. Her aunt seemed a tiny figure standing in the doorway of the cottage, her shawl pulled about her, a terrible grimace of pain flickering about her lips that was not a smile at all, though it pretended to be.

'I will write, so soon as I arrive at Liverpool!' cried Sophie. Sarah nodded, though the wind had whirled away the words. The carriage jerked and the beloved aunt was lost to Sophie's sight, though she still tasted her tears on her lips and cried bitterly herself for the first ten miles.

Then a countryside she had not seen before began to reveal itself: beautiful, though bare and bleak with winter. Sophie put away her handkerchief and, for a while at least, stopped grieving for the painful loss of what was old and dear, and turned her attention to the prospects opening before her.

2

Landfall

On the *Blackbird*, at sea, 6 February 1795

Dearest Aunt Sarah,

     I must thank you heartily for the box of remedies you sent after me. It reached us at our lodging in Liverpool. I have laid the cypress wood shavings among my garments in the chest as you instructed and hope thereby to avoid moths, worms and maggots. But I have not needed to dose myself with any of your tinctures or decoctions yet. In fact I can report myself in reasonably good health, and I hope you continue so and are not too lonely.

     We are still at sea, almost half-way through our voyage, I should guess, being four weeks out. I was only sick for the first two days coming out of Liverpool, and so soon as I was strong enough to walk on deck, I found the fresh air helped to settle my stomach to a surprising degree, so my face is become brown. George says it is disgraceful, that I look like a leathery old admiral! But I don't care.

     When we arrive at Sabato I will send this letter back with the ship. Although I can't speak of Sabato yet, I can at least assure you we are well and have had a safe passage so far. There have been no storms, indeed nothing disagreeable the whole journey. Or at least – there has been one strange thing which upset me, indeed the memory of it returns in my dreams.

     From time to time the sailors catch sharks with salt beef and pork bait. We eat shark often and it is most welcome to taste fresh fish, though it is tough and the colour is rather darker than I am used to. But one day a school of fish called dolphins came alongside, their green skin sparkling in the water. (Not like the mammal with the smile, which you shewed me in the book about Greek vase-paintings, but a fish of the same name.)

The sailors threw out their bait and a dolphin was landed. I watched, and as it died on the deck, it turned all the colours of the rainbow. I felt quite paralysed – it fixed me with its eyes and I longed to help it, but rescue was impossible. I could only watch the men's cruelty. How could I speak? They would ignore a girl's opinions. I had to go back to my cabin, and it took me some hours to recover my spirits.

George laughed at me and called me a cry-baby. I am not sure whether I like George quite so much as I used to. He is become very proud of himself, and lords it over me at every opportunity. He thinks he is such a great fellow, just because he has already been in the West Indies once. You would think, to hear him speak, that he had been a planter for years. I am almost ashamed of him sometimes, which is a very strange contrast to what I used to feel. It is disturbing.

16 March, I think – I have lost track of the days.

I am in the greatest excitement possible! For after a tedious passage of sixty days, last evening we caught our first glimpse of Sabato! First it was a faint smudge on the horizon, like a brush stroke of dark blue ink on a wet sheet of paper. We knew we were getting near, for great quantities of gulf weed had been floating on the ocean for some days. I have marvelled at the crowds of flying fish, their wings about six inches long. Huge birds are wheeling overhead. George told me they are called the magnificent frigate birds: their wing-span is about seven feet across: can you imagine anything more grand?

I was so thrilled by the birds and the first sight of land that I stood against the ship's rail for hours, and by the evening we were close enough to the island to see that the whole place was covered with trees. Its mountainous shape, and the canopy of trees, made it look rather like a gigantic animal lying curled up asleep, covered with dark fur. I stared and stared at it till my eyes ached, and George came up on deck

13

and informed me that I had missed supper, but I didn't care, I was far too excited to eat.

I've spent a lot of time on deck, though George has passed whole days playing cards. I hope he has not lost much money at it, but it is impossible to tell from his manner, which as you know is always jaunty and devil-may-care. I must put aside my letter now, for it is almost dark, and this candlelight very trying to my eyes. It gets dark very abruptly here, at about six o'clock. There is none of the gradual English twilight, though the softness of the air, here, is wonderful, even at sea: the nights have a velvet quality.

It is now morning, and I have been up on deck again, to find we are sailing alongside the coast, a bare few hundred yards from land. Strange tall trees fringe the beach, which George tells me are coconut trees, and the surf crashes on to a dazzling strip of yellow sand; I would attempt to paint it, but my paints are packed; indeed everything is packed, for we disembark later today, as soon as we have rounded the point and come into Douglastown Harbour.

There are more wonderful birds to report: pelicans flying along the coast beside our boat. When they have sighted fish, they perform a strange upward loop to gain height, then abruptly crash down with an undignified flop and a splash. It is so amusing to watch them: I laugh aloud and even Miss Brindle (a formidable starchy lady who has looked down her nose at me the whole journey) is forced to smile.

George says that at Douglastown we shall take a small rowing boat round to Mount Grace: apparently it is a journey of a few hours, depending on winds and weather, but Mount Grace is on the leeward side of the island, so the strong Atlantic gales and seas are gently modulated, and I hope to avoid seasickness.

Though I am so excited to be here at last, I cherish my memories of our days at Hempshott. Dear Aunt! You have taught me almost everything I know and I miss you more than I can express. I often think of what you said about the Abolition of slavery. Your words made a deep impression on me and I am eager to see and hear for myself how things are.

I will write to you whenever I can and be your faithful reporter.

Could I in turn beg a favour of you? That you tell me more about the Abolition movement. I wish you had mentioned it before. Do tell me whatever you can. I feel frustrated by my ignorance.

George sends his love and I will send you news of Mamma's health so soon as ever we arrive at Mount Grace, which may be tonight. Oh, I do hope so! I long to see Mamma again.

Your very devoted Sophie.

Please convey my best love to both the grandmammas, my other relatives and friends, and be sure and give the Kellys' spaniel a lot of fussing from me, next time you go down to the canal.

About five in the afternoon – an hour before sunset – a small boat came ashore on the western side of the island. As it neared the beach, four of the slaves who had been rowing dived out, and ducking through the turquoise waters, guided the boat through the surf. George followed and held out a hand to her; Sophie jumped eagerly, her shoes sank into wet sand, and a playful surge of surf buffeted into the backs of her legs. She staggered and was thrust forward on to her knees.

'I must give thanks for our safe delivery!' she laughed. 'You see, the island demands it!' But George had turned to give orders to the slaves, and did not hear.

In the privacy of her mind she did give thanks, and heartily, for she had found the last few hours in the small boat more uncomfortable than the whole two-month passage across the ocean. Now on land, however, her queasiness was forgotten: she scrambled to her feet again, advanced a few steps up the beach and looked about her. The sudden stillness of the earth beneath her feet felt very odd, and sheltered now from the sea breezes, a heavy wave of tropical heat enveloped her.

Palm trees swayed and creaked above her head. Some leaned out crazily across the shore, as if welcoming the sea. The surf boomed behind her like the slow beating of a great heart and the gentler breezes encircled her, gently stirring her ribbons and playing with tendrils of her hair. A little way inland Sophie could see rough wooden huts peeping from a riot of huge leaves.

Suddenly a white man, aged about thirty, came striding down on to the sands. He was tall and lean, with a weather-beaten face beneath a large straw hat.

'Craig!' shouted George, and the men met and embraced heartily, laughing.

'I spied your boat with my telescope,' Craig smiled, 'and I thought I would come down and welcome you.'

'This is our neighbour, Charles Craig,' George cried to Sophie. 'Craig, this is my sister Sophie.'

Charles Craig took Sophie's hand and bowed low. 'My dear Miss Wetherby, I am delighted to make your acquaintance.'

Sophie smiled and greeted Charles Craig politely, but was irritated to discover she had been spied on when she was feeling seasick in the little rowing-boat. Nor did she wish, at this moment, to be distracted from the extraordinary landscape by the demands of etiquette. The last thing she wanted to receive was a bow and a show of civility from an Englishman.

So, despite her duty to be polite, she was easily diverted by a small pig which came snortling out of the grove of coconut palms and nosed about on the beach, where a little fresh-water creek ran down to the sea. A black child, aged about four, ran out after it with a stick, but seeing her, he stopped.

'Good-day, my dear,' said Sophie softly. The child stayed for a moment, squinting into the sun, which was even now setting behind Sophie and turned her damp curls into a fiery halo. The child gave a little frightened cry and ran away, disappearing behind some trees. Sophie was disappointed. She had never been frightening before, and she did not like it.

One of the slaves who had rowed them round from Douglastown, a tall fellow called Lucas, walked past her with a heavy bag balanced on his head and led the way up to Mount Grace.

3

Carried Away

'Miss Wetherby! Would you not like a mule, or a pony, to take you up to the House?' Charles Craig was at her elbow. 'You've had a long day in a hot boat, do let me arrange for a mount for you. It can be done in an instant.'

'Thank you, Mr Craig, but exercise is pleasant after sitting so long.'

Suddenly a black boy ran up to Charles Craig and burst into a torrent of wild speech. Sophie could not understand a word; she saw from Craig's frown, however, that he was irritated by the message. He sent the boy back and turned to her.

'Some confounded problem or other, I'm afraid – my manager, Higgs, has a fever so I'm much busier than usual up at Belmont. Do forgive me, Miss Wetherby, but I must take my leave – my land is next to yours, up there – I must take this path. But I hope I may call on you soon?'

'Why – of course! That would be delightful.'

'And please give my respects to your parents.' Charles Craig bowed and disappeared up a rough track behind some trees.

George, who had been supervising the unloading of the luggage, came up and looked doubtfully at his sister. 'Old Craig's right,' he said. 'It's quite a climb, and you're only a girl –'

'*Only!*' cried his sister, 'you're an insolent dog to say so, George! I could out-walk you any day when we used to ramble in Miller's Dale. If you can walk it, so can I.'

'We'll see . . .' mused George, with his most irritating smile, offering her his arm. Sophie was forced to take it after a few steps, for the path was exceedingly slippery. But George soon tired of

17

teasing her, and turned to the more gratifying business of displaying his knowledge and experience.

'Craig's a good fellow,' he observed, as they passed along the dirt track which ran inland alongside the creek. 'An excellent shot, has the most tremendous eye. We've had great sport together. Thank God he's a bachelor. If there was some awful little wife dangling about in the background it'd spoil it all.'

'Oh, would it, indeed?' said Sophie sharply, but her brother was oblivious to her tone.

'He inherited his estate from his uncle about five years ago – mad old dog, he was, so Father says. Craig's a younger son, and was kicking his heels rather, so I expect that legacy came in well. Quite odd, the fellow's not married,' he pondered. 'And he's past thirty. Can't think why. He's handsome enough. Perhaps he don't like women much, though he was civil to you, no doubt because as my sister you are a person of some importance here. And Father's daughter, of course,' he added as an afterthought.

Sophie did not want to be a person of importance because she was somebody's sister or daughter. She would rather not be a person of importance at all. Back in Hempshott, her Aunt Sarah's neighbour Mrs Carstairs had worshipped persons of importance. 'Miss Currie and her sister Mrs Murgatroyd are, of course, very superior people,' she had whispered to Sophie once, when, walking in Buxton, they had spied two fat, spoiled-looking women, all ribbons and lace and satins that whistled importantly as they waddled along.

Two girls in rags went by in the dusk, carrying baskets of some kind of fruit. Sophie heard stifled whispers as they passed.

'We have to walk through the slaves' quarters, I'm afraid,' said George. 'We settled them down here beside the creek and the path home leads straight along.'

'But I don't mind at all,' cried Sophie, then lowering her voice, 'as long as they don't mind – it's all so interesting and new to me, don't forget, George.'

'As long as *they* don't mind!' George laughed loudly. 'You are a wonder, Sophie.'

Round the next bend in the creek were small huts made of wattle and daub and thatched with dried palm leaves. Here and there women were taking advantage of the last rays of light, carrying water from the creek to their young plants.

'They each have a small garden, as you see,' George pointed out. 'And we've given them a larger provision ground a little higher up. They grow vegetables and fruit, and so forth. It reduces the expense of feeding them. Damme, don't they stink, though! I'd quite forgot that.'

Sophie felt a spasm of embarrassment. 'I can't smell anything unpleasant,' she retorted. 'Only the earth, and the smoke, and the dung of animals.' However, she had to admit to herself that here and there the smell of human excrement was overpowering, worse than anything she had ever experienced, even in the streets around the docks at Liverpool.

Flies clustered around their heads as they walked; tethered goats gazed at them through clouds of mosquitoes. An old man sat at the door of one of the huts, his face disfigured by a huge sore. The flies were troubling him, too. Sophie noticed that one or two of the slaves had lost fingers or toes, and saw a blind child sitting on her mother's knee, white eyes writhing in her dark face.

But many of the slaves seemed healthy, and some of the younger ones especially were beautiful. Women were washing their children in the stream, feeding chickens or folding up clothes which had been spread on the bushes to dry. Smoke curled up in the still air from makeshift ovens which had been built alongside the huts. The smell of strange food hung in the air: it caught at the back of Sophie's throat.

Whatever they were busy with, the slaves all greeted George and stared at Sophie as she passed, pausing for a moment in the midst of their work. She felt a hundred pairs of eyes on her. Occasionally George would exchange a few words with a particular slave, but he did not stop. Though it was getting darker by the minute, the heat seemed to increase. They began to climb. Sophie's mouth felt parched, sweat ran in rivulets down her sides and the flies bothered her more and more. She began to wish she had accepted Charles Craig's offer of a mule. The hours spent in an open boat had weakened her more than she had realised.

'How much further is it?' she asked, pausing for a moment to wipe the hair off her face.

'Not far. Jove! It's hot, isn't it? Like a damned oven. I'd quite forgot. Still, we're past most of the slave settlement now. We can cut across the corner of this field, and then it's just a little climb and we're there. Hold on – I'll send Eli for a lantern. Eli!' A tall, shadowy figure appeared in the doorway of the nearest house. 'Run up and fetch us a lantern from the House, and meet us and light us on our way.' George's voice rang out loudly above the sleepy crooning of chickens. In the background, the peculiar singsong chat of the slaves paused for a moment. They were listening. And watching – though as the dusk deepened, they themselves seemed to disappear into the air, only the whites of their eyes or a flash of teeth betraying their presence.

Sophie's fair skin shone; her light dress glimmered; she gleamed with heat and importance. It felt uncomfortable. Had it been necessary for George to speak so loud? Eli was standing not three yards away, after all. He obeyed, his thin frame disappearing swiftly up the track ahead.

'He's a quick fellow,' said George. 'He'll soon be back. Come on. Here are the cane fields, you see. The path is more level, here.'

They were past the last of the slave huts, now. The valley had broadened out into a wide expanse of flat land, some two hundred feet above the sea. It was encircled on the landward side by steep mountains clothed in dense forest. The sheltered valley had been cleared and planted. The darkening cane looked like gigantic grass, taller than the tallest man. This strange plant had paid for her education, her clothes, her food.

'When the wind blows, it rattles.' George told her. 'Quite a curious noise. If you hear it in the night, don't worry. It's not the ghosts of dead slaves rattling their bones!'

Dead slaves. Some mute, unexpected alarm leapt in Sophie's body. But of course they must have died. In their hundreds.

'Where are they buried?' she enquired awkwardly.

'What? Who? – Oh the slaves. They have a burial ground over behind the lemon grove; we passed it on the way here. They're mostly Christians now of course, we've knocked all that pagan African nonsense out of them I think. When father first came out here twenty years ago he says a lot of them were still worshipping graven images. Such barbarians, just imagine! Of course a lot of our slaves are born here now. They take to the work better, they're not forever pining for their native land. This is their native land instead, so to speak.'

'Massa George!' a girl's voice came out of the dark, so sudden it made them start.

'What is it? Come here to me!' George replied.

A dark shape emerged from the rustling cane. Sophie could only see her eyes, but the voice sounded young. 'Massa George, you welcome home, you gone long time, yo' see de King? Mi got t'ing to tell yo', Massa, mi got plenty t'ing to say –'

'Ah – it's Ruth.' There was recognition and annoyance in George's voice. 'You shouldn't be in the cane fields at this hour. Get along home to your mother.'

'Nero beat mi Mother,' Ruth went on, although shifting her ground a little towards the slave settlement. 'Him hit her in de mout', she lose t'ree of her teeth, mi got t'ing to tell you, Massa George, you welcome home, plenty happen while you in Englan', mi speak wid you now?'

'Not now. I am taking my sister, Miss Wetherby, home. She's tired. Go away, Ruth.' The girl vanished into the night.

'Who was that?' asked Sophie.

'Oh, just a slave,' sighed George, 'a rather tiresome one, in fact. Always trying to detain one with some nonsense or other.' And he coughed, and swished at a plant with his stick. 'Ah, here comes Eli with the light. Let's wait here for him. The next bit's something of a climb.'

A bobbing light descended the hill ahead of them, taking a zigzag path. Sophie looked back along the way they had come, refreshed enough by the slight pause to take an interest in the landscape once more. The sea lay below them, reflecting the faint amber glow of the western sky. The shapes of the slaves' roofs and the palm trees were silhouetted against it.

'It's very beautiful,' said Sophie quietly.

'I like a good sunset,' agreed George, 'and it's a very pleasant climate, once you get used to the heat.'

Eli arrived, and led the way with his lantern up the path, half-paved here and there, but slippery too. Sophie followed, noticing in the lamplight the flash of his naked heels.

'It's treacherous when it rains,' said George. 'It's really the dry season now, but we do get the odd shower. There's another rough track going round the other side of the fields and up to the House. That's how we get the crop home – in wagons. But it's miles too far to walk, especially in the dark.'

Sophie did not answer. She was beginning to feel tired again, even ill. She had been quite seasick on the boat, and had had nothing to drink since.

'Not far now, old girl,' promised George. 'You must be quite fagged out.'

Sophie's head started to spin, and she clung to her brother's shoulder. 'I feel . . . rather dizzy, George – faint, I'm sorry.'

George steadied her and she sank for a moment to the ground, not wholly unconscious, but her head swimming in the dark, and the faces of George and Eli looming and melting in the lantern light above her.

'Here, you carry Miss Wetherby, Eli, and I'll take the lantern,' said George. 'I'm sorry, Sophie,' he added, giving her an awkward poke – a gesture of brotherly concern. 'I'd carry you myself but I'm so damned unfit after all those weeks on the boat. Don't mind Eli touching you – none of your Buxton manners here, you see.'

Sophie felt herself gathered up and carried towards some distant lights. As her head cleared, she clung to Eli's neck. The sweat from his shoulders anointed her cheek. She heard him grunt and felt him slip with the effort of carrying her.

'I'm sorry, Eli,' she whispered. 'Thank you so much – I'm just so tired – the heat –'

'It a'right, Miss,' he answered quietly, and she felt his breath on the hairs around her temple. He gasped as his foot hit a root, and he staggered. His breath smelt of cloves.

'Here we are,' George's voice was further away, up ahead. 'Carry her in, Eli.'

'Oh my darling Sophie! Put her down there, Eli.' It was her mother's voice.

Suddenly there was bright candlelight, and she was laid on a sofa, and Eli disappeared, and her mother's face was before her, and she felt her arms around her, and smelt Mamma's perfume. Violets.

'Oh Mamma!' she whispered. 'I'm all right, only a bit tired, and so very happy to see you!'

They embraced, and she felt tears on her face. Isabella Wetherby drew back and wiped her eyes, then beamed at her daughter, her head cocked on one side.

'Some sorrel juice first and then some tea, Flora, and a bowl of water and a sponge.' Her mother loosened Sophie's garments, and stroked her face, and a black servant girl brought some red juice with a bitter-sweet taste. Sophie sipped and was revived.

'You poor thing! We did not expect you till next week. Your father's away until tomorrow, he would never have gone if we had known you'd arrive today. You made good speed, George.' Isabella Wetherby was delighted to have both her children to fuss over. 'Why George, you have grown some great whiskers, I declare. They make him look like a highwayman, don't they, Sophie?'

A bowl of warm, sweet water came, and Sophie sponged her face and hands: so did tea and she sipped it, and then a plate of fruit, which her mother cut up and fed her, bit by bit, as if Sophie were a pet monkey.

'Here's some pawpaw, try this: you know pineapple, of course, Lord Hanscombe used to grow them in his glasshouses at Gresham, he always used to send us one when you were little, do you remember? Try one of these little bananas, dearest, they taste all Garden of Eden.' Sophie took the yellow fruit. It had a curving shape, something like a broad bean pod, but fatter. Her mother showed her how to peel it and Sophie tried a timid bite. The flesh was thick, soft, extraordinary, delicious.

Sophie's mother rejoiced to see the improvement in her daughter's looks and spirits. There was nothing wrong that a good night's sleep would not mend. Sophie was pale, but beginning to look around curiously at her new surroundings.

She saw a wide and elegant room, with a floor of polished wood and recognised the dark ruby-red rug which had been in front of the hearth in the library at Hempshott. And the Chinese jars stood on a sideboard, with jasmine cascading out of them, filling the room with its scent.

Other doors led to other rooms, but on both sides were windows, with slatted shutters that let in the night air, but kept out the largest of the moths.

'I'd love to see the whole house,' said Sophie. 'But I'm so tired, I think I'd better go to bed. Where is Papa?'

'He's gone across to see Mr Dawson at Belle Garden, about some cattle. He'll be back tomorrow. We didn't expect you so soon, my love.' Sophie's mother caressed her brow. She caught her mother's hand and kissed it, then noticed something.

'Why, Mamma,' she exclaimed, 'you never used to bite your nails.' The fingers that used to be so elegant were now ragged and raw, the nails gnawed down to the quick. Isabella laughed in embarrassment, snatched her hands away, and hid them behind her back.

'It was the anxiety, the anxiety about your journey, my dear,' she explained. 'Now you are safely arrived, I shall be at ease. Now, come along, I'll show you your room, I have had such fun getting it ready – haven't I, Flora?'

Flora, a young house slave with a mournful brow, followed as her mistress led Sophie through double doors of polished wood, along a short passage and into a room that was furnished all in white.

The bed had posts carved of mahogany and was hung with white muslin; the counterpane was a cotton patchwork of different shades of white and palest pink. A jug and ewer of white china with pink and gold roses on it stood on a small rosewood washstand beside the window, next to a walnut linen press. Her mother opened it.

'Oh, cinnamon!' The scent filled the room.

'It grows here.' Her mother smiled. 'We must parcel some up and send it to Aunt Sarah for her store.'

'What?' exclaimed Sophie. 'Does cinnamon grow on trees, then?'

'Well, where did you think it came from, my love?' Sophie marvelled. She had never before thought about what cinnamon was, or where it came from.

Not everything was strange and new, however. Beside the bed was Mr Robertson's portrait of Sophie and her mother, which had hung in their old house at Hempshott. The likeness had been taken when Sophie was twelve. Mother and daughter sat, arms around each other, in the honeysuckle bower. She smiled to see it, admiring her mother's dark curls in the portrait. Now, by the light of a candle burning in a glass hurricane shade, she saw that a few grey hairs had appeared on Isabella Wetherby's head: at the temples. It shocked her: stupidly, perhaps, for some of her school friends' mothers were completely grey.

'What is it, my dear?'

'Oh nothing – nothing, Mamma. I'm just so tired – I was dreaming, standing up.'

Sophie was skilfully undressed by her mother and maid: she felt two pairs of hands easing her out of her stays and petticoats and into a clean nightgown. Her mother's fingers were quick and cool; Flora's were warm and slower. Sophie sank down at last into her West Indian bed and thin curtains of finest lawn were drawn around her.

'To protect you against the mosquitoes,' whispered Isabella through their misty folds. 'If you hear a scuttling in the night, don't fret. We think there's a rats' nest under the house. A fellow is coming with some dogs tomorrow to get rid of them. But there are no poisonous snakes on Sabato, so if you see a snake, there's no need to worry.'

Too tired even to care about rats or snakes, Sophie smiled as her mother glided away. Then Flora blew out the candle. Sophie stared, hypnotised by fatigue, as the girl's lips pouted to kiss the room into darkness. The candle left an acrid smell drifting through the curtains, but Sophie was instantly asleep.

The smoke from Eli's fire curled towards the stars. Ashes spiralled up like moths from it. Eli yawned, stretched and rubbed his muscles.

'Eh! What a fat ass that chile got on har! She hab nuff pudding in Englan'! Mi a'most break mi back.'

His companion grinned briefly, poking the fire. 'What she smell like?'

'Sweet pork an' dumplin's.'

The men laughed. A few yards away, a stick cracked in the dark. They were instantly alert, but heard only the continuous high-pitched throbbing of the frogs and insects.

'Who dat?' cried Eli. A nightjar flitted lightly off, with a loud, high call which sounded like who-*is*-that? It seemed to mimic Eli's words. 'Mi thought someone listenin'.' He dropped his voice. 'When de boat come in dis evenin', Massa George an' Missy come up de beach, me see dat Ruth, she run away up an' hide in de cane field, wispa an' chat wid 'im.'

'She always a fool roun' him.'

'Dat mout' o'hers nebba stay shut – don't tell her yuh bizniz.' Eli's eyes flared in indignation.

His companion shook his head and brushed away the idea of Ruth with his hand, as if it were a mosquito. He stared into the dying fire. A silence spread. They could hear Eli's woman snoring in the hut.

'Yuh fool, Julius,' whispered Eli. 'Yuh miss yuh chance. While Massa George gone. When Mr Kendrick sick. De ole man on his own here. Massa Fred on his own. Mi tole yuh, yuh nebba lissen.'

'Force-ripe fruit ent got no taste.' Julius shook his head.

'What yuh waitin' fuh? Don't wait for rain to fall, den pick up wood. Massa George come home now, an' Missy here, ent goin' to make it easier.'

'Why not?' Julius looked up, challengingly. 'What you understan'? Massa George is a fool, him make mistake. Massa's mistakes is gifts for us, Eli. Missy too, mebbe: she distract Massa Fred, him never see her since she was pickny.'

Eli nodded, but sceptically. 'Yuh chile is yuh weakness, eh. But when we goin' to act?'

'When we ready. We nat rush it. We got to prepare good.'

Eli sighed. Unlike Julius, he could remember Africa, and felt he could hardly be more lost, whatever happened.

4

Taming and Naming

Out of a dream of boats and pelicans, a strange sound coaxed Sophie awake: a sound like a child with a penny-whistle, then the creak of a door. Her eyes opened. All around her the bed-curtains stirred in a faint breeze; a grid of light fell through her slatted shutters on to the wooden floor.

For a few moments she enjoyed the blessing of a large bed that stayed still, unlike the cramped bunk on the ship. The smell of tar and salt had gone; instead, a sweet, acrid scent hung on the air, that reminded her of bonfires and Aunt Sarah's jam-making.

She got out of bed and walked to the window. The floorboards were warm beneath her bare feet. She fumbled with the unfamiliar shutters for a moment, but suddenly they swung open and she gasped at the sight awaiting her. Lush, arching trees, covered with red and pink blossoms, grew around the house, intermixed with tall palms whose leaves glittered and thrashed in the wind. Her room was at the back, looking east. The mountainous interior of Sabato faced her; high above, clouds hung on the steep, forested slopes.

Then she was distracted by a nearer sight. The strange creaking sound which had woken her was bird-song, coming from a tall tree about fifty yards away. Nests hung from its branches, looking like fibrous balls suspended in nets. Suddenly a large yellow-and-black bird arrived, landed on the branch, imitated the penny-whistle and the creaking door, and dived head first down into the nest, arriving with a final jaunty cuckoo! Sophie smiled, beginning to understand a new language. The bird's cry was a sort of greeting, a celebration: *I'm home.*

She felt the sun warm on her cheek, like somebody's hand, and heard faint sounds from around the estate: footsteps, distant shouts, snatches of song, the hum of engines, a thrashing, crushing sound, and that burning-sweet smell, stronger now. *I should sing the song of that bird*, thought Sophie. Because despite this dazzling view which hurt her eyes, so different from the shy, subdued English light, this place was home now.

A light cotton gown had been laid out for her. Sophie washed first. The water standing in the ewer was pleasantly tepid, not like the icy splash at Aunt Sarah's. Washing was a pleasure here. She dressed quickly and combed her hair, impatient to explore. There was a knock at her door.

'Come in!' cried Sophie.

It was Flora, the house slave. Sophie admired the girl's soft brown skin. Yesterday, the men who had rowed her and George round the island to Mount Grace had been darker. Mahogany and ebony. Flora's complexion was lighter: a coffee colour. Really it was absurd to call these people 'the blacks' as George sometimes did. They were all the colours of the earth: just as in England, people's complexions varied, from the deep red-streaked apple cheeks of their old gardener Sam, to the parchment pallor of the Misses Cartwright, who had settled near Buxton for the sake of their livers. The slaves were no more black than the English were white.

Sophie knew that in England it was considered beautiful to be white-skinned, but now she was not so sure. There was also beauty in skin the colour of the earth, of the woods, of the rocks.

'Good morning, Flora.' She smiled. 'I'm up late, you know, because I had no sleep at all on the last night on the boat, I was so excited.'

'Yes, Miss.' Flora dropped her eyes modestly.

'Have you been on a sea voyage, Flora? It was so long and tiring, all the way from England.'

'No, Miss.'

'How old are you?' The girl shrugged. Her ignorance of her own age seemed extraordinary to Sophie, for whom every birthday had been a great event. 'Well, I'm eighteen – almost. My birthday's in June. The tenth of June.' Flora made no reply.

'Do your mother and father work on the estate?' Flora raised her eyes to Sophie's with a strange, twisted look, and shook her head.

28

The girl's enigmatic silence aroused her curiosity, but Sophie hesitated to intrude.

'So you're alone?'

'Mi got brother.'

'And what's his name?'

'Julius.'

'Ah! Named after Julius Caesar, no doubt. How interesting!' Instantly Sophie regretted her foolish words. What could Flora know of Julius Caesar?

'Well, I'm glad you have a brother.' She knew she was rattling on, but felt she must fill the silence. 'A brother is the best of all friends, isn't he? My own brother George was the greatest comfort and help to me on the journey. He made all the arrangements and never seemed to feel the heat as I did! I am glad you have a brother, Flora. So glad.'

Not just empty words, but lies. George's behaviour on the voyage had been irritating, even mortifying at times. Sophie fell silent, dismissed Flora with a nod and ventured out, soon finding herself in the large hall where she had recovered yesterday on the sofa. It was a long room, running from the front door, which opened on to the verandah, to a door at the back, which led to some steps down to the garden. Both doors were open, so the room glowed with subdued light but was not dazzling, though the air was hot.

'Come here, little one,' her mother's voice called, coaxingly, from the verandah at the front. 'Come! Here's a crumb for you. Serafina's corn-bread. You know it's your favourite.'

Curious, Sophie followed the sound and found her mother sitting on a cane chair on the verandah. Through a tangle of flowering bushes, and between the majestic palms, Sophie looked down the tumbling hillside to the glint of the sea far below. A gardener's boy was sweeping the path.

'Sophie! Hush! Look, here is my mot-mot come to share breakfast with me.' Perched on the balustrade was a beautiful bird with a turquoise crown and a strange tail: two long feathers stretching out behind it, ending in round shapes rather like tennis racquets. Sophie cried out in amazement and delight, and the bird flew away.

'You've scared him off, you naughty thing!' Her mother laughed.

'But he'll soon be back. Henry always has breakfast with me. He's a great one for fruit. He adores mangoes. I have almost got him to eat off my hand.'

Sophie bent to kiss her mother's brow.

'But you must be hungry, my darling – Serafina!' There was a moment's pause, and then a plump slave came out of the house with a slow, slopping walk, swept back a spiral of hair from her brow, sighed and waited for orders.

'Now what would you like for breakfast, my dear Sophie? Some of Serafina's corn-bread? Sorrel juice? Or tea?'

'Oh, just some juice and fruit, Mamma, thank you.' Sophie smiled.

'I'd like some more tea, too, Serafina, and bring us some of the tiny bananas, please.' Serafina nodded and vanished. She did not return Sophie's eager smile.

'We seem to have a lot of servants here, Mamma,' remarked Sophie. 'More than ever we had at Hempshott, I'm sure.'

'Yes, and I'm glad; the house slaves have an easier time of it than their brothers and sisters out in the cane fields. Though they can be sulky. I hope Flora is looking after you well, my love?'

'Oh yes! But she seems very silent, Mamma. Not at all like Lucy at Hempshott, who would tell us all her secrets. What happened to Flora's parents?'

Her mother looked up, startled. 'Happened to them?'

'Where are they? Are they dead?'

'The mother . . .' Isabella picked crumbs off her skirts and flicked them to the floor '. . . was sold, before I came. To Mr Ashton over at Pelican Bay. She was a troublemaker, I believe. So Papa said. So he sold her.'

'Does Flora see her on her days off?'

'On Sundays, you mean? Why no, dearest – it is much too far to Pelican Bay. A day's journey. More in the rainy season.'

'And what about her father?'

'He is dead. Died long ago.'

Two small children ran into the garden below the verandah, talked to the gardening boy and pulled him about in their exuberance.

'How pretty they are!' exclaimed Sophie. 'I think I shall start a school here. If Flora knew how to write, she could send letters to her mamma.'

'No, Sophie!' her mother almost cried out, then seemed to recollect herself. Caught by her warning tone, Sophie stared, waiting. She was puzzled. Mamma was usually all effervescence and gaiety, and had often been called a rattle at home. No silences had a chance to develop in the old days: Mamma always filled them with a joke, or a musical sigh, an alert question or a vivid idea. This was odd.

For a moment Sophie felt as if a cold coat had been placed quietly on her shoulders. She longed for Mamma to break the spell and soon she did, but with a strange look: loving, but with a slant of difficulty.

'I understand just how you feel, Sophie, and it does you credit that you should propose such a scheme. Indeed, when I first arrived I was so struck by . . .' Her voice tailed off and her eyes wandered beyond the verandah, beyond the trees. Sophie waited. She knew her mother's moods. One must never interrupt, just be patient.

'I thought I might set up a little school, to teach the slave children to read and write, but Papa – thought it unsuitable.'

'Unsuitable? But it would be so useful, surely. I mean, to Father as well as the slaves themselves. They could be much more use to him if they could read and write.' There was a pause.

'There are some things your father would not wish them to read.'

'What things?'

'Pamphlets, preaching rebellion . . . urging slaves to rise up against their masters. There have been conspiracies on some islands, Sophie: revolts, even. Fortunately not here. Papa believes our best chance of avoiding trouble is keep the slaves innocent of such ideas.'

'But surely the most important thing is to make them happy?' puzzled Sophie. 'For if they were contented they wouldn't rebel at all.'

Her mother did not answer, only reached out and squeezed her hand. 'You are a dear sweet creature.' She smiled. 'Look, here is the mot-mot again. Sit still now, and see how tame he is.'

Sophie obeyed for a while, though her mind was rather discontentedly busy. She was reluctant to give up her argument about educating Flora. But she would not mention it again to her mother, for a while.

'Mamma, do you know what happened to Flora's father?' Sophie asked in due course. 'What did he die of?'

Her mother raised her hand slowly to shield herself from further questions, as if to fend off the heat of an invisible fire. 'Hush,' she murmured, 'you'll frighten the birds. Look! There's a little humming-bird, by that bush over there. The forest is full of them.'

Sophie watched the tiny creature hang in the air, held there by the power of its wings, which beat audibly with a high fierce throb like a minute engine. 'I must see the forest!' she whispered urgently, not wanting to disturb the bird. 'Can I go there today, Mamma; just for a short walk?'

'Not today, my dear,' her mother answered. 'You shall see my garden, though. I have a fine bird table there.'

'Tomorrow, then?'

'I think not, darling. Father would not like it. You are so new arrived from England. You must take things slowly and get accustomed to the climate. Remember how quickly you got ill last night.'

'Oh, I won't get ill again!' cried Sophie. 'That was just because of the journey. Don't nag, Mamma! Aunt Sarah packed a whole box of medicines in my chest and I never touched one the whole voyage out.'

'Well, let's hope we never need them.' Her mother smiled. 'Ah look: your breakfast has arrived.'

Sophie welcomed her fruit and juice with a hearty appetite, but afterwards, though her eyes were turned towards the sea, she felt distracted by the strange whoops and high whistles echoing in the forest canopy behind the house. At her back she sensed the massive bulk of the mountain. Clouds hung on its face. Sophie's feet burned with the effort of keeping still.

'Couldn't I just go for a very little walk, today?' she pleaded, squeezing her mother's hand like a child begging for a treat. 'Oh please, Mamma!'

'Not today, dear, but you have a pleasure this afternoon to look forward to.'

'What's that? Is it indoors?'

'Well first of all, Papa will come home. Won't that be exciting? You haven't seen him for years. You're quite strangers. When he last saw you, you were a baby; look at you now!'

'Yes, I'll be glad to see Papa, though I'm rather nervous of it.'

'Well, he's longing to see you again, you can be sure. And after Papa gets back, there's another treat.'

'What's that? Something as good as walking out in the forest?'

'Oh, much better, and not half so dangerous. Charles Craig from Belmont, our neighbour, you know, has asked if he may call. You met him yesterday, George tells me, down on the shore when you landed, but he was called away. I think he must have been quite struck by you, my darling. He doesn't normally come and see us from one week's end to the next. Now to the most exciting question of the day.' Her mother's eyes sparkled teasingly. 'What will you wear?'

5

Quite a Pig

'There's no need to put on your stays here, Sophie.' Her mother was helping her unpack the boxes which Aunt Sarah had prepared with so much care. 'I have quite left off mine, for comfort and coolness.'

'Oh good!' cried Sophie. 'I'll burn them, then. Horrid things; I hate them.'

'Don't be so rash, my dear, you'll need them when you return to England.'

'If I needn't wear stays here, that's a good enough reason for never going back to England again.'

'Look: we've made you this loose dress of Barbados cotton. I have an excellent seamstress here, Juno. She is Flora's aunt. See – it's that shade of pale green that suits you so well. Though I fear those measurements Sarah sent me were not quite right. You have grown, my dear.'

Her mother shook out a dress that had been folded in the linen press. Sophie dived eagerly into it and Flora laced it at the back. It had short sleeves, was gathered under the breast and fell in liquid folds to Sophie's feet. After the stays and petticoats she was used to, the feeling of freedom was exquisite.

'I wonder if it's not too low in the front,' pondered Sophie's mother.

'Oh no, Mamma, I like to feel the air on my skin.'

'Ah, but the sun, my dear; promise me you won't walk about in the heat of the day. Your fair skin will get dreadfully burned. But wait! Juno did make you a white short jacket, here . . .'

Sophie tried on the jacket. 'Well, mother, I promise I'll wear the jacket when I go out, but I'm already too hot in it, so you mustn't

34

mind if I take it off now.' She flung the jacket off again. Flora folded it and put it back in the cupboard.

'I must say,' Sophie's mother looked critically at her daughter's figure, 'you have developed a lot since I saw you last. I am sure you don't take after me in that way.'

'No Mamma, you're as tiny and trim as a swallow.' Sophie smiled. 'It's Father's family where the great bosoms are. Not that Papa himself sports one, but I've often noticed that Grandmamma's bosom comes around the door some time before Grandmamma. Oh dear. I suppose I can't escape it, then.'

Sophie glared at her reflection in the looking-glass. To her a bosom was merely a nuisance, something that got in the way. She had always tried to ignore hers. But this green dress had a curious effect. True, it emphasised and half-revealed her breasts, but Sophie was struck also by something subtler. It seemed to make her look more womanly in general. Her shoulders, neck and throat shone like alabaster against the shadows of the shutters behind her.

'I know that *décolletage* is very much the mode,' pondered Sophie's mother, 'but I fear this is a little too much so. Your father might not like it. I think I will ask Juno to set in a little lace ruffle, to run all around the neckline, for modesty's sake.'

'But mother! I want to wear it today. I love it.'

'Well, you may wear it today, as it is, and Juno shall put in the ruffle tomorrow.'

'Oh good!' Sophie pirouetted about and smiled at her reflection. 'I've never felt so comfortable in my life. Horrid old stays! I shall never wear them again. You're so lucky, Flora; you've never had to wear stays, have you?'

Flora's lithe figure moved sinuously in her thin chemise. She was small and slender, and her walk had a relaxed music which Sophie envied. She had always felt gauche, herself. And yet this dress helped. Standing still in it, she looked almost presentable after all.

'There is something strange,' mused Isabella Wetherby, gazing at her daughter's mobile form, 'in first seeing one's daughter as a young woman. You have grown up a lot, it seems to me, in the last eighteen months.'

'Ah, but you know Mrs Rouse's Yorkshire puddings,' Sophie laughed. 'And her goosegog tarts and preserves. Grandmamma was forever stuffing me – I think she was fattening me up like a Michaelmas goose.'

'She always liked to see young people bonny,' nodded her mother. 'Indeed, I think she thought me quite a useless little thing.'

'Well, you're smaller than me now,' said Sophie. 'And thinner – really, you have lost weight, Mamma.'

'Sometimes I am a little disordered – in the stomach,' Isabella murmured, examining the back of the dress. 'You must be careful what you eat, here. But it's nothing. Most of the time I am well.' Reassured, Sophie kissed her mother, but then caught Flora's eye in the looking-glass, and felt guilty at her own happiness.

'But Mamma,' she whirled around, 'Flora must see her mother again soon, mustn't she, please? It's the first thing I shall ask Papa for, when he arrives.'

'You mustn't bother him with anything at all when he first arrives,' warned her mother. 'He will be tired and hot from his ride.'

'I'll be tactful, I promise. I'm determined Flora shall see her mother, though – I missed you so much when I was away, even though you've done nothing but lecture me since the moment I arrived!' Mother and daughter laughed, and embraced again. But Flora looked away.

At half-past two Sophie heard the sound of a horse's hoofs in the yard behind the house. She ran to the corner of the verandah, peeped into the yard and saw a man dismount, but it was not Papa: this man was quite grey-haired and stout. He handed his horse to a black groom and, mopping his brow with a huge handkerchief, headed for the steps up to the house.

Sophie flew back to her mother's side, not wishing to be seen by the stranger. 'Mother!' she whispered. 'It's not father, it's a visitor. He's coming up the steps now!'

'No need for panic.' Her mother smiled. 'I expect it is Mr Higgs come to talk to Father about the horse-breeding.'

But a few moments later, unannounced by anyone, the stout, middle-aged gentleman appeared on the verandah, threw off his coat, kissed Sophie's mother boldly on the cheek and then turned to Sophie and stretched out his hands. 'So this is my little daughter,' he exclaimed. 'Good God! You have quite grown up, my dear.'

Sophie was staggered. Father? Surely not. She had cherished his likeness from a miniature, taken when he was a young man. The years, and the tropical sun, had done their damage. His face was wrinkled and weather-beaten. He looked almost an old man; Sophie felt dismayed.

'Quite the young lady . . . quite the young lady,' he marvelled, admiring her at arm's length. 'And did you have a good journey, my love? No storms, no seasickness?'

Sophie assured her father that the voyage, though tedious, had been without danger and that she was delighted with her new home.

'The birds are astonishing,' she exclaimed. 'I want to study the Natural History of Sabato. I'd like to go out into the forest, Father; I want to see the birds and animals that live there.' There was no point in deception, and he looked so genial and pleased to see her that she suspected plain speaking would only endear her to him.

'Oh, no need for that.' He waved the idea aside. 'I can think of something much better. Julius can make you a big birdcage, and whatever bird you fancy, we can get the fellows to trap you some, and you can have all the pleasure of them here, without the least exertion.' He smiled indulgently and stroked her hair. Sophie hesitated. A warning look from her mother implied that she must not pursue the subject, or contradict her father about it.

Sophie's heart rebelled. She hated birds in cages. Years ago, cousins of hers had kept a goldfinch in a cage. Left alone for a moment in their parlour, Sophie had opened the poor creature's door and placed the cage next to a window. She wanted it to fly straight out into the air and disappear over the meadows, but strangely, the bird had crouched on its perch and ignored the opportunity. Her cousins, coming in just then, had alerted her parents, and Sophie had been sent to her room for the rest of the day: imprisoned herself for trying to assist an escape.

'What a good idea!' cried her mother. 'We could make a big, airy cage, Sophie dear, like that aviary we saw in the park at Buxton, with branches in it and room for the birds to fly up and down. Julius is extraordinarily clever at making things.'

'Oh yes – he's Flora's brother, isn't he?' Sophie recollected. A sharp look from her mother warned her not to raise the subject of Flora's absent mother.

After a few grumbles about the state of the cane harvest and the need to mend a roof of one of the stables, Mr Wetherby walked indoors to rest and wash. His wife went to the kitchen to give Serafina orders for supper. Charles Craig was coming to sup with them: taking tea had been thought too transient a pleasure to offer their neighbour. Sophie enjoyed her half-hour of solitude on the verandah by taking out her sketchbook and beginning to trace the shape of the nearest tree, though she was still not used to the heat and every action, even sitting down, seemed an effort and had to be performed slowly.

There was a step behind her: George arrived on the verandah. He pulled her hair gently, then admired her sketch and afterwards her dress. 'I say, Sophie, that dress is a stunner,' he exclaimed. 'Take care you do not pop out of it tonight, or Craig will choke on his callaloo.'

Sophie blushed furiously. She had forgotten everything except the perfect coolness and freedom of her dress and had been sitting carelessly sprawled in her mother's old cane chair; now here was George winking and ogling at her like an old lecher, forcing her to be polite and careful and public again. She leapt to her feet and smacked him hard across the nose with her sketchbook. 'Don't be so vulgar,' she snapped. 'I hope Mr Craig has better manners, and if he hasn't, I'm sure I hope I never see him again.'

Charles Craig did have better manners, of course. His eyes never wandered once from Sophie's glowing cheeks and freckled brow. She seldom spoke, except to add a detail to George's account of their journey, or answer a question of her father's as to the health of his relatives in Derbyshire, but when she did, Charles Craig's eyes seemed to turn in her direction with the greatest calmness and civility.

Whilst he was engaged in discussing business matters with her father and George, Sophie studied his face. She could see that he would be thought handsome, even in England where there were so many more men to compete for female attention. She liked the bright sky-blue of his eyes. They made him look astonished and innocent when he was surprised: qualities she was not used to associating with the male sex.

His nose was perhaps a little too long. His mouth, though thin, fell easily into a smile. The smile was crooked, but she liked it the more for that. Sophie was not interested in classical perfection. There was a hint of untidiness which pleased her. His fair hair was thick and unruly, and often fell across his face when he dived into laughter. Sophie noticed that his were square working hands, not the soft manicured paws she had seen on some men of leisure.

All this, together with the conviction that though he was thirty he had not as yet lost a single tooth, would have recommended him to any young woman as an agreeable companion at table. She was contented to admire him in a quiet way, though she hoped that she would not find herself expected to carry on a private conversation with him later in the evening. Grown-up men and women talked in a particular fashion which Sophie had no interest in acquiring: a game in which nobody said what they really felt and everything was pretence.

Sophie was still enough of a child for the food to interest her greatly. They began with a soup called callaloo, made, as her father explained, from the leaves of the dasheen plant. It tasted earthy, something like spinach, but Sophie liked it more at every spoonful and accepted a second helping.

'Very good, Serafina,' smiled her mother, as the comely cook and her assistant, a gawky girl called Viola, cleared the soup dishes. It was her mother's finest Worcester china, Sophie noticed. She was surprised that it had been brought out for only one guest.

Next came baked chicken, something Sophie had always adored, served with some fried vegetables.

'Plantain and christophene,' explained her mother quietly. 'Sophie is new to West Indian cookery, of course.'

'And how do you like it?' Charles Craig smiled across the candles.

'Sophie loves any sort of food, she is always a pig over my Aunt's apple dumplings,' George grinned. 'Don't you think she is grown quite plump, Mother?' Sophie burned with indignation, and her mother frowned at her son.

'Every mother, no doubt, thinks her daughter a beauty,' she remarked sharply, 'and I confess I would not have Sophie altered in any particular.'

'Amen to that,' agreed Charles Craig, and with perfect tact he

39

smiled gently at the mother, not the daughter, sparing her the ordeal of a stranger's eyes at such a moment. Sophie was grateful.

At length she and her mother withdrew to her dressing-room to repair the ravages of the evening, leaving the men to talk business.

'Powder your shoulders, Sophie,' suggested her mother. 'You are all shiny. I shall ring for Flora to see to your hair.'

Sophie saw, in the looking-glass, that strange new self she had met earlier, her white body gleaming with the heat. It looked like a woman pretending to be her, and Sophie found the reflection half-enchanting, half-unnerving. She had seen how a tropical climate had worn out her father's looks in a decade. Was she herself now going to ripen and rot with the same haste?

Viola was washing the dishes. Julius, who had called in to the kitchen to see his sister, had been prevailed upon to bring in more water from the pump. Serafina, carrying in some dirty pudding plates, immediately noticed that her assistant had been distracted. 'Yuh rinse out dis pat again, Viola,' she exclaimed. 'Yuh leave grease on dat, Missus gib me a bawlin'. And don' drop dis china, dis de bes' china, if yuh break eben a little piece, we all get a beatin'.'

Flora was sitting at the kitchen table, finishing the last scraps of left-over baked chicken. Her brother leaned across and stole a morsel from her plate. 'Dem hardly leave us eben a scrap,' he remarked.

'Dat Miss Sophie, she eat like a young hog.' Viola, who though timid before company, was malicious in private, grinned. 'When she marry, she husband goin' to put de ring on har nose – stop her diggin' up de neighbour's eddoes.'

'Eben har mammy tell har she grown too big,' added Flora, cleaning her plate with a morsel of corn-bread. 'If she laugh too much tonight she goin' to bust outta dem clo'es.'

'What she look like naked?' asked Julius mischievously.

'Please nat talk so in mi kitchen!' insisted Serafina, folding her big arms and glaring at him. 'If Missus hear one word o'dat, she get de switch out and then yuh gonna feel dat smartin' good.'

'She look like every woman do,' shrugged Flora.

'What she say to you? She hard on you?' asked her brother.

'No, she just curious. She ax mi dis, ax mi dat, where mi mammy, where mi daddy and so.'

Viola sniggered, but Julius silenced her with a glare. 'Keep yo' mout' shut,' he said, sweeping all three women with a severe look. He walked towards the door.

'Where yuh goin' now?' asked Flora.

'Meetin' at Belmont.'

A bell rang.

'Eh, they finish dinner now. De ladies want yuh!' cried Serafina, ever alert to the possibility of punishment. Flora leapt up, wiped her hands hastily and sped off to her next task.

6

A Degree of Liberty

Sophie applied powder to her shiny shoulders and Flora repaired her hair; then she and her mother went to sit in the library, drank coffee and remembered old jokes about old Mr Worden, one of their neighbours at Hempshott. Eventually they heard the men's footsteps in the hall and the door was flung open, and somehow Sophie feared that Charles Craig was going to come and sit beside her – yes! Here he came, blue eyes shining in the candlelight, and the request, courteously made, that he might sit between the ladies on the sofa, was granted by her mother.

She felt his weight and warmth arrive next to her, and she smiled, stupidly she felt, at her knees. Sophie's father engaged his wife's attention and George busied himself about some books at the other end of the room. Sophie realised she was now going to have to make conversation with Charles Craig; it was entirely her own responsibility and the awful burden of it, as she turned to face him, struck her quite dumb.

'So . . .' Charles Craig smiled at her. 'How do you like Sabato, Miss Wetherby?'

'Well, I've been indoors all day . . . Mother says I must get used to the climate slowly and it is indeed so hot – It's beautiful, what I've seen, not that I have seen much, you know.' Sophie bit her lip. She was stammering like a schoolgirl. It was hard to return Charles Craig's steady gaze. She felt like an impostor somehow.

'Yes. It is the most beautiful island of all, I think.'

'Oh? You've seen others then?'

'Well, yes, Antigua and Barbuda, where I went to see some cattle. And of course Barbados.'

'George told me you inherited your estate from your uncle?'

42

'Yes. I hadn't a thought of it. He had much nearer relations. But he was a strange old fellow. Quite a recluse. I came out here to see about getting a contract for my father – Barbados cotton – we are manufacturers in Lancashire. As I was hereabouts, I came to see my uncle, stayed a while, gave him some company – he liked me, I suppose.'

'And what is your estate like?'

'I like the situation. It's higher up the mountainside: cooler, more secluded. You must come and see Belmont so soon as ever you are . . . able.'

'I would like that above all things.'

This was politeness: what Sophie wished to do above all things was to go into the forest. But perhaps the path to Belmont lay that way. She wondered when permission would be granted for this excursion.

'I hope George may bring you.' Craig sipped his coffee. His eyes never left her face. 'George is always coming up to see me. We hunt in the forest, we play cards . . . I think your father must be concerned that I am leading his son into dissolute habits.'

'What?' Sophie's father caught Charles Craig's last words. 'What d'ye say, Craig?'

'Am I leading your son astray?' Charles Craig fixed Frederick Wetherby with a mock-innocent appeal.

'Well, sir, if you are, I can't think of a man I'd rather entrust with that duty.' Mr Wetherby beamed. They all laughed.

'Education has always attracted me,' said Craig. 'And if we get another hurricane, and the crop is destroyed, and we're all bankrupted –'

'Which Heaven forbid!' cried Sophie's mother. 'Don't speak of it, Mr Craig, I beg, or it may come to pass!'

'You aren't superstitious, are you Mother?' cried George, grinning.

'Oh certainly I am, George – I have thrown the salt over my shoulder a thousand times, you know. But Mr Craig, do go on – I interrupted you, it was most impolite, I am a horrid old rattle.'

Sophie was glad to see that since the arrival of Charles Craig her mother's spirits were sparkling again.

43

'Well, I was saying if I am ever bankrupted, I think I shall turn schoolmaster.'

'What! In Latin and Greek and drinking and shooting?' laughed George.

'Would you go back to England, then?' asked Sophie's mother.

'Possibly. But I'd rather start my own school, somewhere in a drier climate. Buenos Aires perhaps.'

'Why not start a school here!' cried Sophie. 'I mean, not just if we're all bankrupted – why not start one in any case?'

'A school, my dear? What, do you miss yours so much?' Her father winked.

Sophie sensed that she was venturing into dangerous waters, but she plunged on. 'No, it wouldn't be for me; I'd like to teach in it. Teach the slaves, I mean. I want to teach Flora to read, but . . . mother says I mustn't.' A glance passed between Mr Wetherby and his wife. There was a pause.

Sophie's father hesitated for a moment, then decided on a smile. 'Look at the girl! She only arrived yesterday, and already she's directing us into good works. You'd better keep away, Craig, or she'll have you building a hospital and an orphanage as well.' The men laughed. Sophie wished she had not spoken.

'A certain amount of education, perhaps, would do no harm –' ventured her mother. 'And the old ladies at Good Hope have a small school there, I believe – I must really go and see them, but I dread the journey.'

'A school! Why, Isabella, it is nothing but a shack by the ocean, no, not even that – an awning only, and Miss Hambledon gathers a few children there now and then, and I suppose it gives her something to do, though I thought she was mad as a March hare, last time I was there. Her sister is a sensible old dame, however.'

'Could I go and visit them?' asked Sophie.

'There is no road,' her mother explained. 'To get there, you'd have to go out from our shore in a small boat, my dear, and have a couple of fellows row you down the coast a little way.'

'Oh.' Sophie did not relish the thought of another journey in a small boat quite so soon after her last ordeal. 'That's a pity. But why could we not have a school here, Papa?'

'My dear, I am proud that my slaves here at Mount Grace are the most nearly converted to Christianity of any on the island. When old Hetty died last month they had a very decent funeral, none of that barbaric yelling and breast-beating.'

'I must disagree with you, Mr Wetherby.' Sophie sensed, by the sudden tension in Charles Craig's voice, that a serious subject had been broached.

'And why, pray?' demanded her father. 'No religion could be more suited to their condition. I find they are become infinitely more docile in the past ten years. They know that any suffering in this life, if patiently borne, will be rewarded in the kingdom of heaven.'

'I see dangers there.' Charles Craig shook his head. 'Beyond your good intentions. I would not attempt it.'

'Why not, sir?'

'There is such a profound difference between us,' Craig turned to the women on each side of him, 'is there not, ladies – between us Europeans and our slaves. In appearance, in habits, in beliefs, in every way. I appeal to the ladies because the female sex is in my opinion the most refined part of our civilisation. I ask you: could you live as they do? Could our womenfolk labour in the cane fields, under that sun, for hours? Could they cook outdoors on a heap of sticks; sleep on a dirt floor? Not for the world. No. The very foundation of plantation life lies in the difference between us and the Africans, and anything we do to bring them closer to our condition of life is dangerous.'

'How can it be dangerous for them to hear about the Gospels, the teachings of our Lord?' thundered Frederick Wetherby.

'Give them our religion and the question naturally arises: what else of ours will they feel entitled to? Baptism today; freedom tomorrow,' warned Craig.

'But Mr Craig,' Sophie's mother burst out, 'of all the gentlemen we know, you are one of the most tender-hearted to your slaves! George has told me of an occasion when you dressed a slave's injuries yourself, with the gentlest care.'

'I may have done so.' Charles Craig flinched for a moment, then recovered. 'But, Madam, it is beside the point, if you will forgive me. My slaves are African in origin, even if many of them are now born here. I practise my religion; they practise theirs. One of my slaves was sick two years ago; an obeah man came from Moriah and cured him with some kind of herbs – when there was nothing I could do for him and the poor fellow seemed doomed.'

'More fool you, to tolerate obeah on your property!' cried Mr Wetherby. 'It's nothing but barbaric nonsense, claptrap. They're lunatics, these obeah fellows. Transportation's too good for them – they used to be burned alive, and if I had my way, they would be still.'

Sophie was alarmed. She wished her father would not shout so. But Craig insisted on prolonging the argument, though he tried for a quieter tone.

'You can't stamp it out: it's what they believe in. You might as well tolerate it and use it for your own purposes.'

'Damned nonsense, man, of course you can stamp it out!' cried Frederick Wetherby. 'That's what we've done here at Mount Grace. Our slaves have left all that superstitious hocus-pocus behind them.'

There was a brief pause. Sophie cringed. She hated her father's anger, and wished she could leave the room. But she was fixed there: bound to endure this argument, but not expected to join it, nor daring to, either.

Charles Craig took a deep breath. Sophie heard it and dreaded it. She knew that he had not given up and feared worse might be coming. 'Forgive me, Mr Wetherby, but I am not as confident as you are of your success.'

'What do you mean, sir? Explain yourself!'

'I heard something a couple of weeks ago. Drumming, in the night. I got up and went to investigate. It wasn't Saturday night or Sunday, when they generally dance and make merry. It was a Wednesday, I remember. I followed the sound a little way into the forest. Behind my cistern, you know, there is a path leads in, and I saw a group of them round a tree, drumming, and dancing themselves into a frenzy. I disturbed them and they fled – most I recognised as my people, but the leader, I am sure, was none of mine. He looked very like that tall fellow of yours: Eli.'

'He'd better not be an obeah man!' roared Frederick Wetherby. 'I'll search his hut first thing in the morning, and if I find anything

46

there – any damned herbs, or beads, or cats' skulls, or teeth, or any such witchcraft trash – I'll have him flogged till he begs for mercy.'

An awkward, prickling silence spread through the room. Sophie trembled. Eli, who had carried her up to the house on the night of her arrival, who had grunted and stumbled and hurt his bare feet, dashing them against rocks and roots for her sake, now threatened with flogging by her own father! Her pulsed raced. She did not dare to look at anybody.

Frederick Wetherby cleared his throat, rumbled a bit, and glanced at his wife, as if for help.

'Well, now you've got that off your chest, I'm sure you feel better, Frederick.' She smiled nervously. 'Frederick's always very fierce against witchcraft. He made me burn my broomstick when we married!'

Dear Mamma, thought Sophie as everybody laughed, clever Mamma, you've rescued us.

Talk turned for a while to Isabella Wetherby's plan to paint the verandah, and the difficulty of getting the right sort of paint, and how well Mr Ashton over at Pelican Bay had done up his house, so it was scarcely recognisable. Sophie remembered that Mr Ashton was the man who had bought Flora's mother, but she knew better than to make any reference to it, or indeed any remark at all. The embarrassment left by her father's rage still seemed to hang in the air, like fumes after the eruption of a volcano, and the party broke up early.

'I hope, Miss Wetherby, I may have the pleasure of showing you Belmont soon.' Charles Craig took her hand and lifted it to his lips, and for an instant she felt his warm breath on her fingers. Sophie was not used to having her hand kissed. She felt confused, but again her mother flew to the rescue.

'Sophie would love that, I'm sure, Mr Craig. George will bring her up in a few days, when she's got used to the heat.'

He bowed, his blue eyes washed over her for a moment, then he was gone.

Alone in her room, Sophie did not feel she could go to bed. Flora came and asked if she wanted any help, but Sophie dismissed her. She walked up and down, her mind racing. Suppose Eli did have something in his hut that her father would think was evidence of

47

witchcraft? She could not bear the thought of him being flogged. There was nothing she could do, except go to bed and try to stop thinking about it. But still she walked up and down, stopping occasionally to stare out at the stars. Were they holes in the floor of heaven? Would it help to pray? If Eli had his own god, would her God still help him? Her mind tired of stumbling through these tangled thoughts and returned hastily to practical matters.

Perhaps she had done wrong to dismiss Flora. If she had told her what her father intended to do in the morning, Flora might have been able to go down to Eli's hut and warn him. But it was too late now. Flora had gone to bed. Sophie did not know where the house slaves slept. There were no sounds of human activity in the house, only the shutters rattling in the wind, and outside the odd chirp or whoop of some night creature. A thought came into her head: a hope, a reckless urge. She must go down and warn Eli herself. She knew the way and she remembered which was his hut. She tiptoed out of her room and hesitated. The house was still. As she crept to the main door some boards creaked, but nothing stirred, so she hastened noiselessly on and stepped out into bright moonlight.

For a moment she paused, getting her bearings. She trembled, but not just with fear. Out of doors at last! And at a time when nobody would be about to stare at her or stop her from doing as she wished. The atmosphere was not in the least sleepy: the air, though soft and warm as a caress, smelt fresh; the stars seemed to blaze down with a brilliance she had never seen in England, and all around her throbbed a chorus of high-pitched, liquid sounds. This orchestra must be composed of the voices of thousands of tiny creatures – she bent down and peered in the moonlight, followed one loud call to its source and discovered a tiny frog, no bigger than her fingernail, sitting under a leaf.

But now was no time for Natural History. She found the hillside path and scrambled down it, stumbling now and then, clutching on to trees for support and trying to make no noise. She did not want to alert any dogs; she had no excuse to be here, and if her father found she had left the house she would have to face his fury. It would have been unthinkable even in England to leave the house at night, though as a child she had enjoyed some freedom in the daytime, allowed to ramble about with George at Hempshott.

48

But this was different. Apart from the strangeness of the place, the unknown dangers of climate, birds and beasts, deliberately scrambling down the path to the slave village was bad enough; that she was on an errand which subverted her father's authority would make her adventure an outrage in her parents' eyes, she knew. All the same, she went on. Soon she was at the foot of the hill, then sped along the edge of the cane field. Here were the first slave huts. She recognised Eli's by the scarlet creeper which hung in festoons around the eaves.

She tiptoed through his little garden and tapped on the door, which was a thin sheet of woven palm leaves. 'Eli!' she whispered. 'Eli!'

Something stirred within: someone spoke. Sophie did not understand the words, but it was a woman's voice. There was the rustle of movement within, the door twitched open and the tall figure of Eli peered out, almost naked in the moonlight. He looked astonished to see her.

'What you want, Miss?' he hissed.

'Oh, I'm sorry, Eli, I'm sorry to disturb you, but somebody told my father tonight that you were – a – I can't remember the word, is it obea? Obi? Anyway, he means to come and search your home first thing in the morning, I wanted to warn you – if he finds any – any suspicious things, he means to have you flogged. I'm sorry, I'm so sorry, but I just wanted . . .' Sophie backed away, her message done.

'Go now,' whispered Eli. 'Yuh go now. If Massa see yuh here . . .' He rolled his eyes in foreboding.

'Yes, yes,' Sophie nodded. 'Good-night!' and she flitted back up the path.

Soon her progress slowed, however. The climb was hard; it was late. Sophie managed it better than on the evening when she had first arrived, but she had to stop several times to catch her breath. On one occasion she heard a rustle in a bush nearby and a huge rat-like shape darted across the track less than a yard away. Sophie suppressed a cry. There had been rats in Grandmamma's barns at Hempshott and she had watched George's dog, Tess, ratting in the stable yard. There was no excuse for hysteria now, just because it was dark. She must compose herself.

She was still shaking slightly, though, when eventually she reached the top. The white mansion glimmered in the moonlight;

the scent of jasmine hung everywhere. The contrast with the dark huddle of slave huts was striking. Sophie sped up the steps and tried the front door. It was locked. Panic flew through her. Who had locked it? Did they know she had gone out? Excuses swarmed through her mind as she crept down off the verandah and skirted round the side of the house. There was still the back door to try – the one conveniently nearer to her own room. As she passed some rough shacks at the edge of the yard her eye was caught by a movement among the buildings where the sugar-processing was done.

A door opened and closed; a shadowy figure emerged, slithered through the bushes and ran silently towards her. It was too late to hide. Sophie was paralysed. It was George.

'Sophie! What the deuce are you doing out at this time of night?'

'I was just talking a walk. I couldn't sleep and Mamma wouldn't let me out all day, you know.' Sophie lied boldly. 'But I might as well ask what you're doing yourself?'

'I couldn't sleep either,' said George. 'I'd left some papers in the office – I wanted to check something about the new engine – so.' He gave her his bold, daring stare. 'That's that. The parents wouldn't understand it, though, so – if we both keep silent, no harm will be done – hey?'

Sophie agreed and they went up the back steps together. She'd had to lie to George, but she was annoyed that George had lied to her. He was certainly up to some mischief, but it was a waste of time speculating about his secrets. As she got into bed, she was simply glad to have managed her errand without discovery. She was grateful to Eli for carrying her up to the house, the day of her arrival. It would be unbearable if he were flogged. But perhaps now all would be well.

7

What a Life

Sophie slept late the next day. The escapade of the previous night had exhausted her, following so soon upon the exertions of her long voyage, and the climate seemed to sap her strength. She wallowed in sleep. It was noon when she joined her mother on the verandah.

'So. You've slept well I hope, my darling?'

'Yes thank you, Mamma.' Sophie yawned, settled herself beside her mother and enjoyed a breakfast of fruit and chocolate brought by Serafina. In the high trees, the black-and-yellow birds were flying to and fro, uttering their strange creaking call.

'What is that bird?' asked Sophie.

'I think, my dear, it is called the Golden Orupendula.' Her mother smiled, looking around her with satisfaction. 'Although I've heard the slaves call it the Pogga, I think. Ah, what a life this is! With nothing to bother us save the naming of birds – Oh by the by, Sophie, I have asked Julius to come and see you this afternoon so you may give orders to him about the making of the birdcage.'

Sophie nodded, but she was preoccupied: burning to know if her father had searched Eli's hut, as he had threatened to do, and whether he had found any incriminating things. But at the moment she did not dare to ask.

Her mother noticed her abstraction and thought it was due to Sophie's misgivings about birdcages. 'We can make it a very large cage, my darling,' she said. 'This verandah is quite wide. They will have enough room to fly up and down.' Sophie nodded, without much enthusiasm. 'Just think, you might be able to make a pet of one of those Orupendulas! They are about the size of jackdaws, aren't they? Do you remember that boy at Hempshott who had a tame jackdaw? What was his name?'

'Antony Rogers.'

'Ah yes. What a memory you have! Well, wouldn't you enjoy having an Orupendula as tame as Antony's jackdaw? To sit on your hand and feed off the fruit you gave it? It might even learn tricks, you know.'

Sophie sighed. 'Yes, but I would rather see the birds in their own homes, Mamma: in the trees and the forest. I don't want them tame and doing tricks. What interests me is how they behave, where they make their nests, what they feed on, how they sing and call.'

'I know, my pet. You are a serious student of Natural History, aren't you?' Her mother smiled, and popped a morsel of mango into her daughter's mouth. 'I'll order some books for you from London and we shall paint the birds together. If you like, you can keep them in the aviary just for a week or two and then release them, and get the fellows to catch you some different ones.' Sophie plainly understood that she could not escape the birdcage.

'Papa is so taken with the idea of your having it,' her mother explained gently. 'It would give him so much pleasure to see it made for you.'

Whatever Frederick Wetherby wanted to give had to be given, and gratitude expressed by the recipient. Grandmamma Wetherby was the same. Sophie had learned long ago that it was more blessed to give than receive.

'I shall be glad to talk to Julius about it,' she said, reconciling herself with a sigh. It would at least be interesting to see Flora's brother.

Serafina cleared away the rinds and husks of the fruit, and the dirty cups. A sleepy silence spread over the verandah. But a distant thrashing and grinding echoed on and on from the sugar-mill on the other side of the house.

'Don't they ever have a rest?' asked Sophie.

'Oh yes. I should think so, anyway, my dear. No doubt they work in teams and one team takes over whilst the other rests. But at this time of year we have to keep hard at it all day, until the crop is all gathered in.'

'Can I go and see the mill?' asked Sophie.

'Oh, no, dearest, not at this hour. Never go out under the noonday sun. Stay here with me. I think I shall have a little nap. You know,' her mother settled deeper in her chair, yawning, 'you should rest, too.'

Sophie hadn't the slightest desire to rest so soon after her long sleep. The question that had been burning in her brain finally chose this moment to burst out. 'Mother, did Papa search Eli's hut this morning? Has he been flogged?'

'Oh, don't upset yourself over that,' her mother murmured, her eyes already closed. 'I haven't seen your father at all. I don't know where he is. You mustn't get too involved with details of the running of the estate, Sophie. You must leave all that to Papa. To speak plainly,' she opened her eyes for a moment and gave her daughter a very direct look, 'there is nothing we can do to alter things, and the way the plantation is run may seem to you a little hard, at first. But I have come to see that it is necessary.' She looked about her for a moment, to make sure there were no slaves within earshot, then sat up, leaned forward and continued in a whisper. 'We are but four, here, in our immediate family, and only the manager, Mr Kendrick. The overseers and slave-drivers are blacks or half-breeds. I'm not confident we could trust them in all circumstances. We have more than two hundred and fifty slaves. Think how they outnumber us, and how easily, if they were stirred up to riot, they could overpower us. On other islands, plantation owners have been killed.' She glanced about, wide-eyed and furtive, at the conclusion of her speech.

'But surely,' Sophie pondered, 'that makes it even more important for us to treat them well. If they love us, they would never do us harm.'

'Don't argue, Sophie. You are so tiring, my dear.' Her mother fell back in her chair, closed her eyes with an exhausted sigh and fanned herself.

'I'm sorry.' Sophie thought Mamma was sometimes more irritable here than she had been in Derbyshire. Perhaps it was the heat. 'Sleep well, dear Mamma.' She got up and kissed her brow.

'Where are you going?' asked her mother dreamily, catching her wrist as she left.

'I'm going to read in my room till the heat of the day is over,' said Sophie.

'Good girl.' Her mother's arm drifted downwards, as she surrendered to sleep. Sophie tiptoed away.

But she could not concentrate on her book. The sugar-mill thrashed and hummed outside; her mind thrashed and hummed also. For a while she walked up and down, up and down. Questions wheeled round like restless cogs in a machine. What had happened to Eli? Was her mother right about the slave rebellions? Was there a real danger? How were the slaves treated here? What would Aunt Sarah have thought of it all? She was beginning to realise how much she had depended on her aunt for the direction of her thinking. She had enjoyed her aunt's encouragement almost without noticing it. Here, there was the contrary feeling: that everything she thought or said was wrong in some way. Her brain seemed to boil in this close confinement. Seizing her jacket and a parasol, she left her room.

She avoided the front verandah where her mother was dozing and walked down the hall to the back door. Passing through the belt of trees which surrounded the house, she arrived in the yard and was engulfed in activity. Hammering, grinding, throbbing and the crushing and splintering of the cane filled Sophie's ears. A great water-wheel turned, driving the machinery. Nearby a cart was being unloaded; great bundles of cane were carried to the mill and fed between the three vertical rollers.

Slaves were busy everywhere: fetching, carrying, heaving, pulling. The stench of sweat hung over the yard. Smoke stung her eyes; beneath a rough roof on the eastern side was a forge and the yard rang with the blacksmith's hammer.

'Out of the way! Out of the way, Miss!'

Sophie turned to see a pock-marked white man with ragged teeth – Kendrick, the manager, she supposed – supervising a gang of slaves rolling barrels towards one of the buildings. Hastily she stood aside, feeling awkward. Quite plainly she was in the way here. Perhaps she should go back indoors. Yet despite the heat, the noise and the smell, she was reluctant to give up her expedition. Suddenly George emerged from one of the buildings. She ran to his side.

'Oh George!' she cried. 'Will you show me how it's all done? I want to see the works.'

George had been preoccupied with something, but was tempted by the opportunity to show off his knowledge and power. 'Well, come along then. I haven't got much time to spare, but I can at least show you round for a few minutes.'

'Oh, thank you!' Sophie seized his arm and George led her across the main yard. She was anxious to get indoors out of the blazing pressure of the sun, but as they drew near the sugar-mill the noise and heat increased.

'Here we bring the cane to be crushed,' shouted George above the din of huge wheels. 'We've got water-mills here of course, because the rivers rush down off the mountain, but they have windmills on Barbados and Antigua, and in some places the wheels are turned by oxen. Father's seeing an engineer about getting us an improved machine.'

Sophie stared at the half-naked slaves who fed the sugar-cane through the crushing rollers. Their bodies were glistening with sweat. She marvelled that they could go on working in the heat. She was beginning to feel faint just standing and watching in the suffocating din.

George led her through all the buildings, showing her where the sugar was processed, and rum made. The liquid crushed out of the cane ran in channels into the boiling house, where the heat was unbearable. Great copper pans bubbled and smoked. Everywhere the slaves were supervised – usually by black overseers, but Sophie saw how Mr Kendrick kept control of everything. He had the hard face of a man whose business was the exercise of authority. One slave paused for a moment to look at Sophie and Kendrick bawled at him and cuffed him on the head with the handle of his whip.

Sophie felt dizzy. 'Thank you, George. I've seen enough.' Desperate to escape, she almost ran out of the boiling house, walked briskly across the glaring crucible of the yard and did not stop until she gained the shade of a tree, clutching at its trunk as a child holds on to its mother's skirts for reassurance. Here, the smells and sounds of the processing factory were muted. She could hear birds and smell flowers.

George came up, laughing. 'Poor Sophie! It's a good job you're not a slave. Kendrick would give you ten lashes for running out like that.'

'Poor slaves, I say,' she burst out. 'To have to endure that every day! I wonder that they don't just drop dead.'

'Oh, they do sometimes,' said George, still in a jocular mood. 'But Kendrick soon resurrects them again.'

'Don't joke, George! I feel very sorry for them.' Sophie looked back towards the terrible buildings.

'You shouldn't,' said George briskly. 'Some of those slaves are the most skilled we have, the boilers and the distillers. And they get rewarded accordingly. The British navy depends on our rum. It's a great part of father's fortune.'

'Where do the women work?' asked Sophie at length, partly prompted to the thought by the sight of three young women, two of them heavily pregnant, who passed close by carrying baskets of clothes on their heads. They disappeared round the side of the house.

'They're going to the laundry,' said George. 'Women work in the house, in the field-gangs, anywhere, depending on their strength.'

'But not when they're expecting a child, surely?'

'Why not? They're not like us, Sophie. They're used to the sun, remember. It's hot in Africa. Damned hot.'

'I'd like to see the field-gangs. I want to get to know some of these women.'

'There aren't enough women at Mount Grace,' said George. 'Not near enough for breeding. Of course what we need most is strong young men, and over the years that's what father has bought. They don't breed very well, of course. The proportions are all wrong. I think we need to buy more young women, but father doesn't agree. If they bred more successfully, we would reduce our expenses very much, you see. We'd get new slaves for nothing instead of having to pay good money for the devils, and those slave-traders are a pack of damned scoundrels – they can make a half-dead slave look like a Hercules: you pay a great price for the beggar, and he dies on you the first evening.'

Sophie was distracted from this tale by the arrival of the two pregnant women returning along the path, their baskets empty now. They smiled shyly at George.

'Good-day Massa George. Good-day Miss. Massa George, you got dat little t'ing you promised me? Dat knife, little knife you say you got for me, cut me fish, trim de wood, cut me rope, peel de stick?' Sophie recognised the torrential speech of Ruth, whom they had met in the dark cane field the day of their arrival.

'Not now, Ruth. Get along with you, now! Don't waste time.' The girls disappeared. George shooed them away like hens.

'Well, at least those two are with child,' said Sophie. 'With luck, perhaps they will have healthy babies.'

'I doubt it, my dear. A fearful number of infants die here. Well . . . I must get back to my business.'

'And I shall go in again – the sun makes me light-headed.' Sophie thought she might write to Aunt Sarah. She did not dare to confide her first impressions of the sugar-mill to anyone else.

'Oh, wait,' said George. 'There's Julius. I'll ask him to take the measurements for your birdcage.' A muscular young man was strolling across the yard, a wooden measure in his hand. He seemed to enjoy a certain amount of independence. No overseer bawled at him and he looked about him with a level gaze. 'He's an able fellow, for a slave,' George went on. 'He's a rare carpenter, and though I've heard him talk to the others in their infernal babble, he's mastered our way of speaking to an extraordinary degree. Just listen to this, now – Julius!'

Julius turned, saw George beckon and came across. He did not smile. He had large eyes and a fine, straight nose and chin, and though his skin was darker than his sister's, it was still much lighter than most of the other slaves'.

'Sophie, this is Julius. Julius, my sister Miss Wetherby.'

'Your servant, Miss.' Julius bowed coolly.

'Julius knows all about birdcages. He could make you anything in the world. He's a first-rate carpenter,' said George. Julius inclined his head at the compliment. 'In fact, I think if there were another great flood, he could make you an ark every bit as fine as Noah's. Couldn't you, Julius?'

'I'd like to try, Master George.'

'He likes a challenge, as you see, Sophie. So tell him your wildest desires in the birdcage line and he will satisfy them, you may be sure.' With a light-hearted wave, George set off back towards the factory.

Sophie turned to Julius. His brown eyes were fixed on her, his expression remote, proud and enigmatic.

'Come, then, Julius, I'll show you where my father thinks the birdcage should be.'

She led him up the steps, through the house and out on to the balcony. Her mother was fast asleep in her chair, a book spilled at her feet. Small birds flickered about the table and flew off at their approach. Sophie smiled at the sleeping figure, but Julius showed no response. There was something hard in his look, at which her spirit quailed a little.

'We mustn't wake her,' whispered Sophie. 'Now, could you build a cage at the end of the verandah, beyond the window of my father's office?'

'Yes, Miss,' replied Julius, and immediately began to measure the area. He noted down the measurements in a little book with a stick of charcoal.

'Can you read and write, then, Julius?' she asked softly.

'A little, Miss,' he replied. 'How high you want the cage?'

'Oh, as high as possible, I think. I do hope the poor creatures will have room enough to fly.' Julius was still for a moment, looking attentively at her. 'I love birds so much, you see.' Sophie's eyes shone. 'I've never seen such birds as there are here. I so much want to go into the forest and watch them. But my mother won't let me go at present. She says I must get used to the climate. Are you interested in Natural History?'

'I know all the birds, where they nest,' said Julius quietly.

'Oh, how I envy you!' cried Sophie. 'I wish you could show me. I know! When Mamma is convinced I am used to the heat, I'll ask if you may take me into the forest and teach me all about them.'

Julius stared at her in surprise. This girl was very different from what he had seen and heard so far about Englishwomen. Isabella Wetherby stirred in her sleep. *Oh no!* she muttered. *Not this!* For a moment the young people hesitated, watching to see if she awoke. But she sank deeper.

'Mustn't wake mother,' whispered Sophie again, smiling.

Julius thought of his own mother, working over at Pelican Bay on Alexander Ashton's estate, working in the fields under the brassy sun. His mother had never idled away a whole morning, dozing in the shade. On Sundays, the slaves' rest day, he knew she would be up even earlier than usual, getting her produce ready for the market.

'When would you be able to take me?' Sophie persisted, looking at him with enthusiasm and anticipation. No white woman had ever looked at him in this way. It was unsettling, but not wholly disagreeable.

'Sundays is our rest day,' he said.

'I shall ask if we may go one Sunday, then,' said Sophie. 'And perhaps your sister, Flora, might come too. She's a beautiful girl, isn't she?'

Julius was silent for a minute. These compliments, this eagerness, perplexed him. He had no ready answers. He was prepared always, as all slaves were, for reproof, disdain, dismissal. Sophie admired his serious eyes, the wide lips, the high cheekbones.

'Flora don't like the forest,' he said. Sophie looked disappointed. It gave him an unusual feeling of pleasure to disappoint her. Encouraged by her openness, his eyes wandered boldly over her, in a way he had never dared to look at a white woman before: her dark curls, her white neck, over the close-fitting jacket that revealed the shape of her generous bosom and trim waist; over her elegant arms and her slim freckled hands. Sophie felt herself tingle slightly as he looked.

'I am white, aren't I?' she said awkwardly. 'I hate it, really. I'd rather be brown, like you. I'm white as a ghost.'

This statement was incomprehensible to Julius. No one in his world would ever dream of thinking such a thing, so deeply was the assumption shared by masters and slaves that white was the desirable, black the inferior colour.

'Look.' She held out her hand towards his. He hesitated, then placed his beside hers. The edges touched for a second like leaves thrown together by the wind. 'You're the colour of the earth. I'm just –'

'Like a cloud,' he said, despite himself.

There was brief moment of delight in this idea, then she withdrew as a wave of strange feeling washed up through her body. She looked away, recollected herself, remembered something she longed to ask. 'What happened about Eli?' she whispered. 'Did father search his hut? Did he find anything?' She glanced round quickly. Everywhere was quiet and still. Her mother's mouth had dropped open a little in deep sleep.

'Eli's all right,' he said. 'Cause of the jumbie came to warn him.'

'A jumbie? What's that?'

'A spirit. Eli told me a spirit come to his hut last night and warn him Massa was going to search his place in the morning.' Sophie understood and blushed.

'So all was well?'

At last it seemed as if Julius would permit himself to share a smile with her. Sophie's whole body seemed to dissolve in relief. But the smile was scarce begun when there was a sudden convulsive jerk from her mother's chair.

'Good heavens! I was asleep. What a dream! My neck is all stiff – Oh, hello, Sophie. Have you given Julius his orders? Then perhaps you can call Serafina to bring us some tea. What a dream I had! I was falling over the edge of a cliff and I was so terrified, I almost fell out of my chair. I hope I did not let out any secrets by talking in my sleep?'

'No, Mamma.'

For the moment, at least, everybody's secrets were safe.

8

To Live Like Angels

'Come on, Sophie! I'm to take you up to Belmont this morning!'
George's voice floated across the polished floorboards of the hall.
Sophie, out on the verandah as usual, went indoors to find her
brother standing in the doorway at the back of the house, fanning
himself with his hat.

'But I was waiting for Julius to come and make the birdcage . . .'
she faltered.

'To hell with that! He's busy repairing a cart behind the yard. I've
just seen him. Your fancy birdcage will have to wait for another day.
Come on! Craig says he wants your advice about some curtains –
God knows why – anyway Father approves, we are to go up there to
dine and come back at nightfall. Let's go! It's getting hotter by the
minute.'

Sophie ran to her room and put on her shoes. She had to admit
that the prospect of a visit to Charles Craig's house was enticing.
Advice about curtains, however, was an unwelcome challenge.
Sophie had never so much as noticed a curtain in her life.

She paused for a moment by the looking-glass, and was annoyed
by her anxious expression and the shine of sweat on her face. Never
mind.

'Come on, Sophie!'

'Coming!' First she must say goodbye to her mother, who had
kept to her bed that morning with a headache. The blinds were
drawn.

'Enjoy yourself, my dear.' Sophie's mother raised herself on her
elbow. 'Charles Craig is such a good fellow. You'll have a splendid
day. Don't walk about too much in the sun, though – promise me.'

'Of course not, Mamma! And you rest and get better!'

Flora came into the room carrying a pitcher of water.

'Flora will take care of me. See you tonight, sweetheart.'

Sophie ran to the back door, where George was lounging, sticking a purple flower in his buttonhole.

'You've got to stop this dashing about, Sophe,' he remarked, giving her his arm as they set off. 'You're in the tropics now. Slow down, girl. Whoa!'

'A moment ago you were telling me to hurry up!' cried Sophie, laughing indignantly. 'I think you just like finding fault with me, George.'

'Somebody must keep you in order.' Her brother grinned. 'Right, let's go. And remember: slow and easy, now.'

'Do you say that to the slaves in the field?' asked Sophie on a sudden impulse.

George frowned. It had only been a half-joke on her part, but he seemed really cross. 'I hope you haven't been infected by this blasted Abolitionist nonsense,' he growled. 'Aunt Sarah is a silly old fool sometimes. She understands absolutely nothing of how things are here. Our slaves have well-regulated lives. They have a rest day. They have their recreation. They work in the fields, yes, but remember they're Africans. Used to the heat. They're not like us, Sophie.'

They turned right, passed the kitchen garden, and crossed the yard. The sun hammered down. Sophie was glad of the shade of her wide-brimmed cotton bonnet and her white jacket. All around her the slaves worked half-naked in the sun, unloading another cart of cane.

'No,' she said quietly. 'They're not like us – in some ways. But they must feel as we do. Couldn't we arrange for Flora to visit her mother, George? Or for her mother to come here?'

'Stop meddling!' snapped George. 'You've only been out here for a few days and already you think you can manage things better. You don't know what you're talking about.'

Sophie dropped his arm. Now they had started up a slippery track through the forest she had longed to explore. But locked into this argument with George, she could not look about her with any pleasure. 'I know exactly what I am saying! I've talked to Flora!'

'Well, you shouldn't talk to slaves too much. You're encouraging her. She'll start getting above herself now, I expect. Giving herself airs. Taking liberties. We'll probably have to turn her out from the house in the end – send her out to work in the field-gangs. And much good your precious influence will have done.'

'George! All I said was that she misses her mother.'

'They don't have those feelings, Sophie. Because you're tender-hearted, you think Flora is, too. Slaves don't behave as we do. They don't even live in families. It may be shocking for you to think of it, but they don't marry. The men and women associate together like animals. The children don't even know who their fathers are half the time, let alone love and honour their fathers as we do ours.'

Sophie was silenced.

'You really must have the patience to learn a little before you start criticising. And the most important thing you must remember is that we Europeans have a civilised way of life. We respect and cherish our womenfolk. Why, Father worships Mother. You can see that. It's a holy bond. There's a sacrament between them. That's what you and I should try and emulate. The slaves' lives are bestial by comparison. It's our job to show them the meaning of decency, of purity, of refinement. They live like animals. We must do our best to live like angels.'

Sophie sighed. If George ever tired of plantation life he would make a passable preacher. He was certainly tedious enough. She said nothing, however. It was no use arguing with George. She had to let him blow himself out.

Instead she looked about her as they climbed higher and higher through the forest. A rough path had been cleared and trees felled. Here and there, where the gradient was steep, rough steps had been made with branches. It was hard going. Sweat poured down her face.

Meanwhile, in the bathhouse up at Belmont, Charles Craig was preparing for his guests. He stood naked under a stream of tepid water which splashed on to his head from a pipe. The water, warmed by the sun in a tank set above the little shed, cascaded down his slim flanks and gathered in little beads in the blond thickets of his pubic hair. He washed himself dreamily: armpits, navel, groin, buttocks, genitals. He paid particular attention, for the first time for years, to his fingernails. One of his slaves had made a washing lotion with coconut oil. He massaged it into his dripping thighs.

He was alone. He had dismissed Cassie. Craig closed his eyes and let his imagination conjure up a vision of Sophie Wetherby, in her white dress, as she had looked the other night. He was sitting on the sofa next to her, looking down at her. She leaned forward to place a coffee-cup on the table. Her heavy breasts swung forward in her low-cut bodice. He glimpsed the faintest pink edge of nipple before she leaned back again and excitement flashed through him now as it had done then.

At the memory, his cock twitched and blundered upwards. Craig caressed himself. He pushed against the familiar grasp of his own strong hand. But in his mind it was Sophie's hand that held him. They were alone in his fantasy; her family had been blotted out. Now he was unlacing Sophie's bodice. The white cloth parted, and her breasts fell heavy and warm into his waiting hands. He kissed her; he fell to his knees, reaching beneath the skirts where her legs were suddenly bare above the stocking tops. There were no underclothes to detain him; boldly on her own sofa he moved into her, again and again, until the glorious convulsion came and the fantasy wheeled away in fragments. He opened his eyes and saw the bathhouse wall, covered with moss and lichen, and the familiar crack in the whitewash that always looked like a smile.

Whilst his heart and breathing slowed, he washed himself again, spent, soft and relieved. Now her visit would not be so unbearable, perhaps. She was so very young, so vulnerable, so appealing. Apart from her immense sexual attraction, she touched some finer feelings in Charles Craig. Nervous apprehensions fluttered in his chest at the thought that he would see her in less than an hour – a feeling like the wings of butterflies beating, he thought with a smile. Was he really falling in love at last?

'Oh look, George! What's that?' cried Sophie. A huge blue shape flickered in the air among the trees up ahead and vanished in a beam of light.

'Some butterfly,' growled George.

'But it was so large – the size of a man's pocket-handerchief, at least.'

'Ah! That's nothing to what you'll see before you've done here.' He smiled in a patronising way, offering to take Sophie's arm again. She hesitated. It was really easier to walk on her own, but she was glad to be on good terms with her brother once more. She took his arm.

'You are a beast sometimes, George.'

'I just want to keep you out of trouble, my dear. That's all.'

'I know. I know.' Unfortunately all the most interesting things seemed to be trouble.

The track widened and levelled out. They had climbed several hundred feet. Pausing for breath, they looked back, and through the gap in the trees where the path snaked downwards, the sea shimmered far below. A mile or so out to sea was a small island. Birds wheeled above it, and Sophie could see the white surf breaking around it and the soft contours of vegetation.

'What's that little island?'

'Uninhabited. Wilderness. Nobody ever goes there. You couldn't land anyway, because of the surf.'

'What's it called?'

'Demoiselle.'

'What? French for Maiden? Why French?'

'The French were here for years. We kicked 'em out in '76 – just before father came out. Damned Frenchys. And they're worse than ever now, with this revolutionary madness.'

'Why did they call the island The Maiden?'

George set off again, fanning himself with his hat. 'Oh, I don't know. Because it was barren, I suppose.'

'It should be Old Maid, then. It doesn't look barren, though.'

'Look!' George turned away, tiring of Demoiselle. 'There's Belmont!'

A handsome house was appearing through the trees. It was set in a clearing, on a kind of rocky shelf surrounded by forest. By now the sun was high, and Belmont seemed to shimmer and float in the heat.

Near at hand, a gang of five or six slaves appeared, cutting back some vegetation at the side of the path. They were supervised by a swarthy middle-aged white man with a pistol stuck in his belt and a stout cane in his hand. The slaves wielded cutlasses and glanced furtively at Sophie, without ever stopping the rhythm of their work. There was a strong stink of sweat.

'Good morning, Higgs,' said George.

'Morning, Mr Wetherby.'

'Hot work today.' Even here, where the weather was always hot, the English could not entirely shake off their old conversational habits.

'Aye. The master's expecting you. We was just makin' the path a bit more accommodatin' like, fer the young lady. This here danged Razor Grass' – Higgs swished at it with his cane – 'terrible stuff 'tis. Slash yer petticoats to ribbins, Miss, not to mention yer tender ankles, see?' Sophie stared amazed at the grass, which looked harmless enough. But George dragged her on.

'Come on,' he commanded. 'Craig will be waiting.' As they drew away from Higgs, George growled in an undertone, 'I didn't like the familiar way that fellow spoke to you. Ogling, and mentioning your legs like that. I'll tear into him all right, when I next see him on his own. I didn't want to make a fuss in front of you, Sophie, but I'm damned if I'm going to let the blackguard take liberties like that.'

'But –' Sophie faltered. She was going to say that it seemed to her quite considerate of Higgs, or of his master, to think of her ankles and want to save them from being cut, and that out here, where Nature could be so savage, there was something absurd in worrying about the finer points of etiquette, especially with a common working man like Higgs. But a strange heaviness overcame her. She was sure it would only lead to another of George's arguments. So she merely sighed.

'Here comes Craig,' said George. 'He must have been looking out for us.'

Craig was coming down the steps from his verandah. His hair shone in the sunlight, and his white shirt and breeches were fresh, immaculate and of a dazzling brilliancy. They met. He took her hand and bent to kiss it. Sophie felt him tremble and noticed a faint scent of coconut lingering about his head. As he rose again and smiled down on her, the cleanest thing of all seemed to be his eyes: a light, washed blue, pure as the tropical sky.

9

New Fruits

'Come in! Belmont's not half so elegant as your Mount Grace, but I've got quite fond of the old place.' Charles Craig led them up the steps. Belmont was a smaller, squarer house than their own, with an upper storey and a broad roof which overhung a verandah on all sides, giving deep shade. At Mount Grace the verandah was only at the front, as if some architect had decided what view it was acceptable to admire.

'It needs a woman's taste,' said Craig, seating his visitors in comfortable cane chairs on the verandah. 'Your mother has brought grace to Mount Grace. Before she came, it was a ramshackle bachelor establishment like this. Cassie!' A plump young black woman emerged from the shadows. 'Would you like tea, Miss Wetherby, or sorrel juice? Or – wait – have we any passion fruit juice left?'

'Eh, Massa.' The girl nodded, but her lower lip protruded sulkily.

'I'd like to try some of that, please,' said Sophie. 'There are so many new fruits here – it's like the Garden of Eden.'

'Watch out for the forbidden fruit though, eh, Sophie?' grinned George. Then he turned to the slave girl. 'I'll have coffee, Cass.' His tone was familiar. Of course, he had been here often. Sophie was jealous of her brother's previous experience on the island. He had learnt so much, made friends . . . still, she must not be impatient. She leaned back in her chair. The sweat on her back made her dress cling uncomfortably.

'I think I'll have passion fruit juice, too,' Craig told the waiting slave. 'We'll dine at three, and before then, Miss Wetherby, I'd like to show you my new coffee plantation. Although if you would prefer to rest before dinner, Cass has got the guest room ready for you – is it done, Cass?'

'Eh!' It was an odd sound, hardly a word, more of a grunt: an affirmation wrung with difficulty out of her.

'Very well. You may go.'

The girl strolled off into the house with a laboured sigh, letting the screen door slam behind her.

'Sulking today,' said Craig with a smile. 'Still, she's an excellent cook so I put up with her caprices. I think I can out-sulk anybody on earth.'

'I hate sulking!' said Sophie. 'I'd rather people shouted at me if they're cross. It's one of George's worst habits. He can sulk for a week.'

'If you dislike sulking, Miss Wetherby, I shall endeavour to root it out entirely from my character.' Craig smiled. Sophie was rather irritated by this gallantry. It made her feel even hotter.

'I must take my jacket off,' she announced gauchely, struggling to her feet out of the low chair.

'Oh, certainly!' exclaimed Craig, leaping up politely. Sophie wrestled with the buttons which seemed to cling damply to their buttonholes, clogged up with humidity. There was an awkward silence.

'May I – May I call Cassie to assist you?' enquired Craig. His voice shook slightly.

'Oh no!' cried Sophie. 'It's stupid – there!' She managed at last, made self-conscious somehow by being so thoroughly looked at. Off came the jacket, with a clumsy flourish, and Charles Craig took it from her, folded it and placed it on a nearby table. Sophie sat down again – with a jolt. Craig looked at her for a moment or two, then sat down too. There was a moment's silence.

'What were we speaking of?' he asked in a blank tone. George had picked up an old newspaper and was scanning the shipping news.

'We've ordered some cannon from Wilkinson's for a battery down at the beach,' he said absent-mindedly. 'Gregory promised we'd have them within weeks. And some fine new muskets as well.'

'Your sister doesn't want to talk about guns, I'm sure,' said Craig, still smiling at Sophie. She fidgeted. Now the cane chair was scratching her bare shoulders. She wished Craig would not address himself so exclusively to her.

'Oh no, please, do talk about guns as much as you like,' she insisted. 'I'm happy sitting here and watching the birds come and go.'

'You love birds?' Craig pounced on the subject. 'We have some wonderful ones here. Now, which would provide the most beautiful feathers for your bonnet? The blue and red macaw, perhaps.'

'I'll shoot some for you, Sophe.' George grinned.

'You know what I think about shooting birds, George,' retorted Sophie, tight with irritation.

'Good God, we wouldn't dream of shooting any creature you cared for, Miss Wetherby!' exclaimed Craig, giving George a hearty kick on the boot. 'But you can collect feathers by picking up the ones that drop or are moulted. I see fine ones every day, just lying on the ground.'

'Oh, do you?' cried Sophie. 'I do envy you – being able to wander about like that – outdoors, all day, as I did in England.'

Craig frowned. 'But the sun . . .' he said doubtfully, casting a brief glance at her arms. 'And then, it's rough land hereabouts. Stones, tree roots, Razor Grass.' His eyes descended to her shoes, frail and already disfigured with mud. A tiny area of naked foot showed above each shoe. She was bare-legged. His heart began to throb more strongly than before. 'You must not expose yourself to – to dangers. There are snakes . . .'

'Then I shall wear breeches and boots, like you and George,' said Sophie. 'And in any case Mamma told me the snakes are not venomous. What on earth is the point of my coming here if I've got to fret about indoors all day?' She fixed Craig with her most imploring look.

'Well, for a start, I shall be delighted to show you my new coffee plantation.' He smiled. 'I'm confident it's going to make my fortune, George. I got the plants from a fellow on Trinidad. The harvest is a much easier business than sugar.'

'I would like to see your plantation very much,' agreed Sophie. 'But I'd also like to go into the forest.' She stared at him directly, demanding, like the child she had so recently been. Craig hesitated. Sophie leaned forward beseechingly, as if offering herself to him, her neck gleaming softly in the shade. 'Oh please, will you take me, Mr Craig?'

Craig became thoroughly aroused. 'Of course I will,' he replied gently. 'But another time. Not today. Let it be something to plan and look forward to.'

'Well, soon then,' pleaded Sophie. 'For George won't be bothered with it, you know – he's so busy, he hasn't time for me and my Natural History, at all.'

'It will be an honour for me to accompany you into Natural History.'

Sophie leaned back in relief. She thought she might come to like Craig despite his gallantries.

After they had refreshed themselves, Craig was eager to show them his new plantation. They climbed up a track behind the house. The sun was at its height, and George mopped his brow. 'Damn it! I'm out of training,' he puffed.

'I swim in the surf every day, to keep fit,' said Craig. 'You should join me, George. That long sea voyage has made you go soft.'

'I'd love to swim in the surf!' cried Sophie.

Craig hesitated and frowned. 'As to that, Miss Wetherby . . . I think it might not be quite . . . The surf here can be rough, you know.'

'I swam in the river with George, at Hempshott!' Sophie insisted. 'I'm a strong swimmer, too. Aunt Sarah taught me, at Scarborough. I even hauled George out once when he got cramp! Didn't I, George?'

'I was only pretending,' growled George, embarrassed.

'You were not! You nearly drowned! I rescued you!'

'Well, here are my coffee trees,' Craig said hastily, offering a distraction. A grove of small bushes was set out on the hillside, with rows of taller trees planted in between them. The coffee bushes had leathery evergreen leaves, like a small laurel. Sophie admired them, although she thought they looked rather odd and bare set out on the cleared earth, and she preferred the luxuriant variety of the forest beyond and above.

'They need shade to flourish, and they enjoy the coolness up here on the mountainside,' said Craig. 'So I planted these Immortelles to shade them,' he looked up into the branches of the taller trees. 'They will flourish under their protection.'

'Like husbands and wives,' suggested George with a grin. 'Well, thank God for the Immortelles, say I.' He threw himself down and fanned himself with his hat. 'We were fools to come out at noon, Craig. You and your confounded coffee!'

'I'm sorry.' Craig addressed himself to Sophie. 'I was too eager for your approval. Would you like to sit down for a while? Or go back?'

'I want to walk into the edge of the forest,' said Sophie, and struck off boldly towards it. Craig followed, shouting to George that he would escort Miss Wetherby and her brother should rest.

Two hundred yards away, through the coffee plantation, the forest waited. Sophie almost ran to it.

'Don't exert yourself too much, Miss Wetherby.' Craig was at her shoulder. 'You must not exhaust yourself.'

Gaining the edge of the forest, Sophie plunged in, until she stood in deep, dripping shade. She stared up at the tangled festoons of trees and climbers. 'I've had enough of people saying that to me,' she remarked quietly.

'What? Have I offended you?'

'Not at all.' She turned to Craig, who was standing close to her, and alone with her, for the first time. His heart raced, but he managed to keep his breathing level. 'I just don't want to be told, any more, that I can't do this or that: that I must rest and be careful, that I can't swim or explore or do any of the things I used to do at home when I was a girl.'

'You are a young woman of spirit.' Craig poured his cool blue gaze down on her. His eyes shone with attraction, though Sophie was too interested in her surroundings to notice.

'Why do you keep telling me I can't do things?'

'Please forgive me – a simple desire to protect you from harm.'

'Well, I don't mind danger,' said Sophie, aware that she was bragging. It depended very much on what sort of danger presented itself, and how many legs it had. 'I'm not going to change the way I live, just because people call me a young woman now instead of a girl.'

'Quite right! It must be irritating. You can make your own rules, Miss Wetherby.'

71

'You might as well call me Sophie,' said Sophie. 'I dislike formality so much. Here we are standing in the forest together! You must at least call me by my name.' Her brother's friends had always done so.

'My dear Sophie, it will be a pleasure. And you must call me Charles.'

Unable to restrain himself any longer, Charles Craig seized her hand and kissed it fiercely – too fiercely. Sophie was alarmed, drew back – he stumbled slightly, dizzy with desire, floundering under her puzzled stare. Sophie had had absolutely no experience of courtship. She did not understand why his eyes blazed so, or his breath came in great waves.

'I beg your pardon,' stammered Charles Craig, 'but – but I adore you.'

Sophie seized her skirts and strode out of the forest. Craig leant his brow against a tree for a moment before following her. He saw an army of ants swarming down a nearby tree-trunk and snaking off across the forest floor. Millions of living beings, totally unaware of his existence, driven by irresistible instinct. He could feel his own life drawing together around an instinct, too. A short while ago he had been only vaguely aware of the existence of Miss Sophie Wetherby as an abstract idea: his neighbours' absent daughter. Now every thought, every impulse, every ambition, was knotting itself around the thought of her.

I must have her, he thought. And the more she resists, the more desperate for her I shall be.

10

Some Filth or Other

Sophie's heart still raced with embarrassment. They were sitting down to dinner now and she could not any longer avoid Charles Craig's eyes. He had astonished her by his outburst in the forest. Adoration was something Sophie had never experienced before. She had been fairly oblivious even to admiration in the past, when one or another of George's friends had thought her handsome. Sophie did not seek men's eyes. She wanted to look at things, not be looked at.

Cassie and another black girl carried in the food. Craig, desperate to ingratiate himself with Sophie after the moment of madness in the forest, beamed nervously at the spectacle of his own hospitality.

'Cassie is a superb cook, Miss Wetherby. I think you will find her Creole chicken to your taste. The beef here is very indifferent, hardly worth bothering with. The mutton is good and the pork very sweet, because the hogs are fed with sugar-cane tops. And for fowl we have turkeys, guinea-fowls, Muscovy and English Ducks.'

Sophie, feeling some comment was required, declared without looking at him that she was very fond of chicken. Eagerly he offered the vegetable dish.

'These are our own christophenes. Have you tasted christophenes yet? Oh yes, of course – we enjoyed them the other day, at your mother's table. We grow some fine vegetables here at Belmont. Here – try some of our sweet potato.'

Sophie addressed herself to Cassie rather than Craig. 'Did you learn to cook from your mother, Cassie?' she asked.

Cassie looked startled by the enquiry. She was a large young woman, with a rough, slouching manner. 'Eh, Miss,' she drawled, barely polite. The other girl, a tall, thin figure, stared open-mouthed at this exchange.

'And are you married? Or do you still live with your parents?' Cassie glared at Sophie for a moment, but said nothing. Craig shifted uneasily in his chair.

'Answer Miss Wetherby's kind enquiry, Cassie.'

'I sleep under de porch.'

'What! Do you not have a bed?' Sophie was amazed; Craig, uncomfortable.

'The house slaves generally . . . sleep here and there, where they please. I believe it is quite . . . cool and pleasant on the porch.' He hesitated. 'You may go now, Cassie. And Venus. Thank you.'

The girls sauntered off. As soon as they were outside the door, Sophie heard them break into animated chatter. But she could not understand a word and they were soon out of earshot.

'I hope I have not done wrong to mention it,' faltered Sophie, looking at Craig for reassurance.

'No, no, my dear Sophie, not in the least. She is a primitive creature, Cassie, poor thing. It is astonishing how different from ours their lives are, and their notions of comfort.'

Still rather puzzled, Sophie could not think of any response but to smile, and Craig, delighted to be smiled at, allowed his intense admiration of her to blaze out for a moment. This time she understood the look: she knew she was adored, and though there was something unnerving about it, she was not such a puritan as to find it totally repugnant.

Well, he is certainly handsome, thought Sophie. It is odd that he should admire me; I am such an awkward thing. But of course there are no other women here. If we were in Buxton he wouldn't notice me and that would be more comfortable. But he seems kind to his slaves. He's a good man, I'm sure. I must not be impolite.

And then she turned enthusiastically to her baked chicked. It was delicious. Cassie was indeed a superb cook. The brown sugary sauce melted into the chicken's soft flesh, and fried onions and garlic gave the dish a wonderful piquancy.

But Charles Craig had lost his appetite. Sophie, sitting opposite him, was bare-shouldered again. Whenever she took her jacket off he was lost. Her white bosom and swanlike neck shone in the soft light from the window. Without ever looking directly at her he was mesmerised. He was aware of every little movement. His hands

74

could almost feel the moist weight of her breasts, so intensely was he imagining her nakedness.

George was rattling on about guns again, and about the unrest on other islands, and Craig nodded and dropped the occasional word into the conversation, just to keep George going. This gave him a certain privacy in which to admire her. He placed his hands in his lap, and beneath the discreet cover of his napkin he began to masturbate.

Unable to stop himself, he marvelled at the horrible absurdity of his behaviour. But the semi-public situation intensified his arousal. He had behaved like this in school once, whilst gazing obediently at the Latin master. Looking at Sophie, now, was much more helpful. He knew it was madness, but he could not desist.

George was deep in an account of a shooting trip: '. . . and you know of course a mad dog is the worst thing out, has to be done away with, has to be stopped . . .'

Luckily the Wetherbys were fond of their food. George gorged himself shamelessly and Sophie, more relaxed now she was friends with Craig again, was deeply engaged with her dinner, too. Even now a generous portion of chicken was travelling towards her mouth. Her lips parted – but a drop of the sauce fell from her fork and smacked loudly on to the skin between her breasts.

'. . . and there she was,' George went on. '– I had her in my sights –'

At Sophie's annoyed exclamation, the attention of both men was legitimately drawn to her bosom.

George flashed Craig a sidelong grin and, wiping his mouth, finished his story. 'So I let her have it, there and then. Right between the eyes.' He imitated the explosion of a musket. Sophie leaned forwards as she mopped, revealing herself more fully. A shudder shook Craig's frame, but he covered it with an exclamation of sympathy for Sophie's plight.

'I say, Sophie,' cried her brother, 'you are a saucy thing! What a pig you are! You are worse than me.'

Sophie tied her napkin around her neck, protecting herself from further spatterings of sauce and at the same time veiling the distractions of her body from the admiring company. 'Thank

75

goodness you have such good napkins.' She smiled in embarrassment at Craig, who could not but agree.

'They are Irish linen. Part of my mother's dowry.'

'Was your mother Irish, then?'

'No, no, just the linen. My mother was from Northamptonshire, a thoroughly English family. The Arnolds. Sir Anthony Arnold's youngest daughter. She rather disgraced her family in marrying my father – a tradesman, you know.'

'Oh.' Sophie wanted to distract Craig from the embarrassment of her clumsiness with the sauce. 'I wondered it you might have Irish blood.'

'Nothing so exciting. Just very ordinary tame English blood. Though at times it's as much as I can do to cope with that.'

'I knew an Irishman once', said George, 'called Slattery. God, how that fellow loved to fight! Do you know, at school, once, he broke a fellow's nose for a farthing.'

By concentrating very hard on George's stories of his friend Slattery, Craig managed to eat a morsel of Cassie's baked chicken. But his mind was racing away in a parallel dimension. *It will have to be marriage, of course*, he thought. *It will require some patience. There are discreet intervals which must elapse. An engagement. But if I speak to her father in the next few days, I might hope for a consummation within weeks. Or months at the most. She's young and spirited – she doesn't know what she's doing in the world, yet. I must capture her fancy somehow.*

Craig had captivated girls easily enough in the past, but he had the grace to be a little nervous about this challenge to his charms. There was something unpredictable, almost violent about her, like an unbroken horse. But how might that express itself in the marriage bed! She would be ardent, Craig had no doubt of it. But he would have to be careful, stop behaving like a madman. Secretly he admired the extraordinary thought that he might, for the first time in his life, be genuinely in love.

After dinner Sophie accepted Craig's invitation to rest for half an hour on his best bed, carved from Honduras mahogany. He was glad. After she had gone back home tonight he would roll about on that same bed and hope to find there the faintest hint of her scent. It would be the smell of her own body; she was not, as far as he could tell, wearing perfume.

Sophie admired the guest room, though she had no very useful advice to give about curtains. Left alone to rest, she also admired the view: high above the forested valley, looking down on birds flying to and fro. The bed was carefully made, with more good linen. After a quick wash, removing the last traces of the spilt sauce (luckily it had fallen on skin, not the fragile muslin of her dress), she kicked off her shoes and lay down. A faint breath of wind stirred the frail hairs around her temples. Below, bird calls echoed up and down the valley. She felt at peace.

Then there were footsteps below, in the garden. She recognised the voices of Cassie and the other girl. There was the clink of tools. Intrigued, Sophie got up off the bed and tiptoed to the window. They were hoeing between rows of some leafy green vegetable. The moment she appeared they sensed her presence and looked up. Sophie smiled down at them and waved. Cassie immediately scowled and turned her back; the other girl hesitated, cast a doubtful look at her friend, raised her hand briefly to Sophie in a half-hearted salute, then also turned away.

Sophie felt hurt and disappointed. She had imagined she might find a friend here among the slave girls of her own age. But Flora, at Mount Grace, had been reserved and unbending; Cassie, here, almost impertinent. Sophie drew away from the window and lay back down on the bed. But it felt lumpy now, and the afternoon heat stifling. Never mind. She would rest. It was absurd, being upset over this. She would drift away on a river of sleep.

A murmur of voices rose from the garden below, then a snigger. Sophie writhed. It reminded her of her schooldays, when Jane Alsbury had stolen Lucy Webb, her best friend. Now the slave girls' voices were heard in song. The song rose and fell with the rhythms of their hoeing. It was a working song. Sophie supposed. The words did not seem suited to a lullaby, thought she could not altogether make them out:

> 'Shame – what a shame
> Buckra woman you los' de game
> You wear fancy clo's
> You look down yo' nose
> Buckra woman le' go me man.

Oh you scamp Mary Anne
You done me wrong wi' me man,
But she not goin' to beat me,
I goin' to put jumbie on she,
Mary Anne let go me man.'

She fell into a light doze, though in her dream she was trying to find somebody called Mary Anne. She ran through a slave village, calling out to all the women, asking where Mary Anne might be. But they all turned away, some sadly, some abruptly, until Sophie awoke, with a great twitch of the limbs, and found herself in tears. Ridiculous, she smiled, wiping her face. The evening was silent now; the girls had gone.

'George,' asked Sophie as they walked back down the track to Mount Grace. 'What does buckra mean?'

'Why?'

'I heard it in a song. The slaves were singing.'

'I'm not sure.'

'And who was Mary Anne?'

'Mary Anne who?'

'I don't know. A character in a song. The girls sang "Mary Anne let go me man".'

'Some filth or other.' George slashed at the grass with his cane. 'You shouldn't listen.'

The sun, huge and glowing like a red-hot coin, slipped into the glittering sea.

11

Snakes and Monkeys

'Want to come into the forest today, Sophie?' asked George a few days later at breakfast. 'Craig and I are going shooting. He sent me a note insisting I should bring you too.'

'Oh, I'd love to!'

'You must go suitably dressed, my dear,' warned her mother.

'I'll wear an old pair of George's breeches,' said Sophie, excusing herself quickly from the table.

'Breeches! My dear, I hardly think . . .'

'Poo, Mother! She will be all right. Better protection for the legs, you know. Insects and such. Stinging plants. Huge poisonous snakes. Tigers. Elephants. Men whose heads do grow beneath their shoulders . . .' George leaned back in his chair, picked his teeth and laughed lazily at his own joke.

The slave, Ruth, walking past the open window, heard his laugh and paused for a moment as if struck by a sudden thought, but she could not see in: the windows were set too high for that. They had been designed particularly so that the occupants of Mount Grace should be invisible to casual passers-by, like gods living a shining life above the clouds. Ruth's friend pulled her along. They were going to the laundry again.

Up at Belmont, Charles Craig was in a frenzy. He had not seen Sophie for days. It seemed like a year. He was utterly possessed by the thought of her, distracted even from his plantings, indifferent to his food, unable to sleep properly. He prowled around, now, like an angry bear, looking at himself from time to time in the glass that stood on his mahogany chest of drawers. He even hesitated over which shirt to wear, then laughed at himself: a ludicrous thought that Sophie Wetherby would care twopence what shirt he wore. But what would she wear? His head swam at the possibilities.

'But what would Papa say?' faltered Sophie's mother at the thought of Sophie in breeches.

'He'll never know,' said George. Their father had gone to meet a boat at Douglastown and would be away all day.

'And besides, he wouldn't mind,' pleaded Sophie. 'Surely he would want me to be suitably dressed, Mother?'

'I'm not sure whether he would approve of the expedition at all.'

'Of course he would!' cried George. 'Why, if Sophie learns to shoot, she would be twice as much use to us here, you know, Mother.'

'Oh, don't talk like that!' Isabella Wetherby covered her face with her hand for a moment and shuddered. Sophie leapt across the room, fell to her knees and flung her arms around her mother.

'Oh please, dear Mamma,' she begged. 'Charles is coming too, remember.'

'Oh yes.' Her mother was instantly alert, noticing Sophie's use of his Christian name. 'I don't know what he will think of you in breeches, however . . .'

'Think? He won't even notice!' bawled George – innaccurately. 'Come along, Sophie, I've still got some of my old breeches from my schooldays. You shall take your pick.'

Half an hour later Sophie swaggered out on to the verandah, beaming all over her face. Breeches, boots and a long-sleeved shirt of George's had transformed her.

'Why, I have two sons!' exclaimed Isabella Wetherby. 'I hope Mr Craig will not consider it improper.'

'And I have suited her with a light fowling-piece, Mother,' said George, forestalling his mother's objections. 'She will be perfectly safe, I promise. Craig is a crack shot. He'll put her through her paces.'

'So Mother,' Sophie smiled, putting on her broad-brimmed hat with a swashbuckling air, 'you must call me Sebastian now. I'm like a character from a Shakespeare play, aren't I? Rosalind or Viola, Aunt Sarah would say. I love it!' She leapt down the steps from the verandah with masculine panache, and almost landed on top of Julius, who had appeared silently, carrying a bag of tools. 'Oh Julius!' she cried. For a moment his eyes flickered over her strange clothes, but his face remained completely composed. His eyes seemed full of light.

'I beg yo' pardon, Miss,' he murmured, standing aside to let her pass. Sophie felt a curious disappointment that he was looking modestly at the ground. She wanted him to share the joke of her dressed like a man. But perhaps it was offensive to him: to his beliefs, to the way his own people behaved and thought. She was aware of the ears and eyes of her mother and brother.

'I'm going into the forest, Julius,' she said. 'With my brother and Mr Craig.' Sophie felt another lurch of awkwardness, remembering how she and Julius had made a kind of promise to go into the forest together. He had said he would show her all the birds. Now she was going with somebody else. She felt curiously guilty. But his dark eyes did not reveal anything. All he gave her was a courteous glance, made necessary by her remark.

'A' right. I hope it good for you . . . I going to make yo' birdcage today.'

'Oh!' Sophie could not contain a cry of dismay. Double, treble awkwardness. She had looked forward to watching him work. 'I shall miss it. I wanted to see how you did it.'

'Never mind that, Sophie,' growled George, clattering down the steps beside her. 'Come on! We'll be late. I told Craig we'd meet him at the waterfall.'

Sophie gave Julius a last regretful look, but he did not raise his eyes.

'Goodbye, my darling!' cried their mother from the verandah. 'My regards to Mr Craig. Good sport!'

Sophie and George set off down a new path, between towering trees.

'You shouldn't talk so freely to Julius,' warned George when they were out of earshot of the house.

A rebellious flame shot through Sophie's heart. 'What do you mean? I've done nothing wrong.'

'You shouldn't encourage him, talking politely to him like that. As if he were an equal.'

'But Mamma and Aunt Sarah taught us always to be polite to the servants.'

'He's a slave, Sophie. Not a servant. He's not our equal. He's our possession.'

Sophie was silent. In future she must conduct herself carefully in front of George.

'Very well, George,' she replied, with a massive effort, 'but do stop lecturing me all the time.'

'I'm not lecturing you,' George insisted. 'Only trying to keep you out of trouble. If you start being over-familiar with slaves they take advantage. It makes them discontented, too. It's not good for them. It doesn't make them happy. I warned you about it before, with Flora. Just think about it, Sophie. Keep your distance. That's all.'

Sophie was silent for a while. They walked deep into the forest. Birds whistled, hooted and flew about in the great green canopy above their heads. She wanted to detach herself from this argument and enjoy her expedition. George, for once, sensed this.

'You've been looking forward to this, haven't you, Sophie?' He smiled.

'Oh yes!' sighed Sophie. A green bird flashed past on their right. 'What was that?'

'No idea. Craig will know. The waterfall's just around this corner.'

Already Sophie could hear the drumming sound. She looked about her with fascination. There was a delightful ease in walking with breeches on. One could lift one's legs high, climb over fallen trees and take huge steps across puddles. The novelty of it pleased her. But she still somehow could not quite shake off a double disappointment which lay at the pit of her stomach, heavy and indigestible. Julius was not with them. He was working on the verandah at Mount Grace. Sophie wondered how he was getting on. How ridiculous! She had got almost sick of sitting on that verandah in the past few days. She had been consumed with longing to go into the forest. Now, here she was in the forest, and the verandah kept coming into her head. Sophie shook herself and tried, with a large sigh, to establish a rational frame of mind. And then they rounded a bend and Charles Craig was suddenly before her, standing in a shaft of sunlight, with a halo of rainbows playing around his head.

Sophie was mesmerised for a moment. He looked supernatural. Even George noticed the effect.

'I say, you look like a damned ghost with that light behind you,

Craig.' George laughed. But Craig had no time for George's jokes. He was bathing blissfully in Sophie's enchanted stare and drinking in the extraordinary paradox of her clothes. Here was the most beautiful girl on the island, dressed like a boy. But the breeches only emphasised her swelling hips, and the dripping humidity of the place made her shirt cling to her bosom.

Craig lowered his eyes as he kissed her hand and admired the shape of her legs – something which before had only been suggested by folds of muslin.

'I don't know whether to kiss your hand or slap you on the back, Miss Wetherby.' He smiled, perfectly in control of himself despite his hammering heart and all his sexual nerves shooting off like fireworks. He was determined to behave properly. 'Or is it Master Wetherby? Is this your younger brother, George?'

'Yes, Sophie has changed her sex today,' George grinned. 'Looks idiotic, don't she? She was afraid of the snakes.'

'I was not!' cried Sophie. 'It is merely a sensible, rational way to dress. Why should men have all the freedom? I think I shall wear breeches always from now on.' And she gave Craig a bold stare. Let him disapprove if he dare. She did not care.

But Craig met her challenge with a seductive smile. 'Not merely rational, but exquisitely attractive, if I may say so.' He bowed slightly. 'You are a great ornament to our male attire. But Miss Wetherby would look handsome in a sack.'

Sophie blushed. Though flattered by his attentions, she always found them uncomfortable. On the whole she wished he would not stare at her like this. His breath blasted against her eyelashes. She moved away slightly. Sophie had acquired from her Aunt Sarah an instinct that a man's attentions were dangerous – that marriage pinned women down to be displayed for admiration, like butterflies in a collector's cabinet. She shook off this idea, and looked up into the trees.

'We saw a green bird fly across a moment ago,' she said. 'Just down there. What was it, do you think?'

'A parrot, I dare say,' answered Craig. 'There are many different types. Now. What shall we find for you today, my dear Sophie? What is you heart's desire? Feathers for your hat? Or a beautiful pelt to make you a bag or gloves?'

Although Sophie had been shooting with George once before, in an English wood, she now followed the men rather doubtfully into the forest. Her heart was heavy. She had hardly even seen a bird yet. Already George had made the gun ready and kept stopping to squint down his sights, whenever a distant branch quivered or a bunch of leaves tossed overhead. All around them were calls, but the musicians seemed shy. Sophie was torn between her desire to see a bird and her dread lest the men would shoot it.

Suddenly a purple shape burst out of a dome of leaves and flashed across the sky. George fired.

'Damn it! Missed! No hope unless we catch something sitting, I fear.'

Sophie's ears boomed with the echo and shrill alarm calls swirled around their heads. 'Please don't shoot the birds!' she faltered. Craig was alert to her distress; George oblivious, reloading the charge. 'It seems so cruel – surely there's no need.' Craig was instantly at her side. She reached out, pleadingly; he took her hand.

'My dear Sophie –' he began, but was interrupted by George.

'Ah, we've got a monkey here!' he cried. There was a scampering in the branches above, George aimed, and as Sophie shouted a protest another loud report echoed through the trees.

A moment's silence, and then a stricken tumbling amongst the leaves: something heavy fell from branch to branch, then dropped to earth with a thump. A horrible screaming broke out.

'You ass, George, it's got young,' said Craig. A few steps brought them to the place; there, pathetic in its bed of leaves, the creature lay inert, the young one clinging to its mother's fur, shrieking and shaking. It turned its face to its destroyers with an expression of absolute terror.

'May as well finish the young 'un off,' said George, raising the butt of his gun like a club. 'Won't survive. Cruel to let it hang on.'

'No!' howled Sophie, and scarcely knowing what she was doing, she turned and ran. She heard the men's voices call, ignored them and, pulling off her hat, she crashed back along the track, past the waterfall, down through the trees, until at last, panting and weeping, she saw the roof of Mount Grace below her.

She stopped here for a moment. Her mother would be on the verandah; if she arrived distraught, it would be an end of forest

84

expeditions for ever. So for a moment or two she stood still, recovering her breath, wiping the rivers of sweat from her face, removing the evidence of tears. Then, with a great shuddering sigh, as all her episodes of weeping had always ended, she walked the last few hundred yards with her hat on her head, refusing to think about anything.

She heard hammering. Julius! There he was, his broad back bent as he set the foundation for her birdcage in the corner of the verandah. Her mother's chair was empty. Sophie felt a wave of relief. No lies were necessary. She collapsed into the empty chair as Julius, hearing her approach, got up and turned round. They looked at each other for a moment, then tears burst from her. Julius moved closer; he looked about him for a moment as if not sure what to do.

'You want Flora, Miss?'

'I don't want anybody,' said Sophie quietly, dashing away her tears. 'Is mother in her room?'

'Yes.' Julius's voice was soft. 'She went in to sleep.'

At this assurance of privacy, Sophie threw back her head. More tears were on their way. With strange ceremonious grace, Julius knelt by her side. He said nothing, but his eyes were fixed on her. His silent presence strengthened her.

'I – I'm upset,' she said, 'because – they shot a monkey. And it had a young one.'

Julius nodded in sober sympathy, observing the paradox of her masculine clothes and tender tears.

'It's foolishness, I know,' said Sophie, recovering herself gradually. 'I mean, I knew we were going shooting, and I've been shooting with George before – in England. I should've known –' She stopped, sniffed, and shook her head.

Julius's eyes seemed to grow as she looked into them. 'You need a drink,' he said. 'You run back. That wrong. When you come with me in the forest,' he lowered his voice to a mere murmur, 'it all be a' right.' Sophie felt all the sorrow drain out of her.

Then the sound of footsteps broke into her head. Julius looked up, and Sophie saw his face become public again. Charles Craig clattered up the steps, out of breath and anxious.

'My dear Sophie! I am so very sorry. You should not have run off like that – I was anxious – if I had known you would be distressed –

George didn't kill the baby – here it is – don't touch it – it might bite, and it may have teeth already. You shall have it for your own pet. You shall be its kind mistress. They can be tamed, you know.' Craig began to get his breath back and sat down beside her, the small monkey still in his hand. 'You shall give it a name.'

The small creature shivered in his hand, its eyes huge and scared. For the first time since his arrival, Craig noticed the presence of Julius, who had withdrawn tactfully to his carpentry in the corner.

'Here, you, fellow, be off, will you?' Craig said. 'Miss Wetherby wants a bit of peace. And here – take this creature, get it taken care of in a cage or something. See to it. It is to be Miss Wetherby's creature.' Craig handed Julius the monkey. Sophie saw the white fingers brush against the black as the helpless animal was passed across. For a moment Julius hesitated, then he slipped the tiny creature inside his shirt and was gone.

'Almost looked like its father, didn't he?' grinned George, arriving as Julius departed and slumping into a chair. 'The blacks eat monkeys, you know, Sophie. That's the last you will ever see of your pet – Flora! Bring us a drink! – Well, Sophie, you have ruined our day's sport. I hope you're thoroughly ashamed of yourself.'

'Yuh look after dis creature fo' Miss,' Julius instructed Ruth and Mary, handing over the monkey. Ruth gave him a taunting look.

'Viola say she see yuh talkin' wid Miss on de verandah las' week, makin' sweet talk, Miss standin' real close an' gib yuh kissin' looks, like she thinkin', "Mi wonda how dem big black lips o' Julius taste!" '

'Don't talk out o' yuh rassa!' Julius flared. 'Fool talk, no better dan fartin'!'

'Eh, shut yo' mout', chile,' Mary warned, controlling the monkey under one arm and pulling Ruth away with the other. 'Rememba dis man tempa, he goin' to be vex wid yuh.'

Julius stalked off, but Ruth could not resist a last tormenting call.

'Tajo, tajo, tajo! What yuh gettin' fo' yuh dinner? Little bitty white bubby? Breast or leg, mi dear? Tajo, tajo!'

12

Beastly Hard Work

'Good shot, Sophie!'

Sophie looked up and peered into the distance. The wooden target which George had set up on a wall was winged on its right side. Charles Craig smiled approvingly at her, took her musket and reloaded it.

'I admire your nerve, Madam.' The 'Madam' was bold, flirtatious. 'Most women, after what happened this morning, would retire to their room with a fit of the vapours. Not you. Oh no. You rise to a challenge, I can see.'

Sophie flinched at his heavy barrage of compliments. At her side, George fired, and cursed through the puff of smoke.

'Missed! Damn it!'

'You're a better shot than your brother,' Craig continued with a mocking smile at George. 'I can't believe you've never touched a gun before.'

'Well, I have,' admitted Sophie. 'I went shooting with George when we lived at Hempshott. But I want to learn properly. I like doing things that are supposed to be only for men.' She was still wearing her breeches, despite her mother's protests.

'You should have been a boy.' Craig laughed, pulled her gun to full cock and handed it to her again. He leaned close to her, as if to peer down the gun, and whispered, 'But I'm glad you're not.' Then, louder, 'Here, bring your arm round a little . . .' And his hand closed over hers. Sophie felt the warmth of his body all down her back. She heard his breath deepen. George, preoccupied with his own performance, did not notice their closeness. Sophie felt paralysed by Craig's enveloping arm. She could not decide whether she liked it or not. It embarrassed her.

She could admire his eyes, but his lips disturbed her. They were thin and mobile. She feared them, somehow. They were always active: framing compliments; arranging themselves into smiles; and in the forest, when they had flown down and fastened on to her hand, her soft, plump, defenceless hand, it had almost been as if it was their prey they were seizing upon.

'I wish I were male,' she admitted heartily, seeking to disarm him by emphasising her impatience at her female destiny. 'Women can do nothing. How would you like it? Needlework, and supervising cooks, and polite conversation . . . I would never shoot monkeys, though, even if I were a man. I wouldn't shoot any creature, unless it was dangerous.'

'Why learn to shoot at all, then, Sophie, you goose!' called George, reloading.

'In self-defence,' said Sophie. 'Not for sport. I don't mind wooden targets, though. And I like wearing breeches. I feel free.'

'You could be still more free,' murmured Craig.

'How?' Sophie turned to him, intrigued by the idea. His face was so close she could see tiny flecks of black in his sky-blue eyes. 'Why!' she exclaimed, distracted for a moment, 'your eyes are just like thrushes' eggs!'

It was the surprised observation of a naturalist, but to Craig it sounded more like the delighted cry of a lover. He felt a thrill of encouragement; teaching her to shoot had been an excuse for the most exquisite intimacy. And now she was admiring his eyes. After the early difficulties of the courtship, Craig glimpsed the distant harbour where he would willingly drop anchor for the rest of his days. He was dizzy with desire and, for once, speechless.

Disturbed by his dumb gaze, Sophie quickly abandoned her study of his eyes.

'How could I be still more free?' she asked, genuinely intrigued.

'Were you – in the course of time – to choose a husband,' faltered Craig, 'you could escape your father's authority and do just as you liked.'

'Oh no,' Sophie replied. 'Then I would have to do just as my husband liked.' And she returned to her scrutiny of the target.

'Permit me to say,' the words tumbled from Craig's lips, though he struggled to order them and hide his trembling, 'that any man of sense and feeling, favoured with your hand, would – would respect your freedom and independence, and cherish your fine spirit.'

For a moment Sophie considered the idea. Inexperienced in courtship, she did not dream that Craig was within a breath of proposing to her. He admired her, she knew, but she thought he spoke generally. So it was not Belmont which she conjured up in her mind, no particular house, but it was somewhere on Sabato, on a hillside, surrounded by echoing forest. In this vague, dreamlike place, Sophie imagined herself getting up when she wanted, eating and drinking when she felt like it, wearing what she wished and going off for hours with her sketchbook. The admiring husband was a shadowy figure, preoccupied with business. She had no interest at all in imagining him.

'You would,' murmured Craig, as George fired again, 'prove a mother of magnificent sons, I am sure.'

A flash of annoyance scattered the last shreds of Sophie's dream. Did Craig really cherish the idea of her independence? No! Like all men, it seemed, he could only imagine women rocking the cradle. Pregnancy, probably repeated pregnancies: she had seen it happen often enough.

'I don't want sons!' she burst out. 'I can't think about children, yet. I was still at school myself last year. And if I ever do have children, I hope they're girls.'

Craig was stung. To have felt within moments of a declaration, even with her brother a few yards away – and then to have his compliment childishly rejected. She certainly had a temper. He walked away for a few moments and pretended to study the targets. Sophie shot and missed, aiming badly in her anger.

'Hah!' cried George, observing her for a moment. 'Well done, Sophie! Shot like a woman, by God! I think you hit that bird's nest in the Immortelle tree.'

'I've had enough,' said Sophie abruptly. 'I'm hot. I'm going in.' She put down her gun and walked away to the house. The men watched her go: George with amusement, Craig with a mixture of irritation and longing. George's old school breeches were tight across Sophie's generous buttocks and the effect, as she marched off, was not as dignified as she would have wished.

'What's wrong with her now?' asked George. 'She goes off like fireworks sometimes. What did you say to upset her, Craig?'

'I don't think she likes me,' said Craig, wiping his brow. This being in love was beastly hard work. He thought perhaps he should chuck it in while he had the chance, before he was utterly lost.

'Like you? Of course she likes you! And if she don't, well, what does it matter? She's only a silly girl . . . I say, didn't she look comical in those breeches?' George burst into peals of long-suppressed laughter and Craig, with some sense of relief, joined him.

'Eh! Yuh see dat chile wid de man's clo'es on?' Eli laughed with a high, soaring sound, slapping his thighs. 'What she doin' next? She some crazy t'ing!' Julius laid another stick on the fire. Eli noticed, and instantly interpreted his friend's unusual stillness. 'Hey! Don' think yuh haul dem breeches down. All o' we has thought o'that, sure, but no nigga's ever gonna do it. Don' be distract, Julius! You want a fuck, take Viola to de wood. Don' be hypnotise by white ass. It bad meat, make you sick, fatal, dat de end o'yuh.'

'What yuh mean?'

'One fuck an' yuh hang, fo' sure. Remember yuh mission. Yuh de man for we people. Yuh not goin' to find we freedom up Missy's ass.'

'Don' give me dis hot-mouth,' Julius retorted. 'What yuh think, mi crazy? That ain't pon mi mind at all. Dat girl wild. Dat wildness interest me. No mo so.'

'What yuh say? What wid her wildness?'

Julius raised his eyes to the trees, standing all around in the darkness; growing, breathing witnesses – the only ones he would trust with his most secret thoughts. The slaves hid from their white masters behind deliberate mysteries, and sometimes even friends could trespass and have to be kept at arm's length. 'Always one parrot fly out o'de flock,' he remarked. 'Dat de one de hawk get.'

Next day Sophie ventured through the library to the door of her father's office.

'Papa . . . ? May I come in?'

Frederick Wetherby was in his study, where he had spent a lot of time since returning from his trip to meet the boat. He looked tired and preoccupied. Papers lay scattered everywhere: letters, bills, old newspapers. Her father was evidently not a tidy man.

'What is it, my dear?' He looked irritated by her intrusion. Sophie recognised the palisade of lines on his forehead, and hesitated.

'Perhaps I should . . . I won't disturb you.'

'No, no!' He shook off his preoccupied air and managed a smile, took her hands and seated her in the other chair. 'How is my Sophie? How do you like Sabato? I have hardly had time to get to know you, since you arrived. Matters – business matters – have distracted me.' His eyes wandered off to the pile of papers and the lines deepened again in his brow.

Sophie wondered briefly what was worrying him, but she was so full of her own errand that she had no appetite for anything else.

'Oh I love it here, Papa!' she cried. 'I'm getting used to the climate, now. I like it. In England I used to feel cold half the time even in summer. But –' She hesitated; she was nearing the dangerous part of her interview.

'What, my sweet?'

'I was wondering . . .'

'You are after something! Speak out, and if it's a reasonable request you shall have it.'

'I only wondered . . . please could I go out into the forest?'

'What, alone? I think not, my dear. The forest is a dangerous place.'

'No, not alone – with – with a guide. Julius, Flora's brother, you know. He knows all the birds and plants and –'

'Yes, yes. But don't expose yourself too much to the sun, my dear –'

George suddenly appeared at the door. 'Father,' he exclaimed, out of breath, 'they've arrived. The six-pounders you ordered from Gregory. The boat is out in the bay, and Kendrick's taking a gang down to help get them off. And there's some letters for you, from Barbados.'

Sophie's father stood up, seized the letters and broke the seal of the first one. 'Run along now, Sophie,' he said. 'Play with your birds, my dear.'

Sophie went, and George closed the door behind her, closeting himself with his father. After a couple of steps, Sophie heard her father's voice, 'Hell and damnation! This is bad news, George.'

'What, sir?'

'They've had news in Barbados of a rebellion on St Domingue. Fanshawe writes that thousands of slaves are armed.'

'The devils!'

'They're sacking and burning the plantation houses. And looting and raping. Raping white women. The planters' wives. A Madame Lefèvre . . . Hang it! Fanshawe's writing is so bad, I can scarce make it out.'

'By God! Ours must not hear of it,' said George.

'No newspapers, George, no pamphlets must be allowed to circulate – if you see any, bring 'em to me instantly.'

'None of ours can read, though.'

'Julius can. And Lucas. Mind you, they are loyal fellows. Julius has too much to lose. But word will spread . . . Thank heaven the guns have arrived. Let's go and see to it.'

Sophie pretended to be studying a book as her father and brother swept past. When they had gone out, curiosity drew her into her father's room. The letters were scattered, open, on his desk. She hesitated, not daring to touch them. She was perturbed at the thought of unrest on other islands, but in England, and so far here, too, she had enjoyed a life of serene social order and could not imagine anything else.

Then her attention was caught by a movement beyond the window, out in the yard. Julius strolled into view. She saw her father arrive, call him to his side and speak to him for several minutes. Then Julius walked more purposefully off towards the blacksmith's forge, disappearing behind a wall. Sophie wanted to rush down to the yard and tell him he could take her into the forest, that they had permission – but it was not the moment. With a sigh, she went to her room and started a letter to Aunt Sarah. It was time to share her first impressions of Sabato.

Up at Belmont, Craig was watching Venus clear the dinner plates. Odd that she was called Venus. She was tall, rather awkward and skinny, with buck teeth. But there was something erotic about her, nevertheless. Craig admired the swing of her full breasts under her skimpy bodice. It was the contrast between her thin frame and her generous bosom that interested him.

'Venus,' he called. 'Come here.' Leaving the plates on the table for a moment, Venus came with downcast eyes.

Craig reached up and tugged the single string that held her bodice together. It parted in the middle and fell away down her arms. Her breasts, generous and curiously pointed, hung level with Craig's face as he sat in his chair. He reached up and squeezed and caressed them. Their slight greasiness aroused him. Pulling her down towards him, he bit her till she gasped and felt his breeches tighten unbearably. He looked down at his lap.

'Let me out, Venus,' he whispered. Obediently the girl unlaced him, released the erection and waited dumbly for her duty. He pulled her down on to his lap, her slim thighs splayed, her arse hopelessly bare beneath the frail rags of her skirt. Craig savoured the feeling: he was a tingling column inside her. Venus moved up and down as she knew he required, sending her spirit up to the ceiling where it would nestle against the beams for a few minutes and avoid the violation. It wouldn't be long now. His smile had arrived: that smile she always recognised as the prelude to her release.

Behind the smile, Craig was a primed cannon. I shall blow her to pieces, he thought. His eyes were still closed. He was imagining Venus was Sophie. Venus's eyes were closed now, too. She was thinking of Africa. A hut by a river. A tall man in a boat, shooting fish with a bow and arrow, against a flood of light.

By the end of the following day George and Frederick had supervised the unloading of their battery on the beach. They had also brought up to the house two crates of muskets, shot and powder, which they carried up to the attic room under the eaves which was to be their armoury. It had windows on all sides and overlooked the yard and all the outbuildings – giving them an all-round defensive view from the house.

'Weren't those cannon a trim piece of kit, though?' marvelled George. 'Carriage, wheels, ropes, ladles, swabs, the lot – even the stones they sit on.'

'Yes,' his father agreed, 'we ought to be somewhat safer from the French now, in our little bay – and the damned privateers, always skulking about, God rot 'em. Still, I wish our house were on a promontory, like Ashton's.'

'But then you are so exposed to the storms.'

'Aye – much easier to defend yourself if there's any trouble from the slaves, however. Ashton's slave huts are quite far off, remember, on the shore – and he's got stores enough, he tells me, to withstand a siege of several weeks – fowl, and beasts, and a fine cellar, and I know not what.'

'Still, I think we are pretty safe now, considering,' mused George, admiring one of the weapons.

'Yes, to be sure. I feel more secure now,' said Frederick Wetherby, admiring his armoury and caressing the heavy key to the lock which Julius had fitted the day before. 'There's nothing like a good store of arms, my boy, to help you sleep sound at night.'

'Yes, Father. We won't let the forces of darkness run riot here.'

'Indeed not. Bestiality will not triumph here, no matter what happened at St Domingue. What! Insult our women! Let them try it. Let them try.'

13

So Very Bad

'In England, on Sunday mornings, all the church bells ring,' said Sophie, surprised by a sudden memory of Derbyshire. Julius and Eli looked curiously at her. They were sitting by the waterfall, resting for a moment before going deeper into the forest. Eli was carefully folding a large net.

'Church where yuh go sing for de God Almighty?' he asked, his long legs tucked up under his chin, squatting as he worked. Eli was restless, his long fingers always busy. Now he turned to toy with the fastening of a cage Julius had made, with a carrying handle. It was woven of thin cane in a zigzag pattern. Julius sat in stillness, watching the falling water.

Sophie hesitated. Her father had boasted to Craig that many of his slaves were converted to Christianity, but even Julius, who could speak such apparently educated English, had talked to her about jumbies – spirits. How could they possibly imagine the sights and sounds of Derbyshire? And what was the point of asking them to? She was annoyed with herself.

'Well, church is where we sing to our God, yes,' she admitted. 'But I'm very interested in your god, too. Tell me about him.'

The young men exchanged glances.

'We sing fer yuh God, too, Miss,' said Eli, rising to his feet with languid grace. 'We love de God Almighty King George.'

Sophie laughed, and then wished she had not. Far-away God; far-away King. What was the difference? But perhaps Eli was pretending to be ignorant. Perhaps it was a deliberate joke. It was hard to tell. Such an abyss divided her from the slaves, and conversing with them was like edging forward across a frail bridge made of vines.

95

'But I want to know about your gods, Eli,' she insisted, scrambling clumsily to her feet. She was wearing a dress again – Father had forbidden the breeches.

'Our God is the same as yours,' said Julius with sudden authority, drawing a line under the subject. She felt she had irritated him. Not wishing to repeat the mistake, she fell silent.

'What sort of bird you want?' enquired Julius, looking round.

'I don't know, Julius.' She shrugged. 'I don't know what sort of birds there are. They all look beautiful to me.'

'We'll go further in,' said Julius, setting off up a steep path and cutting back the vegetation with his cutlass as he went. He was naked to the waist and his skin gleamed as the sweat ran down between his shoulder-blades. Sophie could not help staring. She had not often seen men half-naked, except in pictures: especially George's prints of prize-fighters. Julius's torso was broad and heavily muscled, his chest covered with black, curly hair. It reminded her of her first glimpse of Sabato, from the boat: dark, mysterious and overgrown. She smiled to herself.

'Come.' Julius stopped, up ahead, and beckoned. Eli stood aside to let her pass. 'That nest there – what creature do you think make that?' Sophie stared. The nest was a great ball made of mud hanging off a low branch. It was larger than a human head.

'Not –' she pondered. 'Not a bird, surely?'

Julius shook his head. Then he pointed to the trunk of the tree: a column of huge termites was pouring up it towards the nest and another column coming down. The ones on their way up carried tiny fragments of leaf. They flowed across the path. A living stream.

'Army ants,' said Julius. 'You must be careful, nah. They bite strong.' Sophie lifted her skirts and jumped across. She had never been completely comfortable about insects and could not help wishing these were not quite so large: they were as big as earwigs in England.

'We stop here,' said Julius, a few minutes later. A tree had fallen and the tangled mass of its dead branches, together with the living vines that hung down from neighbouring trees and festooned it, formed a perfect hide. Julius climbed up on to the tree, crouching under a canopy of leaves, and reached down to pull Sophie up. His hand was hot and strong. Sophie felt herself soar up like a fish caught on a line. She settled herself beside him. Eli waited, holding his net and looking around at surrounding trees.

'Waaak waak waaak!' came a harsh, gabbling cry, and a flock of green parrots flew over, with shallow, rapid wing-beats.

'Oh!' cried Sophie in delight. 'What are they?'

'Them Jacquots,' said Julius. 'You want one?'

'Not Jacquots,' objected Eli. 'Loros. Him got red throats, nah.'

'You blind as a pig's ass,' retorted Julius. 'Go catch one for Miss. You see.' Eli slipped away between the trees.

Other bird calls drifted around them. The echoing laugh of a woodpecker, not unlike the ones at home: some descending notes, like a child playing a scale on a recorder; and the mournful coo of a dove. Then another call resounded: 'Co-loro . . . co-loro'. Julius was immediately alert. He whistled softly. At once an answering whistle came from Eli, hidden some distance away.

'We got Tocoloros here,' said Julius looking pleased. 'They're very beautiful. Eli can catch them easy. Lazy birds. You put them in a cage, they don't care.' He understood her aversion to the cage.

'Oh, I would like that most of all! To have birds to study, just for a few days, you know – then I would let them go again.'

A few minutes later Eli approached, grinning and flourishing the cage. 'Mi got a pair for yuh!' he boasted.

The Tocoloros's heads were royal blue, their backs green, their bellies white with a vivid scarlet slash just above the legs; the wings were barred black and white and the long tails a buff colour edged with blue. The colours at the tip of the tail merged mistily together. Sophie wondered if she could capture the effect with her water-colours, to send to Aunt Sarah.

The birds sat and blinked in their cage, seeming stupefied by their capture. Suddenly there was a loud hooting call: Whup whup whup! A small brown-and-white owl swooped low over them and vanished into a bush.

'Oh, an owl! cried Sophie, glad to be able to recognise something at last.

'Jumbie bird!' whispered Eli hoarsely.

'Take it easy, a' right, Femi,' said Julius.

But Eli stood up and looked fearfully in the direction where the owl had disappeared. 'Mi got to get herbs now, eh,' he said. 'Mi get mi herb.' He slipped off swiftly between the trees.

'What's happening?' asked Sophie. 'What's the matter with him?'

'He's scared of the bird,' explained Julius, picking up the cage and getting ready to go. 'That bird, the Jumbie Bird, Eli thinks it's spirit o'the dead, an omen, so he's got to get the herb protect him.'

'But it was only an owl!' exclaimed Sophie. 'He shouldn't be frightened.'

'Owl? Ghost? Who can say?' Julius frowned. 'How do you know? You're a very clever woman, but you don't know all these birds. You tell me, you don't know any of them.'

Sophie thought for a moment. 'I'm sorry, yes. It's all a mystery to me. What was that word you said to him? Femi? What's it mean?'

'Just our language,' said Julius. 'Our own words for me friend.'

'I'm sorry,' Sophie apologised again. 'I didn't mean to – intrude. It's none of my business.'

There was a brief silence. Julius allowed his gaze to play over her. She felt stilled, almost hypnotised.

'You're not like buckra people,' he murmured.

'Buckra!' Sophie remembered. 'I heard that word too, in a song. What's it mean? If you don't mind my asking?'

'Buckra', said Julius reflectively, 'means white. White man. White woman. You're buckra.'

'Why do you say I'm not like other white people?' asked Sophie.

Julius looked away. 'You won't like what I say.'

'Why not?'

'I don't want upset you.'

'I wont be upset. I promise.'

Julius sighed. His eyes moved reluctantly back towards her. Sophie wanted to dispel this difficulty. Why was it often so hard to talk, when one most wanted to share one's thoughts? 'Come on, Julius!' she urged playfully. 'Is it so very bad?'

At last he favoured her with a long look. But she felt her gaiety wither at his solemnity.

'My mother lived in Africa before I was born. White men came. They take everybody in the village. Throw us in stinking ship. Bring us across the sea. Nowhere to shit, just little buckets, ill people shit where them lie. Every day they take you up on deck, make you dance while some little whitey plays the fiddle. They call us monkey, devil. Beat us. Many of us die. My mother tell me all this and it still happening now. All the time.

'When we get here, we're sold. Like beasts. We got to work. If we don't work, we whipped. We answer back, we whipped more, till the bone show. Whitey do what he likes with us. No court for us, Miss. No law for us. A black life not worth a cuss. Whitey has our women when he wants, he gives us disease. My sister had a baby, but she killed it so it won't have to live in slavery.'

He stopped for a moment and drew a long, shuddering breath, like one who had cried for hours. Sophie was silenced. She struggled to confront the idea that Flora had killed her own child.

'So, Miss, you ask is it so very bad? I say yes, 'cause whitey stole us from our home and make us hate our lives.'

'You must . . . hate white people, then?' enquired Sophie timidly, shattered.

'Most of them,' Julius nodded, giving her a bleak stare. 'Yes, I hate them, when they're cruel to us. I hate all the time. It like a fire burning in the gut. I hate when I'm making the chairs for Massa, I hate when I'm making the desk and so on.'

'And my birdcage?'

'Even you hate the birdcage,' Julius reminded her.

'Do you ever . . . not feel this hate? Can't you sometimes feel happy?'

Julius looked up at the forest canopy. 'In here with the birds,' he affirmed. 'Here I feel a' right.'

Sophie felt battered by his speech, though it only laid clearly before her things she had half suspected and tried to ignore. Her mind tiptoed among the crushed stalks of her high spirits, wondering how she might frame a limp apology to Julius for making him hate his life.

'This makes me very sad,' she murmured at length. 'I can't tell you how much I regret . . .'

'I told you, you're not like other white people,' said Julius.

'Aren't I?' asked Sophie with a faint spurt of hope. 'But perhaps – the others aren't so bad as you think – I'm sure Mamma . . . I'm sure she feels . . .' But she had to abandon this speculation. She realised that, since arriving at Sabato, her mother's feelings had become a mystery to her: tangled, folded, hidden. Before, in England, all had been open, daylight, loving and giving.

'Your mother's a sweet lady sometimes,' affirmed Julius slowly. 'When she first came here, she tried to be kind. She comforted my sister when mi mammy was sold.' His lapse into slave speech for a second made him seem like a little boy.

'I wonder what I could do to help you?' pondered Sophie. 'I can't bear not being able to. At least Papa should let you and Flora go and see your mother, surely. Perhaps I could come too. We could take a mule.'

They were quite alone. Eli had disappeared. Nobody could have overheard Julius in any case, in this hooting, throbbing forest, but yet he looked around before replying. 'My mother.' He hesitated. 'She's a wild woman. She's not obedient. She's a strong character. She makes trouble. Your father don't like her. He'll be angry if you say her name. I don't want you to get in trouble.' Sophie was puzzled. But she was learning to subdue her impulses. She sighed and abandoned the idea. For a moment they stood in silence. She sank under the weight of everything he had said.

'You don't hate me, then? Not as much as the others?'

His face suddenly softened for a moment, the dark eyes glinted behind the curling lashes. 'No. I don't hate you so much as the others.' The smile faded, leaving his eyes fixed on her, but painfully. A strange wave of feeling swept down through Sophie's body, as it had on the verandah: a kind of somersault of blood. 'Any time you want you can come with me into the forest,' said Julius, so softly that his lips scarcely moved. 'Come at night, see the Jumbie Bird and Oil Bird and Potoo. You see the waterfall in the moonlight. I'll show you.'

Sophie knew she would not be allowed out at night. But she had already discovered how easy it was to slip away after dark.

'I'd love to. Everything is even more beautiful at night.'

'Next time the moon's strong,' said Julius, 'I'll send you a sign. I'll send you a new bird. That means I'm waiting for you by the waterfall.'

Suddenly, above his head, a darting flash of iridescent turquoise appeared and hovered by a huge scarlet trumpet-flower. They both looked up. It was a humming-bird, balancing on the air with its buzzing wings, daintily sipping the nectar with its long curved beak.

'She's the Ouanga-Negresse,' said Julius. 'She loves to suck that sweet stuff.'

'And what does Femi mean?' insisted Sophie. 'That word you said to Eli? I promise I won't tell anyone.'

'You're like a little dog got a bone, won't let go.' Julius smiled faintly. 'Come on, we got to go.'

Some return to ordinary activity was a comfort. She welcomed the small tease he had permitted himself. Indeed, she almost wished she were a little dog. Better to be a loved dog than a hated master.

'What about Eli?'

'He'll come his own way.'

He wanted to recover himself: to withdraw again. He had told her too much, perhaps. He had almost told her Eli's African name. That would have been unforgivable. He must defend himself more successfully. She seemed to melt his resolution. Even now she required help: as they started off down the muddy track, she slipped. Julius held out his hand, as he knew he must.

Sophie took it eagerly. She wanted to feel his human warmth; she wanted him to feel her goodwill. She was buoyed up and vibrating like the humming-bird poised to sip the nectar, but wounded by his hatred of her kind, by his sufferings. She could not ever remember feeling such delight and agony at once.

Thank God we are alone, at least, she thought, *with only trees around us. There's nothing, here, that makes him a slave.* All too soon they would be back in the yard, with the apparatus of slavery all around them. She must savour this moment. She had just opened her mouth to share this thought with Julius, when around the corner came Charles Craig, alone, and as it happened, thinking of her with some anguish.

14

Dark Secrets

It was an awkward moment. Craig stopped and stared; Sophie clasped Julius's hand determinedly and performed a somewhat ostentatious slip on the mud.

'Good morning, Mr Craig!' she cried. 'I've been looking for birds with Julius and Eli. Look! We have got some – what are they, Julius?'

'Tocoloros, Miss,' said Julius quietly.

'Trogons, you mean,' said Craig, recovering from the shock of seeing her. 'I'll escort Miss Wetherby, fellow – you take the birds and go on ahead.' He offered Sophie his arm and fought against his feelings of outrage that she should have been scrambling about the forest with this slave, covered with sweat and mud. 'You've got wet,' he reproached her.

'Oh yes, but what does it matter? It's so warm on Sabato,' cried Sophie. She sensed the need to placate him, but resented it.

'If I had known you wanted another expedition, I should have accompanied you with the greatest pleasure,' he said.

'Thank you!' Sophie smiled. 'But I would not wish to impose on you.'

'No imposition in the least,' Craig assured her. 'It is my greatest delight to be in your company, as you know.'

Sophie smiled briefly, avoiding his eyes, but found nothing to say. She looked ahead to where Julius was passing the waterfall.

'I don't think that fellow is quite the thing,' remarked Craig.

'Oh, but he knows all the names of the birds, and how they live!'

'He might do well enough as a guide, if we go another time,' conceded Craig, not wishing to irritate her too much, but unable to contain his feelings. 'But I hardly think he is responsible enough for you to entrust yourself to him. The blacks are ignorant and unreliable as a rule. You could have exposed yourself to all kinds of dangers.'

'Well,' Sophie bit her tongue, 'I'm quite all right, as you can see. But I am obliged to you for your concern.'

They did not speak again until they reached the verandah, where Sophie's mother had come out to admire the birds as they hopped about on the perches of the new aviary.

'Good morning, Charles!' She was delighted to see him. 'I'm so glad you could escort Sophie back. I'm sure we all hope you will dine with us?'

Sophie excused herself and went off to change her clothes, leaving her mother flirting with Craig. Julius, having delivered the birds, had disappeared.

'You want help, Miss Sophie?' Flora appeared in the room as Sophie was pulling off her wet dress. She paused, noticing that Flora's face seemed sadder than ever.

Sophie recollected herself; she could not bring herself to speak of the dead baby. 'Thank you, Flora. I'll have the cream muslin gown, I think, if you could lace me up the back – I've just been on a walk with your brother. He knows all about the birds. He is so clever.' Her words sounded like empty gabble, but she could not face silence.

Flora poured water into the large china basin and set it on the floor, so Sophie could sponge the mud from her legs. The sun-warmed water soothed her. Objects gave comfort, here; conversation often seemed painful.

It was an extraordinary contrast to her old life with Aunt Sarah in Derbyshire. There, feelings had been effortlessly shared and delight taken in experiences old and new, but the external world was often cold and forbidding. Sophie had frequently struggled through stinging hailstorms to the warmth and security, the loving words and smiles of her mother and aunt. Here, it was the words, and beyond them the silences, which wounded, and the mind, not the body, which was bruised.

'You and Julius are very . . . very clever, Flora.' The word sounded cheap, wrong somehow. But she struggled on. 'I wish I could have met your parents.' Flora sighed, but did not oblige with any response. 'Julius told me a little about your mother. What is her name?'

Flora looked around for a moment and spoke very softly. 'She Mrs Murphy.'

'And her Christian name? – That is – her first name, I mean.'

'Mimba. African name.'

'Yes, yes, I understand. Mimba. Mrs Murphy. You know, it sounds, well – Irish.'

'Her husband Irish man.'

'So your father was a white man?' She had noticed that Flora and Julius had lighter skin.

'Him drunkard. Massa throw 'im out. Him die long time back.'

'So you really hardly knew your father at all?'

'No, Miss.'

Flora handed Sophie a towel. As she dried her toes, Sophie realised that she and Flora had shared a similar experience: growing up without a father. Papa had been a stranger, but he had written often to her and sent her presents, and she had loved him because her mother loved him and spoke so fondly of him, and told stories about his adventures. Sophie's father had seemed like a hero. Poor Flora had to admit her own father was a villain.

'I told Julius I would try and get permission for you both to visit Pelican Bay and see your mother,' said Sophie. 'But Julius warned me it wasn't a good idea.' Flora shrugged, and emptied the water out of the window. Sophie sat on the floor, staring at her feet and feeling that the air was particularly heavy today. The very furniture seemed to sweat. 'Oh well,' she sighed, clambering up. 'I suppose I'd better get dressed. It'll soon be dinner time.'

Sophie was hungry after her exertions and the thought of some delicious dish of Serafina's was enticing. She might not have to make much conversation with Charles Craig, either, since her mother was in good spirits and would rattle away happily to him for hours. This suited Sophie, who felt that since she had come back out of the forest her spirits and energy had sunk away.

'But Frederick, you told her she could!'

Sophie's eyes opened in the dark. Her parents' bedroom was next door to her own, and the sound of their voices drifted out of their open window and in through hers. It was late; the moon was high, and Sophie had already been asleep and dreamed she was back in Hempshott again, with a young leopardess as a pet, when her mother's sudden cry had awoken her. The voices continued, but obscurely. Catching the sound of her own name, however, Sophie shook off her drowsiness, leapt out of bed and crept to the window where she could hear more clearly.

'And why not? Julius is a perfectly capable fellow,' her father was grumbling.

'But Charles was disturbed by it.'

'And who the deuce is Craig to tell me how to run my household? What should I care what he thinks?'

'Don't be foolish, Frederick. You know you respect him very much.'

'I'm glad that our neighbour is a gentleman, certainly. But if I choose to let my daughter explore the forest, escorted by two trustworthy slaves, he must accept it. She came to no harm.'

'But Frederick! You don't understand. He is very struck with Sophie.' A nerve of alarm leapt in Sophie's throat.

'So he should be. So should any young man. She's a fine-looking girl. He's welcome to admire her. But that doesn't give him the right to criticise me.'

'I don't mean that he – criticised you. Just – he was upset, to find her in the forest, alone with Julius. Her safety means a lot to him.'

'She was perfectly safe.'

'Frederick! Just think. He is the only eligible man hereabouts. They make a very pretty couple. And I am sure Sophie likes him.'

'Then she will know how to please him.'

There was a silence and a sigh. Sophie heard soft footsteps in the room next door, and the chink of a glass against a jug.

'What is it now? Another damned headache?'

'No.' Her mother's voice sounded stiff, silted up. 'It's just that – I would have thought, after what I have suffered, since my arrival here – though I seldom speak of it –' She broke into a sob. Sophie's eyes flared in astonishment at the sound of her mother's weeping. Without realising what she was doing, she bit the edge of her own hand in agitation.

'Oh, let us be spared all that again, Isabella! I beg you!'

'. . . I would have thought you would want to please me.'

'I do want to please you, damn it!'

'Then please – have a care that Sophie does not get too wild. If she takes to running around with the slaves, no eligible man will look at her. And the news from St Domingue . . .'

'Ah!' Frederick Wetherby groaned. 'There you have me, Isabella. Very well.' He sighed. 'We will clip young Sophie's wings.' There was a pause, in which Sophie almost cried out in indignation. 'I would not have her come to harm,' her father continued in a low voice. 'Not for anything in the world. Come.'

There was a shuffle and a creak, as if her mother had gone back to bed. But Sophie could not, at first. She was boiling with curiosity and outrage. Was she to be confined to the house, now? And what had her mother meant about her sufferings? Sophie's brain raced, but could produce no idea capable of explaining the mysteries of the past, nor any hint of what might be to come.

Eventually she lay down again, but the darkness seemed to thicken around her: even to whelm up from within. An hour or so later, she heard distant thunder roll around the mountains and within five minutes it was pouring with rain. The dull hammering of it on the roof was soothing, however, and she sank into sleep at last, weighed down with sheer exhaustion.

Up at Belmont, Charles Craig dozed and dreamed, unable to dive deep into sleep as he usually did. He had returned from Mount Grace in an uneasy mood. Her mother had assured him that Sophie had been escorted into the forest by two slaves, and he well understood that she had been in no danger, but he could not shake off the irritation he had felt when he saw her appear, holding Julius's hand. Most of all he was annoyed with himself for feeling this absurd jealousy: a few grains of grit chafing in the pit of his soul.

Arriving at Belmont he had found further cause for vexation. Higgs reported failure in certain horse-breeding plans he had been pursuing. Craig was hoping to mate one of his mares with a jackass, to produce a mule suited to the climate and terrain. He had bought several on a trip to Barbuda, but wished to breed them himself.

'He wouldn't have nothin' to do with her, sir,' Higgs had

lamented. 'Obstinate bugger! We tried blindfoldin' him, and we tried givin' him a glimpse of a she-ass just afore he was blindfold and then bringin' the mare in instead, but he wasn't havin' any, miserable little cuss. Oh no! He knew better.'

How could they get the wretched animal to cover the mare? And how could any creature of discrimination prefer a she-ass to his neat little grey? The truth, Craig knew, was that the jackass preferred his own kind. And if dumb brutes could be so cussed in their affections and revulsions, how much more intricate was the wretched business of human courtship.

Had Sophie been cold towards him as they returned from the forest? Or had he imagined it? Perhaps he had shown his displeasure and jealousy in his face and she had not liked it. She would not, of course, welcome the intrusion of his opinion. Her actions ought to be admired and it was usually easy to do so. The trouble was, he had no power at all over her conduct.

Influence, he might have, perhaps, through her mother; though he feared it as much as he desired it. He knew how apt girls were to shun suitors proposed by their mothers. And she was headstrong, that was clear enough. Not easily broken or brought to manage. Patience was required. He did not want to wing her, to bring her down; he doubted if he could do so with any violence of authority. But this freedom of hers must be challenged somehow. He must be patient. He must prepare an irresistible lure.

He drifted into sleep. In his dreams he was in the forest again. She was up ahead, out of sight, in someone else's company. He shouted her name, struggled to catch them up, but only heard their voices through the trees. Vines clutched at him; roots tripped him; thick tropical vegetation knitted itself about his limbs; he was caught, he struggled, in a living net.

An escape: fresh English air and the gentle curve of a hillside. Dorset perhaps. Good brown earth. It had been ploughed. He admired the deep regular ridges; this was soil that could be tamed, good country, fat country that felt the plough and carried the marks of it all winter long.

'Good land,' he said to some companion – a man with grey whiskers, his uncle perhaps, he was not sure – 'long in cultivation, it will bear well.'

He blinked. He was somewhere else, lying down. Ah! Of course. In bed at Belmont. But the ploughed field remained, too close, out of focus. No! It was Cassie's broad back, scored by the scars of past floggings, six inches from his face. Not his floggings, he had never flogged her, he had been too indulgent no doubt. With a sudden surge of disgust he threw himself out of bed and slapped her lightly on the buttocks.

'It is broad day, Cassie, you idle creature, get up and get my coffee on. I must sort out this horse business today.'

When Sophie woke up it was noon and Flora was folding up some freshly laundered clothes and putting them in the closet. Sophie found a tray on her bedside table, with a slice of pineapple and a glass of sorrel juice, and an orchid and a note from her mother. 'I hope you slept well, my darling,' it read. Sophie smiled. The sun had come out again. She could smell wet vegetation; below her window the garden steamed. But her parents' words, overheard last night, still hung in the air.

'Good mornin' Miss,' said Flora, smoothing the bed-cover and plumping up Sophie's pillows. 'Yuh want mi do somet'ing?'

Sophie wished Flora would smile. She hesitated for a moment. 'What's your favourite thing to eat in all the world, Flora?' she asked suddenly.

Flora frowned. Once again, Sophie felt the effort of communication. 'Mi like pawpaw,' the girl admitted suspiciously.

'And pineapple?'

'Eh.' She nodded, still frowning.

Sophie picked up the plate of pineapple and handed it to the girl. 'Have this, then,' she said. 'Do! I like to see you smile.' Flora backed away a little, almost alarmed, as if Sophie had suggested something indecent or dangerous. 'Don't you want it? Take it to please me.'

Reluctantly, and plainly embarrassed, Flora took the slice of fruit and bit into it. The juice ran down her chin. But there was no smile. Sophie felt she had broken another unspoken rule and given pain instead of the pleasure she had intended.

She picked up the note her mother had written. The handwriting was pretty, but hasty: the letters, however, were clear. 'Look, Flora,' she said, 'this is the letter A. It is the first letter of the alphabet.'

Flora shifted uneasily about. 'Mi can read a'ready.'

'But I thought you couldn't!'

'Mi brother teach mi.'

'Julius! Ah yes. And have you got many books? You may borrow some of mine.'

'Mi got no books,' said Flora, edging towards the door. 'Mi brother teach mi read wid a prayerbook.'

'Would you like to borrow one of my books, then? Take your pick!' Sophie gestured generously at the bookcase where all her favourite novels had been housed.

Flora paused and looked exasperated. 'Mi got no time for readin', Miss. I work till dark.'

'What about Sundays? You get Sundays off, don't you? Do take a book and try it for half an hour next Sunday.' Sophie was irritated by the way that all her kind overtures, here, were turned somehow into bullying.

Flora sighed, went across to the shelves and took a book at random, without looking at its title. On the way back to the door she gave a token nod. 'Thank you, Miss,' she said and quickly left the room.

Sophie lay back and looked at the ceiling. The episode had left her more melancholy than ever. She had made friends easily in England. Here, she felt prevented by obstruction and resentment, and if she tried to hack her way through, the more strongly it seemed to spring back up again in her face. She turned her face to the pillow, her open and sociable soul quailing with a sudden bitter sense of solitude for almost the first time in her life. A tear ran down her nose into the warm cloth.

'Aunt Sarah!' she whispered, like a small child lost.

15

Difficulty of Breathing

'Come, dearest. I need your help today,' Mrs Wetherby smiled her sweetest smile at her daughter. She was determined to charm her, to disarm her; and Sophie having overheard her parents' midnight conversation, knew why. 'I want to set about some linen for you; we must hem and embroider these sheets.'

Mrs Wetherby had laid out a collection of needlework stuff on a large mahogany table in the breezy hall.

'Didn't you have a slave who was good with her needle?' objected Sophie. 'Flora's aunt, wasn't it? Who made my dress?'

'Yes, Juno. But she's not here today; her husband is very ill. She has to nurse him. It's a nuisance.'

'Couldn't we go down and help?' asked Sophie, eager for a chance to revisit the slaves' dwellings.

'No, no.' Her mother laughed. 'You need a quiet day at home, for once. You must help me with these sheets.' Behind her playful tone was a determined will.

Sophie sat down with a sigh. 'Couldn't we at least – work on the verandah?' she asked.

'Oh, very well, go out and see your birds.' Sophie cheered up somewhat and ran out. The Tocoloros were sitting together, quite still on the highest perch. They observed Sophie suspiciously but did not react to her whistles.

'They're certainly beautiful,' remarked her mother. 'But extraordinarily still, aren't they? I'd expect them to be darting frantically about for the first few days in a cage. Trying to escape. But no. They seem quite resigned. Come along, darling. We must work.'

'Julius said they were lazy birds,' said Sophie, casting a last look at the captives as she followed her mother. 'Perhaps they won't be much fun. Sitting around and waiting to be admired all day. Like girls at a ball.'

Her mother cast her a sharp glance as they sat down by the needlework table. She did not like this sardonic tone of Sophie's, though she herself, when young, had developed sarcasm as the only weapon allowed. But she must not sympathise too much. She would distract her daughter instead.

'I saw Julius this morning –' Sophie was instantly all attention – 'and he said that young monkey Charles rescued for you – some girls are taking care of it. I forget who. Mary, I think he said. Then, when it doesn't need so much cosseting, they'll bring it up here for you.'

'I could cosset it myself, couldn't I?' Sophie frowned, threading her needle.

'I think not, darling. It's still quite wild. It might bite. A friend of ours in Grenada died of a monkey bite.'

'Well, then, the girls ought not to be put at the risk, either.'

'Please don't argue so much, Sophie! You are always objecting to things since you came here. I don't know what has got into your head. Aunt Sarah must have spoilt you, though I can hardly imagine her doing such a thing. It is very galling and I wish you'd stop.'

Sophie was chastened by this unusual outburst. For the next two hours she sewed till her eyes ached, her neck was stiff and her fingers thoroughly pricked. Her mother talked of England, of childhood adventures, and Sophie answered civilly without being drawn into the subject. Her imagination was completely captivated by Sabato and busy with it, secretly, the whole time.

'Well, these will make you a very pretty pair, for best,' yawned Isabella Wetherby at last, setting her work aside. 'Your wedding sheets, my dear.'

'I don't want to get married.'

'Perhaps not at present. But one day, maybe . . . if someone captures your fancy, you may think differently. Has nobody appealed to you yet?'

Aware that she was being intently watched, Sophie packed away her needle and thread with a deliberate tidiness she did not normally manage. 'Oh, I have thought fellows handsome, to be sure. But I have not felt anything particular for them, Mamma.'

'Dear me! what an odd girl you are! When I was your age, I had been in love a dozen times already, I am sure. Never mind. Goodness! My back aches. I must go for a nap.'

'So will I.' Sophie got up, yawned and stretched. 'I am half-way through a novel and if I can't sleep, I'll read.'

'Do darling. Is it a love story?'

'Somewhat. It is a comedy, too.'

'Ah, splendid! Enjoy it. I will see you at supper.' Isabella Wetherby trailed off into the dark depths of the house. Sophie heard her speak to Flora, who then came into the room to put away the linen.

'Flora!' said Sophie urgently. 'I was sorry to hear your uncle is ill.'

'Yes Miss.' Flora folded the sheets and laid them in the chest.

'Is he very bad? What's the matter with him?'

'It his breathin'.'

'And your aunt is nursing him? Juno? I wonder . . . I have some English medicines. Perhaps I could go and offer them? What do you think?' Flora stood reflecting on the idea. It was impossible to read her thoughts. Sophie had never seen a face so veiled.

'Yes, Miss. If you like.' Flora shrugged. Sophie strove to assert her will against the girl's inertia. 'I'll take them some of my aunt's remedies, at any rate. Where do Juno and Bacchus live?'

'Down by Eli.' Flora jerked her head to the right.

Sophie decided her best plan was to enquire again nearer the place. She heard her mother call for Flora. 'Go to my mother,' she whispered swiftly, 'but don't tell her where I'm going. Tell her I'm asleep or reading.'

Flora nodded, but with no expression of solidarity. Sophie was not sure she could trust her.

All the same, she slipped quickly into her room, rummaged in the bottom of the trunk Aunt Sarah had packed and found the medicines. Aunt Sarah had included a list of ailments and details of the appropriate remedies. Sophie soon found something that sounded suitable.

'Horse-tail, says Gerard in his *Herbal*,' Sophie smiled at Aunt Sarah's swift and curling script, which seemed to conjure up the energy of her character, 'with his roots boiled in wine is very profitable for difficulty of breathing.'

Yes! There was a small bottle labelled 'Horse-tail', and when

Sophie held it up to the light she saw fragments of leaf or root floating about in it. Quickly she put on her jacket and bonnet, hid the bottle in her pocket and slipped out of the house.

It was a quiet moment, in which the heat seemed more intense than ever. Some men were arguing in the yard, but they were too busy to notice her. She slipped away down the path between the lemon bushes. Crossing the corner of the cane field was simple, too: there was a gang at work but they were over on the far side, and she was easily hidden by the towering cane. Soon she was at the corner of the track; here was Eli's house, and a child showed her Juno's shack, beside a heliconia bush.

Though she had been so eager to come, now she had arrived Sophie did not wish to intrude. She hesitated by the door, nervous and flustered, before knocking. There were stirrings within. Suddenly the door opened and a middle-aged woman peered out, squinting against the light. Her brow was deeply creased and her hair was cut short. Two brass rings glinted in her ears, but they were her only adornment. She was tall and square, with a masculine air.

'Are you . . . Juno?' asked Sophie softly. The woman nodded. 'I'm Sophie – Miss Wetherby.' She hesitated. It was foolish to introduce herself, she supposed. Every slave must know who she was. Still, she stumbled on. 'My mother told me your husband is ill. I'm so sorry. I've brought a medicine which might give him some relief. Could I see him?' Reluctantly, the woman stood aside to let Sophie in. She stepped into the darkness.

Gradually she made out the figure of a man lying on a ragged blanket wrapped around some dried leaves. Sophie heard him before her eyes could focus on him: he inhaled with a great, rasping effort, every few seconds, and let his breath out with a groan.

Something moved at the foot of the bed; Sophie suddenly realised that Eli was there as well, squatting on his haunches with his knees drawn up under his chin.

'Hello, Eli,' she murmured. 'Poor Mr Bacchus! I've brought him some medicine.'

'He had mi herb, Miss,' said Eli. 'Mi pick 'im in di forest yesterday.'

'Of course.' Sophie looked round for a table where she might place the bottle, but there was none that she could see: just the bed and a box, where presumably Juno had been seated. Sophie handed her bottle to Eli. 'I don't suppose it'll do any good,' she said. 'But here it is, in case you want to try it, later.'

Eli looked suspiciously at the bottle and placed it on the floor beside him.

Sophie approached the bed. 'Mr Bacchus,' she murmured. 'How are you feeling?' Bacchus groaned.

'Him can't speak, Miss,' said Eli. 'Him nat talk six days nah.'

'Oh dear. I am so sorry.' Sophie gazed pityingly at the heaving wretch. Then she noticed something odd. He had no ears. Instead, there was a scarred twist of gristle and flesh on each side of his head. The sight gave her a physical shock. She could not help staring for a moment and felt quite stupefied and dumb.

Eli got up, and Sophie sensed it was time to go. She placed a sympathetic hand on Bacchus's shoulder, frustrated that she could do no more. Then she turned to Juno. 'I'm so sorry,' she whispered. 'If there is anything I can do . . .' Gently she squeezed the woman's arm. Juno acknowledged the gesture with a dignified nod. It suddenly occurred to Sophie to thank Juno for making her the dress and jacket. 'By the way,' she added softly. 'I am wearing the clothes you made, Juno, and they are very skilfully done. I am very much obliged to you.'

'It mi work, Miss.' Juno shrugged, looking away at her suffering husband. Sophie felt ashamed at having made such a trivial remark to a woman whose husband was probably dying. She bit her lip and slipped out of the door.

The sun struck her full in the face like a great gong. Through the tossing heads of the coconut palms, the sea had turned to gold. It was late. Eli came out too, and stood by her side. 'Yuh want mi take yuh home, Miss?' he asked.

'I don't know – perhaps you should stay and take care of him – I'm sorry if I said the wrong things; I am so awkward; I hate to upset people. But . . .' Sophie could not entirely get rid of her curiosity, 'Why does the poor fellow have no ears?'

'Him ears cut off.'

'Cut off?' Sophie gasped in horror. 'Why?'

'Massa say Bacchus done wrong. Him nail him to tree with one ear. An hour later he cut 'im ear off. Then he nail him to tree with other ear. Then he cut other ear off. Long time ago. When I a little boy.'

'What!' Sophie gasped and almost swooned. 'You mean my father did this?'

Eli took her arm and supported her. 'Sit down under de tree, Miss.'

'No. No. I'm quite all right. I was just – shocked.'

'Yuh go home now, Miss.' Eli looked about furtively. 'It get dark soon. Yuh nat want mi come?'

'No, no, thank you.' Sophie was not sure which would be considered worse: associating with slaves or walking alone. But alone she was less noticeable, perhaps. Although her white clothes, and her white skin, made her horribly apparent. She felt like a wrong thing, walking among the dark tree-trunks: a mistake. The slaves somehow always seemed graceful in their rags, whilst she floundered clumsily about in her finery.

She hesitated, not wanting to return to her house or see her father just now. The urge to linger in the slave settlement was irresistible, but feeling like an intruder, she needed a pretext. Then suddenly she remembered the monkey. It was down here somewhere, being cared for by the girls. She asked Eli if he knew where it was and if she could see it. He nodded and led her along a path at right angles to the main track, to three small huts fenced about with a flowering vine.

'Come in,' he said, opening a makeshift gate. The garden was planted with beans and corn. Eli did not knock on the door, but went round the back. Sophie followed, curious. Two girls were sitting behind the house, looking down across the sea. Sophie recognised them as Ruth and Mary, the pregnant girls who sometimes worked in the laundry at the back of Mount Grace.

'Good day, Ruth,' she said quickly, and Ruth greeted her with an eager smile – the first she had received from any slave so far. 'I don't think I know your friend's name?'

Ruth's friend smiled sheepishly and stood up. Sophie noticed a baby swaddled against her back.

'Mi friend Mary,' said Ruth.

'I see you have had your child,' cried Sophie with pleasure. 'Is it a boy or a girl? What is its name?'

Mary said a word, but her voice was thick and Sophie did not understand.

'Him name Joshua,' Ruth was quick to interpret. 'Him a boy, him big fella, when him cry, mi baby jump in mi belly, goin' to be him playmate.'

Eli said something sharp to the girls in their own language, at which Ruth threw him a curse and then fell silent. Sophie watched as Mary stooped to open a small wooden box which lay beside them.

'Oh! The monkey!' exclaimed Sophie with pleasure.

Mary handled it gently, stroked its head and then, to Sophie's astonishment, she pulled up her bodice and offered it the breast. 'Mi take good care o'yuh monkey, Miss,' she said with a good-humoured growl. Sophie began to understand her speech. 'Eli say mi got nuff milk for two babies. So mi feed mi chile and then mi feed yuh creature.'

Sophie was dumbstruck and could only watch as the monkey suckled. 'I – I'm very much obliged to you,' she stammered.

'When it bigger, we bring it up to yuh,' said Eli.

Suddenly George appeared round the side of the house. 'Sophie!' he exclaimed, in outrage. 'What the devil are you doing? Eli, you are to report to Watson. You should be in the boiling house. It'll be stripes for you, my friend. Get along!'

As Eli went, George cut him across the back with his riding crop. Sophie opened her mouth to protest, but George seized her hand and, ignoring the stream of salutation which had erupted from Ruth at the sight of him, dragged his sister roughly homewards.

16

Velvet Obedience

'Let go, George! You're hurting me!'

'What were you doing down there?'

'What were *you* doing down there?'

'Don't be so damned insolent! Did you have permission?'

'I went down to take some of Aunt Sarah's medicine to Juno's husband Bacchus. He's very ill. I'm afraid he's going to die.'

'He'll be no loss. The fellow was always trouble. And that confounded Eli is going the same way.' George nodded at Eli's lanky form, climbing the path up ahead of them.

'What do you mean?'

'Always slipping off if he gets the chance. Father suspected him of being an obeah man and I'll wager it's true.'

Sophie knew Eli had picked herbs when they were in the forest and treated Bacchus with them. 'He told me he worshipped God Almighty,' she insisted.

'God Almighty King George, you mean. The blacks are hopeless. Ignorant dogs. Some of 'em can't tell the difference between God Almighty, King George, and me.' George pronounced this with sarcasm and a hint of satisfaction.

Sophie thought bitterly that George behaved, sometimes, as if he thought he was a king or a god. And this place seemed to offer every encouragement to such delusions. She rubbed her wrist, still painful from his rough handling. The idea of her father cutting off Bacchus's ears returned with new vividness to her imagination, though she tried to banish it from her thoughts as she began the long climb back up to the house.

As they crossed the corner of the cane field, an old man stumbled into their path. His eyes were clouded and he walked with a stick, feeling his way.

'Stand aside, Pompey,' said George.

'Good evenin', Massa,' growled the old man, moving to let them pass. He wore a thin waistcoat, hanging open, and Sophie noticed with a sudden flash of astonishment that there was a scar on his chest in the form of the initials F. W.

'If he's called Pompey,' she whispered as they climbed on, 'why are the initials F. W. marked on his chest?'

'Frederick Wetherby, you ass.' George laughed. 'Our father, remember?'

'But why – how did Father's initials get on to Pompey's chest?' Anxious apprehension raced across her skin.

'He was branded. Long ago. We don't do it now.'

'Branded? How?'

'With a hot iron. Like farmers mark cattle.' At the violence of this idea, a cry flew from Sophie's lips. George ignored her. 'To prove he's father's property. Some of the slaves run away and the devils are so cunning they change their name, and appearance – but they can't change that. It was damned convenient, I can tell you, and I wish we did it still.' Sophie was silenced. Every day, and now every hour it seemed, brought new things she did not dare to think about: her father's initials branded on the chest of a blind old man; the horrible stumps of gristle where, at her father's instigation, Bacchus's ears had been cut off; Flora's baby, freed into death.

As they arrived in the yard, Kendrick, the manager, was hauling Eli about. He hit him a savage blow on the head with the handle of his whip and Eli fell to his knees.

'Oh – don't!' Sophie cried helplessly, half to herself. But George only gave a grim approving nod.

Suddenly Charles Craig was at her side. 'George, Sophie!' He bowed. 'Your good mother has invited me to sup with you.' Then he followed Sophie's agonised gaze and understood the situation.

'Eli only – was only showing me that monkey you gave me,' cried Sophie. 'And – I asked him to escort me down there to visit old Bacchus, who is dying. Must he be flogged, Charles?'

Her use of his Christian name went straight to Craig's heart. 'Well, George, one does not wish to be unjust, old man,' he said, holding up his hand as a signal for Kendrick to wait. Eli knelt in the dust, his shoulders drooping like a sick bird's wings.

'Why didn't you tell me that, Sophie?' grumbled George, going across to the manager. 'It's all right, Kendrick. The fellow was about Miss Wetherby's business.' Then he glared down at Eli and gave him a kick. 'Next time Miss Wetherby asks you to escort her, get leave from your overseer. Or you'll get the flogging of your life. Understand?'

'Yes, Massa.'

'Very well. Now go back to work. All right, Kendrick.' George turned to Craig and Sophie. 'I've got something to see to in the office.' He sighed. 'You must entertain Craig for a while, Sophie. If you'll excuse me, old man?'

Craig was only too glad to be left alone with Sophie.

'Thank you,' she whispered and took his offered arm with gratitude.

Craig sensed a territory where he could impress her, and it corresponded with his own aspirations. 'I hate that sort of thing,' he murmured. 'Needless cruelty. A fellow suffers through a misunderstanding. We try to avoid that at Belmont. It's easier, of course, because the estate is so much smaller. If there is any dispute, I settle it myself.'

'Do you . . . brand your slaves?' asked Sophie, as they climbed the verandah steps.

'Good God, no. That sort of thing hasn't been done hereabouts for over ten years. It's barbaric, don't you think?'

Sophie was flattered by his enquiry. Her opinions seemed to matter to him. 'Oh yes! And it must have made them hate us.'

'And of course it gives more ammunition to the Abolitionists. If we can show them that a plantation can be a model of civilisation, all this public outcry at home will die down and we can go on in peace and prosperity – which is better for us, better for England and better for the slaves, too, don't you think?'

'What public outcry?' asked Sophie, as they arrived at the verandah and Craig handed her into her chair. She had wished Aunt Sarah had been able to explain more about the Abolition movement in England. Now perhaps Craig could.

'Oh just, you know – people making a fuss about things they don't understand. I'll explain it some other time. Here comes your mother.'

Sophie was frustrated by his reply, but the arrival of Isabella had saved Craig from a most delicate subject. And Sophie was aware that his presence excused her from some awkward questioning about where she had been. So with Sophie subdued and grateful, and Craig and her mother charmed by each other as usual, they spent a pleasant hour or two before supper, though Sophie could not quite banish to the basement of her mind all unpleasant thoughts.

As she went to dress for dinner, she paused to feed her birds with some slices of mango. They had not moved, it seemed, all afternoon, but sat quite still in their cage, watching with incomprehension the caprices of their captors. Tomorrow she would try to paint them, then let them go.

Next day she was distracted, soon after she had dressed, by a strange hammering in the house. Hammering had, in the past, been associated with Julius, so instantly she followed the noise and found him fixing a huge bolt to the front door.

'Good morning, Julius.' She smiled. 'How are you?'

'Very well, thank you, Miss.'

'What are you doing?'

'Just fixin' new locks an' bolts.'

'Why, it's like a fortress.' Sophie was puzzled. Julius would not look her in the eye. 'The birds seem sad,' she said. 'They just mope about all day.'

'Not sad,' replied Julius. 'They're just lazy.'

Sophie was not convinced. 'When will the moon be strong enough to see the night-birds?' she asked softly, certain that no one could be listening.

'Soon.' Julius's eyes rose to meet hers at last. 'I send you a bird when it time,' he whispered. 'I send you a little blue bird. He shines. He's called the Azulito. When you get him, you know –' He heard her mother's step in the next room.

'To meet you by the waterfall,' whispered Sophie, 'when the moon is up. Yes.' Then she raised her voice again. 'I hope you've got a new bolt for my room, too, Julius,' she joked. 'To keep the ghosts away.'

'Oh yes, I got a lock for your room too, Miss,' said Julius, showing her a pile of locks in his toolbag, 'but no lock keeps jumbies out. They come thro' the walls.'

'Sophie!' Isabella Wetherby's face appeared round the door of the library. 'Don't distract Julius from his work. Come and help me with the linen. I am sewing in here, to be out of the noise.'

Sohie went, without a backward look and with every appearance of eagerness. She was learning to dissemble.

She felt relieved by the few intimate words she had managed to steal with Julius. Their trip to see the night-birds shimmered seductively in her imagination. Amongst the many sad and shocking things she was discovering, anticipating it was her one delight. And Julius had not forgotten. He must be thinking of it sometimes. It was fortunate she did not know that most of the time, Julius was thinking of guns and hostages.

'My dear,' began Isabella Wetherby when they were seated. 'I was sorry to hear from George that he found you down among the slaves' dwellings yesterday afternoon, after I had suggested you rest.'

'I only went to offer some of Aunt Sarah's medicine to Juno for her husband,' said Sophie with a sweet smile. 'And then it occurred to me to ask to see the monkey Charles gave me. I am so very fond of the little thing.'

Her mother hesitated. She had meant to reprimand Sophie severely, but of course Craig's attentions were of the greatest value. And Sophie had appeared genuinely pleased with him yesterday evening; more than ever before. 'If you want to go out again, why not ask Charles to escort you?' Isabella said. 'George too – as you did when you went shooting in the forest. But if George is too busy – I'm sure there is no need for a chaperone hereabouts. Charles is a perfect gentleman and an excellent companion, I find.'

'Oh yes!' Sophie agreed with enthusiasm. 'He has a kind heart, Mamma, and you know, I think that is worth more than anything.'

Isabella Wetherby was very struck with Sophie's positive expression. She was sure her daughter was beginning to soften and respond. The planned rebuke was translated, in this promising atmosphere, into the gentlest of suggestions.

'Father is worried about the rebellions on some other islands,' she murmured, keeping her voice low. 'So I'm sure you will understand, darling, if I suggest that you do not go on any solitary expeditions for the immediate future – neither on your own, nor with slaves, however trustworthy. You are so very precious to me.'

'Of course, Mamma,' answered Sophie, and reached across and stroked her mother's arm.

Isabella Wetherby was surprised by Sophie's velvet obedience and attacked the embroidery with renewed enthusiasm. Perhaps it was not going to be so very difficult to be the mother of a daughter after all.

'What yuh doin'?' Eli asked.

Julius had set a peeled banana and a slice of pawpaw on an old treestump, in a corner of the slaves' provision ground. It was the following Sunday and many of the slaves were working on their gardens. But in this remote corner, at the forest's edge, there were no rows of beans or corn, just a few fruit bushes. This suited Julius's purpose well.

'Mi goin' to catch de Azulito,' he announced.

'Ah!' Eli nodded. 'De banana, it de bait.'

'No,' Julius replied, smearing a trace of honey over the banana and smiling faintly to himself. 'De Azulito, him de bait.'

For the next few days Sophie discovered that a routine of activity had been arranged for her. Needlework or drawing every morning, then a rest after dinner, and every afternoon Charles Craig arrived to take tea, and sometimes stay to supper. Any further expeditions seemed out of the questions. The only slaves she saw were Flora and Serafina. Flora told her that Bacchus was still ailing, but somehow Sophie hesitated to ask Flora how her brother was. She had evidence of his activities, at any rate. Her door was ornamented with a stout new lock.

'To keep you safe at night, my dear.' Her father had smiled at her. The lock was the sort which could be operated from both sides. For the time being, the key was at her disposal. Sophie was not locked in. But the threat was there.

She submitted silently to this empty routine, sensing it was time to reflect. She found that she was looking forward to Craig's arrival every day. He made George relaxed and playful, and seemed to provoke her mother into her most vivacious behaviour. Things became amusing when he arrived. His visits to Mount Grace were more comfortable these days. They were never alone together, so there was no opportunity for the awkwardness she had experienced in his company before. She began to feel that, in company at least, she liked him above all men.

And he always brought something for her: a beautiful feather, or a flower picked on his walk down from Belmont. One day he brought her a great conch shell. 'That's from the beach.' He smiled. 'I found it after my swim yesterday, and immediately thought of you.'

Sophie raised it to her ear and heard the faraway roar of the sea.

'The slaves have a way of blowing the conch shells,' Craig went on.

'Oh yes. They're called to work in that way, in the morning, aren't they?' Sophie had heard the melancholy sound.

'Yes, and they blow them at their high days and holidays. Celebrations and so forth. I'm damned if I know how they do it, though.'

'Give it here,' cried George, but he puffed in vain.

'I think they alter the shell in some way,' said Craig. 'Cut an extra hole in it or something. I'll ask Claude. He's my tame musician,' he explained to Flora. 'I must get him to play for you. They have the most striking way of singing, you know, in harmony. Mournful. Touches your heart somehow. Claude and two or three of his friends. And on Saturday nights, an old fellow of yours comes sometimes. A blind drummer. Pompey, I think his name is.'

'Oh yes!' cried Sophie. 'I have met him.'

'You must hear them one day,' said Craig. 'I will invite you to supper. But at present my hospitality is limited – we are improving the kitchen at Belmont. A new stove is being fitted. Then I will issue an invitation and you shall dine to the rhythms of Africa.'

'I should like that very much!' cried Sophie. She longed to hear the slaves sing. She had heard the sound of their drumming and the hypnotic wail of their voices on Saturday nights, but only at a distance, in the dark. She looked forward to this trip to Belmont to see and hear at close quarters.

After supper that evening Craig suggested Sophie might like to go out on to the verandah to admire the moon.

'I'll come, too!' said George. 'I've just received a box of Havana cigars, from Andersen, you know. The fellow I played cards with on the ship.'

'No, George!' His mother gave him a warning look. 'I'll not have you smoking those things next to Sophie. You will make her dress smell like a bonfire. Go and smoke out at the back.'

'Very well, Mother.' George bowed demurely and withdrew.

As Sophie and Craig went out on to the verandah, Isabella shot a tender and hopeful glance at her husband. But he had fallen asleep in his chair. 'Close the door behind you, my dears,' she cried, 'or the moths will fly in and bother us.'

Craig understood her tact and was grateful for the privacy she provided. He knew he could depend on her support. But whether her daughter's response would be as positive, he was doubtful.

'The moon is almost full,' he remarked trying to compose his spirits.

The night was silken and the presence of Sophie close beside him, in opulent folds of cream satin, was most disturbing. Looking at her out of the corner of his eye, he could not discern where her bare shoulders ended and the fabric of her dress began. Her skin was cream satin, too.

She was staring at the moon, washed with its pale light. 'The moon seems bigger here. Is it because we are so much nearer the Equator?' she asked.

Craig smiled to himself. She was still hankering after Natural History and Geography, when all the other girls he had courted would by now be panting in his arms. Not than any of those girls had inspired in him a serious passion, like this.

'It's the atmosphere, perhaps,' he said. 'The humidity, which gives everything a glow. It's even more striking from the verandah up at Belmont. We see the sea more clearly from up there. You must come soon – you and George. I will invite you to sup in a few days, when my kitchen is restored, and you can both stay the night, I hope, to admire the moon and the stars. I have a telescope you might like to try.'

'Do you?' Sophie was immediately interested.

'Ah yes. And I forgot, last time you came up, to show you my egg collection.'

'Oh, that would be interesting!' cried Sophie. 'What colour eggs will my Tocoloros's be – if they do lay?'

'I'm not sure. I can't remember. You shall explore my collection for yourself.'

Craig was getting a little tired of Natural History and wondering how he could steer the conversation around to a more urgent subject. There was a pause as they both looked at the moon. Then he turned to her. 'My dear Sophie,' he murmured. 'May I ask you something?'

17

A Seductive Vision

Sophie flinched. A heaviness in his voice bore down on her. But only her eyes could escape; they searched restlessly through the darkness. She dared not look at him. Her heart was beating in her ears and she could only cling tightly to the rail of the verandah and do her best to remain calm.

'I think you know how I admire you,' he whispered. 'You must know. I have never concealed it. In fact I think I have often been too bold with my compliments and embarrassed you. I have expressed my feelings without consideration. You have felt uneasy because of it and I hate myself for that. The last thing I would ever want to do in all the world would be to cause you a moment's uneasiness.' He stopped for breath, and to wait for some kind of response.

Sophie did not know what to say. The massive leaps of her heart frightened her. The moon, riding above the clouds, was pale and calm, but sent no help. It was not a Virgin Goddess, protector of maidens, as the Greeks had believed, but a remote disc of reflected light.

After a couple of seconds' hesitation, Charles Craig continued, 'I feel we have come to know each other quite well, my dear Sophie, and as I have discovered your character I have been most struck by your generosity, your high ideals, your modesty, your intelligence. You are a very unusual young woman.' He paused again.

'Thank you,' murmured Sophie rather hoarsely, finding she had to cough. 'But I think I am quite ordinary. My friends at school were no different.'

'Then it must have been a remarkable school,' Craig smiled. He was relieved that she had made some response. It was a start. 'Your reply only illustrates that modesty which I so much admire. In short, you are the most –' he faltered slightly and his voice shook. Although Sophie was afraid of these signs of emotional struggle, she was somehow glad of them as well. She did not want to feel that he was in control; so much older, so much more eloquent, knowing exactly what he planned to say, in a prepared speech, whilst she trembled helplessly at his side.

'– The most delightful, the best of young women. I mean . . .' His voice trailed off, and he loosened his collar. '. . . The fact is, Sophie, do not be frightened by this, but . . . I have fallen in love – deeply in love with you.' Sophie's arms and legs seemed to melt. Although she had always scorned the idea of swooning, she feared at any moment she would fall to the ground.

'I hope this does not alarm you, or shock you. Indeed I am sure that you have already suspected it. Above all I implore you, let me hope.' He waited for a moment, but Sophie was unable to reply. 'Do you hate me?' he asked. Dumbly she shook her head. Encouraged, he went on, 'I realise this may be the first time anyone has spoken to you in this way. You are probably confused, not knowing what to think. Don't feel you have to say anything at all.' Sophie felt some of her terror drain away, and was grateful.

'Bless me!' he cried, striking himself at the side of the head. 'I have said it all wrong. I have quite forgot –' He laughed aloud for a moment. 'Forgive me, but I am so agitated, what I meant to say, of course, was to ask you to be my wife.' Then, with a sudden movement which startled her, he flung himself down on his knees and seized her hand. 'Marry me, Sophie, oh my dear Sophie, and make me the happiest man in the world!' He kissed her hand fervently and then, recollecting himself, gently released her. For a moment they stared at each other.

'Now I have to get up again.' He smiled. 'The etiquette guides don't warn you that after the proposal, there is the clumsy business of stumbling to your feet again.'

Sophie smiled, glad of the joke.

Craig surged up on to his feet. He still moved like a boy. 'There!' He dived into her smile. 'I may have the creaking limbs of an old fellow of thirty, but I have the heart of a passionate eighteen-year-old.' He grew serious again. 'And it is full of you.' He stared down earnestly at her. His eyes were full of fierce energy that she feared.

Sophie felt dizzy. She could not imagine what he would say next. But he had told her she did not have to say anything and he had made her laugh. The proposal was not as paralysingly awkward as she would have thought. There was something graceful about the way he was conducting it.

'I – don't know what to say,' she stammered at last.

He seized her hand. 'Permit me – say nothing. I would rather you said nothing than told me there was no hope. If all you can say is that you could never care for me, then I would rather you remained silent for seventy-five years.' Again he coaxed a smile from her. 'No need to say anything, Sophie. But there is something more I wish to mention, if you will allow me?' Sophie nodded.

'I know your life here is a great delight to you. Naturally you love being with your mother and father after such long separations. But if you were to become my wife, you could still see Mamma and Papa every day. As you know, a mere stroll separates Belmont from Mount Grace. So you must not feel that you would lose the precious company of your family. There would be no loss of anything to you.

'But there might be gains. Perhaps you would like more freedom to explore the island, make your study of the natural history?'

A thrill of excitement burst through the paralysis of her embarrassment. 'On my own?'

'Oh, not entirely alone,' said Craig. 'There are dangers in the forest, even of the mundane sort. A slippery bank – a twisted ankle – you would not like to be alone if you were unable to walk, with the army ants marching nearby.'

'No,' admitted Sophie. 'But I do so want –'

'Yes. You are a serious student. I understand. Perhaps you will write the first Natural History of Sabato. I would be the proudest man on earth if you did. Of course I would wish to accompany you myself on our expeditions. It would be the greatest joy, for me, to explore with you. But if business detained me, I would be happy for you to go into the forest if you were accompanied by a trustworthy slave.'

'There is . . . Julius.' Sophie hesitated. 'He knows the names of all the birds and their habits. Where they make their nests, and their courtship, and –' At the mention of courtship, she became embarrassed.

Craig, touched by her enthusiasm, thought for a moment. 'I would give you anything in the world, my dear Sophie,' he said. 'But I am not sure whether your father would agree to part with Julius. He is a very skilful carpenter. But perhaps, as a wedding present, he would allow the fellow to come to us, as your guide and bodyguard. Or he might permit me to buy Julius, which of course I would be only too delighted to do.'

'Oh!' cried Sophie, fighting off for a moment her vertigo at the bizarre notion of men buying and selling other men, 'If you could, I know I would be very happy!'

Charles Craig took this almost as an acceptance to his entire proposal. He could feel his blood dancing around his body, even though he was aware that in his desperation to encourage her he was saying the wildest things, at which his more sober senses might later rebel.

'Anything that makes you happy, you shall have,' he promised, squeezing her hand. 'And I fancy you would like a little school, too. There are children at Belmont who would find you a kind schoolmistress, I am sure.'

'Could I really have a school?' Sophie was amazed. A seductive vision of life at Belmont was forming in her imagination. 'I would adore it!'

'What's more,' added Craig, grinning in anticipation of his triumph, 'I would be only too glad for my wife to wear whatever clothes were rational and suitable for her situation. Breeches and boots, Sophie would be yours whenever you wished. I do not see it as a husband's right to comment on his wife's clothes, except to compliment her, which you may be sure I shall do every day, no matter what you wear.'

Sophie could not help being fascinated by the possibility of the freedom he described. He raised her hand to his lips and kissed it fervently. Then with hypnotising slowness, he turned her hand over, kissed her upturned palm and allowed the tip of his tongue to brush delicately across her skin for a moment. She gasped, perhaps in surprise; this small sound of hers destroyed his self-control.

'Oh Sophie!' he cried and hurled himself around her. Sophie, weak and spinning, felt herself trapped in his hard arms. She lifted her head up and suddenly found his face massive and close above her, blotting out all but a few framing stars. She opened her mouth, to protest, to gasp for breath, but felt his lips on hers, smelt her father's brandy on his breath, heard him groan and felt his body hard, shaking and surging all about her. Frightened, Sophie struggled, but drunk with the fulfilment of his fantasy, Craig pushed his tongue into her mouth.

She was suffocated by it. Strong and muscular, like a snake, it curled about hers. The fumes of alcohol filled her head and she felt Craig's hand squeeze her left breast, pushing himself against her and groaning.

She threw him off with an instinctive rush of strength and he turned away, ashamed. In the last moments, releasing so many hours, days, weeks of pent-up anguish, when he had at last felt her skin and tasted her tongue, he had come in his breeches.

'I beg your pardon,' he panted, not daring to face her for a moment. 'Now I've spoilt it all – I was carried away – That was a terrible liberty to take. My dear Sophie, say you forgive me. It won't happen again. I must have frightened you.'

Sophie was silent, shaking and winded. It was true, it had frightened her. His fierceness was unwelcome; she was angry with him for speaking so sweetly and then, it seemed, leaping upon her and devouring her.

'You hate me now, I'm sure,' he said, turning to her with a tormented face. 'And yet you shouldn't. It was your fault, you know. You shouldn't be so beautiful. It drives a fellow mad.'

Sophie was dumbfounded. She did not like this kind of talk.

'I'll never touch you again,' he whispered urgently. 'If that's what you want. Not even when we're married. I promise.' He was talking madness and he knew it. He was desperate not to have thrown his triumph into disaster by losing control for a moment. Sophie was still silent. He was filled with dread.

'I can see I've offended you,' he said, backing off towards the steps down into the garden. 'And I don't blame you. You want me to go away, don't you? And never come here again. Don't you? Admit it. I have made you hate me. And you want me to disappear.'

'No –' It was hesitant, but it was enough. 'Don't be silly. Of course I don't.'

'Will you forgive me, then? Forgive me my hot-bloodedness?'

There was a pause. Sophie was still too giddy to speak rationally. The violent extremes of his behaviour puzzled her. But she could not entirely banish the vision she had of a life in breeches, exploring the forest with Julius and teaching in a little school.

'Yes. But you frightened me.'

'To tell you the truth, I frightened myself.' He smiled and she responded gratefully. Again he helped them out of difficulties with his sense of humour. 'I won't come back in now,' he whispered from the verandah steps.

Sophie shrugged. 'As you please.'

'I'm not in a fit state for polite conversation. Please bid your parents good-night for me and thank them for their hospitality. I will come and speak to your father tomorrow morning, if I may?'

These words seemed to strike Sophie like a portentous blow. Must it be tomorrow? she thought. She wanted more time; she was not ready. She did not feel, yet, what she ought to feel. 'I need – time to reflect,' she stumbled.

'Of course. Of course.' He moved backwards into the darkness. 'I won't come again. It is up to you. Summon me when you have an answer. I shall try to lay my head down on the block with as much courage as King Charles. My royal namesake, poor fellow.' Another joke eased his passage.

Sophie was lost: he lurched from a threat to speak to her father tomorrow, to a promise never to come again until she wanted him. But at least he had responded to her plea for more time. She was grateful for that. It was the first requirement. 'Good-night,' she called. Her voice sounded weak and small in the blackness. A chorus of frogs, insects and night-birds seemed to engulf her words.

'Good-night, dearest Sophie!' His voice came from the dark. He had disappeared.

Sophie took a deep breath. She was glad to be alone. She leaned against a post; she must stop shaking before she went back indoors. It was a mercy, now, to have a moment to herself; a blessing to be unobserved.

But she was not quite as unobserved as she might have hoped. The whole interview had been seen and heard, and within twenty-four hours every slave withing seven miles, from Belmont to the north, down to Good Hope in the south, would know what had passed between Massa Charles and Missy out on the verandah, under the indifferent stars.

18

Radical and Strange

At first, that night, Sophie was too disturbed to sleep. Her mind buzzed round and round the notion of an independent life up at Belmont. She could get up early, put on her breeches and go out, with sketchbook and notebook, into the forest – perhaps with Julius. She would return and, in the heat of the afternoon, put in order her discoveries of the morning. The idea of writing a Natural History of Sabato had taken root.

She would dine on some exquisite dish prepared by Cassie, and since she was now Cassie's mistress, the sulkiness would have vanished. Yes. She would win Cassie over with a mixture of kindness and education. In the last two hours of daylight she would teach the little blacks to read. No, perhaps it would be better to teach them in the morning. Or in the evening? But she knew she would have other obligations. Behind all her delightful fancies of an independent life the figure of Charles Craig was hovering. He would, she supposed, want to do more of that kissing and embracing. She was surprised at how violent it had been. She had rather imagined love-making as sweet and soft. Perhaps that was why she had had so little interest in it. Charles was in love with her, she plainly understood that. But she was surprised at the pain it seemed to cause him. She had supposed that love would bring happiness, serenity, delight, not a groan and a shudder.

It was all so odd. Was she in love with him? She did not know. She looked forward to his company; she appreciated his kindness to the slaves. She admired his head and felt she would like to draw it. Its clean, straight lines appealed to her. His blue eyes were also striking. She wondered if she would be able to capture that blue with her paints. She might have to mix Prussian Blue with Cobalt and lighten it a little, somehow.

Yes, she was probably in love with him. Or she would be soon. Or in the end. She would get used to the embracing, perhaps. She might lose her fear of his lips. Or, as he grew more confident of her, he would be less desperate, less hot and shaky. Perhaps even calm. She had noticed that, at home: new-married couples always did a deal of billing and cooing. Two years later, things had usually visibly cooled. Comforted by this thought, Sophie fell asleep. She could discuss it tomorrow with her mother, who was so wise about love. Indeed her overpowering interest in it had occasionally irritated Sophie in the past, but now it would be useful to her.

The Wetherbys were at breakfast on the verandah: Mr Wetherby was devouring one of Serafina's omelettes and Sophie was picking at a piece of pawpaw. Mr Wetherby was explaining his plans for a new venture. He planned to grow some cocoa-trees along the edge of the forest, where they could be shaded by its canopy.

'We could build a drying-shed,' he pondered, 'on the land behind the slave dwellings on the south side, overlooking the sea.'

'What?' asked George, looking surprised. 'On their provision ground?'

'Well, at the moment it is their provision ground,' admitted his father, 'but we can easily give them a scrap of land somewhere else. That's good land there, and it's level, which is a great consideration when you're building, and frankly, lad, it's wasted using it to grow a few beans for blacks.'

Serafina poured some more pinapple juice into Sophie's glass. At this moment a sturdy but untidily dressed white man arrived at the verandah steps, hot and out of breath, and delivered several letters to Frederick Wetherby, who hastily wiped his mouth and seized them.

'Go round to the kitchen, Mr Weekes, and Viola will give you some breakfast,' said Sophie's mother. Serafina was serving an omelette to George as his father tore open the first letter.

Delicately Serafina arranged a garnish of sliced tomato, pawpaw and green leaves on George's plate. Sophie watched in fascination. There was an artistry in her fingers which Sophie could only admire, but never emulate. She loved eating, but hated cookery.

'Good God!' her father muttered.

'What is it, my dear?' Sophie's mother sat up. Her husband tossed the letter down and opened the next. As he read this one, the familiar fence, the vertical stakes of anxiety, appeared on his brow. Nobody dared to speak. George bolted down his omelette in haste, sensing that he must get it out of the way. Serafina's long black fingers removed the dirty dishes.

Worried, Isabella Wetherby picked up the letter and scanned the first paragraph, then seemed to choke.

'Oh!' she cried. 'Mrs Herbert and her five children! – Mrs Herbert, you know, George, who sailed with us two years ago on her way to Barbados – all murdered! – With an axe!' she threw the letter aside and fanned herself violently.

Sophie leapt up. 'Shall I fetch the smelling salts, Mamma?'

'I have them here –' her mother scrabbled in the reticule that hung by her side.

'You can go, Serafina,' said Frederick Wetherby, glowering at his wife. As soon as Serafina had disappeared, he exploded. 'Damn it, Isabella! How many times have I warned you? You must not say such things in front of them. By noon every slave we have will know there has been a murder on Barbados.'

'But our people are so good!' cried his wife. 'Serafina would not harm a fly. She's the gentlest creature in the world. And she's loyal, I'm sure.'

'None of them must be assumed loyal these days,' commented Wetherby grimly. 'We need more overseers. We've only got Kendrick and those two mulattoes Ben and Jeremiah. I don't trust them. It's not enough. I must recruit some more sound white fellows.'

'Can we afford it?' asked George. 'They're damned expensive. A trustworthy slave costs you nothing to arm; these white scoundrels know their value. They drive a hard bargain.'

'Some things we must afford,' snapped his father.

'Still, there is no unrest on Sabato,' said George. 'Damned dozy bunch, our blacks are. I can hardly get them off their backsides to work sometimes. They'd not rebel. Too much effort.'

'Don't talk like a fool!' thundered his father. 'This,' he waved the second letter, 'is from Ashton over at Pelican Bay.' Sophie pricked up her ears. 'He says that damned woman has run away.'

'What? Mimba Murphy?' asked George.

'Flora's mother?' cried Sophie.

'Damned meddlesome, trouble-making bitch!'

Sophie recoiled at the insult to the mother of Flora and Julius. Isabella recoiled at the language.

'Please, Frederick!'

'I'm sorry, my dear, but we are living in dangerous times. Worried men cannot be expected to speak in a mealy-mouthed way, as if we were all seated at some filigree tea-table in Buxton!'

His wife was silenced. She sniffed at her bottle of smelling salts, then closed her eyes and rested her head against the back of her chair. Her husband looked keenly at her for a moment, trying to judge her mood, and then he turned urgently to his son. 'This gang that killed the Herberts as Speightstown – they were armed with axes, swords – even some guns. I think we should search all the slaves' dwellings. Today, whilst they're at the fields. We'll see if any of them has any damned books or pamphlets stowed away, too.'

'I'll tell Kendrick to be vigilant in the boiling house – and Ben and Jeremiah in the fields. They might overhear something,' suggested George.

'Yes, and tell them to make sure that everyone knows that any slave who reports any trouble brewing, and identifies the ring-leaders, will be handsomely rewarded. You and I will have to perform this search ourselves. I wish we had more trustworthy men.'

'Shall I ask Craig to send some down?'

At the mention of this name, Isabella Wetherby opened her eyes and scrutinised her daughter, who betrayed no emotion. Sophie was still mesmerised by her father's words. So slaves were to be rewarded for spying on one another.

'No, Craig has enough troubles of his own. But we must get the militia mobilised. Denton, too – if we can wean him off his damned bottle. And Greene – the poor fellow is infirm, but I'm sure he can still carry a gun.' Frederick Wetherby drank the last dregs of his coffee and stood up. 'I wish I'd despatched that damned Murphy witch when I had the chance,' he muttered. 'God knows I had cause.'

Then he riffled through the remaining unopened letters. 'Bills . . . bills . . . a letter for you, my dear, from your sister – and one for Sophie.'

Her father tossed the letter across. Sophie blushed. Somehow, for a crazy moment, she thought it would be from Craig. But of course he had only left her the night before, and these letters had been brought by the untidy Mr Weekes, presumably from a boat arriving at Douglastown.

'Oh!' exclaimed Sophie, reading the sender's address on the back, 'It's from Aunt Sarah!'

'I have one from Sarah too!' cried her mother, tearing open the seal, and the men withdrew, leaving Sophie and her mother to devour Aunt Sarah's words.

My Dear Sophie,

I take up a pen on the day your ship sailed from Liverpool. I wish you Godspeed, and trust that, by the time you read these words, you will be safely arrived on Sabato and reunited with your dear mamma. You will also be making the acquaintance of your papa – almost for the first time. I trust you are pleased with each other and I am sure Mamma is contented to be restored to the bosom of her loving husband after so many years' separation.

If can spare a few moments to write, I cannot express how eagerly I would welcome the most mundane details of your daily life. What is your house like? The land around it? The landscape, the people, the whole business of plantation life? It interests me exceedingly, as you know, for there is much debate about the whole subject in England at the moment, in the coffee houses and in Parliament, and with pamphlets, engaged in furious argument, appearing every day.

Moreover, we hear every week of new riots and rebellions in the West Indies. This causes me a great deal of anxiety on behalf of you all. Do, my darling girl, at least send word to assure me of your safety; and beyond that, more, if you have time and attention to spare.

I am most interested by a certain question, Sophie. Do

your slaves worship our Christian God? Has your father converted them? I am sure they must be converted. And if they are, perhaps the hope that they will one day obtain rest and ease in heaven will help them bear the heavy burden of their daily tasks, poor souls.

But my dear, I preach to one whose personal experience must already have taught her more than I in all my readings can discover on the subject. All the same, I am taking the liberty of enclosing a little pamphlet which you might care to peruse in your leisure hours. My old schoolfellow sent it – Elizabeth Morton, you know, who lives in Buckinghamshire. She is a Quaker, and has always been a person of deep convictions and a restless conscience.

I hope in sending you this, and in what I have written, I have not caused you any anxiety or distress. I only send you such thoughts as I feel may help to illuminate your situation, and in a continuing attempt to answer your question about the Abolition movement.

Tell Mamma we have set the shallots, a task she was always glad to preside over in her warmest coat and bonnet, and as the winter is remarkably mild here, they have already begun to shoot.

There followed some endearments and news of neighbours, which Sophie perused with a fleeting eye, for the pamphlet interested her exceedingly. It was entitled *The Case for the Oppressed Africans* and was published by the Quakers. But no sooner had she opened it than her mother took it swiftly from her daughter's hands. A frown flickered across her brows.

'Your father would not like this.' Her hands trembled as she toyed with the publication. 'Sarah was always so hot-blooded, so . . . You do see, don't you, darling, that this is going to upset Papa, especially with his present anxieties.' She rubbed her throat and looked about her. Below them, a cockerel crowed suddenly in the dust in the stillness, and Isabella Wetherby jumped at the sound. Her nerves were ragged.

'Shall I burn it, Mother?' asked Sophie, on a sudden impulse. 'I'll burn the letter and the pamphlet, if you like.'

'Oh, yes please, my darling!' Her mother seized her with gratitude and kissed her cheek. 'Take it to the kitchen, throw it in the stove. Do it yourself, don't let Serafina see it. I don't think she can read, but still . . . I hardly know what else we can do. Sarah's opinions are so very . . . so very radical and strange. I don't think she is quite reliable on this subject, somehow.'

Sophie said nothing, but she hid the letter and pamphlet in the folds of her skirt. She must distract her mother and drive all thoughts of Aunt Sarah's ideas out of her head. Luckily she knew just how to achieve it. 'Mother,' she whispered, nuzzling her head against Isabella's shoulder, 'I have a secret to tell you. Last night Charles Craig asked me to marry him.'

With a great, glorious crow of delight, Isabella folded her daughter in her arms. The cockerel looked up from the grain of corn he had found and gave voice again in reply.

19

Strolling About

'Oh, my dear!' beamed Isabella Wetherby when Sophie had told her the whole story of Charles Craig's proposal. 'And did you accept?' She assumed, because of her daughter's smiling eyes, that the proposal had not been unwelcome to her.

'Well, Mamma, I said I'd think about it.'

'Well done, my darling! Mustn't accept too quickly, of course. Keep him in suspense for a day or two. Harder won is dearer.'

Sophie stared at her mother in surprise. 'And I do need to think about it, Mother. Really. I'm not sure that I love him.'

'Not being sure is all right, sweetheart. If you knew you disliked him, that would be different. But you don't – do you? He's a delightful man.'

Sophie wondered whether she should mention that she did not always quite like his lips, but decided against it.

'I do look forward to his visits.'

'Of course! And it's much better, quite frankly, to be a little wary, not to fall in love headlong. That's how I used to be. Foolish! Then things can only cool off. But to approach it cautiously, be sure you like him and love him a little, and let love grow over the weeks and months, well, that's a different matter entirely. So much better. You are clever, Sophie.'

'It's not cleverness, Mamma. I just don't know. What does love feel like?'

'How can I describe it? It's – well, one day you'll see him and you'll feel your heart turn over. Then you'll know.'

'I see,' said Sophie. 'I don't think that's happened yet, exactly.'

'Well, don't fret, my dear, because it certainly will. Oh, Sophie, I am thrilled! He is such an excellent fellow. And you will be just next door! We won't lose you at all. How soon – I expect he would like it to be soon?'

'He didn't say.'

'And you? What do you think?'

'I'm not sure.'

'Then it had better be soon. Long engagements are tiresome things. Especially in this climate.'

Sophie wondered what difference the climate made.

'Did he say he would come and speak to your father?'

'He said he would come when I wanted him to.'

'There, isn't that typical of the fellow! So considerate towards your feelings! I'm sure, if I were you, Sophie, I'd be quite mad for him by now.'

Her mother sighed in a nostalgic way and fanned herself joyfully. All the turmoils of the morning were forgotten – Aunt Sarah's letter, the murder on Barbados, all blown clear out of her mind by the sumptuous typhoon of Sophie's news. Already her mind was running wild on the subject of wedding dresses. She must write to her friend Lydia, Lady Melrose, who lived in London. Lydia would provide something stunning.

Although it would take such months – no, far better to have it made here. Juno would do an excellent job. On one of his trips to Douglastown Frederick could find some white silk. There was a little Portuguese merchant who had a shop down by the docks. He kept linen and stuffs. Lace, too, some of it straight off the ships from the East Indies. Sophie would look remarkable on her wedding day. They would get the priest up from Douglastown and invite all the local planters.

'I think I will go to my room now, Mamma,' whispered Sophie, kissing her mother's hand.

'Yes, yes. Go and write to him. Don't keep the poor fellow in suspense.' Her mother smiled, caressing her hair. Sophie smiled too, but did not commit herself to an immediate reply. She supposed she ought to give Charles Craig his answer, but something made her want to delay just a little longer. It was painful to let go of girlhood. But then, the freedom of the forests was beckoning her. *I mustn't think of it as the end of girlhood*, thought Sophie. *I must think of it as the means to achieve my breeches.* She smiled wryly to herself as she entered her room.

Flora was sweeping her floor and crying. Sophie instantly asked what was wrong.

'It me uncle, Miss.'

'What, Bacchus? Oh no! He's not – worse, is he?' Sophie's spirit quailed.

'Dead.'

Sophie felt a stab of pain, though the news was not entirely unexpected. It was more than a simple grief. She knew that on her visit to Bacchus she had been distracted and ineffectual, of no help or comfort, merely an intruder despite her best intentions. Then, when she had learnt how her father had tortured Bacchus, she knew she ought to have visited again, and struggled against every difficulty of communication until by some means, by her words or actions, she had made what amends she could.

Instead, in the week or so since her visit, she had tried not to think about it; events in her own life had blotted out the consciousness of Bacchus's illness, and now it was too late. Tears burst from her eyes, not merely that the sad travesty of his life was over, but of regret at her own cowardice.

'Oh dear. I'm so sorry.'

Flora sniffed and wiped her nose on her chemise. Sophie handed her one of her lace-edged handkerchiefs, a gift from Aunt Sarah. Flora wiped her eyes.

'When will the funeral be?' asked Sophie.

'This evenin'.'

'I must pay my respects,' said Sophie hurriedly. She put on her jacket and bonnet and, to Flora's obvious surprise, strode out of her room without any further discussion. Not even thinking that she ought to stop and ask permission, she was halfway down the winding path to the slave dwellings before she realised that she was breaking the new rules about not going out on her own. She only knew she must go, must perform some ceremony of regret which his widow at least might understand. Otherwise she would feel nothing but contempt for herself.

She paused for a few moments to pick a bunch of orchids which were growing on the stump of a tree. Some men were cutting logs in the forest, and as she passed, she heard them sing a mournful tune which brought tears to her eyes.

> 'The birds in de bush
> They bawl qua-qua
> Are time fo' man go home.'

Swiftly she crossed the corner of the cane field, ducking down as she went, as the field-gangs were nearer this time, and soon she was at Juno's gate. Inside the hut was the sound of loud lamentation. Sophie hesitated. She had visited the bereaved with her mother in Hempshott and seen the grief of simple people before, but she had never heard such wailing. A high-pitched ululating cry rose and fell, and every time it fell there was a deep groan, in which several other voices joined.

Sophie was embarrassed and stood there for a moment, holding her bunch of flowers and desperately searching for her few shreds of courage. At last she knocked and went in. An old woman rose to greet her; when Sophie's eyes got used to the darkness she could make out the weeping form of Juno draped across her husband's corpse. As she lamented, Juno raised her head and threw it back, then dashed herself forward on to him again. The old women joined in the crying, and the waves of sound tossed to and fro and seemed to lift Sophie off her feet.

She laid her flowers down at the bedside, wiped her eyes and squeezed the withered old arm of the woman who had met her. Then, suddenly, a brusque oblong of bright light fell across the mourning tableau. Someone had opened the door, and a harsh European voice called out: 'Come out! Come along! The Master needs to look in here!'

For a moment Sophie did not recognise her brother's voice, but the next instant he was beside her, saw her and glared at her. The old women scrambled to their feet, but Juno still lay across her husband's corpse, oblivious to the disturbance.

'What are you doing, George?' hissed Sophie indignantly. 'Bacchus has died, this is a house of mourning, you can't just –'

'Don't tell me what we can't do!' snapped George. 'Father and I are searching the slave dwellings, everyone one of them, and after what we've found, you should be damned grateful.'

143

He hustled the old women out and bending over Juno's body, shook her by the shoulder. 'Come along, Juno!' he called. 'Master is inspecting the house. Outside for a moment, please.'

'George!' cried Sophie, her heart crackling with indignation and outrage. 'Juno's husband has just died!' George thrust his sister aside, and for a moment Sophie's whole body seemed to glow with white rage and she almost flew at him; her teeth and nails ached for violence. Then a movement from Juno distracted her. Very slowly and stiffly Juno rose and walked to the door, looking scornfully into the distance with eyes red from weeping. George poked about in the mattress underneath the body of the dead man, then knelt down and felt behind the rough bed.

Sophie stared in at the body, disfigured in death as in life by the loss of its ears. The twisted look of suffering had faded from his face, but George's business around the corpse seemed the most hateful indecency.

'Father tortured him when he was alive, and now he's dead you can't even leave him in peace,' she hissed. 'This is disgraceful conduct, an offence before God, and I hope he punishes you for it.'

George ignored her and completed his search by ransacking the few modest pots and pans ranged along the wooden shelf and turning out the two boxes which served as seats. A few pitiful objects fell out: needlework things, a few lengths of cloth, a couple of knives and forks, a bundle of herbs, a small drum. George picked up the knives and left the other things scattered on the floor. Grimly he seized Sophie's arm and steered her out into the sunshine. Their father, standing in the strip of garden, was astonished to see his daughter.

'Look what I've found,' observed George sarcastically.

'I was paying my respects, Father,' said Sophie defiantly. Fury at her father's past cruelty gave her courage and she was faintly conscious of an increase in confidence since receiving Craig's proposal. She was not so utterly and finally her father's chattel any more. She could see a way out. 'Bacchus died, and Flora was upset. So I brought some flowers.' She waited for a rebuke, but none came. Her father squinted down at her, his head against the sun. She could not read his expression.

'Alone?' he asked in a neutral tone.

'Yes, but I am quite safe, as you can see, Papa.'

'Go back home now,' said her father. 'We will speak of this later.' He would not chastise her in front of the blacks. Sophie understood that. She turned and walked off towards the cane field, her heart still vexed in a bitter knot. Behind her, Juno and the old women went back to their funeral rites, and Frederick and George Wetherby continued their search.

It was hot work, climbing back up to the house. Anger gave way to exhaustion and desperate thirst. Instead of going up on to the verandah, Sophie went round to the back of the house, where a coral dripstone stood: a device perfected in Barbados for the production of pure water. She drank deep from a cup made of coconut shell, then sluiced her head under a stream of water from the pump. The coolness streamed down, soaking her clothes.

Then a strange sound, a kind of deep moaning, came from the open door of the laundry. Dripping and refreshed, Sophie went in to investigate. She found Ruth lying on the floor, a stick clenched between her teeth, and Mary and another woman attending her.

'What's wrong?' asked Sophie.

'De pickny comin' – de baby,' said Mary.

'But – can't we get her to a bed –' faltered Sophie '– to the house – to my bed, perhaps. Surely she shouldn't be on the floor –'

The women ignored her, as an increasing wail broke from Ruth.

'Aieeee! Dat man, dat put me t'rough dis, mi belly gwine to break, him kill me, I gwine to die –'

Sophie started to shake with terror – what could she do – she knew nothing – there was no physician by – blood and mucus on the flagstones alarmed her – another terrible howl and a stream of curses burst from the poor sufferer. Sophie's head swam; she looked away to compose herself, horrified at the thought she might do more to hinder than help by a foolish swooning. The older woman noticed and reassured her.

'Ruth fine, Missy.' She was a thin, busy character with triangular filed teeth. Her smile, though of ferocious appearance, somehow gave confidence. 'She doin' a' right. Her last baby born here.'

'You mean this isn't her first?' gasped Sophie incredulously. She was sure Ruth was younger than herself. Surely she could not be more than sixteen.

'This her third, Miss,' said the thin woman. Mary's own baby, sleeping in a box under a table, began to wail.

'What can I do to help? asked Sophie. 'Shall I soothe your baby, Mary?'

'Eh, Miss. Gib him yuh thumb to suck.'

'Come, then, Joshua!' whispered Sophie, lifting him out of his box with shaking hands that had never felt more ill-equipped for the precious charge of an infant. He was sopping wet and some of his rags fell off. At the strange sight of Sophie's white face so close, Joshua let out a fearful scream of terror and would not be pacified, so Mary took him away to quiet him, and it was Sophie who helped deliver the child, and found in the action of sponging Ruth's brow and holding her hand some relief from her own disastrous agitation.

'One las' push, nah!' called the midwife, and with a supreme effort Ruth delivered her child. It almost flew out.

Sophie looked – and with an extraordinary shock saw a white baby lying on the flagstones, linked to the mother by a rope of blood. The cord was cut, the child soon wrapped in clean rags, laid at her mother's breast, and Ruth was sitting up and smiling.

'Look at mi girl!' she kept saying. 'Look at mi little white chile! Look she sweet, look she fine, a'most as white as Missus!'

Sophie stared. She supposed Mr Kendrick, the manager, must be the father.

'I hope the father will take his responsibilities seriously,' she said, admiring the child's sweet face, the gentle curves of its African features given an unusual emphasis by the light skin. The other women giggled.

'Mi like yuh name, Miss,' said Ruth. 'Mi call mi baby Sophie, Miss. Mi beautiful chile.'

After making sure there was nothing more she could do to help Sophie walked into the house and met her mother in the hall.

'Sophie! Where have you been?'

'Only down to express my condolences to Juno. Bacchus has died, you know. I saw Father and George down there. Then, when I came back, I went into the laundry and found Ruth giving birth. So I helped – did what I could.'

'We really cannot have you strolling about the place like this,' complained her mother, vexed at this intrusion of life and death into her daughter's serene hour of betrothal. Then her face softened. 'Still.' She smiled. 'That will be Charles's concern soon enough, won't it, my dear? I quite give up on you – he will be the man to bring you to heel, my girl.' And linking her daughter's arm in her own, she escorted her in to admire the latest needlework.

20

Billing and Cooing

Two day's later Sophie sat down with her pen and ink. She must write to Charles Craig, her mother absolutely commanded it, the poor fellow could not be left in uncertainty any longer. He would go mad. Sophie must give him her answer, then he could come and see father, it would be settled and they could all rejoice. Sophie hated to disappoint her mother. But when the time came, she found herself instead writing a different letter, to a different person altogether.

Dearest Aunt Sarah,

It was a joy to hear from you. I am so interested by everything you say about slavery! I have been trying and trying, ever since I arrived here, to understand it, but it is horribly difficult. It is hard for me to believe, for instance, that my father can have ordered a man's ears to be cut off, or have his initials branded on another's chest, but I have seen the evidence with my own eyes. Though of course, I say nothing.

Such cruelty is not practised nowadays, or so George tells me. I have not seen the slaves working in the fields – at least, not close to – although I have been near enough to hear their songs and the occasional shouts of the slave-drivers. We have an English manager here, and two mulattoes who are overseers, and some trusted slaves are promoted also to the office of slave-driver, but I am not allowed to go out into the cane fields yet, because Mamma says the sun will be too strong for me. I have hardly spoken two words to Mr Kendrick, the manager, since I arrived. He lives by himself in a small house across the yard and keeps his own company – though I believe he plays cards a lot with Mr Higgs, the manager up at Belmont, our next neighbour.

Oh, by the bye, I quite forgot to assure you that we are all in health, and to thank you for the pamphlet, which I have hidden, though Mamma told me to burn it, for everybody seems very anxious that the slaves should not see anything unsettling.

As to religion, Papa had a great argument with our neighbour, Mr Charles Craig (who owns Belmont, of which I spoke) and Papa said that all our slaves are as near as may be to being Christians, but Mr Craig said it was a bad thing to convert them, for it would surely make them restless and dissatisfied. Papa disagreed. I fear our slaves must be restless and dissatisfied: what human being would not be, subjected to a life such as theirs is, with no hope of freedom? My maid Flora carries about with her a most mournful atmosphere, which I have tried to dispel with friendly overtures.

Her brother Julius is our carpenter, such a clever fellow! He took me into the forest and taught me all about the birds. If he were English I'm sure he would be a professor or a scholar. He can read too and he taught his sister to read, though I could hardly persuade her to borrow one of my books, as she said she has so little time for it. The slaves' lives must be terribly hard. I want to teach the children in a small school and soon I may be able to, because . . .

Here Sophie's flow of ingenuity dried up. It was curiously hard to describe her engagement – almost as daunting as drafting her reply to Charles himself. She pushed her letter to one side, and took a fresh sheet of paper.

'Dear Charles,' she began. Or would 'Mr Craig' be more appropriate? Though she was sitting alone in her room, her heart began to race. This must be the beginnings of love. All the same, the ink dried on her pen before she could write a single word.

Eventually, encouraged by the thought of putting on her breeches and going out into the forest, she found some words, though the letter was a queer, stiff thing; hardly one to set a young man's heart alight:

> Thank you for your proposal of marriage which I have been thinking about with great care. I will, with my father's permission, be glad to accept. Yours sincerely, Sophie Wetherby.

'You darling girl!' cried Charles Craig to the letter, when it reached him, and it was no sooner in his hands than on his lips. Cassie, who had brought it, gave him a sour look as she sauntered out of the room, but Craig neither noticed nor cared; he must to the bathhouse, he must array himself in clean linen and walk down the hill all ablaze, like a bridegroom, to obtain her father's permission.

What a funny letter! So short and formal. It had aroused him sexually all the same; some exhalation of her physical presence seemed to cling to the large, childish handwriting. How he adored her! He placed the letter in his Bible, smoothing it flat like a sacred relic. Perhaps children of theirs, or even great-grandchildren, would treasure that letter, their great-grandmother's acceptance. The thought of his and Sophie's children thrilled through Charles's veins, as he strode off for his shower, impatient to rehearse the first begetting.

Three days later the Wetherbys gave a small dinner to celebrate their daughter's engagement. Isabella sought to repair her previous neglect by inviting the old ladies who lived down the coast at Good Hope and, Mrs Dodds and Miss Hambledon accepting the invitation with eagerness, Charles Craig undertook to supervise their travel and offer them hospitality at Belmont. The arrangements for this event preoccupied him somewhat: a visit to the old ladies was necessary to ascertain their needs, so Sophie hardly saw her fiancé in the intervening days and was left to admire her engagement alone.

She was intrigued by the idea of meeting the old ladies. She recalled her father mentioning that they kept a small school at Good Hope and, since she was now privately cherishing a plan to teach the young slaves up at Belmont, she wanted very much to question them about their establishment.

Her mother was in a lather of excitement about the dinner. Apart from Miss Dodds and Miss Hambledon, she persuaded her husband to invite Alexander Ashton, who owned the large estate up at Pelican Bay, on the north side of the island. His acceptance bestowed, in Isabella Wetherby's eyes, an elegance and importance on her daughter's betrothal, for Ashton was the local representative on the island's council, the principal landowner on Sabato, and had caroused on Barbados a few years previously with Prince William Henry, when the prince was serving as a naval captain on the Leeward Islands Station.

In the event, however, business detained Alexander Ashton; all his hostess's anxious agitation could not secure the longed-for arrival and the Wetherbys were obliged to begin their dinner without him. What the company lacked in distinction, however, was amply compensated by the effusive warmth of the old ladies. Like old ladies everywhere who have little to occupy their time, they had arrived early, from a desire not to miss a glance or a crumb that might prove diverting, and when Sophie entered the room they almost leapt on her with delight.

She saw a small, round old woman, and a tall, thin one, both with long noses and bright, darting eyes, that gave them the air of rodents.

'My dear!' exclaimed the stouter, vole-like one, 'we are quite thrilled to make your acquaintance at last. I am Anne Dodds, it's a short name, if you cough you'll miss it, but my sister rejoices in her maiden name, don't you Mary?

'Miss Hambledon,' murmured Sophie, dropping a faint curtsy to the taller lady, who took her hand and gave her a gracious smile, spoilt only by two rows of black teeth. Sophie observed that Miss Hambledon had a slight moustache and was more severely dressed than her sister, who inclined to ribbons and bows.

'And here is your handsome fiancé, I declare!' cried Mrs Dodds, seizing both Charles's hands and chafing them in her exhilaration. 'Do you know, we almost crowed aloud when we heard the splendid news, for one hears nothing but bad news these days; indeed, Mary and I hardly ever hear news at all, we live in such a remote spot, and most of our acquaintance is dead!' She laughed at this announcement, in an unexpectedly robust way.

'To be sure, we have lived too long! But I am so glad we have lived to see this! For Mr Craig has always been our favourite young man since he came to see his old uncle, you know, who, by the way, was a great friend of my dear William.' Here she paused for a poignant sigh, and noticing the silence which it caused, gave a great start of guilt and pleasure. 'Oh, but I do go on! You must excuse me: I am a frightful old rattle. Mary says I run on like the Dover mail, don't you, Mary? I must stop, but I just must say many congratulations; many, many congratulations! Oh, I am so happy for you, to be sure!'

The dinner was an occasion saturated in satisfaction. Sophie was aware she had pleased her mother more than ever before in her life. They always dined in the early afternoon, and supped in the evening, after dark, and now, at three o'clock, the sun seemed to lend a mythical quality to the landscape. The dining-room at Mount Grace was at the back of the house, looking out on to tumbling forest and the mountain. Serafina's cooking was excellent and the table was decorated with heaps of flowers. The wine flowed, toasts were proposed and Sophie felt embarrassed but pleased, wishing, in some mysterious way, that she could enjoy these celebrations without being the cause of them.

Her father's brow was smoother than it had been for days; he had always felt fatherly towards Craig and was pleased to have these feelings confirmed by Sophie's happy choice. A daughter was continually a source of anxiety: his lovely girl was not going to wither away into an old maid, nor flourish unseen in some distant place, but bloom at their own gate, a daily blessing to their old age.

Sophie hardly dared look at Craig, whose hospitable duties had recently kept him from her. He was aware that after dinner he would not have the opportunity for a few moments alone with his Sophie, for he must escort the two ladies up to Belmont by mule. He therefore enjoyed the present opportunity to admire her with a kind of desperate hunger. If she cast her eyes his way, she received a glorious blaze. It was like looking into the sun. She was too nervous to eat much – something her mother saw with a smile.

Love had made Isabella Wetherby lose her appetite, years ago, and now Sophie showed the same symptoms. It was a poignant sight, which Mrs Dodds also perceived, though Miss Hambledon looked most of the time at her plate, or out of the window, for her sister talked for them both. When some comment was unavoidable, Miss Hambledon made it in a curious, sighing voice, like a breath of wind, her words disordered and somewhat distracted. She had an unfinished air.

George talked more than usual. Being the least touched by the romantic drama which had unfolded around them, he ate heartily and swore as confidently as usual.

'You should've seen the fuss the blacks were making yesterday,' he said. 'I was going along the stream, down by the grove of tamarind trees, when I heard singing, and I came across Juno and a gang of old women in the stream, washing all Bacchus's things and bawling out some frightful African verses – couldn't hear the exact words, but sounded damned indecent to me. And weren't they furious when I interrupted their barbaric singsong! "Get off back to work!" I told them, and as for black looks – well, their black looks are blacker than most, of course. Haw haw!' George was exhilarated by his father's wine.

'You shouldn't have disturbed them, Mr Wetherby,' exclaimed Mrs Dodds. 'That was one of their most important rituals, you know. Washing the dead-bed, they call it, don't they, Mary?'

'So I – believe.'

'Ah yes. An important ritual. It's the women's job, of course. A very tender ceremonial. No men allowed. They sing songs which – ah – well, let us say they are a vigorous celebration of life, are they not, Mary?' She blushed and patted her mouth with her napkin.

Her strange threadbare sister twitched. 'So we – are – have been – so we heard,' she sighed. 'Some African dialect. I do believe – although – the ones born here, perhaps . . .'

'But no men allowed, Mr Wetherby!' cried Mrs Dodds with renewed vigour. 'A purely female ceremony! You should not have been there! You are a rascal! I shall have to give you a scolding, I can see!' George looked demure. Sophie was grateful to Mrs Dodds for this rebuke.

'If you ask me, Mrs Dodds,' said George slyly, a moment later, deciding that a challenge would be entertaining, 'you're too indulgent to these savages.'

'It costs us nothing to respect their . . .' Miss Hambledon

unexpectedly seized the initiative, 'their customs – especially when it is . . . a funeral. Death is so . . .'

'Amen to that, Madam!' cried Craig, looking at Sophie for approval and encouragement, which she willingly provided. 'If they're about some ritual or other, and it's not violent, "leave well alone" is my motto.'

'The fact is, my dear Mr Wetherby,' Mrs Dodds bore down on George with her busiest smile, 'you think one way, and my sister and I think another on the subject of slavery, and there is no point in provoking an argument, for I know you are about it. Your father and mother would like to talk about something else, I am sure.'

Frederick Wetherby seemed to have fallen into a slight reverie, but his wife was grateful for the opportunity to share her thoughts.

'How can we get some music for the wedding?' she burst out, unable to contain her voluptuous imaginings any longer.

'Doesn't Greene have an overseer who is musical? I remember the fellow had a fiddle,' said George.

'Yes, Hayes has a band I think,' said Craig. 'It may be a bit Irish, but so much the better.'

'Old Greene is bound to fall asleep during the ceremony.' George grinned. 'You mustn't mind if he drowns your vows with snoring, Sophie, and really, it's better if he dozes, for when he's awake he has a curious habit of growling to himself all the time, which is worse.'

'Don't tease Sophie so!' cried her mother. 'Mr Greene is a charming old man, and Montparnasse is such an elegant house – he invited me to dine when I first came out and we had a capital evening.'

'Oh yes!' cried Mrs Dodds. 'Dear Henry Greene! His manners are so perfect, one really does not mind the growling and snoring.'

'Whom else else ought we to invite?' Isabella asked her husband.

'Christopher Dawson, I suppose, over at Belle Garden.' He picked his teeth and cast about in vain for any of his acquaintance that might add elegance or accomplishment to his daughter's nuptials.

'What, Dawson?' cried George. 'Surely not, Father! Why he is nearly always blind drunk by noon.'

'We had better have the ceremony at ten in the morning, then.' His father smiled. 'For there's no one can sing the bass line more resoundingly than Christopher Dawson, and I suppose we must have a hymn or two.'

'A hymn or two!' cried his wife. 'A half-dozen, I should hope! – But I suppose we shall all have to travel to Douglastown? St Mary's is the only Anglican church.'

'I dare say, then,' suggested Mrs Dodds, 'you would ask Mr Somerville to play the organ? He is an accomplished performer, you know. He was at Trinity College, in Cambridge, many years ago.'

Isabella Wetherby hesitated and looked at her husband. 'Must we invite the Somervilles?'

'Why, I think so, my dear. Why not?'

'Well – his wife . . .' Isabella looked at the table and toyed with her handkerchief.

'Ah!' said Mrs Dodds. 'You would not like that, I suppose?' There was a brief, embarrassed silence.

'What is it?' asked Sophie. 'What wouldn't you like, Mamma?'

'Somerville's wife is a mulatto, my dear,' her father explained briskly. 'A half-caste.'

'And she's got nostrils on her like a great heifer!' George laughed. Sophie noticed that the old ladies had become very still and composed.

'And even though Mr Somerville did play the organ at Cambridge,' her mother took up the subject with obvious distaste, 'he has been here so long, and married to that woman, he has picked up a most unattractive singsong way of speaking – almost like a slave at times.'

'But I am sure Mrs Somerville is a very decent sort of woman,' said Craig, taking a daring initiative, 'and as I recall, she is a friend of yours, Mrs Dodds – is she not?'

Sophie saw her mother start and blush, but Mrs Dodds was too generous and polite to let her hostess suffer embarrassment for a moment. 'She is indeed a most accomplished lady,' she cried, 'but a little robust in her ways, perhaps – her manner, in company, can be loud – she only reveals her excellent qualities over the years, and of course, you have not had the opportunity, I am sure, to make more than a brief acquaintance.'

Sophie's mother nodded, grateful to have the awkwardness removed.

'Well, but what about the music?' Craig turned the conversation towards more beguiling topics. 'Not in church, I mean, but afterwards, for I am sure our guests would appreciate some diversion. It may be too hot for some to contemplate dancing, but I am sure Sophie and I would like to stand up together.'

'The slaves sing beautifully, in harmony,' said Sophie, struck with a sudden thought. 'I heard some men singing the other day, whilst they were chopping wood. There was something . . . haunting about it.'

There was a brief silence, then George laughed, rather wildly. 'You can't have blacks singing at your wedding, Sophie!' he cried.

'Why not?' asked Sophie.

'It would not be seemly, dear,' soothed her mother. 'Although I admit that they have a rare talent for music.'

'Aye,' agreed George. 'You can hear them on a Saturday night drumming away and shrieking and mopping and mowing like things possessed.'

'I do agree with you, my dear,' said Mrs Dodds quietly, and reached out and squeezed Sophie's hand for an instant, as if she were consoling her. 'Their singing can be very fine. My sister and I like to hear our dear people sing on their Saturday nights, don't we, Mary?'

'Oh!' cried Miss Hambledon, gazing rapturously at the side-board, 'to be – sure, we –'

'But perhaps not for a wedding, you know.' Mrs Dodds cast a diplomatic glance at her host. One look from Mr Wetherby was enough to convince Sophie that it would be out of the question for slaves to sing at her wedding. It was a disappointing detail in what seemed to be a pleasant prospect opening up before her. Although she did not entirely like the thought of all these eccentric planters assembling to celebrate her marriage. She wished she could get married quietly, at Mount Grace. She might suggest it to Charles, who could undertake to broach the subject with her mother.

Any further thoughts on the topic were prevented by the sound of a booming voice and ringing heels, which announced the arrival of Alexander Ashton, a huge figure, quite a head taller than Frederick Wetherby, with a great red sunburnt beak of a nose. He strode directly into the dining-room, still wearing his muddy riding boots, and seized Isabella Wetherby's hand with a confidence and éclat which reminded Sophie of the villain in an opera.

'My dear Madam! How can you forgive me this impudence? I assure you, I shouldn't have been so damned late if I could have helped it, you know – I find you in blooming looks, and I hope, in good health, hey?' Isabella answered this braying enquiry politely and Ashton, with a somewhat brutal briskness, turned his attention to each of the company in turn.

'My dear Mrs Dodds! What a very great pleasure! And Miss Hambledon! Delighted, dear lady! Ah! Now this must be your daughter, Wetherby – enchanted to make your acquaintance, m'dear!'

Sophie felt her hand roughly taken and kissed; she noticed the scrape of his unshaven chin, saw his grey eyes wash over her and turn indifferently to the menfolk.

'May I congratulate you, Craig! The young lady is a beauty! Much better than you deserve, I dare say, you dog, you sly dog, but then, you always were a sly dog, hiding your best bones away and keeping them for yourself! Haw Haw!'

Sophie was not entirely flattered to have herself compared to a bone, though she consoled herself with the thought that most of the company would perhaps have missed the allusion. Certainly her mother had forgiven him it, as she would have forgiven Alexander Ashton anything. She was even now stirring herself to see if his dinner could be resurrected, as Ashton himself, without even a brief absence to wash or repair his travel-stained clothing, sank into her vacated chair, leaned back and addressed Sophie's father in the kind of bawling voice convinced of the superiority of its words to any other sound.

'Tell you what, Wetherby, part of the reason I was so late, look 'ee – apart from your track round the east side, which is in a damnable state of disrepair, you dog, you must send a gang out to mend it if you can spare any fellows from the harvest – Humphrey – my horse, you know, dear ladies, a most tremendous fellow – almost broke a leg on one of your confounded potholes – anyway – thank you, Madam, a little claret will refresh me – I will withdraw directly and make a brief toilet, if I may – but I was about to tell you, Wetherby, I have been plagued with the most troublesome pack of runaways! On

Tuesday I lost four, including my cooper, which is a wretched piece of ill-luck, for I am almost out of hogsheads, and to lose him in mid-harvest, well! – Your health, ladies.'

He lifted the glass to his lips, and since no one else dared speak, all were obliged to listen to the sound of his drinking, which was almost as loud and unedifying as his speech.

'But I tell you who I am convinced is behind all this, Wetherby: that damned witch you sold me, Mimba Murphy. Good God! The woman's a cunning devil, and no mistake – if you have any others such, don't attempt to foist 'em on me, you cunning swine, you can keep 'em to trouble your own head next time.'

Sophie was immediately alert at the mention of Julius's and Flora's mother, and prayed that Mr Ashton would see fit to confide more details, but learned no more beyond what she knew already: that Mimba Murphy had run away into the forest a couple of weeks previously. After a few more curses, Ashton embarked on a conversation with Frederick and George about the progress of raising the militia.

Shortly afterwards the party broke up, for the old ladies were anxious to make their mule-journey up to Belmont before dark. Sophie went out to bid them goodbye. Craig kissed her on the cheek and gave her a look which eloquently expressed his regret at having to depart. Sophie smiled, looked modestly down at the earth and, catching sight of a small lizard sunning itself on a stone, wondered for an instant if the creature could behold their actions, or understand their words.

'You must come to Good Hope!' cried old Mrs Dodds, as her mule set off, and Sophie called her thanks after her and assured her she would love nothing better. She still had not found the opportunity to ask them about their school.

'Come, Sophie!' her mother summoned her urgently from a window. 'I want you to entertain Mr Ashton!'

Sophie turned obediently to do her duty, but could not help feeling that she would rather spend the rest of the day listening to Mrs Dodds rattling and her sister stuttering than Alexander Ashton's braying, no matter how many princes he had caroused with.

21

Hammers and Pistons

Two days later, after having escorted Mrs Dodds and Miss Hambledon safely back to Good Hope, Charles Craig returned to Mount Grace, and after dinner was granted the private interview with Sophie for which he had been longing. George had stumbled off for a nap, promising Craig he would walk home with him at half-past five and pass a bachelor evening agreeably at Belmont with cards and cigars. Frederick Wetherby retired to his study; his wife, with many a knowing smile, declared she needed her after-dinner nap and left Sophie and Charles alone together on the verandah.

Sophie's heart began to flutter – and so, of course, did Craig's. They sat for some minutes in silence. Sophie felt quite dizzy with embarrassment, deserted by words. Eventually Craig drew closer to her in his chair and leaning forward, picked up her hand.

'My dearest Sophie,' he whispered. 'Permit me to tell you the ecstasy into which your acceptance has thrown me. I have scarcely been able to eat for the past few days; just now with your family I could barely talk intelligibly. My only desire is to be with you, hear your voice, look at your lovely face and thank God for my happiness. You are like an angel, and I can only kneel and worship.' Sophie kept her eyes down and said nothing, only squirmed silently in some invisible inner place.

'Look at me, please,' he begged, modulating into a more informal tone. 'Just a little look. Only a quick peep. It won't hurt.'

Sophie obliged him, but found his eyes fearfully ablaze. 'I wish you wouldn't –' she faltered, 'talk so – I am not accustomed –'

'Forgive me!' cried Charles Craig. 'I forget myself. Of course, you are not used to hear a lover. I will not embarrass you any more – only permit me one kiss and we will talk about something else. Just one kiss.' Remembering the first kiss, Sophie was afraid, and offered him only her hands. But pulling them towards him, Craig drew her closer, until she felt his breath on her face again, and the blue of his eyes closed over her like the surface of a pool. Sophie was afraid she would drown, like last time, but she felt only the lightest of touches: his lips brushed over hers like a feather drifting across.

This required a huge effort of self-control on his part, for his tongue quivered to its roots with the desire to invade her, and his heart and groin surged and throbbed with desire, but Charles Craig was determined to offer her a dainty kiss that she might enjoy. Once she learnt to appreciate his delicate caresses he could give in, little by little, to the tempests which racked him when she was nearby.

For her part, Sophie felt the dry, maidenly kiss with relief, but in the very heart of it, when her ears warned her that somebody was walking up the verandah steps and would disturb their dalliance, she pulled herself away and hastily stood up, glad to be excused.

It was Julius, carrying a small birdcage. Craig, still dazzled and distracted by the smell of her skin, sat stunned for a minute.

'Oh Julius!' cried Sophie, 'Is that the little bird you promised me?'

'Yes, Miss. The Azulito.' For a second Julius looked straight into her face. This was the sign. They would meet by the waterfall tonight, when the moon was up.

'Thank you so much,' said Sophie, tortured by her inability to say more.

'Sorry to disturb,' murmured Julius and turned on his heel.

'Not at all,' cried Sophie, feeling a curious sense of guilt that Julius had come upon them together. She wished he would stay for a moment, but he was down the steps and away before Craig could say a word.

'That fellow has a damned cheek,' he muttered.

'Oh, it's only a bird,' said Sophie, suddenly driven to cunning. 'You know me and my birds, Charles. Come – let's see if my Trogons are billing and cooing!' And, smiling into his face, she held out her hand and he was instantly tamed.

The Trogons – or Tocoloros, as Sophie secretly thought of them, were still sitting hunched up together on their branch, looking rather miserable.

'They don't seem very happy together,' observed Charles. 'Not like us!' He squeezed her hand.

'Perhaps they're not suited, poor things,' pondered Sophie. 'Imagine being cooped up together in this cage, if they don't really like each other! I must let them out soon, but I haven't managed to paint them well enough yet. I've tried many times, but my technique is so poor they hardly even look like birds sometimes.'

'Try again tomorrow,' said Charles, with an intimate smile. 'And I will assist, if I may, with encouragement and praise.'

Eventually George reappeared from his sleep, and declared he was ready to walk up to Belmont. Reluctantly Charles left Sophie's side, with many a fond backward look, promising to return tomorrow for the watercolours. George seemed unusually sober and affectionate towards his sister – he kissed her on the cheek and congratulated her on having betrothed herself to such a decent fellow. Then Sophie went to her room, and found Flora sweeping.

'Oh, Flora!' Sophie felt propelled into another world. 'Did you know that your mother has left Mr Ashton's place at Pelican Bay? Mr Ashton told us, when he came to dinner the other day.' Flora looked up, paused for a moment, shrugged, and then resumed her work. What she knew, she would keep private – that much was clear. 'I thought I had better tell you,' Sophie went on, washing her face. 'In case – I suppose it's possible – your mother might want to come and see you here. If she does, you may be sure that I'll say nothing about it. I'll help, if you like. If I can.'

Flora frowned slightly. 'A' right, Miss. No need.'

Once again Sophie felt herself excluded. She sighed and buried her face in a towel. She would have to persevere, that was all.

Night fell, and Sophie took a light supper with her parents, George being up at Belmont with Craig. There was some sense of anticlimax after the animated dinner earlier in the day and nobody was really hungry. Sophie was nervous, however. As soon as the moon was up, Julius would be waiting by the waterfall.

'An early night, I think, my love,' said Sophie's mother, smoothing her daughter's hair and bathing her in a mild smile. 'You need a good rest after all this excitement.'

Sophie kissed both parents and went to her room. Moonlight fell on to the floor. She lit a candle and closed the shutters. Moths batted about, attracted to the light. One ventured too near the candle flame and singed its wings. Sophie blew the candle out again and opened the shutters. Restless, she walked up and down. In the moonlight, the face of her watch said eight o'clock. It had been dark for almost two hours.

She lay down under the muslin nets, in case her mother should come in. She prayed that her parents would go to bed early. Yes! There was a tap on her door. Sophie froze in anticipation – she heard her mother's light step – and the nets were swept aside and she felt her mother's lips on her brow. Then she was gone, leaving the faintest scent of violets.

Distant sounds of music drifted up the hill from the slave dwellings: drums and voices and a violin. It was Saturday night. Julius would be waiting. Sophie hated deceiving her mother, but she would never have been given permission to go out. And her engagement had made her bolder. She could see an end to her father's authority and she felt that Craig's would be altogether more elastic.

There was still half an hour to wait and, to Sophie's relief, the faint sound of her father's snores suggested that getting out of the house unobserved would be easy. Swiftly she threw off her dress, arranged her pillow under the sheet to resemble a sleeping body and pulled on her shirt and breeches. Carrying her boots, she padded barefoot out of her room, along the hall and on to the verandah in perfect silence and ease. The moonlight washed round her ankles like a lagoon and she savoured the feeling of the night all around her for a moment.

In England, the nights were cold, threaded with savage cries: the blood-curdling bark of a vixen echoing across a frosty field, or the sudden shriek of an owl in a nearby tree. Here, the night seemed to glitter with sound, as millions of insects, frogs and toads throbbed like tiny engines. The air was as warm as breath. She moved off confidently on her strong boots. Walking was easier at night, though, in the glare of the day it required some effort to push through the sodden wall of humidity.

But penetrating the forest was not so easy in the dark. The moonlight fell in patches, illuminating a tangled mass of lianas here, a suddenly flapping leaf there. Sophie was frightened despite herself and ventured slowly forward, her hands in front of her face, groping and tripping over roots and pools and anthills. Suddenly a hand closed over hers; she gasped in shock, but instantly recognised the warmth and strength of Julius. He appeared before her, or at least, the whites of his eyes did, and when he spoke, his teeth flashed in the dark.

'I came to meet you,' he said.

'Thank you so much, Julius! I was having difficulty, I admit.'

'You got your breeches on, good,' he observed.

'Oh! How can you tell? Can you see in the dark, like a cat?'

'I can see you easy in the dark.' She heard a smile in his voice. 'You shine.'

He led her deep into the forest, until they stopped by a slight clearing where a huge tree had crashed down. Julius touched her arm and pointed.

'Look Over there!' A bird's eyes flashed in the moonlight for an instant as it swooped through a gap between trees. 'That's the Potoo. He's called "Poor-me-one". He hunts for insects. Moths. Listen!' Sophie waited, and heard a soft, breathy call, like a child playing a descending scale on a recorder. 'Poor-me-one,' confirmed Julius.

Sophie heard more birds than she saw: the 'chuck-wit-wit-wee-oo' of the nightjar, and the soft purring hoots of owls.

'Smell this flower,' commanded Julius, 'it's strong at night.'

Sophie obeyed, and a rich scent filled her nostrils. 'How delicious!' she sighed. 'It makes me feel happy.'

Julius picked the flower, and fixed it in her hair. She could smell the sweaty musk of his body beyond the flower's scent.

'Now you can take the happy smell with you,' he said, standing back respectfully after the necessary closeness of the hair-adorning.

Sophie knew she must tell him about her engagement to Charles Craig, and how, quite soon, Julius would be her official guide and bodyguard and escort her through the forest. They would make a complete study of the wildlife. If I do ever write the book, thought Sophie, Julius's name shall be on the title page as well as mine. I suppose his name is Murphy, Julius Murphy and Sophie Wetherby. Oh no! Of course, my name will be Craig. Sophie Craig.

She opened her mouth to tell him of her engagement, but some other words came out.

'Julius . . . have you got a wife?'

'No, Miss.'

'Have you ever . . . been in love?'

'Once I had a nice girl. Belle. But she died. She got sick. A bad sickness called yaws.'

'I'm so sorry. And you've had no sweetheart since Belle?'

There was a hesitation. As an accomplished craftsman, and a clever and handsome fellow, Julius had considerable status on the plantation and many young women were available to him. He had accepted their overtures at random, from time to time, over the past years, though now that he had become engrossed in more serious plans to improve the lot of the slaves at Mount Grace, he felt he had little time for such distractions. None of these thoughts were to be shared with Massa's daughter. He was irritated by her questions, yet flattered by them. Her interest in him as a man was obvious and disturbing. He was thinking of her, these days, much too much, and when he was alone with her his heart rioted.

'No, Miss. I haven't got a sweetheart. I don't feel it in me heart.' That was true enough.

'I'm so very sorry, Julius.' She reached out, in the dark, found his hand and squeezed it. He uttered a tiny sound: a faint gasp or sob, she was not sure what. She could not see his face, and felt she must let go of his hand again.

'I don't mean to remind you of unhappy things,' she whispered. 'I'm so happy here, with you showing me these wonders . . . I wish you could be happy too.'

'I am very happy, Miss.' His voice was low, but true. 'Very happy here in the forest always.'

Beyond the occasional whoop and purr of night creatures, she heard the faint sound of drums. 'Is that the sound of our slaves?' she asked. 'Where are we, exactly? Could we go and watch them dance?'

'That not Mount Grace music,' said Julius. 'That Belmont.'

'Oh, really? Are we so near Mr Craig's house? I would love to see his slaves dance and listen to their music. Can we go?' There was an obstruction; she could sense it.

He struggled with his own destructive intentions, for he had

164

deliberately led her this way. He had heard of her engagement to Charles Craig with an inward burning, a bitterness which he knew was ridiculous. His first response to her arrival on Sabato had been that she might be useful to his cause, somehow. Now a more personal desire to hurt her was gathering in him. Her open, ardent nature exerted an appeal which he could not altogether shake off. He could, with tremendous effort, resist her beauty, perhaps. Her humanity was more dangerous.

Sophie was desperate to learn more about the slaves' music-making and tried to dispel whatever doubts he was entertaining. 'We don't have to be seen by them,' she insisted. 'Just go a bit nearer. So we could hear the words of the songs. And you could tell me what they mean.' Julius sighed, caught by a desire to wound and an irritating impulse to protect and console.

'A' right, Miss.'

Sophie wished he would call her by her name, but it seemed an impossible thing to ask.

They followed the sound of drumming and soon saw that it came from Belmont itself: from the Great House. The lamps were lit; slave voices rose and fell in a lively rhythm.

'Why, the slaves are singing in Charles's house!' cried Sophie. 'Let's go closer – although I must take care not to be seen, of course.' Julius hesitated but Sophie would not be stopped. 'Come,' she said. 'We can peep through the window there; they'll never hear us. Now I come to think of it, George is up here tonight. They're playing cards and gambling, I dare say. They'll be drinking, too; they'll never see us. How delightful for them to have the slaves singing to them; and just think, George told me today I couldn't have slave music at my wedding.'

'At your wedding?' asked Julius quickly. Sophie's heart leapt: she felt caught out.

'If I should ever – marry,' she stumbled, astonished at her inability to acknowledge her engagement. Julius was astonished too. This was more madness. He knew she was engaged. All the slaves knew. Why deny it? For a moment she seemed almost guilty. Then she recovered her authority. 'Come, Julius! We can watch for a moment and then slip away again.'

Nimbly she glided through the dark garden, up the steps and on to the verandah and, concealing herself against the side of the house, peered in through the window, with Julius at her side.

First she saw two male slaves, seated on the floor, drumming and singing. Two women beside them provided a fierce swaying harmony. Two other women, whom Sophie recognised as Cassie and Venus, were dancing whilst George and Craig watched, sprawled in their chairs. Though the slave girls had been clothed when Sophie had visited Belmont, now they were naked to the waist. Sophie had seen slave women half-naked before, working outdoors, gardening and feeding their babies, but the way these women moved, now, disturbed her.

Venus, though thin, had large, pendulous breasts, which shivered and shook as she shuffled along, hips undulating. She moved like the sea, approaching Craig and retreating in a teasing way. Cassie, whose breasts were small and triangular against her large torso, turned her back towards the men and, drawing her skirt tight, shook her arse at them. Sophie began to feel sick. There was something wrong about this.

George was grinning in a loose and foolish way. And the same look was creeping into Craig's eyes. Venus approached again, tantalising him by shaking her sweating torso. There was no mistaking the invitation of her dance, though her face was curiously blank. Craig grabbed at her but she leapt back, and he leaned forward, beckoning for her to return.

Venus approached again, lifting her skirt this time, inch by inch, revealing her fine, slim thighs. Sophie watched, mesmerised, gnawing her fingers and whimpering in horror.

'Come away, Miss,' muttered Julius in her ear.

'No!'

She had to watch. She had to feel this sense of looming defilement. She was fastened to the sight.

Finally Craig rose up out of his chair, threw Venus in the air and caught her up in his arms, with her legs wound around his body. He carried her to the table and laid her down backwards upon it; unlaced his breeches and let them fall. The drum thrashed on and the women's voices rose in an erotic wail.

Craig, with every appearance of confidence and long practice, spat on his hand, made Venus ready and entered her. As he did so his breeches fell around his ankles and Sophie beheld the buttocks of her fiancé, lightly furred with blond hair and framed by the elegant black legs of his mistress. The whole spectacle was monstrous, ludicrous, painful.

She was aware that George was doing something similar to Cassie, also on the table, but with Cassie turning her back and being served from behind, like the heifers in the meadow below Aunt Sarah's garden wall. Only compared to the brief sexual acts of cattle, which was all Sophie had previously witessed, this horrible spectacle seemed to go on and on; the men were pumping like machines. Hammers and pistons. Surely they would kill the women? How could they bear it?

Venus, propping herself up with her arms behind her, shook and winced at every thrust of Craig's; her breasts bounced, which Craig watched at first with a greedy, carousing air, and then he threw his head back and shut his eyes. Both actors were now closed off in their private world. Repelled by the violence of their coupling, Sophie could imagine neither their physical sensations nor their thoughts. She would never have believed that Craig was thinking of her, even imagining it was her body he was possessing.

All she saw was the man who, four hours ago, had assured her she was an angel whom he only wanted to kneel before and worship. And now he was behaving like some hooved creature from the darkest pit of hell. She ran from the verandah into the night. After a few yards, she had to stop suddenly. A strange feeling gathered in her stomach, something unfolding. She recognised nausea, and as she vomited felt Julius's hands sustaining her.

A few moments later, when she had recovered from the paroxysm, he found a smooth green coconut, lopped the top off with his cutlass and gave it to her. She drank a little, then let it stream down her face, neck and shoulders, raising her head to the moon to be cleansed.

22

A Hard Time

'Mr Craig is your man?' enquired Julius softly. They were back in the forest, sitting on a fallen tree-trunk. Sophie lifted her head.

'He asked me to marry him.' Why did it feel like a confession? 'My mother encouraged it. He said if I married him I could do what I liked. He said I could wear breeches and come out into the forest and learn about all the birds. He said . . . he said you could take care of me. Teach me things.' It was not quite the truth, but it was what Sophie wanted the truth to be.

'When he saw us before in the forest, he don't like it.'

Sophie blushed. 'Oh no, he didn't mind at all – it was just that – he was rather angry with me about something else.'

'No. You don't understand. I understand fine. He don't like me near his woman.'

'I'm not his woman!'

'You told him you'd marry him.'

'I won't now! I'd rather die than even speak to him again.'

'You'll speak to him again, fo' sure. You'll marry him anyway.' His tone was bitter, almost taunting.

'How can you say that? It's an insult!' Sophie was astonished at her anger. Why was she shouting at Julius? 'I thought you understood me – You don't understand me at all! I won't marry him. They can't make me. I'm not a possession.'

But Julius was. Her words sprang backward treacherously and stung her. Sophie's indignation stumbled.

'No. Not like me. They can make me do anything. Even eat my brother's shit. That's what your father made me do, when I was a little boy and I naughty. He make Eli shit in me mouth.'

His eyes burned like phosphorous. Tears overwhelmed her, but he did not comfort her. She drew up the hem of her shirt and howled into it, not caring about the noise she made; not caring what a spectacle she might be; not even caring if Julius might still be there when she was finished. But he was.

'I hate it all,' she said, tearing at handfuls of leaves and hurling them about. 'I can't tell you how much I hate it.'

'You're part of it.'

'I still hate it. What's the use of being a woman, though? You can't do anything. They control me absolutely.'

'They control me more,' declared Julius. 'Massa controls you, maybe, but you control Flora, me, all o'we slaves.'

'But I don't want to control anyone!' cried Sophie. 'You must believe me! George told me I mustn't get too friendly with you. The hyprocrite! To tell me that – and then to come up here . . . He's certainly made friends with those girls.' Now she was spitting scorn.

'No. That not friendship.'

'It looked like more than friendship to me.'

'Not friendship. Rape. Specially for Venus. Cassie, she likes Mr Craig some, but not Venus. Venus she shy girl. Only one man she liked, Stefano, he was the mule-driver. But Mr Craig sent him away. If Mr Craig likes a girl, he don't want anyone else to touch her. Venus has to do what he wants every time, even if she's ill.'

Recovering from his bitter outburst, now, he worked on her feelings with some relish. It gave him exquisite satisfaction to see the beautiful white face turned up to him, attentive and responsive to his words, and to know he could play her like a fish on a line.

'Many time, black girls get taken up by buckra man. You just seen that. So most of us, we got no girls to be our sweetheart.'

Sophie paused for a moment. She felt her heart thudding against her ribs. 'I'm sure you could find a sweetheart if you wanted one, Julius. Easily.'

There was a moment's stillness. She could hear his breath. As he thought what to say, his tongue moved in his mouth and she heard the soft wet click of his saliva. A frail thrill fled up the skin of her neck and hid itself in her hair.

'I don't want a sweetheart.' His voice was very soft. Sophie's mind knotted itself around his words. They gave her both comfort and pain.

'No,' she agreed eventually. 'Nor do I.'

He moved away slightly. She knew she needed to shift the ground of their talk, too.

'Well, my brother won't be able to lecture me any more – now that I know he's got a slave girl for a mistress.'

'And more than she.'

'What?' asked Sophie sharply. 'What do you mean?'

'He don't just sex with Cassie an' Venus. He's got three girls down at Mount Grace, too. Ruth, she just had a baby, you know? That baby called Sophie, like you. That baby is your brother's child.'

Sophie gasped. 'George is the father of Ruth's child?'

'Yeah. You saw the baby. Her skin's white like yours. Where you think that come from?'

'I thought one of the overseers . . . Kendrick perhaps.'

'No. It was your brother did that.'

Sophie was winded for a moment. Then she drew a great breath and with it found some energy. 'I must go home, Julius,' she said. 'I've got to think. tomorrow I must . . . It'll be a horrible day.'

They walked down through the forest in silence, then paused at the edge of the trees. The roof of her house glimmered below them. A faint sound of drumming drifted up from the slave settlement down by the sea.

'They – you – dance all night,' mused Sophie.

'We got one day a week belongs to us,' explained Julius. 'When you got one chance, you drink, you dance till you drop. You don't waste that with sleep, 'cause you know next day you're going to be breaking your back for Massa again.'

Sophie could see Julius quite clearly now. Moonlight fell on his hair. She stared at its dense spirals, wondering what it felt like. The light threw into relief the muscles on his shoulders.

'You look like a statue, Julius,' she whispered.

'I'm not a statue. 'Cause I got feelings in my heart.'

'What feelings?' she whispered, standing close. He could hardly believe the tender invitation which shone in her face – and could not help feeling a surge of response. But he must repel her. Eli's warnings, and his own instincts, still preserved his resistance.

'Pain and hate I got.'

'Only that? Why are you kind to me, then?'

'Somebody's got to look after you. You crazy.'

'Crazy?' She ought to be offended, but could not help feeling curiously pleased instead.

'Why did you say you marry Mr Craig when you don't love him? That's crazy.'

'I didn't – I wasn't –' A blush burned across Sophie's face. Thank God it was dark. 'I thought I might come to love him one day.' Julius was silent. 'Is that crazy?' she asked. He did not reply. 'Yes, I suppose it is. Well, I've learnt a useful lesson tonight.'

'I still think you're going to marry him.'

A flare of anger scorched through her. 'Don't say that! I tell you Julius, I will never marry that man. It's impossible. I'm more likely to marry . . . Eli than Charles Craig.'

Julius seized on his chance to taunt her. 'You like Eli? He's handsome, for sure.'

'No! That's absurd. I just want to show how impossible it is for me to marry Charles Craig.'

'Impossible for you to marry Eli, too. Massa would whip you and hang Eli if you tried.'

Sophie's soul was stung by this. They seemed to be saying things to hurt each other.

'Julius – I'd like to help Ruth's baby if I can . . .'

'You want to make a pet of her?' Julius seemed determined to annoy her. The moonlight sparkled on his wet lip and glowed in his eyes.

'No, of course not! Just – I think men should take responsibility for their children. And if he won't – I will. I could be her – her godmother.'

'Godmother. What dat?'

Was he being ignorant on purpose? She felt he had slipped into slave talk deliberately, to obstruct her. But of course what she'd said had been stupid. She felt her slender filament of energy snap and hung her head.

'Oh, no matter. I'm just being foolish. As if I could help, or ever be any use. I'm just a girl. Worse than a slave, in some ways. At least you have Sundays at leisure. At least you're not a slave on Sundays.'

'You talk outa yo'ass, Miss.' He gave her the slave drawl again, to be doubly offensive. 'We slaves every day o' our lives.' Sophie sighed. Could she say nothing right? She slumped against a tree for a moment. Fatigue crept over her.

'You may go, Julius.'

'Ah, you sendin' me away now? So I'm a slave to you after all?'

'What have I said wrong now?'

'I thought we meet in the forest like we friends.'

'Yes. Of course.'

'You don't talk to me like I was your slave. You talk to me with respect.'

'I do respect you.'

'Just now you tell me to go away.'

'I'm sorry. I didn't mean it. I'm so tired.'

He reached out and brushed a tendril of hair off her sweaty brow. 'I'm giving you a hard time. This was a bad night for you. Bad things you've had to see. You're tired. I'll go.'

'No! – Wait!' She could see the roof of her father's house glimmering below them in the moonlight. She could not bear him to go yet. 'When shall I see you again, Julius?'

There was something utterly helpless about her appeal. He knew he should discard her now, but he could not find it in his heart.

'If you want me, you hang a shawl out of yo' window. When I see that, I come to you. If you not in the house, I come to the waterfall.'

'Thank you, Julius.' Sophie stared into the white discs of his eyes. He seemed to be a part of the night: moving, breathing darkness.

'You not be too upset, Miss.'

His words moved towards kindness; they were about to part. Despite the difficulty of talking tonight, she dreaded losing his company. She wished he would touch her hair again but knew he would not. She raised her own hand to her head and found the flower he had fixed there earlier. It was withered.

'I'll pick you another, next time.'

'When will next time be?'

'When you want. I'll be lookin' out for you.' He took a step back into the forest. 'I'll whistle if I come. Like the Poor-me-one.' He whistled to show her: four sad, descending notes. 'You hear me. Easy.'

'Thank you, Julius,' she whispered, raised her hand in an awkward kind of salute and tore herself away from him and the forest. She walked down across the land her father had cleared, slipping along in the shadows of his buildings and gliding across his threshold like a ghost. And indeed she was beginning to feel that her obedient life with her parents was something she occupied in a transparent state of being, as if she were a creature with no heart, brain, passions or instincts: a mere yard or two of empty muslin.

Back in her room, she laid her head down, expecting tears to come. But there was only a dry throbbing, and Sophie, instead of dissolving, felt herself on fire with rage. Like someone branded.

23

Poor-Me-One

'Mother, I must talk to you.'

Isabella looked up in alarm at the dull sound of Sophie's voice. She saw red eyes and a pale face: the picture of suffering. 'What is it dearest? Are you ill?'

'No, but I must talk.'

'Of course! Let's go in. Come into the dining-room.'

Serafina was hovering on the verandah, laying breakfast things. Birds flew here and there. A tiny yellow Bananaquit landed on the balustrade and flirted its wings expectantly.

'Don't you want anything to eat or drink, Sophie?'

'No, thank you, Mamma.'

Her mother picked up a glass of sorrel juice, carried it in and set it on the mahogany table in the library. Then she turned and shut the doors.

'Father's gone to Montparnasse to see Mr Greene,' she said hurriedly. 'About the militia. And George spent the night up at Belmont. So we are quite alone.' At the word 'Belmont' Sophie felt an angry blush flood across her face. 'What is it? Tell me, Sophie.'

'I can't marry Charles Craig.'

'What?' Isabella Wetherby was struck to the heart. 'Why, in heaven's name? What nonsense is this?'

'It isn't nonsense,' sighed Sophie. 'I just can't, that's all.'

'Why not? You were happy enough in his company yesterday.'

'I feel different today.'

'I hope this is not some silly caprice, Sophie.' Her mother's tone hardened.

'I assure you, Mother, I have good reason.'

'Then tell me what it is!'

174

'I can't.'

Her mother got up and walked around the room, wringing her hands in perplexity. 'Just as everything . . . You'd made me so happy. How can you hurt me like this?'

'I'm hurt too, I assure you, Mamma.'

'Then tell me about it! Let me help!'

'You can't help. Nobody can.'

'Why not? What has he done?'

'It's simply –' Sophie hesitated in anguish. How could she speak of what she had seen? Never in the world. 'It's simply the man he is.'

'What nonsense, child! We all know him for a splendid fellow, an absolute darling, a fine man, a gentleman. And though I say so myself, Sophie, I consider you are a lucky girl to have caught his eye.'

Sophie said nothing, but looked straight ahead, out of the window. A small breeze stirred the shutters and they swung slightly to and fro on their hooks. Beyond their dark slats was a brilliant grid of light and colour: the vegetable garden. Some slave girls were hoeing there. Their voices rose and fell in song. Sophie remembered how Venus and Cassie had sung under her window at Belmont, sung a taunting song aimed at her. She understood it all, now. 'Buckra woman let go me man.'

Her mother looked tired and bewildered. Sophie could not bear to hurt her. But what else could she do? Her throat ached, and her nose filled, with suppressed tears. She sniffed, and her mother's heart softened at the childlike sound.

'But, my darling . . . we all like him so much. He is such a good influence on George –'

Sophie could not contain her feelings any more. Suffocated by violent sobs, she ran out and locked herself in her room. She lay down on her bed and wept scalding tears of indignation. If her mother knew how George was behaving she would die of humiliation. Poor mother! Watching slave girls going past with babies slung on their hips and never knowing those babies were her own grandchildren. Young Englishmen preached sermons in public and acted like apes in private. She could not bear to see Craig again. How could she ever forget the lurid images of his pleasures up at

Belmont? If she saw his clean, polite smile bearing down on her, she might scream. The hours passed, and she was left alone.

At about noon, she heard footsteps in the hall, and George's voice rang out: 'Hello, Mother! Where are you? I've brought Craig down for dinner. Where's Sophie?'

Sophie heard the swish of her mother's skirts pass her door and sweep along the polished boards, and then the low murmur of voices.

'What?' exclaimed George. 'Let me –'

'It's no use!' cried her mother. 'Leave her alone.'

'Starve her into her senses,' growled George. 'That's the ticket. Come on, Craig. Let me get you a glass of claret. Cheer up, old man, She'll come round. Vapours!' They moved off, away out of earshot.

Sophie's heart slowed to its previous sombre beat and she walked to the window. Outside, the landscape lay still, flattened by the weight of the sun. Nobody was working in the garden.

On this side of the house there was no verandah, only a drop of some ten feet on to the dirt path that ran round to the laundry. With a rope Sophie might manage to climb out, at night, wearing breeches. She longed to speak to Julius – even a few whispers here, at the window. Remembering what he had said, she threw a shawl over the window-sill. Surely he would come, and say something that would make her feel better.

Certainly at night she could escape, even if she were locked in – although her parents slept in the next room and any unusual sound might wake them. Sophie sighed and rested her brow against the window-frame. The wood was warm, like the body of a living thing. It comforted her slightly in her misery.

The distant sounds of people having dinner drifted around the corner of the house. Civilised life, George would call it. Sophie was beginning to hate civilised life. She ached to be back in the forest. The ants and the birds and the snakes did not tell lies. They fought, perhaps, hunted each other, killed and ate each other, but that was at least honest.

Suddenly, a movement out in the garden caught her eye. It was Ruth and Mary, sitting under a bush, feeding their babies. They were too far away for Sophie to hear their voices and their dark limbs blended in so exactly with the shade cast by the vegetation that she had not noticed them at first. They were enjoying a brief break from work in the garden, she supposed, sitting in the shade eating fruit, with their babes at the breast. Sophie felt a violent pang of envy.

An hour later, there was a knock at her door. Her mother's voice, sounding mortified, appealed to her once more: 'You will let me in, Sophie, and explain yourself. Open the door, please.' Sophie neither moved nor spoke. 'Julius is here,' her mother went on. Sophie flew to her feet, her heart thudding. 'And if you do not open the door yourself, I shall ask him to take the lock off, which will cause a great deal of damage and make Papa very cross.' Sophie unlocked the door, but she did not open it.

The handle turned and her mother came in. Though her voice had been angry, Isabella Wetherby's face collapsed with sympathy when she saw Sophie's tear-stained cheeks. She took her daughter in her arms.

'Don't be upset, my darling,' she whispered. 'Wash your face and come out. There's nobody here but Charles and myself. George is asleep. Papa is still at Montparnasse.'

'You said Julius was here.' Sophie looked about her.

'I had to threaten force, or you would not have let me in. It's Sunday, Julius is not at work.'

The knowledge stung Sophie. She should have remembered. And she was angered by her mother's trick. She shrugged off her embrace. 'So you're lying to me, too, now,' she snapped.

'Has Mr Craig lied to you?' enquired her mother in an urgent whisper. 'If so, I'm sure it was a mistake, and that you can settle any misunderstanding if you will only speak to him.' Sophie shook her head. 'You owe him an explanation,' Isabella Wetherby insisted. 'Yesterday you gave him to understand you were looking forward to being his wife. Now you won't even speak to him. He is distraught, Sophie. You're breaking his heart.'

'He hasn't got one,' growled Sophie.

Her mother turned her head away in exasperation and closed her eyes for a moment.

When she opened them again, however, she did not immediately turn back to Sophie. She seemed to stare at something on the floor and a frown crept across her brow. Sophie looked – and saw, crumpled on the boards where she had thrown them off last night, her muddy boots, breeches and stained shirt. Her mother grasped both her arms and glared into her face. 'Have you been out again, Sophie?' A storm of anger seized her. She threw her daughter aside and picked up the clothes. 'The mud's still wet,' she hissed in a furious whisper. Sophie sensed that Charles Craig was outside the room and might hear. 'You were out last night, weren't you? How could you? After everything we said?'

Tears sprang to Sophie's eyes, but she refused to cry. Why should she feel guilty? What had she done wrong? She clenched her teeth. She would say nothing.

'Tell me, Sophie!' insisted her mother. 'Where did you go?' Suddenly, from outside, came a fatal sound. Just below her window, the whistle of the Poor-me-one: four descending notes. Julius had come.

Isabelle Wetherby flew to the window and flung the shutters back. 'Julius!' she cried. 'What are you doing here?'

'I'm trying to catch a bird, Missus,' came Julius's voice, hesitating more than usual. 'The Poor-me-one. For Miss Sophie.'

'Miss Sophie has enough birds for the present! She has more important things to think about! Go away!'

She pulled the shawl in, slammed the shutters to and confronted Sophie in the sudden dimness. Both women were shaking.

'What have you done?' snapped her mother, eyes flaring. 'Where did you go? Who were you with? That fellow Julius? Tell me!' At last all Sophie's accumulated anguish rose up and flew out in a great hoarse scream.

'I – have – done – *nothing*!' she roared, almost tasting blood, and threw herself on to the floor, rubbing her face and hands against the boards and wishing the splinters would penetrate her brow and palms. She felt her mother's skirts sweep over her.

Isabella Wetherby stepped across her daughter's body, walked out and locked the door. 'If you behave like an infant,' she snapped, 'you shall be treated like one.'

Low voices sounded elsewhere in the house; footsteps came and went, and eventually silence fell. Sophie sensed that Craig had left and a small part of the immediate horror of her situation seemed to ebb away. She went on lying face down on the floor until it got dark.

There seemed some kind of cruel satisfaction in it. But as the frogs started up their nocturnal song, she got up and washed her bruised face. Life had to go on.

She hesitated by the window for a moment, listening to the night sounds. Should she attempt to get out again tonight, or should she go to bed? A great yawn spread over her, insisting that the body rest. If there was a state of war between herself and her mother, she must restore her energies for the struggle ahead.

Before blowing out her candle she stared briefly into the glass fly-catcher on the table, in which insects were lured to their death by the sweet smell of molasses. Moths batted against the curtains; rats scuttled behind the wall; huge bugs appeared on the ceiling sometimes. Creatures in the forest did not alarm her, but she wished they would not come indoors, blundering and circling in a way which was half aimless, half sinister. She shuddered and retired to her curtained bed.

24

Into the Cage

Bird-song woke Sophie early. Refreshed, she decided she would take an initiative. Dressing quickly, she went out to the verandah, where her father was drinking coffee. He looked startled to see her. Sophie bent down and kissed him in her usual calm, obedient way.

'Good morning, Papa,' she said.

'What was all this nonsense yesterday, Sophie?' he asked. 'Your mother was quite distracted when I got back last night.'

'I can't marry Mr Craig after all,' said Sophie, keeping her voice even and reasonable. 'I'm sorry, Papa. I thought I liked him but I was mistaken. I'm particularly sorry to have upset Mamma.' She waited anxiously for him to digest this overture. Had her mother said anything about the muddy boots, or Julius whistling under the window? Her father folded the paper he had been reading, and set it aside.

'What the deuce has Craig done to offend you?'

Sophie hesitated. 'I'm sorry, Papa. I can't say more.'

Her father gave her a most searching look, then shrugged his shoulders and sighed. 'So be it, then. Next time, please have some consideration and don't encourage advances until you're quite sure they're welcome.'

'No, Papa. I am most heartily sorry. Although –' Sophie could not help spoiling the apology with a hint of protest: 'I hardly encouraged him at all. Indeed, I think he urged me too strongly. Truly. I am not used to it, Papa. I felt . . . hunted.'

Her father peered at her, observing her brows, wrists, ears and neck as if judging a beast at an auction.

'I don't blame him. You've become something of a beauty, Sophie. At least, by the standards of this place. Craig hasn't seen a passable white woman for months, probably – not a marriageable one, I mean. So have a care, next time.'

Sophie subsided into stillness.

Quiet footsteps brought Isabella out. She had heard voices and was surprised to receive Sophie's dutiful kiss and apology for having caused her mother distress.

'She's dead set against Craig, though, still,' commented her husband, 'so you'd best not waste any more time on that, Isabella.'

'Oh Sophie!' exclaimed her mother, but her father interposed.

'No more of it! Sophie is entitled to a mistake or two. We have all made them.' Her parents exchanged a slanted look. There was a moment's chill. 'We must mollify the fellow, however. You must at least write him a note, Sophie. Common courtesy demands it.'

Sophie did not make any observation about the common courtesy due to an innocent fiancée, though her tongue burned with indignation. She nodded.

'I've got to go up to Belmont, today,' her father went on, as George appeared, looking rather crumpled, and glaring at his sister as he slumped into his usual chair. 'Greene had four runaways to report to me yesterday, and when I arrived back here Kendrick told me that Eli and Walter have gone.'

'Gone where?' Sophie blurted out.

'Into the damned jungle,' sneered George. 'To join their cousins the apes.'

'George!' cried his mother, as Serafina appeared with a tray, 'that is not the sort of thing we say.'

'She should know where they've gone, anyway.' George glared at Sophie. 'Always slinking about.'

'Slinking about?' Sophie's father was alerted. 'What do you mean?'

'Well, she's always slinking about, isn't she?' cried George. 'Down at Juno's the other day, and round at Ruth's hut, I found her once – you're keeping bad company, Sophie, and that's the truth.'

'How dare you speak to me like that!' Sophie leapt to her feet. 'You damned hypocrite!'

'Sophie! Be quiet!' cried her mother.

'Silence, both of you!' roared their father. 'Serafina, go!' The slave dropped her tray in her confusion and scuttled off. Mr

Wetherby turned to Sophie. 'You will go to your room, Sophie,' he commanded. But George heaved himself out of his chair and confronted his sister.

'You'd rather go skulking about making friends with your precious slaves than behave decently to Craig!' he said. 'You fawn all over them and flatter them and make pets of 'em, in your damned do-gooding ignorance – I tell you, Sophie, if we get any trouble on this plantation it'll be your fault!'

'Well at least I don't . . .' Sophie paused, on the edge of a terrible cliff. The words seemed to reel away into silence and for a moment she fought for air, before launching herself over the abyss. 'I don't father their children!'

'What?' screamed her mother.

George lunged forward and hit her a stinging blow. Sophie gasped. She could taste blood. Mr Wetherby seized George by the hair and forced him against the balustrade.

'Don't you ever – ever strike a woman again, sir!' he grunted into his son's face. Then, with an awkward, frenzied heave, he threw him to the floor. George lay there, paralysed by the extraordinary situation more than by physical pain. 'Isabella, see to Sophie.' Mr Wetherby strode towards the verandah steps. 'George, you will join me up at Belmont in half an hour. We must discuss this expedition with the militia. And Sophie –' He turned suddenly to his daughter, who was pressing a handkerchief to her lips. 'If you can't behave in a civilised manner you will be sent back to England. A boat leaves on Friday. I've a mind to pack you off home. I've enough to plague me without your hysterics.' He strode down the steps and was gone.

George picked himself up off the floor and dusted down his shirt. Sophie and her mother watched in silence. Eventually George favoured Sophie with a long and blistering look.

'She-devil,' he said quietly.

'You're the father of Ruth's child.' Having said it once, Sophie found it surprisingly easy to repeat. 'You know you are.'

'So Ruth's claiming that, is she? Stupid whore. She should be flogged. It's Kendrick's. The fellow's as horny as a goat.'

'George!' his mother protested. 'Please!'

'I'm going.' George pulled down his cuffs importantly. 'There's work to be done. Something's brewing. Don't listen to anything this lying chit says, Mother. The sun's addled her brain.' He slouched off.

His mother turned, numbly clawing her way through the mystery.

'What on earth was all that, Sophie?' she whispered, still shaking.

'It's true. George is the father of Ruth's child.'

'My dear, you must not think any more of the idea. Even if it is true – and I am convinced it is not – it is not something a young woman should concern herself with.'

'But he has responsibilities!' insisted Sophie quietly. 'To the child and its mother, I feel – guilty on his behalf.'

'You must not concern yourself with it. How did you come to hear about it?'

'Somebody told me.'

'A slave, I suppose. You mustn't believe anything they say, Sophie. The best and dearest of them are the most outrageous liars.'

'I believe I was told the truth.'

'Well whatever they say, you should disregard it. They are not reliable. Always trying to cause trouble . . .' Isabella Wetherby walked to and fro, fanning herself anxiously. The sun was climbing higher. Beads of perspiration broke out on her lip. 'And if anyone ever says anything of that sort to you again, anything indecent, you should simply ignore it. Act as if you have not heard it and walk away. Remember the wise monkeys, darling. See no evil, hear no evil, speak no evil.'

'So I am to see no evil, even if it is my own brother who has done it?'

'Forget it, please. Put it out of your mind. Come now. You must write to Mr Craig – if you are still so set against him.'

'I am,' confirmed Sophie. 'I shall go and write to him now.'

'And I shall dress, then. Dear me! Nobody has touched any breakfast.'

Going off to her room, Sophie could not resist a faint smile at this last silly lament.

Having surveyed her split lip in the mirror, and felt curiously proud of her wounds, Sophie took pen and paper.

'Dear Mr Craig,' she wrote. 'Forgive me for misleading you. I

183

thought at first that we might have been suited, but I find, upon further reflection, that we are not. Please consider yourself released from any engagement to me. Yours sincerely, with apologies and regrets, S.W.'

Apologies and regrets, thought Sophie savagely. The currency of civilised life.

'Flora!' she called. 'Will you see this letter is taken to Mr Craig directly?'

Her mother, hovering outside, put her head round the door. 'Why not ask George to carry it?' she suggested. 'Then it will go all the more quickly. Take it to Massa George, Flora – he is only changing his boots, I think.'

George took the letter, and Isabella Wetherby left her daughter to her own thoughts for a while.

They met again at dinner: a meal for which neither had any appetite. Sophie picked at a melon and her mother sipped some coffee. It was the hour of silence and stillness. Sounds of industry had ceased in the yard and the shadows shrank to pitiful pools as the sun enjoyed his moment of absolute ferocity.

'My dear,' ventured Isabella. 'Please tell me one thing, truly.'

'What, Mamma?'

'Why was Julius outside your window?'

'I don't know.' Sophie blushed.

'You must not become too friendly with him, my dear.'

'Mamma! I have never done or said anything – with anybody – that I would not be happy to do or say again in front of you.' Sophie flung herself down on to her knees and fixed her mother with her most intense look. 'I promise. You have my word.'

'You're not – the least bit interested in him, then? In – in the wrong way, I mean?'

'Of course not!'

'Oh thank God!' her mother collapsed into relief, fanning herself. 'I'd been afraid – there could be absolutely nothing but evil come of it, my darling, if you were – it's quite, quite out of the question. I was thinking – you see, when I was your age, my head was so easily –'

'Mamma! I'm not like you. I'm only interested in Natural

History. That's why I value Julius's company. Don't you understand? How can you cross-question me like this, when George has actually –'

'Don't say it!'

'Why not? We're alone. He's the father of Ruth's child, Mother. Believe me.'

There was a short silence.

'It's different for the men,' Isabella Wetherby sighed weakly. 'I'm shocked, perhaps, at what you say George has done, but not really surprised. They have such passions – such violent passions, you know – that perfect chastity is, I think, beyond them. So in those years before marriage – and I don't think George has met anyone yet who has seriously taken his fancy – in those years, we must expect a few little indiscretions, my dear.'

'Indiscretions? But he fathered a child!' cried Sophie. 'And he has several mistresses here. Julius told me.' Instantly she regretted her words, but it was too late.

Her mother's eyes flashed and she seized Sophie's hand. 'Julius told you?'

'Yes; why shouldn't he?' But her tone was broken. Sophie knew it was all up with her now.

'You have no business talking to Julius in that way. That kind of conversation is indecent.'

'My conversation is indecent?' gasped Sophie in outrage. 'What about George's conduct?'

'A young woman must be above suspicion,' her mother persisted. Her hands had started to shake again. 'Julius should know that. He's behaving very impudently to say such things to you. Quite out of character, and he's betraying a very great trust and responsibility here, which your father has given him.' She rang a little silver bell. Flora came in.

'Bring Julius here,' commanded Isabella. Flora nodded and withdrew. They sat in silence, waiting. Sophie's heart thudded. What was her mother planning now? She dared not to open her foolish mouth any more.

Ten minutes later Julius arrived, slightly panting. He bowed respectfully to Mrs Wetherby, and gave a quick nod to Sophie, without meeting her eye.

'You want me, Missus?'

Isabella Wetherby drew herself up in her chair and stared levelly at him. He was wearing a loose waistcoat, open at the front. Sophie noticed a small droplet of sweat, like a tear, detach itself from his neck and trickle down his chest, losing itself in the thickets of his hair.

'My daughter tells me you have had some conversations with her.' Julius nodded. He did not look at either woman. His eyes were fixed on the wall. 'These conversations are at an end.' Sophie's breath shrivelled. 'She is of marriageable age and it is important that her reputation remain spotless.' Julius bowed. 'You must not meet, in future, or speak together in a friendly way,' her mother went on. 'And you must never comment again, to anybody, about my son's affairs. Do you understand?'

'Yes, Ma'am.'

'Now go and get your carpentry tools. I have a job for you.' Julius obeyed. Sophie was silent. She felt her spirits soak into the earth like spilt blood.

Three hours later, up at Belmont, Frederick and George Wetherby took their leave of Craig and he was alone with Sophie's letter. He took it to his study and locked himself in. His heart was pounding. At the sight of her handwriting, his cock rose its foolish head and his whole body gathered itself up for sex, though his brain knew it was an execution note he was about to examine. He ripped open the seal.

It took only a second to read the three short sentences with which she despatched his hopes. Rage surged up in him; he clenched his teeth like a trap and saliva spurted into his cheeks as if he would eat monsters, coals, poisons.

'Lead me on, then stab me to the heart, would you?' he growled, glaring at the helpless paper. 'You bitch!'

He dropped the paper on the table and undid his breeches. Closing his eyes helped to clear his head. He was breaking into Mount Grace, breaking into her room, splintering that stupid, locked door of hers like matchwood. She was sitting at her desk and leapt up fearful at the sight of him. Effortlessly he ripped her flimsy dress away and she clutched helplessly at her naked breasts, which she had tried to keep from him, but in vain. He'd squeeze them, he'd bite them till she shrieked and shrieked, the bitch.

Bitch! Her muslin skirt was easily torn off and he threw her backwards on to her bed, forcing her legs apart. It was easy, easy, easy; the bitch, she'd have to have him now, to hell with it all, to hell with her, he'd smash her into pieces for his pleasure, the silly little bitch. His eyes snapped open again as he jerked uncontrollably over the table, defiling her letter with a pool of hate.

Craig slumped down into his chair, utterly spent. He had wanted to kill her. But now he hated himself for wanting it.

Sophie and her mother sat white-faced in the sound of hammering. Julius was obeying Isabella Wetherby's instructions and nailing bars across her daughter's window. The women sat on the verandah till he was done. Sophie stared, dry-eyed, out at the canopy of tropical trees and the glittering sea far below. She knew that when he had finished his task, Julius would depart without a backward look and leave her to sulk to death in her cage.

His work completed, Julius left the house with turbulent feelings. Before Sophie had arrived at Mount Grace he had made his plans with a steadiness of purpose. Her arrival had unsettled him. At first, he had seen her only as a weak point in her father's defences: an opportunity for ransom, perhaps. She entrusted herself to him with ridiculous openness, fearing neither for her life nor her honour. It would be easy to take her prisoner and he trembled, sometimes, at how effortlessly he might enjoy her body. Perhaps she had been sent by some malicious spirit to distract him from his aims.

Now the time was approaching when he must act. The slaves at Mount Grace expected it: he must fix his mind upon a settled plan, or all would be lost. And yet still Sophie rolled around his mind, a possible factor in events. Should he simply ignore and exclude her, as Eli urged? Or should they smuggle her away from her father's house in the dead of night and drive a hard bargain for her release?

She was beginning to be suspected by her parents; that was obvious. Their association had been forbidden, and in the strongest terms. Yet the girl seemed to possess a dauntless energy. He was sure she would try to come to him again, despite all the locks and bars. Some magnetism drew her, not merely sexual, though the consciousness of that troubled him more and more. Beyond her womanly instincts, and her curiosity about the forest and its creatures, there seemed to burn an indignation and sympathy towards the slaves that might find eloquent utterance and influence the minds of others. Julius could not decide what to do; he ran down past the slave village and hurled himself into the sea, hoping that the turquoise waters breaking over his head would instil into it something of their own lucidity.

25

Runaways

Sophie went to bed as soon as it got dark. Her mother escorted her, took the key out of the lock and pocketed it.

'Good-night, my dear.' Sophie obediently brushed her lips against the pale cheek, set down her candle, walked to the window and ironically admired Julius's handiwork. The bars were securely screwed across. 'Think of it as a means to protect you.' Isabella was still hesitating in the doorway, trying to smile. 'We do love you so much, my dear.'

Sophie turned away and sighed. 'Thank you, mother,' she said emptily, impatient to be left alone. Distant sounds suggested the arrival of the men; Isabella swiftly departed. Sophie heard her father's voice.

'Craig has had runaways, too: three of his best fellows. Damn it! There seems to be an epidemic of it.'

The voices grew more distant; they had gone out on to the verandah. Sophie tried to read, but could not concentrate. She was a prisoner. She marvelled, now, at the perfect freedom with which she had crept out only a couple of nights ago. She hadn't appreciated her liberty, then, but now it had gone, she felt a if her guts had turned to stone.

Perhaps it would be better to go back to England after all. Here she was, with all the creatures of the night calling to her, and there was no hope of getting out to them. Her breeches and shirt had been taken away. Her active life had been stolen. What would she hope for from life from now on? Needlework, cards, music and the painting of caged birds. Sophie threw herself on the bed with an exhausted sob. Lying there, she could smell her own sweat. It seemed particularly bitter on this hot and frustrating night.

Next day she meekly performed the hated needlework, replied to her mother's questions in as composed a voice as she could manage and waited for the rage in her heart to die down. She longed for the sun to set, not that she could escape, now, but simply to avoid the ordeal of conversation. Supper seemed endless, and after supper the men discussed the possibility of unrest among the slaves.

'It was a good idea to show 'em the guns,' said George. 'In fact, I think I'll have a bit of target practice again tomorrow, behind the yard. Want to join me, Sophie? It's all hands on deck, now, you know.' Sophie hesitated. She did not want to be part of a swaggering parade of fire-power, to scare the slaves into obedience. But learning to shoot might prove useful.

'Yes,' she said suddenly. 'Why not?'

'Oh, Sophie,' cried her mother, 'I wish you wouldn't be such a tomboy!'

'My dear,' her husband reproached her, 'in our situation a woman who can shoot is particularly welcome.' Isabella was silenced.

'When shall we get this hunting party out, then, Father?' asked George.

'Oh, good!' smiled his mother. 'You gave us a fine piece of pork last time, I recall.'

'Not pig – Maroons.'

'Not yet.' His father picked his teeth. 'We must have a care. There must be a lot of them by now – if they're congregating together.'

'What are Maroons?' asked Sophie.

'Runaway slaves,' her father informed her. 'Living rough in the forest. We know there must be some around here. The ones in Jamaica have been free for years. They live in the jungle around the Blue Mountains. The Government had to accept the situation and grant them some land of their own. Jamaica's a vast place, of course, not like Sabato. They've got plenty to spare. So the Maroons are tolerated in Jamaica. But not here. Hence our hunting party.'

'But you're not going to – shoot them?' faltered Sophie.

'Why not? It'll be a pleasant change from shooting pigs,' said George, lounging back in his chair. 'I like an intelligent quarry. Better sport.'

'We won't attempt it yet,' warned his father. 'Not till we've got the whole militia together. The rest of the fellows are coming over on Friday – we can make an expedition then. We'll be eight guns. Safety in numbers. And it is not to be regarded as sport, George. Our situation is not without its dangers – I think I need not say more.'

'But how will you find them?' asked Sophie, terrified.

'Ah! There, my dear, we have been clever. We've had some Cuban hunting dogs sent over. They arrived at Douglastown last week. Fearsome brutes. And they set up the most unearthly howling. The dogs will sniff them out all right. Don't worry.' Frederick Wetherby looked pleased with himself, pushed his plate away and smiled at his wife. 'And now, my dear, I'd like to hear you play. And bless me! I have not heard our Sophie sing yet.'

Serafina was called, the table was cleared and Isabella Wetherby sat down at her piano – her pride and joy, especially shipped across from Liverpool. The humidity had warped certain parts of the works and it was a difficult task to keep it in tune, but George performed this office for his mother when he was too lazy to go out shooting and too wakeful to lie snoring.

Trembling, Sophie shuffled through the pile of music. How could she sing, knowing that her father and brother would soon be hunting Mimba Murphy and her companions as if they were wild animals?

'What shall we do, Mamma?' she asked.

'My dear! No need to be so nervous. It's only Papa and George – and George will be asleep by the third note, you know.'

Sophie's shaking hands tossed the music about, but she could recognise no titles, saw nothing except guns and dogs.

'Come along, darling, let's have Elisa's first aria from *Il Re Pastore*. You know I am always trying to persuade Papa to like Mozart.'

'New-fangled stuff!' boomed Frederick Wetherby. 'Give me dear old Handel any day. No, I'm joking, my dear. Let's have *Il Re Pastore* by all means.'

Isabella struck up a few introductory chords and Sophie nerved herself up, with tremendous effort, for the aria. Her mother had translated the verse from Italian and as Sophie sang, the words, creeping curiously into her brain, seemed to offer some secret consolation,

'To the forest, to the meadow, to the spring,
I shall go with the beloved flock,
and to the forest, to the spring, to the meadow,
my idol will come with me.

In that cramped, rough hut
which will give us shelter,
with joy and delight
innocence will dwell.'

Frederick Wetherby ws pleased with his daughter's recital. His thoughts, however, were not completely at rest. He was all too aware of the frailty of this moment: the European confidence of Mozart's cadences frayed and thinned in Sophie's boyish voice. The notes drifted out through the shutters and were devoured by the slumbering darkness, drowned by that huger concert of night-birds, the screams of nocturnal creatures and the ceaseless throb of insect life.

His daughter's brow plunged down towards him for her good-night kiss; he bestowed it, expressing the hope he would soon hear her sing again. He held on to her wrist for a moment and admired her honest eyes. Coming here had already caused her some pain. The business with Craig. Unfortunate. He prayed, for a moment, that his fine and accomplished daughter, whose occasional clumsiness and enthusiasm made her all the more dear, would not be exposed to anything worse. For all his guns up in the armoury, it seemed to him for a moment that Mount Grace was not a stronghold, but a dolls' house made of card and paper, which the slightest tremor of the earth or breath of wind could sweep away for ever.

Sophie kissed her mother good-night and went to her room. Flora helped her undress, folded her clothes, closed the shutters, arranged the hanging nets around the bed and filled the fly-catcher with water.

'Thank you, Flora,' sighed Sophie. She longed to ask how Julius was, but could not find the courage. Flora hesitated, however, in an unexpected way, drew a scrap of paper from her pocket and, without a word, placed it on Sophie's pillow, before leaving the room.

Sophie was hypnotised for a moment, then seized and unfolded it. The message was in a hasty, upright hand, one she did not recognise. 'Two of your floorboards are loose,' it said. 'I have marked the place.' Julius must have written this! Sophie's heart skipped, though at first she did not fully understand the significance of the words.

Hastily she locked her door, then bent down with her candle and found two small chalk crosses beneath the cotton rug at the foot of her bed. Cautiously she touched the boards and they moved. Sophie could see where the nails had been drawn out. Julius must have done it when he was putting the bars across her window. She leapt up and rummaged in her drawer for some tool with which to lever up the first one. She found a paper-knife shaped like a Turkish dagger. Excellent! But would it be strong enough?

Delicately, and as quietly as possible, she inserted the blade and pushed down on the handle. The floorboard instantly rose up into the air. It was not a long section of plank – in fact, it had been sawn deliberately short, quite recently. It was an easy matter to remove the neighbouring board, then Sophie lowered her candle down and stared into the black space under the house.

Like many houses in the West Indies, Mount Grace was built raised up on pillars, partly for coolness, and to provide a storage space underneath which was open to the air, not blocked off like a cellar. Staring down into this space, Sophie saw a small frog leap across the dirt below – far below, it seemed. How could she get down? But wait! There was a box conveniently placed underneath. She had not noticed it at first in the darkness.

Sophie pulled on her dress and shoes, blew out her candle, and with an agile swing she was through the hole and had found the box with her feet. She climbed off and, once her eyes had got used to the darkness, crept out from under the house. Stepping into the flood of moonlight, she closed her eyes for a moment to compose her mind. Serious duties awaited her: she must warn Julius about the plan to hunt the Maroons. She set off without hesitation towards the forest path which led to the waterfall. Having made the journey by night once, and several times during daylight, she was beginning to know the track and progress through the bushes, over fallen logs and under trailing vines was much quicker than before. Though encumbered with a dress, she pulled the back skirts up between her legs and tied them round her waist, like a pair of Turkish trousers.

The sound of the waterfall drew her on and soon it was before her, glinting and foaming in the moonlight. But no Julius. Her heart sank. She had been sure he would be there. She sat down beside the pool and tried to digest her disappointment. All around her the ceaseless chirping of frogs and insects vibrated; she had tens of thousands of living companions, yet had never felt more intensely lonely.

She cupped her hand and brought some water to her face, sipped and washed her temples and neck. She would look for birds and night animals, enjoy the freedom; then she would have to go home and climb back up into her cage. She would have to try and warn the Maroons by sending a message through Flora instead.

Something touched her back. Sophie leapt, and suppressed a scream. She turned.

'Sorry I frighten you, Miss.'

She felt a flare of disappointment when she saw it was not Julius, but Eli. Tall and graceful in the moonlight, wearing only a loincloth and carrying a cutlass, he looked more than ever like an African warrior, almost as if he belonged in the forest. Sophie recalled that he was a runaway – as, in a sense, was she.

'Julius send mi take yuh back,' he whispered. 'Him can't come. Him want yuh go safe home.'

'But I don't want to go home!' objected Sophie. 'I've only just managed to get out! And I must get a message to the Maroons. My father is planning to hunt them. Do you know where Mimba is? Is she with the runaways?' Sophie wondered where Eli was living, now he had run away from Mount Grace.

He stood fixed in thought for a moment, doubt and suspicion issuing from him in a kind of long-drawn-out gutteral sigh. Then he tossed his head to indicate she should follow. It was a long walk, along a route Sophie had never travelled before, and she completely lost her sense of direction, except that it seemed to her that they climbed up beyond Belmont, round the back of it and curved westward again towards the coast. She stopped for a moment to get her breath. Eli paused patiently but said nothing.

'Is it very much further?' she asked, panting. Her dress was plastered with mud and dew, and sweat was running down the back of her neck. Eli shook his head and set off again. Ten minutes later they passed some huge rocks and suddenly, through the trees, Sophie saw a fire. There was a clearing, surrounded by a few rough shelters made of leaves and branches, and Sophie could make out three people sitting round the fire. One got up – the firelight shone from below on his strong jaw and neck. It was Julius, at last. Sophie felt her heart turn over. She paused, half-paralysed for a moment, remembering what her mother had said about Craig: 'One day you'll catch sight of him and you'll feel your heart turn over.'

Julius came up to them, took her hand and shook it in an odd, formal way. Sophie felt a double shock: a seizure of pleasure at the warmth of his hand and a curious feeling that for the first time they were meeting as equals.

'Why have you come here?' he asked, with a despairing shake of the head, and a tone of voice one would use for a small child.

'I asked Eli to bring me,' she said. 'I have news – my father's plans – I had to warn you of the greatest possible danger to you and your people here.'

Julius understood that Fate had delivered her to him. In an agony of indecision he had sent Eli to escort her back to Mount Grace, not trusting himself to confront her. It was extraordinary that she should have struggled so far, enduring exhaustion and thirst for their sake. He could not help being touched by it.

'Come meet me mother,' he said, and led her to the fireside.

Sophie felt a surge of agitation, fear and guilt. Mimba was the woman she had heard so much about: the one her father had hated and sold to Alexander Ashton at Pelican Bay. She was, the men had agreed, a notorious runaway and trouble-maker. Sophie saw a thickset woman with wild, greying hair. The firelight threw into relief her sharp cheekbones and expression of fierce intelligence. There were some tribal markings etched on Mimba Murphy's brow.

'So; you Frederick's Wetherby's chile.'

'Yes. I'm very pleased to meet you, Mrs Murphy.' They shook hands, and Mimba drew Sophie down beside her and continued to scrutinise her thoroughly.

'You nat look like yo' father at all. Not at all.'

'No, I know. I'm more like my mother, I believe.'

Mimba reached down and squeezed Sophie's thighs in an approving way. Sophie was surprised, but not displeased. It was not the sort of thing that was often done in Buxton. But then, Sophie was beginning to feel that almost nothing was done in Buxton – at least nothing that interested her.

'Good legs,' Mimba reported to her son. 'Strong girl, she. Show me your teeth, darlin'.' Sophie obliged. 'Good teeth,' commented Mimba. Sophie could not help laughing.

'It's as if I'm a horse and you're buying me,' she explained.

'Horse – or slave,' agreed Mimba. 'That what yo' father do to me, when he buy me, twenty years ago. Legs, teeth and worse. He look up me arse, see if I got de bloody flux.' Sophie was speechless, but Mimba laughed easily, completely unembarrassed. 'All de planters do that. Sometimes de slave-traders got a slave wid de flux, they put a bung up de arse so no blood come out, sell 'im, run off wid de money, slave drop dead, I seen it happen plenty time.'

'How horrible.' Sophie shuddered. 'But Mimba, many people in England are trying to stop the slave-trade now.'

Mimba nodded. 'We read de pamphlets come from Barbados,' she said, expertly turning some pieces of meat she was cooking on a kind of skewer. 'We hear King George want to give us three days. Three days a week fuh ourselves. De planters try keep us workin'. Beat us, brand us, rape us, kill us. Dem take no notice of King George. Dem say, he across the sea, him never know what we do, we carry on. But King George, him order dat – so we goin' to claim our right.'

Sophie hesitated. She wasn't sure if Mimba's information was entirely correct. And even if it was, there were rumours that the King was not in perfect command of his senses.

'I must warn you, my father is getting a band of men together, and they're planning to come out and hunt – and look for you. On Friday.'

Mimba's eyes narrowed. 'They never find us in dis forest, chile.'

'But they've got dogs – Cuban hunting dogs! I heard him say. They're already at Douglastown. They're bringing them here.'

Mimba's face changed. She looked at her son. 'We got to move we place, Julius.'

'Out to Demoiselle,' said Julius immediately. 'Dogs can't sniff us across the water.'

'We got two days.' Mimba poked the fire. 'Thanks to dis girl. You good, brave girl to warn us, darlin'. You clever girl. Kind heart to help poor slaves. You help us more?' Mimba cocked her head.

Sophie could not help being alarmed, though she was ashamed of it.

'I'd be glad to,' she faltered. 'That's to say, I couldn't do anything to harm my family, but anything I can do to help you. I will.'

'Dis girl scared,' said Mimba abruptly to Julius. 'She no good to we. She got de heart of a mouse.'

'No!' cried Sophie rebelliously. 'What do you want me to do? I want to help. To make up for the bad things – the bad things that have been done at Mount Grace.'

'She's not scared!' Julius growled at his mother. 'Why you say that? She jus' escaped out o' the house, come here to warn us, could be big trouble for her with Massa, she's brave, you said so yo'self.'

Mimba laughed in acknowledgement, hit her son playfully on the shoulder and lapsed into thought for a moment, regarding Sophie, who was glowing with Julius's praise.

'It yuh bizniz,' she told him, suddenly shifting her ground and shrugging off her authority. 'Keep her here, take her back, ax her help, not ax – and what yuh ax her do – it yuh biznuz.' It seemed that nobody knew quite what to do with Sophie.

'What's going to happen?' she asked.

'Him tell yuh dat.' Mimba threw Julius an artful glance. 'Him de main man, ax him.' Julius stared into the fire, evidently not ready to say anything yet. 'But first,' Mimba went on, breaking into a deep grin, 'you eat, get strong and brave. What you want to eat? Opossum? Iguana? Or monkey?'

26

A Perfect Gentleman

Julius picked up a piece of meat on a skewer and offered it to her. 'Chicken,' he said. Sophie gratefully accepted it. 'Cooked with honey from the tree. We got a bees' nest in that Mammee Apple.'

Sophie looked up at the great bunches of leathery leaves. 'It's not a real apple tree, is it?' she asked. 'What's the fruit like?'

'What you mean, real?' Julius picked up a spherical fruit with a rough, brown skin and cut it in half. The flesh was golden, like an apricot. He cut a slice for Sophie to taste. 'It's a good tree,' he said. 'Flowers smell good for to put in your hair. Timber strong for me furniture. I made a desk for your father from the wood of the Mammee tree.'

'Why's it called Mammee?' asked Sophie. 'Is it because your mother's sitting under it?'

Mimba Murphy burst out laughing and slapped Sophie affectionately on the thigh. 'Dis girl a clown,' she said approvingly. 'She make me laugh. I need dat.'

Sophie finished her supper, and drank from a young, green coconut which Julius handed her.

'Take de girl home nah,' commanded Julius's mother, getting up heavily and sucking the last fragments of food off her fingers. 'I got to sleep. I commander, darlin', you see,' she pulled at Sophie's arm and confided, grinning, in her ear. 'I de chief warrior, my soldiers all asleep.' She indicated, with a sweep of the arm, the little ring of shelters where, Sophie supposed, more runaways were at rest; then turned to her son, enfolded him in a great embrace and murmured something in a private language, at which Julius gave a great shout of laughter. Finally, with a last wave to Sophie, Mimba Murphy retired behind a palm-leaf screen.

'You want to swim first?' asked Julius.

'Oh yes! – Could we?'

'Sure. The bay's just down there.' He nodded through the trees. Sophie, hot and dirty from her walk, and bedecked with smuts from the fire and grease from the roasted meat, longed to plunge through the surf. Julius led the way.

'Are those people with your mother all runaways?'

'Yeah. Some from Belmont, some from Montparnasse, they come few days ago. Some from Pelican Bay. They all hate Mr Ashton.'

'Isn't it very dangerous for them? Wouldn't they be punished if they were found?'

'They won't be found – 'cause you warn us. Tomorrow we move camp, we cross to Demoiselle.'

'Why are you telling me this? Shouldn't you keep it secret?' Julius stopped and looked straight into her eyes. He said nothing for a moment. Sophie stared back, hypnotised. Strange feelings leapt up inside her, like a waterful launching itself into space.

'You're right. I shouldn't tell. You make me behave different. Well, I'm telling you because you're a good woman.'

'How can you know?'

'It shows in your face. You good to me sister. You good to Juno an' Ruth. You're not like other white people.'

'I wish I could do more for you. How could I help?'

'You know what I want for you?'

Sophie's heart gave a kick. 'What?'

'I want you to go away back to Englan'. On the ship. She sails on Friday. Go back home.'

Sophie felt stung. 'Why? Why do you want me to go away?'

'I don't want you get hurt.'

'Why might I get hurt?'

Julius shrugged, and averted his eyes for a moment.

'Trouble's coming for sure.'

'But if trouble's coming, I want to be here with –' There was a silence. Sophie began to shake. Julius's eyes were steady on her again. They seemed to pour a kind of warmth into her, which swarmed up and down her limbs.

'With your family?'

199

'With –' Sophie's mind reached blindly into the dark and grabbed at the vague shape of the word that was waiting, '– with you.'

'No.' Julius's voice trembled. 'It's no good.' He stepped back a little.

'Don't turn away, Julius!'

'I got to.'

'Don't you like me?' Sophie was astonished at the words which burst from her, but she could not stop them. Julius's eyes moved here and there in mysterious distress. Suddenly Sophie felt a column of strength unfold within her. She reached out, boldly, and touched the side of his head. His hair felt crisp and dense, reminding her of the wool of young lambs she had stroked up on the moors above Hempshott.

Julius closed his eyes and uttered a deep sound, like the string of a cello when the bow is drawn across. Sophie felt the curving beauty of his cheekbone, the temple, the fine whorl of his ear, his neck. She was dizzy with pleasure. Now she had dared to touch him, she realised how long she had wanted to.

'I like you so much, Julius,' she whispered. 'I can't help it. I'm sorry if – you don't –'

He opened his eyes. Her fingers moved delicately towards the swelling shape of his lips. Tears seemed to gather in his eyes. Had she upset him? She took her hand away and moved back a pace or two. For a second they were both frozen, apart, caught on each other's eyes.

'Don't stop,' breathed Julius. A tear fled down his cheek. She touched it, then tasted her fingers.

'I want to taste your tears.' She smiled.

Julius caught at the little jest. 'How I taste?' he asked.

'Salty,' Sophie teased him. 'Let me try some more.' And putting her arms around his neck, she gently drew him down to her. First she kissed his moist eyelashes, but then he raised his head and she felt his lips: huge and soft after the thin hardness of Charles Craig's. At first he kissed shyly, like a child, but soon his tongue ventured out to greet hers.

I am kissing Julius, she thought. A glorious chord broke out all over her body; music that was felt, not heard. When finally, reluctantly, the kiss ended, she hung in his arms, limp and panting.

'What have you done to me?' she croaked, from some pit of bliss. 'You've turned me inside out.'

'Everything inside out, yes,' he replied. 'An' upside down. Come on – we got to swim.'

The track began to drop and they reached a place that was slippery with mud. He took her hand and Sophie, grasping it, swung around into his arms again.

'You some hot woman.' He grinned. She drew his head down to hers and kissed him again, at first tenderly, then more deeply, his breath crashing around her face like a gale.

As their mouths parted, Sophie's body felt like a map bursting magically into life: the lines which had tracked the path of rivers were welling up and liquifying, trickling and surging towards deltas and oceans where cranes flew and sailing ships scudded about, their sails bellying in a warm western wind. She wasn't a map, now, but a landscape: moving, changing, alive.

She felt his large hands move down her back and round her buttocks, squeezing her against him. He was a mixture of softness and hardness, of saltiness and sweetness. His breath smelt of mango and his sweat tasted musky, like the woodsmoke from a fire of scented pine. She wanted to engulf him and be engulfed by him; she was intoxicated when he groaned; she wanted to feel his skin against hers, all over.

'I want to eat you up!' she whispered, and he grinned.

'I'm goin' to tell you a secret in your ear,' he replied. His lips moved around the side of Sophie's head, and now his breath roared in her ear and his tongue explored the intricate channels there, and for some reason this was delectable and made Sophie writhe in longing. She felt his thigh between hers, and adoring its strength and thickness, she pressed herself voluptuously against it whilst they kissed, until a sudden strange feeling seized her, deep within her belly and seemed to draw her inside out through a series of blazing hoops.

She froze for a moment in fear; was she going to faint? Had she hurt herself? What had happened?

'Oh Julius!' she gasped. 'What was that? I felt something most – peculiar. And wonderful.'

'It's all right.' Julius smiled into her face. 'You're a hot woman,

201

that's all. Passionate. That's your sex feelings. Your pleasure.'
Sophie held on to him for a few moments, still feeling rather giddy.
Julius withdrew a little.

'We've got to go,' he said. 'Got to get to the sea.' He led her down
a steep, moonlit path and soon Sophie saw, immediately below
them, a tiny curve of sand, its rim of surf shining white. Julius
offered her his hand to help her down the last few slippery steps,
then she kicked off her shoes and felt the sand beneath her feet. The
bay was closed off at each side by rocks and the forest tumbled
thickly down all around them. The sand glimmered in the dark and
the surf seethed invitingly a few yards away.

'You're the first white person to see this bay,' said Julius. 'It's our
bay. We call it Marlidoundoun. Name of a drum. Sea come in,
waves come in, beating like a drum.'

'Marli – Is that an African name?'

'Yes.' Julius ran forward a few steps, into the edge of the surf.
'Sea's not rough here. Gentle, 'cause of the island out there.' Sophie
looked and could just make out the dim outline of a small island a
mile or so across the water.

'Is that Demoiselle?' she asked.

'Yes.' Julius turned to her. 'You want me to hide while you swim?
I'll go over there, sit on that rock, look the other way.'

'Oh, no, Julius. I'd like you to swim with me. I know you're a
perfect gentleman.'

Julius grinned. 'Yeah. Ah certainly am.'

He walked a few yards off and turned away as he slipped out of his
breeches. Then he ran down to the water's edge and dived, dolphin-
like, through a wave. Sophie admired his naked grace. She had never
seen a naked man before, only pictures of Greek statues in Aunt
Sarah's book about antiquities. Even judged by this exacting
standard, Julius's physique was splendid.

Sophie only hesitated for a second. Modesty seemed to be
irrelevant here. Swiftly she wriggled out of her dress and ran into the
surf. It lifted her up, it was warm. Sophie, who had previously only
dipped a toe in the sea at Scarborough from a bathing machine, and
almost perished with cold, could not believe the loving embrace of
the Caribbean Sea. She swam out beyond the breakwater, to where
Julius was waiting. Every wave lifted them up, then dropped them

back again. Sophie felt an inner thrill each time it happened. It was like the silent somersault she felt whenever she saw Julius.

He swam up to her. The moon danced in fragments on the water all around them. Sophie reached out and found his hand. He drew her close; she clasped her arms across his shoulders and her legs wound themselves round his torso. The water clothed their nakedness and swirled around their embrace as if they were a single creature.

Julius spun round and round and Sophie, letting go of him with her arms, felt herself stream out backwards from him, safely locked on to him with her legs. She screamed with delight. He slowed and gathered her back into his arms and the whole universe seemed to be spinning as they dived into a salty kiss.

Stumbling out of the sea, later, they collapsed laughing in the edge of the surf, ticking each other and rolling over and over. Then Julius engaged her in a serious kiss. Lying on her back, with her hair full of sand, Sophie could see the stars all around his head.

'You make me happy,' murmured Julius, kissing her eyelids. 'Make me feel alive again.' He was glad that he had abandoned his resistance. It was a great relief to have given up that stern self-denial. He did not think of the future; he rejoiced in the moment of bliss.

'You make me feel alive – for the first time,' whispered Sophie, stroking his broad brow and tracing the voluptuous curves of his lips with her fingers. His mouth opened; her fingers crept inside and stroked his tongue. He dropped his head down towards her; kissed her eyes, nose, ears, neck. Sophie felt herself melt and liquify and begin to yearn for him.

They were both naked; it was easy. His dark head floated across her body like a cloud across a landscape. Sophie's head swam. A great longing was gathering in her belly and a strange shoal of images flickered through her mind. Craig and Venus, George and Cassie, her parents, the bull with his heifers in the pasture below Aunt Sarah's windows, had all felt this urge. Nature seized all its creatures like this: the hen crouches to receive the cock, the cats growl on the dairy roof, the bitch and the dog stand tied in the stable yard after their coupling. Fierce, bizarre but delicious, it shot through her veins like a shock of recognition.

He entered her with his fingers first, his tongue in her ear, then kissing her temple and cheek. His touch was gentle; it made her dance. His tongue inside her, and his fingers inside her, made her long to devour him.

'Touch me.' He nuzzled against her jaw. 'Touch me an' tell me if you want me to come inside you.'

He took her hand and moved it across his thigh, until she found the part of him that fascinated and frightened her.

'Oh dear!' she exclaimed, feeling its weight and purpose. It moved in her hand like an independent creature.

'Let me,' he whispered. 'I not too big. Let me sex wi' you, darlin'. I be very gentle.'

Suddenly he rolled over on to his back and pulled her on top of him.

'Now you take me as slow as you like,' he said.

Sophie obeyed. It was easy, after all. Her body seemed to know how to do it. She engulfed him and revelled in him.

'Slow down!' warned Julius. 'Make it last long time.'

Sophie stopped. The sea roared as if it was a crowd applauding far below, and they were acrobats poised on a golden wire. Suddenly there seemed to be nothing solid beneath them and Sophie was catapulted into space, where she fell, somersaulting, until he caught her and she sank down gratefully on to his thudding heart.

27

Keeping Quiet

They stood at the edge of the forest. Mount Grace glimmered below them in the last shreds of moonlight. A cock crowed suddenly nearby.

'I've got to go now,' said Julius anxiously, holding her at arm's length. 'You won't see me till Friday. Massa will be angry, he'll say I'm a runaway. You keep quiet.'

Sophie nodded. 'But why are you going?'

'I go back to my people,' he whispered. 'Got to help them move to Demoiselle.'

'Can I help?'

'I only ask you one thing.' He hesitated.

'What?'

'Let me in. On Friday, when Massa's out with the rest of the planters, hunting. You know that hole I cut in your floor?'

'For me to get out?'

'Also for me to get in. I got to look at your father's papers. In his study. There's a rumour King George has sent word to all the planters, let the slaves have their three days. Maybe a letter from the King in your father's office.'

'I'm sure there isn't.' Sophie was doubtful. 'I would have heard something about it.'

'Let me look. There might be something else – some other paper – would help us. Will you let me in, sweetheart?'

'But what if Mamma finds out?'

'I'll come when she asleep. Kiss you in your own room. Love my woman, eh?' He touched her cheek.

'I'm just – frightened.'

'We all frightened. Listen. We'll do no harm. We're goin' to send ambassadors to Massa, talk with him. Promise if we get our three days, all runaways come back and no more running away.'

She wanted to believe such negotiation was possible, but Sophie could not imagine any such thing. She closed her eyes and rocked with vertigo.

Julius's hands propped her up, demanded she stand firm.

'You be strong, now,' he murmured. 'You're intelligent woman. You want me to be your father's chattel? Or want me to have respect?'

'Respect, of course,' admitted Sophie.

'A'right. This is the only way. Be brave.'

He kissed her brow and was gone. Sophie stood still for a moment, her body aching to be back on the beach, where everything had been so easy. She dreaded what was to come and almost wished for a moment that things could go on as they were: stolen moments in the forest. Why did Julius have to bring things to a head, precipitate this crisis? She wished he would not. But that was the instinct of a coward. Instead she should admire Julius for his bravery in planning to confront her father. It was the chance for a new start and for the Wetherby family to put right things that were terribly wrong.

Now Julius had gone, exhaustion overwhelmed her. She was too tired to be very much afraid. She limped back to the dark house and spent much of the next day dozing in her room, with a violent headache. Her mother, being inclined to headaches herself, was tender and understanding, and left her to sleep, only appearing from time to time with glasses of water and juice.

Sophie drifted in and out of dreams: of making love on the beach, of Derbyshire, even of her old school. But beyond it all lurked an anxiety about approaching events. It fringed her dreams like the black edging to a letter of condolence, and her waking moments plunged into anxiety the moment she remembered it, overshadowing even the sweet reflection that she had a lover.

Eventually the light dimmed and night came. Having dozed for most of the day, Sophie was now wakeful. She walked out towards the verandah for some air, where she could hear her parents talking, but hesitated in the dark as their words became clear.

'I wonder if you and Sophie should go for that boat,' came her father's voice. 'Something's afoot. There's going to be trouble.'

'I am staying here with you, Frederick,' insisted her mother. 'As for Sophie, all she requires is to settle down and learn how to behave here.'

'I think you should both go home, my dear. That Craig business has unsettled Sophie. She's at a difficult age and she can't have any freedom here, or meet anybody her own age. I don't like her fretting in her room all day like this.'

'No, Frederick! Sophie is perfectly all right.' Sophie heard her mother's words with surprise. 'She wasn't fretting. It was just a tiresome headache. She's better now.'

'Well, perhaps the climate is too much for her.'

'Not at all! I think the warmth suits her very well. She has got used to it very quickly. Really, Frederick, I'm surprised you haven't noticed how Sophie has flourished here.' It was obvious that Sophie's mother was desperate to stay and would say anything to achieve her aim. 'As for the Craig business, I am sure she will soon get over it. There must have been some misunderstanding. She has a sweet nature, perhaps he read too much into her manner. She was such a good girl yesterday. We got Julius up to put some bars on her window and she was very composed.'

'Bars on the windows all round might not be a bad idea,' pondered Frederick. 'I don't suppose you'd have time to catch the Friday sailing in any case.'

'Good heavens, no! The packing! – You men have no idea.'

'Well then, you'd best stay. But if things get worse, my dear, we must think again.'

'Of course, Frederick.'

Silence fell. Sophie crept back to her room.

After this she lay for some time restlessly examining the possibilities. If she could only take Julius with her, she might not mind going back to England. Perhaps there, people would be kinder. He could be properly educated. Sophie tried to imagine him in shoes and a coat. If only they could find somewhere . . . a remote cottage, perhaps. Aunt Sarah would help them, she was sure. If only they could get to England, she would offer them shelter.

Julius would have to travel as her servant, of course. She lay down again, her mind knitting away with speculation. Had a white woman ever married a slave? Was there anywhere in the world where she and Julius could live together as man and wife, with the blessing of the church and of their neighbours? She reached for a handkerchief and mopped her brow. Heat, mosquitoes buzzing just beyond the nets, a skittle of rodents' feet somewhere in the wainscot – the batting of moths' wings against her shutters . . . Sophie felt encircled by taunting lives that had no notion of right and wrong, were not tormented by man-made impossibilities. Eventually, she slept.

More needlework. Sophie had risen late again, exhausted by her nocturnal debate, but she felt wide awake now. Her brain was racing. George was out at target practice and her father was patrolling the estate with Kendrick, keeping a vigilant and visible presence. She feared that Julius's plan to negotiate with her father was hopeless. She longed to contrive an escape for him.

'Mother.' Sophie launched herself at the idea which had been haunting her all night. 'I wonder whether it might not be a good idea after all for you and me to go back to England?'

Her mother looked up in alarm. 'Why do you say that, my dear?'

'I just – if Papa thinks it best, I'd be happy to go, if I could take Flora and Julius with me.'

'Take Flora and Julius! – But why?'

'They are so very . . . such very fine young people.' Sophie hesitated, feeling a blush fly across her face. 'Think how they would benefit from seeing England.'

Her mother was silent for a moment. Her eyes roved nervously over the room, not seeing anything, lost in anxious thought. 'I am going to stay here with Papa,' she said eventually, trying to keep her voice level. 'If you wish to go back, I will arrange it, but not with Flora and Julius.'

'Why not?'

'My dear, think how I depend on Flora here at the house. It would take me months to train up another girl – if I could find someone suitable, which I doubt.'

'Just Julius then. To protect me.'

Her mother gave her a very hard look. 'Sophie . . . tell me the truth. Are you fond of that young man?'

'I admire him, yes. He's intelligent. He shouldn't be a slave at all.

208

He could make his way in the world if Father would give him his freedom.'

'I understand these feelings, Sophie, but it is not possible, not at all. Julius is too important to Father here for him to part with him. But if you really wish to go back to England, we can easily arrange it. I can send someone else to escort you. I know of several English families in Douglastown, indeed I believe Mr Ashton's sister is thinking of returning. You shall travel with her.'

'Oh, no!' cried Sophie. 'It doesn't matter. I'll stay.'

'No, my darling. Not if you're frightened. My place is here beside your father, but you're so young, your life has barely started. Your instinct to go back is quite right, I'm sure. I'll arrange it.'

'No!' Sophie leapt up. 'I want to stay. I must stay.' She trembled.

Her mother scrutinised her face, mystified. 'But a moment ago you wanted to go back.'

'I don't really. It was just an – idea.'

'An idea, Sophie?'

Her mother rose slowly from her chair, a look of discovery creeping into her eyes. She seized her daughter by the arms and peered into her face. 'You only wanted to go if you could take Julius.' Sophie blushed again. 'Good God! I begin to understand – You've taken a fancy to him!'

'A fancy! A fancy!' The word felt like an insult. 'I admire him – and why not? And he deserves admiration, a good deal more than Charles Craig, I assure you.'

Her mother fluttered and sank, like a candle going out. She held on to Sophie now for support, not interrogation. 'You foolish girl!' she gasped. 'You cannot – must not – give yourself up to these feelings.'

'Why not? George has his concubines, but you don't object to that. It's perfectly in order for him to indulge the basest lusts! But if I . . . admire someone . . . it's a crime.' She faltered and fell silent, unable to find words to do justice to her experience.

Her mother seemed to rally, seized the moment and spoke with a savagery that chilled Sophie's heart.

'You must never speak of this again. You must never even think of Julius as a man. He is a slave – a race apart. You could no more marry him than you could a dog. And if there has been any impropriety, Papa will hang him.'

'Impropriety!' shouted Sophie. 'What about George? He and Craig entertain themselves with concubines whenever they like – half the babies crawling about in the dirt here are probably your grandchildren – and you warn me about impropriety!'

'Craig?' Her mother was suddenly alert. 'What do you know of Craig's behaviour?'

'Enough.'

'Do you suspect him of having a – concubine?'

'I know he has.'

'Is that why you refused him?'

'Partly.'

'But that is no reason at all.'

'It's reason enough for me.'

'We must accept that men behave badly at times,' whispered Isabella, trying now to ingratiate herself and squeezing her daughter's hand in an imploring way. 'Believe it, my darling. We women must accept the most painful things, or society itself would disintegrate.'

'Then let it!' cried Sophie, flinging her off. 'Who wants to live in a society based on such filth? Such degradation?'

Isabella was impatient with her daughter's puritanical indignation, and jarred by the rejection of her caress.

'If you go about with such high-minded ideas, Sophie,' she snapped, 'you will never find a husband.'

'I don't want a husband!' cried Sophie. 'Not if he behaves like that!'

Her mother leaned back in her chair and wiped her face with her handkerchief. She felt suddenly exhausted.

'This has been a dreadful conversation,' she murmured. 'It's quite shattered my nerves. We must never talk like this again, Sophie.' Sophie was silent. Since everything she said seemed to offend and upset, she would speak no more. 'I have already told Julius that he must not communicate with you again,' her mother went on. 'And that is final. You understand. I may even have to speak to Papa about it – although he may blame me for not being more vigilant. I must act for the best. Oh heavens! I can't think properly. My poor heart is fluttering like a mad thing. I'm going to lie down. Send Flora to me.'

She staggered out, holding on to the furniture. Sophie watched her sadly. The Mamma she had adored as a child seemed now a weak, confused figure faltering between tyranny and collapse.

Though she was free from her mother's vigilant presence, she could not settle to anything. George came in for dinner, but Sophie could not find an appetite. She was upset by her mother's words, and paralysed with fear about what would happen on Friday, when the militia went off to hunt the Maroons, and Julius would return.

'Are you still counting on that hunting party, George?' she enquired timidly. Perhaps it would be called off. But that would be disastrous – because the men would all be here at Mount Grace when Julius arrived.

'Oh yes. We'll have great sport. Ashton has the dogs. He's got a fellow who used to be a kennel lad in Somerset, you know, and he says he's never seen anything like these Cuban beasts.'

Sophie composed herself. She knew that the Maroons would be safe on Demoiselle by now, so there was no danger to them from the dogs. But what danger there might be to Julius from his own reckless actions she could hardly guess, and did not dare to imagine.

Their father strode up the verandah steps, sweating and scowling. 'That confounded Julius has run away now,' he growled, throwing himself into a chair and mopping the back of his neck with a large kerchief. At the mention of her lover's name, Sophie's whole body seemed to flash with light. She was sure somebody would have noticed. But her father simply went on with his complaint. 'Hasn't been seen since the day before yesterday. Gone to join his wretched mother, I suppose. I might have known. Bad blood. Bad blood. I was a fool to take to him. Ungrateful swine! After all I've done for the fellow, all the favours he's enjoyed – still, they say that the ones you spoil are the most treacherous.'

'We'll make him jump on Friday, Father,' affirmed George, pouring his father a glass of port. 'We'll pepper his arse with shot and teach him to respect his betters.'

'I'll set those dogs on him, I swear.' Frederick Wetherby sipped his port with a bitter glare that froze Sophie's blood. 'And if they tear him to pieces it'll be no more than he deserves.'

Sophie went to bed early. Next day was Thursday. The hunting party was to arrive and stay before setting out at dawn on Friday. Since Julius had left Mount Grace, Sophie had been gripped by a heaviness. Her dread of the approaching events, and a certainty that there was no chance of even a passing glimpse of him going about the yard, paralysed her. An overpowering fatigue nailed her to the ground. Not even the calls of birds could rouse her. She could only wait, dumbly, for the time to pass.

As she crawled into bed and watched Flora arranging the mosquito nets, she noticed that the girl had been crying. 'What's wrong, Flora?' she enquired.

'Nothing, Miss.' The girl's face was a mask.

Sophie knew what was upsetting her. 'Are you worried about Julius?'

Flora shook her head almost sulkily. 'Me brother do what he want,' she said, with a sour shrug. If she knew that Julius was Sophie's lover, she clearly deplored it. Sophie sighed. She would have hoped that his sister would be glad. But jealousy and disapproval stalked her even here.

Long ago, when she had first wondered about love and courtship, she had imagined that when the time came, her mother would share her secrets with delight. In the event, she had received them with repugnance. Sophie's attachment to Julius even seemed to displease his sister. She must speak of something else if she wanted to restore cordial relations with Flora before dismissing her for the night.

'How is your Aunt Juno?' she asked.

'Me aunt upset 'cause she lost her provision ground.'

'What do you mean? Her garden?'

'Massa and the men fencing off the provision grounds this mornin',' Flora informed her, 'where we grow de beans an' corn. Massa say we goin' to have another place for to grow de herb, but he not say where or when.'

Sophie remembered, now, that her father had talked about building a drying-shed on the patch of flat land down beside the slaves' huts, overlooking the sea.

'I will speak to Father about it tomorrow,' she promised. But privately she knew that soon they would be too preoccupied with more dangerous things than the site of provision grounds. All the same, she felt crushed by this new exercise of her father's authority. There was no confronting it. Sophie was beginning to feel there were only two possibilities for her: submit or rebel. And filled with the lethargy that had possessed her since Julius's disappearance, she longed to submit, longed for these passions to drain away into the ground, for human voices to be stilled and for the birds to inherit the earth. Let them pick her bones clean and have done with it. Human life was too twisted. It would never get right.

'It's fear that makes me so lazy and cowardly,' she told herself in the dark. 'I must root it out.'

But it was still there, waiting for her in the morning, the moment she opened her eyes.

28

Barricaded

She heard them first: a deep howling and barking, and voices calling in the thickening afternoon light. The militia had arrived. Sophie watched them through the dark slats of the jalousie. She saw an untidy handful of white men, looking hot and tired. They numbered six or seven. One or two, busier than the rest, were probably servants. A slight sandy-haired man bustled about with the dogs.

'Let them lie under the trees – your place will be properly guarded at last, Wetherby!' cried a towering figure. Sophie recognised Alexander Ashton's great red hook nose.

Sophie's father admired the dogs, stroking their massive heads, and showed the kennel lad where he could take the hounds to drink. Craig was there, too: not asserting himself, hanging back. Sophie noticed a stout man with a face like a great ham, and a small, agile, bald-headed fellow.

'Ashton!' George arrived now, out of the house, shaking hands all round. 'Dawson! Somerville!' So the bald figure was Somerville, who had married a mulatto woman. Sophie was curious to observe him at closer quarters. He seemed a meek, self-effacing character, judging from his actions now; it was Ashton who commanded here. His booming voice echoed around the yards, audible even above the drumming and splintering of the sugar-mill.

Sophie was to share her mother's bed tonight, so the men could more easily be accommodated. Years ago, a night in Mamma's bed had been a treat; now it was an anxiety. Her mother's eyes seemed always upon her. Sophie dreaded muttering out some secret in her sleep.

But first there was supper to be endured. Mrs Wetherby had instructed Serafina to prepare a feast: turtle soup, kingfish, kid and pork were offered. Sophie had not sat around such a crowded table since Grandmamma's tea-parties at Hempshott, but these were all hard, rough men, marked by the climate, whose eyes seemed to stick to her unpleasantly. Luckily they were too nervous about the unrest on the island to bother much with gallantries. Their eyes played over her, but their minds were busy elsewhere. Sophie was glad. She made of herself a thin, pale thing: a plaster figure. Her vital self was elsewhere, too.

'Who'd endure the place, though, were it not for the rewards of the sugar-cane?' brayed Ashton. 'The heat, for a start, is enough to stifle a saint, and then, when the rains come, one is damn near drowned; colossal landslides, last season, along my northern road: near three acres of my furthest grounds slipped into the sea.'

'Ah, do yuh sometimes remember that gentle English rain, now?' murmured Mr Somerville, wiping his mouth, cheeks and shining pate with a napkin already stained with sauce and fat. Sophie was fascinated to hear his singsong speech – echoing the slaves' voices. It was as if she could hear the wife speaking in the husband's words. 'Rain here falls like swords, but the English rain – so soft and grey and timid, it makes yuh feel like it tiptoeing, don't it, Mrs Wetherby? I think so, fuh sure.'

'Indeed, I do miss that smell we get at home – a refreshing shower after a long dry spell – that smell of damp earth.' Isabella smiled obligingly. Sophie thought of the fierce gales which swept down from the moors, shivered privately, and said nothing.

'Some more pork, Mr Dawson?' Mrs Wetherby loved to entertain.

'Aye, I thank you Ma'am.' Dawson was stout and liked his rum. His red face had a curious boiled look, and great sweat-stains spread wider and wider beneath the sleeves of his coat. He said little, but ate and drank with such a solid rhythm, it seemed as if he would never be satisfied, but sit there gleaming and chewing and sipping all night.

'The climate is very disagreeable to be sure,' piped up a little old gentleman who sat at the far end of the table, and who must be Mr Greene from Montparnasse, for he had growled into his soup and dozed over his roast kid. The horrors of the Sabato fauna, however, roused him. 'As to vermin! Mosquitoes, sandflies, merrywings,

215

scorpions –' He shook his head in dismay, and returned, growling, to his roast pork.

'Those damned centipedes!' agreed George. 'They sting like hell! And the cockroaches, although they don't sting, the way they come indoors in the evenings and run all over you, all over the furniture, and your clothes, is confounded insolence in an insect.'

'I confess I do shudder at the cockroaches,' cried Isabella. 'But it is the chiggers I hate most.'

'Oh yes, my dear lady, amen to that!' bawled Ashton through a mouthful of dasheen, scattering dark-green strings and splashes across his chin. 'Why, I've felt the skin of my feet almost flayed with the little scoundrels, at times – I'd have thrust my feet into the bread-oven to be rid of them, I swear.'

They laughed – all except Serafina and Flora, whose faces hung in the background of the brilliantly lit table like two dark planets. No mention was made of the expedition, of course. Though the arrival of the dogs was an obvious sign that a hunt was projected, nothing more revealing could be mentioned in front of the slaves. The talk was all of the torment of life on Sabato: the hostile steepness of its mountains, the torrid tangle of its forests, the venom of its wildlife. Its climate was a simmering stew, the absence of society a dreadful torment; everyone longed for paved roads, it seemed, trim fields walled or hedged about, shops and, perhaps most of all, the reassuring presence of the English regiments.

Fear boiled at the heart of their complaints, which Sophie well understood, though she could not quite forgive her mother who now reviled what she had so thoroughly admired in her letters to her daughter. But Sophie said nothing. This supper was an insane occasion, something to be endured, and useful at least in confirming her feelings of antipathy to these specimens of her race and class. She could not help loving her parents and supposed she always would, but she could not approve of their words or their deeds nowadays, as she had automatically done as a child.

Every waking hour, she had to fight off a longing to see Julius again, but she knew that when she did see him, it would be in circumstances of some danger, and he would be preoccupied with her father's papers. Nevertheless her body yearned for him, and her mind returned again and again to the memory of their embraces. It was a torment not to be able to share these thoughts with anybody and increased her sense of isolation from the company.

Eventually, thank God, her mother caught her eye and they withdrew, leaving the men to their self-important drinking and roaring. Sophie feared she would pass a most restless night, but a glass of claret did the business, and she had dived off down the mysterious reefs of sleep before her mother had even dismissed Flora.

When she awoke next day she was puzzled, for an instant, to find herself in her mother's bed, but then recalled everything, and finding that her mother was up and gone, she hastened to dress and venture out. It was already half-past ten; the hunting party had left and her mother was sitting on the verandah. Kendrick was stationed on the steps, cradling a musket on his knees. He nodded a greeting to Sophie.

'What is that fellow doing?' whispered Sophie in alarm.

'Why, guarding us, of course, my sweet.' Her mother smiled. 'Papa would never leave us unprotected. There are two more at the back door. Alexander Ashton's men. One of them is quite a saucy fellow; I heard him flirting with the girls from the laundry. The other one reminds me of the Rogers boy, who had the jackdaw, you know. He has exactly the same cheekbones. Like a Tartar.'

Sophie did not attend to her mother's ramblings. She struggled to hide the consternation that swept over her. Julius had reckoned without a guard. She did not know when or how he was coming. She could not face any breakfast; such a fury of agitation throbbed in her that she found it hard to sit still for a moment.

'Whatever is the matter, Sophie?' enquired Isabella, setting down her book. 'Do stop fidgeting. You are quite distracting me.'

'I'm sorry, Mamma. I think I shall go back to my room now. I feel rather hot. I shall read there.'

Back in her room, her mind raged. How would he come? When? Would he be shot down by the guards the moment he appeared? How would he get under the house without being seen? On the north side, she supposed, where the garden was most overgrown, a stealthy progress might be made through the deep shade of the guava trees and avocado vines, which grew close up to the side of the house.

The hours passed. She heard her mother retire to her own room for her afternoon sleep. Sophie tossed about on her bed until, exhausted by the heat, she had drifted into a half-conscious dream, when a curious knocking on the floor awoke her with a start. The trapdoor! She flew to it, raised the boards and saw Julius's face, but surrounded by a crowd of other black faces, staring up at her out of the hole in the middle of her floor. They looked for a second almost like a painting framed by the floorboards. She shook herself out of this bizarre hallucination.

Her heart leapt at the longed-for sight of him, but his companions' presence dismayed her.

'Who are all these others?' she asked, full of doubt and fear.

'Me people,' said Julius. 'Let us in, now.'

He held his finger to his lips. His eyes flared to indicate that perfect stillness was necessary. Sophie stood back helplessly as, one after another, the lithe young men hauled themselves up into her room. Soon, they were all in: eight of them stood about her, in a quivering stillness. Their bodies stank with danger, their breathing was harsh and loud and they held clubs and cutlasses.

'What are you going to do?' whispered Sophie in anguish. Her heart was thudding wildly. They must not harm Mamma; dear Mamma, innocent Mamma. It was not her fault.

Sophie had not expected this. Julius's arrival had taken her by surprise. He had led her to anticipate an intimate moment together; he had been tender as well as purposeful. She could not help wondering if he had deliberately misled her – tricked her into letting them in, so they could do God knows what mischief.

'Don't hurt Mamma. Promise that you won't hurt Mamma.'

'We won't hurt Missus.' Julius shook his head irritably. 'She a good woman. We not savages.'

She sensed, for a moment, the authenticity of his indignation. But she, too, had resentment to express.

'Why did you not warn me of this?'

'We change we plan.' Julius looked boldly at her. 'Listen, now: we see three guards. Kendrick at the front an' two at the back. Any mo' men in de house?'

He had fallen into slave speech before his fellows, as if to emphasise that he belonged to them, not to her. She felt rejected.

For a second she suffered a dizzying idea that everything that had passed between them had been a cunning contrivance on his part, to enlist her help at this moment.

'Any mo' men?' Julius repeated impatiently. She shook her head. Her dismay showed in her face. He was quick to understand that her faith in him had faltered. He took her in his arms, felt her slight resistance, and made his assurances more urgent. 'You good woman, good heart. Feel sorry for us slaves, eh?'

'Yes.' Her heart recoiled. She did not like to be touched like this in front of his companions.

'You want to help us get some dignity?'

'Of course.'

'Get our three days King George promise us?'

'I'd like you all to be free. But don't hurt anyone –' She broke away from his arms and looked doubtfully at the knives and cutlasses. 'Please don't hurt Mamma.'

Julius shook his head and, after listening for a moment, motioned his companions out. Noiselessly, on bare feet, they left the room and crept towards the hall, where some turned left, some right, to surprise and overcome the guards who, of course, were concentrating their attention on the distant undergrowth, never expecting an attack from within the house.

Julius stayed behind, hesitating beside Sophie for a moment. They were alone.

'You're taking the house, aren't you?' she concluded. 'You didn't tell me you were planning that.'

'Don't be frightened. We're not goin' to hurt you or your mammy. We only going to defend the house.'

'Defend it? Against whom?'

'Massa, when he comes back.'

'What, defend Father's own house against him?' There was a deep irony in the plan which pained her. This was her doing.

'Only way to make him talk with us.' Julius was firm. 'Go to your mammy's room, now. Tell her not be frightened. Lock yourselves in. Tell her we only make talk with Massa. No fighting.'

A slave entered the room, flourishing Kendrick's musket triumphantly. Sophie stared. The guards had evidently been disarmed with scarcely a sound.

'What have you done to Mr Kendrick?' she asked, faintly, dreading blood and injury.

'We tie 'im up, Miss.' The slave grinned. She now recognised him as Lucas, who had helped to row her round to Mount Grace from Douglastown the day she arrived. 'Knock 'im down an' tie 'im up. Him nat gwine to do any fightin' or shootin' today, no sah!' Lucas's voice was loud with exhilaration.

'Mr Kendrick?' Sophie heard her mother's voice, sleepily calling from the next room. 'Who is that?'

'I must go to her.' Sophie ran to her mother's door.

'Who's there?' she heard her mother cry. 'What's happening, Mr Kendrick?' She sounded tiny and fragile. Sophie felt a pang of pity and a fierce desire to protect her.

'Mother!' The door was locked. Sophie rattled the handle in vain. 'Mother! Open the door! It's me!' Since she had come to Sabato, it seemed there were always locked doors between Mamma and herself.

'Sophie! Good God! What's wrong?'

The key turned in the lock and her mother appeared, wide-eyed with alarm. Sophie pushed her way into the room, locked the door behind her and reached out to reassure her mother.

'What is happening?' Isabella stammered. 'Who is that out there?' Footsteps sounded overhead and the jabber of voices echoed through the thin wooden boards. Both women knew that up in the attic was the armoury, Frederick Wetherby's store of guns and ammunition, so lovingly assembled and stoutly defended with several locks and bolts installed by Julius – who now, with the familiarity of a practised locksmith, penetrated them with ease.

'Who's up in the armoury? Is it Papa? Have they come back?'

'No, Mamma. It's Julius and his people.'

'What do you mean, his people?'

Sophie felt a surge of solidarity with the slaves. Hadn't she burned with rage at their sufferings? Now was her chance to speak for them.

'King George has outlawed slavery, Mother!' she argued, desperate to convince. 'Or at least, I'm sure he will. Our slaves want justice. The way they are treated is wrong. They want an agreement, that's all – they want to talk to Papa – they won't hurt anyone –'

'Why are they seizing our weapons, then?' cried Isabella, hearing increasing activity up in the armoury. 'This is an armed revolt, Sophie. They are going to kill us! Kill us, child!' All the colour drained from her face and she clung to the bedpost. 'Lock the door!'

'I have done. It is secure, Mamma. They won't kill us, I assure you we are safe. Julius has given me his word.'

'His word! His word!' her mother cawed, like a caged bird, caught between terror and ridicule. 'His word! What's *that*?'

'He's an honourable man, Mamma.'

'Honourable? Honourable? To rise up against his master, after so much kindness, such trust reposed in him – he's betrayed us all!'

'No, Mamma, he hasn't. He's a fine man!'

'What has he done to you?' cried her mother in revelation. 'He's bewitched you, you fool!'

'He has not! I love him. I'm not ashamed of it, either!'

Isabella Wetherby fell into a horrible shuddering. 'You mustn't!' she gasped, clawing for the furniture. 'You can't! You can't love him! No, no! Not this!'

'Why? Because he's black?' Sophie's own small rebellion rang out above the rising sounds, elsewhere in the house, of hammering, of things being dragged about, of voices raised in command, in nervous agitation. The jug rattled in its basin on the dressing-table. The looking-glass began to shudder, making the light in the room tremble, as if an earthquake had struck.

'Oh Sophie! – Julius . . . is . . .' Isabella paused and was racked with a kind of dry heaving. The words flew from her, finally, like vomit. '. . . He's your brother.'

Sophie's brain seemed to go dark for a moment. The room rocked; the floor rose towards her; she sank on to the bed. Everything was whirling. She reached out a hand, suddenly feeble. 'What do you mean, Mamma?'

Her mother took her hand and wrung it violently, tears of fury and resentment bursting from her eyes. 'Julius is your half-brother. Papa is his father too.'

Sophie could only manage a faint croak. '. . . How?'

'You know that Papa . . .' Isabella Wetherby wrestled to express herself. 'Papa was on his own here for years. Fifteen years or so, before I came out. Men on their own . . . he had a slave who was his housekeeper. An intelligent woman. He bought her on his first trip out here. Before you were born.'

'Mimba Murphy!' cried Sophie, suddenly discovering a mighty truth.

'Yes – it was she. Oh God! All the planters have favourites among their female slaves, Papa says that Alexander Ashton even – but never mind that – it's horrible, horrible, but I have had to struggle to accept it. When I first arrived here two years ago, Papa had just sent her away –'

'Sold her to Mr Ashton?'

'Yes, where she went on making trouble, it seems. But when I arrived – Flora and Julius were so helpful, I became rather fond of them.'

'As I did, Mamma! How could one help it?'

'Well, since their mother had gone away, I felt almost motherly towards them, not knowing, of course, of their parentage . . . Then I overheard some girls talking in the garden, and I realised –' Her face fell into a grimace and she had to fight off a tide of sobs, as she relived the moment of betrayal. 'I realised . . . that you and George . . . were not Papa's only children.'

The tears returned and it was Sophie's turn to comfort her mother. She saw her hand soothing the shaking shoulders. It looked remote, as if it were someone else's hand.

There was a knock on the door. Sophie unlocked it and Julius himself stepped into the room. She stared in crazed silence at his handsome head; the mouth – she knew the taste of it. Her mind seemed to spin and hurtle off sideways, like a wheel worked loose from a cart.

'We fortifyin' the house, now,' he said. Sophie nodded, not really hearing his words. He hesitated for a moment, looking at Mrs Wetherby. 'Missus upset?'

'It's all right.'

Sophie motioned him to go. He must go. It was too painful to look at him. Julius and his fellow-slaves, and their rebellion, seemed to have been moved a long way away. Everything was muffled and numbed. Julius was her brother.

'Oh God! Oh God! I can't think any more!' moaned her mother. 'If only I could just die now. I can't face any more of it.'

Sophie looked about her helplessly and, with a great effort, managed to find a way forward in attending to the most mundane matters. 'Mamma, you must get dressed,' she said quietly. 'Let us wash our faces and wait for what will happen. We can do no more.'

29

At Bay

They were a weary and frustrated party, straggling back to Mount Grace through the outskirts of the forest. Old Henry Greene was limping badly, and Christopher Dawson lurching. He stopped often to take a pull from his flask. Frederick Wetherby's mouth was set in self-defence. It was unfair of Ashton to blame him.

'Not a single darky! I don't call that sport.' Alexander Ashton slashed savagely at an inoffensive plant with his switch. His servant Preston was carrying his master's gun as well as his own. Frederick felt this was an irritating affectation in the tropics, undermining their solidarity.

'Sophie must have warned them,' growled George. 'Just wait till I see her again! I'll give her the thrashing of her life.'

'You will not lay violent hands on your sister, sir, or on any woman,' snapped Frederick. His temper was frayed. He was distraught. This, his expedition, the strategy of it all his, a fiasco; and George blaming the ruin of it on Sophie, in front of everyone.

'Not even a damned pig,' Alexander Ashton went on. 'Not even a decent monkey! I've had better huntin' in Norfolk.' Frederick Wetherby wished that Ashton were in Norfolk now.

'Well, I guess it might 'a been yo' lovely daughter, sah!' put in Oliver Somerville tentatively. 'If she's friendly with the slaves, she might have told them our intentions, fo' sure.'

What, even faithful old, meek old Somerville daring to criticise him now! Somerville, who was himself married to a hideous half-caste – actually married, the fool. Frederick ground his teeth in rage. Only Craig, at his side, was silent. In his silence, Frederick hoped for a thin sliver of support. But it might have been just buried fury.

Fatigue, and a deeper heaviness, had settled on Craig's limbs like a shroud of lead. Of course he was disappointed that the Maroons had eluded them. These were dangerous times. One must snuff out rebellion. The smallest spark could flare up into a bonfire that would consume them all. But yet – he had not looked forward to this hunt as a sport and the remarks of his companions irritated him. He particularly hated any mention of Sophie and dreaded George's loose tongue.

'Gentlemen, I admit it,' sighed Frederick Wetherby. 'Somehow our intentions were conveyed to them – I cannot say how. It might just as easily have been a word overheard somewhere – at one of your own establishments, if I may say so.'

'Damned right,' spat Christopher Dawson. 'Always lurking and listening. Sly devils! Walls have ears in this place, indeed. Snakes in the grass.' Dawson often resorted to proverbs in conversation, to spare himself the exertion of original thought.

'All the same, I would have thought you'd have watched your girl rather better,' sneered Ashton.

'She's with her mother all the time. In her hours of repose she is locked in – and her windows barred.'

'Ah, but she's bound to have a maid,' argued Ashton, who loved to criticise the establishments of others. 'Whisperings, secrets, messages. Admit it, Wetherby – hasn't she got some house slave she dotes on, tricks the girl up in laces and bows, and calls her pet names, hey?'

'Nonsense,' insisted Frederick Wetherby with a blush. 'The only slave she sees is Flora. A reliable girl of a very austere temperament.'

'And Julius's sister,' George could not help adding, at which his father shot him a venomous look. Why was his son such a disloyal fool? Not whipped enough as a boy, perhaps. Raised by his mother. Bread and milk and kisses and songs instead of obedience and the lash. He did not trust himself to speak.

'What, the sister of your prize man, the runaway, the carpenter?' Ashton grinned. 'Well, there's your daughter's spy network, staring you in the face, man. Miss Wetherby looked so mild last night, and hardly said a word, I hadn't reckoned her to be such a spirited piece.'

'If I ever marry,' vowed George, 'it won't be a woman with spirit. And if I ever fancy one such, I'll take her to the surgeon and have her damned spirit removed.' The men laughed. The outline of Mount Grace was visible now through the trees.

'Well, gentlemen.' Frederick attempted to blot out the fatigues and disappointments of the day, and the humiliation of his bad generalship, by slipping into that more congenial role: the generous host. 'Though we've had a damned hard and dismal day, at least I can promise you a splendid dinner, and a bottle of my best brandy.'

'Ah!' drawled Dawson. 'And we shall do justice to it. I assure you.' He broke into a few bars of song, as they walked out into the clearing at the edge of the garden, for he liked to show off his clear bass voice. 'Here's to the maiden of bashful sixteen, and –'

Suddenly there was a loud crack of musket fire and a puff of dust sprang up only yards in front of them. They scattered and dived behind trees and rocks.

'What the devil –' Peering round from his cover, Frederick Wetherby stared in disbelief at his house. The windows and doors were all barricaded. He could see the weapons poking out from the upper floor, from his own cherished armoury, trained on himself. His heart flooded with terror; Isabella and Sophie – what had happened to them?

'So what's this, Wetherby?' demanded Ashton from behind a Jackfruit tree, still supercilious even when under fire. 'This your splendid hors d'oeuvres, what?'

Wetherby hated Ashton, at that moment, almost to the point of murder. How could the fellow make a triumphant jest at a neighbour's expense, whose family might be lying dead? A spasm of pain seemed to seize his heart and squeeze it. For a few minutes he could only lean against the rock and wait for it to ease. A cold sweat mantled the face and neck, and he was afraid that in his dizziness he would soil himself. But his head cleared and the pain released its grip.

Fire was exchanged for a few minutes, but then George crept across to his father's redoubt.

'We can't go on like this, sir,' he hissed. 'We'll be out of ammunition. And they've got the whole damned arsenal at their disposal.' Frederick wiped his brow. George was right. They had gone out fully armed, but expecting to encounter a group of slaves with nothing more than axes, cutlasses and swords: no fire power at all. Now what they were faced with, at the end of an exhausting day, was a well-defended citadel with its own armoury.

'The women!' his father muttered. 'Your mother and sister . . .'

Craig was beside them; he brought out his handkerchief, tied it to a stick, and flourishing this white flag above his head, he stepped out cautiously into full view of the house. He lifted his hand and the shooting stopped.

'Mrs Wetherby and Miss Sophie!' he called. 'Are they safe?'

'They're safe, yes!' a voice answered from the armoury. Craig recognised Julius's educated tones.

'Prove it!' he cried. 'Let one of the ladies speak to us; show herself.' There was a pause. Craig could hear the buried murmur of voices and the distant thud of footsteps inside the house.

'Tell them to let the women go,' said Wetherby, still too weak to stand up. 'If they let them go, we will withdraw, tell them.'

'Aye, let's regroup up at Belmont, hey, Craig?' suggested Ashton.

'Willingly,' said Craig.

There was a movement at the window just below the eaves. They saw a white hand flutter for a moment and heard Sophie's voice. 'We are safe and well, Papa!' She sounded surprisingly strong. 'They have not hurt us. Mamma and I are both unharmed.'

'Julius!' called Craig. 'Let the ladies go and we will withdraw to Belmont and talk to you tomorrow.'

'No!' The answer was sharp. 'Ladies stay with us till we get our demands met.'

'What demands?'

'Damn them for their impudence,' fumed Ashton.

'Letter waitin' up at Belmont. All we want is in de document.'

Craig walked back to his companions. 'Come,' he sighed, unfastening the handkerchief. 'You know the womenfolk are safe, at least, Fred. If we send a fellow for help to the fort at Douglastown we might get reinforcements the day after tomorrow. Let's go to my house.'

'They foresaw that, eh?' commented Ashton sourly. 'Cunning devils. I'd like to see their impertinent letter. Let the fellow who wrote on it choke on it, Wetherby. Hang the lot of them, I say.'

'We are not in a position to do anything so gratifying, I'm afraid,' snapped Wetherby and set off wearily up the hill, glad only that his pain had left him and that his wife and daughter were alive.

Up at Belmont the letter was waiting. Wetherby did not read it aloud, though any eavesdropping slaves would doubtless have known the contents in any case. The militia passed it from hand to hand. Reading it seemed to increase Craig's weariness, though it aroused Ashton's wrath. Frederick Wetherby felt it enter him like a wound.

> To Mr Wetherby, once our master, now our enemy, but who could be our partner if he so desires; we have taken your house and your wife and daughter are in our hands. We have great store of weapons and ordnance here. If you attack again you cannot defeat us, and the more cruel you are to us, or to our people on the estate, so will we be cruel to yours.
>
> But instead we invite you to agree with us in realising King George's will that the slaves should have freedom and not be constrained by bloody authority; we promise to work for you three days a week, if you grant we may work for ourselves three days and set aside one day for rest. This will bring an end to the tyranny that must offend the God who has taught us that all men are brothers. Julius Murphy.

At the end was a codicil in a fair, round hand, unlike Julius's stiff and upright writing:

> Father, Mother and I are both well. Please do not reject Julius's request. Be kind to them, Papa. We are all human beings after all. I am confident you will see the justice of it – Sophie.

'I'd thrash the gel,' commented Ashton. 'And what an impudent fellow this Murphy must be! Calling the Almighty to support his cause! – I always said you were wrong to convert your slaves, Wetherby.'

'Well, well, perhaps you are right about that,' growled Frederick. 'I gave them the Christian religion, but they only want it as a stick to beat me with.'

'Aye, The lout! Burn him alive for his presumption – he writes a fair hand, however.'

Craig's eyes were still fixed on Sophie's few words. The sight of her writing stirred in him the most painful thoughts.

'I educated Julius,' said Frederick bitterly, also moved despite himself by the sight of familiar handwriting.

'Damned mistake, Father, if you don't mind my saying so.' Frederick regarded his son with a curious, measuring stare. At times he felt that George's education had been even more wasted than Julius's.

They sat down to a frugal supper. Cassie had known the militia would arrive, but she pretended to be surprised and produced, with a great show of sulking, only the remains of a stewed goat, a little bread, some sweet potato and rice. Craig's cellar was well stocked, however. There was plenty of claret and Christopher Dawson was soon drunk. Old Henry Greene fell asleep, with his old hands clasped across his belly. They looked like twigs, frecked with age, the blue veins somehow pitiful. Craig found it hard to bear the thought that such an old man should have to be pressed into active service. But his more urgent concern was the safety of Sophie and her mother. Only Ashton rejoiced in his usual barbarian high spirits; the mood of the rest was sombre.

'Having the damned Maroons living wild in the forest, as they do in Jamaica, would be bad enough,' complained Ashton. 'But the impudence of the beggars! – Taking your house like that, Wetherby. And then demanding three days. You must hang 'em all.'

'I've got to get the devils out first,' snapped Frederick. 'And I'm damned if I can settle on the best course of action.'

'Send to the fort, sah,' suggested Somerville. 'They got cannon, they got small cannon they could bring round in a bum-boat, drag 'em up from the beach in no time.'

'But that could take days! And meanwhile my wife and daughter are in their hands.'

'Besides!' cried Dawson, joining the conversation with a sudden drunken lunge of energy, 'they're all sick at the fort, you know: half-dead of the fever, I shouldn't wonder. A few small Leicestershire boys: tiddlers, terriers, God help them! Mere half-pints!'

'Aye!' agreed Ashton. 'If I'd caught 'em fishing I'd have thrown 'em back! Why, even if they were fit, Wetherby, you could no more defend your place with them than with a pack of chimney-sweeps' boys.'

'Say we tried to take the place by night, now,' mused Somerville. 'D'ye think it would serve, sah? Catch 'em sleeping, eh?'

'Let sleeping dogs lie!' shouted Dawson. 'No, no! Too dangerous, I say. Fools rush in, what?'

'You are right, Dawson,' bawled Ashton. 'Disturb 'em at night, they wake in confusion, some fool draws his cutlass, and there's your wife's throat cut directly, Wetherby.'

Frederick Wetherby quailed at Ashton's brutality.

'Hopeless!' cried George, always impatient with the elderly, the infirm, or the meek – in this case, Somerville. 'We don't know how many we are up against for a start. They'll have a watch going all hours. And their damned eyes are so sharp, they can see in the dark.'

'But we can't see them,' added Ashton. 'Damn it! This is depressing talk, Craig – haven't you got some girls we could fool about with?'

Craig glanced fastidiously at Frederick Wetherby. 'Later.' He shrugged.

'Get Cassie up here – she's got an arse like a great Aberdeen cow.' George laughed.

His father pursed his lips. 'My carousing days are past,' he said grimly. 'And I'm surprised that you can be so lewd, George, when the lives of your mother and sister, your house, your estate, all your inheritance hangs in the balance here.'

'I'm sorry, Father.' George sighed, rather sulkily.

'We must resolve upon a course of action before dawn.' Frederick fidgeted in his chair.

'Get some cannon up from Douglastown!' shouted Dawson in a sudden shaft of drunken enlightenment, evidently oblivious to the fact that this possibility had already been discarded. 'Send to the fort there!'

'They've got fever at the fort,' said Frederick impatiently. 'You said so yourself a moment ago, for God's sake, man! Aren't you ashamed to be drunk at such a moment?'

'I don't mind what moment I'm drunk in.' Dawson chuckled. 'They all seem to serve.'

'What about that new battery you got yo'self down at the beach?' asked Somerville. 'Smart guns from London, I heard. Sure yo' could get it up to the house somehow, eh?'

'You'd better to set fire to the place,' remarked Ashton. 'Smoke 'em out.'

'What, with my wife in there? Are you mad?' Wetherby felt he disliked Ashton more and more. The fellow seemed oblivious to anyone's feelings but his own.

'Then let us take some nearest of their kin,' Ashton went on. 'The fellow's sister, your daughter's maid.'

'What, Flora?'

'Aye, and some others of their brothers and sisters, and tell them we will kill them, one by one, till your wife and daughter are returned to you.'

'And what if they call our bluff?'

'No bluff, you dog! If they don't release the prisoners, we send them their brothers' heads.'

There was a knock at the door, and the kitchen maid, Venus, appeared.

'Bring us some coffee,' said Craig briskly. 'The good sort, not that stale stuff I had yesterday.'

'Come here, gel!' cried Ashton, keenly amorous now that he had supped.

Venus hesitated: Craig was her master. He confirmed the order with a nod. She approached Ashton a pace or two and he pulled her close to his chair and put his hand in her bodice, in a casual, automatic way.

'Good teats, girl!' he leered. 'I'll have to do with you later.' He dismissed her with a playful slap and as a brief afterthought watched her go. 'No arse to speak of,' he remarked. 'Who did you say was well-endowed in the aft quarter, George?'

'Cassie,' said George.

'Send 'em both to my room tonight, Craig, if you would.' Craig nodded bitterly. He had no appetite for women at the moment.

'Smoke 'em out, I say.' said Ashton, resuming his train of thought. 'Your womenfolk will be safe, I'll wager, if your daughter's made a pet of some of 'em. Smoke 'em out, and gun 'em down while they flee. Build yourself a better house on the ashes of the old. And no

231

more damned education for them, man. The lash – that's what they understand.'

'You're right, by heaven!' thundered Frederick Wetherby, giving way to a gathering pressure of frustration. 'That's how it all began. Schoolmasters, college men, tomfool Abolitionists, filling the blacks' heads with nonsense about liberty and brotherly love. Whip the slaves? I'd whip the college boys first, till they screamed for mercy. What do they know of life out here? Sitting in their precious libraries in Oxford, or their fine tea-houses in Covent Garden, gossiping and scribbling – what do they know of hard work? White, soft hands, the whole pack of 'em. Book-men! A day's work under this plaguey sun would kill them. Mischief makers to a man. A pox on them!'

'That's the spirit, Father!' cried George, slapping his thigh. 'Ashton is right: smoke 'em out and gun 'em down!'

'No!' Craig had spoken so rarely, this sudden word had a soaring quality that silenced the others. Even Old Henry Greene jerked awake and stared at his fellow militiamen in a lost, wondering way. 'We must be clever,' Craig explained. 'Subtle. There's no need to risk all our skins – and the lives of the ladies. We know what the blacks want now. Of course, it's impossible. But we don't tell them that. They think their demands are reasonable. We must pretend to agree. I suggest you write back saying that if they give up their weapons we will promise to meet their conditions.'

'What! – Give my word, and go back on it?' Wetherby faltered.

'But, Fred, they are only slaves, after all,' Craig pointed out. He was privately not entirely committed to his own argument, but had a strong instinct to avoid bloodshed, no matter how. 'Slaves that have seized your property and your wife and daughter, and now dare to make these demands. I grant you, to break your word to a gentleman would be unthinkable. But to slaves? To savages? I think not.'

Frederick Wetherby thought for a moment, then walked to Craig's writing desk and took up the pen.

'That's not the way!' cried Ashton. 'Show the slightest weakness and you're done for. The whole island will be in turmoil the instant the notion gets about. Smoke 'em out, you fool!'

'Don't call me a damned fool, you arrogant swine!' seethed Wetherby. 'If you had womenfolk taken, you wouldn't swagger so.'

'Starve 'em out!' cried Dawson. 'A siege, man, that's what you want. More haste less speed.'

'God help us, God help us all! I got a bad feelin' in my spine, sah, about how this going to go!' Somerville shook his head, lamenting.

'None of your wretched foreboding!' commanded Ashton. 'We'll have none of your plaguey superstitions, and glooms, and vapours, now, Somerville. It is a simple matter. By sunset tomorrow they will all be hung, and King Fred will be back on his throne. Ha ha!'

Henry Greene said nothing, only looked round discontentedly at his companions, growling softly like an old dog who can no longer bite. Frederick Wetherby went on writing.

30

Demands

A few hours later, down at Mount Grace, Sophie took up her pen also:

Dearest Aunt Sarah,

I am writing this by candlelight. It is three o'clock and I cannot sleep. The house is full of slaves – there has been an uprising – Papa and George were out hunting at the time, they are gone to Mr Craig's house at Belmont I believe, with the rest of the militia. Whilst they were out, Julius gained entry to the house through a hole he had cut in the floorboards, and with him brought a party of young men who instantly overpowered our guards and barricaded the house.

When Papa's party returned, the slaves fired on them. There was the most tremendous noise of gunfire above our heads, all around us – Mamma and I were so frighened, we crawled under the bed. Yet for all the clamour of muskets and gunpowder, it seems there were few if any hurt, and I hope none in Papa's party. When the firing stopped, I was called up by the slaves in the armoury to shew myself and assure Papa that we were safe.

But what will happen next I tremble to think. I cannot now be confident I will ever see you again, dearest Aunt! It might be that we will be harmed somehow, either by the slaves or by some attempt to retake the house. Mount Grace is built mostly of wood. I cannot think it would withstand a long or violent siege, or offer much protection against cannon. I suppose I might be going to die very soon and my thoughts should be composed and resigned, but all sort of things rush about in my brain, chiefly the desire to escape, and the hope that, if I do die, it will not hurt very much or last very long.

Other things torment me, however, and this is the reason I could not sleep, apart from the constant snores and shufflings and whisperings all over the house, for the slaves are sleeping everywhere, on the floor, sprawled on chairs, even curled up under the kitchen table (where I went to get Mamma a morsel of bread). Mamma has slept well I think. Her steady breathing is a great comfort to me.

But what she told me yesterday has almost broken my heart. She confessed that Julius and Flora are Papa's children. He consoled himself, it seems, for Mamma's absence by taking Mimba Murphy as a kind of surrogate wife. His relations with her must have started on his first short trip to the West Indies, before I was born, for Julius is older than I am. I think Mamma finds this particularly painful – that Papa should have been unfaithful to her so soon after their marriage, and on a voyage which would restore him to her bosom within two years.

She was indeed most agitated, as you can imagine. Her own life must have been blighted by the discovery, and mine is now become a catastrophe, for, dear Aunt Sarah, I hope you will not be shocked by this confession, but I have come to love Julius as much as any man could be loved. To discover he is my half-brother puts an end to all my hopes in the cruellest manner.

Although you will think it extraordinary perhaps that I should have any hopes at all in that respect, since Julius is my father's slave and, as Mamma expressed it, I could no more marry him than I could a dog. And beyond all that there is the extreme peril into which we are all thrown by this rebellion, which Julius and his mother planned and led. No doubt my anxieties at this moment should all concern survival. But I cannot help being haunted by the fact of Julius's parentage and beyond that, by the way my life has been hedged and fenced about with lies.

Lies, from beginning to end. Except from you, dearest Aunt Sarah – you always told me the truth, although I know you hesitated to give your opinion of slavery until it was unavoidable. You hesitated because you knew I was too young to understand and it would grieve me. Alone perhaps of all my acquaintance, I am sure you never told me lies. But think how everyone else I have been concerned with has lied both to me and to one another!

Father writes to Mamma from the West Indies: fond letters no doubt, full of longing and the anguish of separation. Then he puts down his pen and goes off to Mimba's embraces. George lectures me about the necessity of keeping aloof from the slaves, then I discover he has several slave mistresses and probably as many children. Charles Craig assures me I am an angel, then returns to Belmont and indulges himself in the most gross orgies. Everyone lies to me about Flora's and Julius's parentage. Lies are so thick about me I hardly feel I can breathe.

But the lies I dread most, and am least sure of, are Julius's. How could he encourage my feelings towards him, knowing we were related? Was it all a charade, to engage my affection and ensure my support for the rebellion? The possibility tortures me and I have no opportunity of a private interview with him now, for the house is full of slaves and I barely glimpse him, and if I do, there are always six or seven others standing by, or at least Mamma, so I can say nothing.

He might have spared himself the trouble, for my sympathies would have been with the slaves' cause in any case, so long as they did not hurt anybody. I cannot believe he did not mean it, that his loving ways were not genuinely felt. But since I came to Sabato, I have seen how casually and cynically men can use women, without a care for their feelings or the consequences, so I am thrown into a kind of terror of uncertainty.

If by some miracle I am preserved, I cannot imagine what sort of life I will lead, except perhaps that I shall teach, and hope to find in the company of young minds a kind of freshness and grace, as when I was young I found in your loving guidance. But above all I shall endeavour to do two things. The first is never, so far as I am able, to deceive people, for lies are like vermin that find their way into the pantry and eat away at your sustenance whilst you are unaware. I think of Mamma waiting patiently for fifteen years for letters from my father and not knowing that her husband, and in some sense her life, had been stolen away and devoured by someone else. I will not ever tell a lie again if I can help it, though I know how taxing the attempt will prove; I could not respect myself otherwise.

My second resolution is in some ways the opposite: I will not believe anybody, no matter what they say; I will never again be taken in and made a dupe. The first resolution is for the repose of my own conscience; the second is to assist mere survival. But I acknowledge that at this moment the preservation of Mamma's life is my most important aim. Julius has given his word that he will not harm us. I cannot imagine such a thing. But if I am to practise my new resolution straight away, I should be resolved not to believe even Julius.

Writing this letter has helped to compose my feelings. I now feel almost calm and not a little tired. I shall go to bed, dear Aunt! – hoping to dream of you, remembering the delightful picnics we had down by the stream at Hempshott, and confident that, if we do not meet again on this earth, I shall be waiting in a better place to greet you when your time comes, and to kiss your dear eyes and wipe away your tears for ever.

Sophie

Sophie yawned and stretched. It was four o'clock. There were two hours of darkness left; she was weary. She crept to the bed, delicately climbed in and lay close to her mother's back. Dear warmth of life! A tear slipped on to the pillow at the thought of anyone seeking to harm Mamma. She would defend her to the death, even against Julius. But Julius would not hurt Mamma – he had given his word.

Lies. Lies. Her mind was still busy with the word, though more lazily now. It was a curious word. It seemed to buzz in her brain. My mother lies in bed, thought Sophie, and I lie behind her. She drifted into a shallow sleep and found herself in the pantry at Grandmamma's house at Hempshott. At least she thought it must be the pantry, for she recognised the great stone shelves and the flagstone floor, though the place seemed bigger and loftier than usual.

A buzzing disturbed her: she looked more closely and saw, with a sudden shudder, that a joint of meat had been left uncovered; it was crawling with flies. Their black bodies swarmed all over it, flashing with green and blue; other flies hovered and settled, and now she saw eggs, and maggots, and always that horrible buzzing, buzzing in her ears, that made her flesh creep.

I must take the meat away, she thought, *I must get rid of it, cast it on the fire, or throw it away somewhere*. But as she reached for the plate, she saw with a sudden spasm of horror that it was not a joint of beef, as she had supposed, but a human head: the head of Julius. Sophie opened her mouth but could not scream. She strove, with every ounce of her strength, to turn away, cry out, to escape, and her eyes opened with a sudden snap. She heard herself shrieking and saw her mother's face, and knew she was at Mount Grace, in Mamma's room.

'What was it, my dear?' Mamma's arm was around her, comforting her as it had in childhood. Sophie shook like one in a fever, trying to blot out the hideous image.

'A – a bad dream, Mamma – oh, how horrible! I can't – I must not think of it.'

'Come. It is day. They've brought us some fruit and chocolate. You must eat. And Julius has asked to see you. He is up in the armoury.'

'Oh, then I must go.'

Sophie tore from the bed. She was already fully dressed and did not even pause to put on her shoes, so desperate was her urge to see Julius alive, with his head on his shoulders, and obliterate the hateful nightmare. As she left the room she heard her mother exclaim in disapproval at her haste, but her mother's disapproval had become a thing so insignificant it could be ignored.

She raced upstairs to the armoury, where Julius seemed to spend most of his time. He was talking to Eli, who was sharpening a large knife with a whetstone. Lucas, the wheelwright's assistant, was also there, cleaning the musket he had so proudly snatched from Kendrick. Sophie wondered for an instant what had happened to Kendrick and prayed that he had not been killed. It seemed to her, as she arrived, that Lucas looked at her satirically, and she wondered, fleetingly, whether all the slaves knew that she was Julius's half-sister. But the desire to see him soon banished all other thoughts.

He looked at her kindly, she thought, though he was obviously much occupied with a paper he held.

'We got a letter from Massa.'

'What! From Papa? – Let me see!'

She took the paper and tried to read it, but her fingers shook so much and her brain whirled, so that at first she could not understand a single word.

Dear Julius,

I need not tell you how disappointed I was to find that you had not only deserted your duties on the estate, but gathered about you a group of rebels, seized my house, taken my wife and daughter hostage and dared to fire at my returning party. Considering the great favour and responsibilities I have invested in you, your betrayal is the more painful to me. Such behaviour might, in other circumstances and with other masters, provoke the most dire retribution. But after a great deal of reflection, I have decided to show forbearance.

Though most of my fellow-planters have urged me to think otherwise, I have come to the conclusion that your demands are not, in themselves, unreasonable. We cannot here on Sabato endure the same disastrous unrest which has plagued other islands. If your proposal will guarantee me labour for three days a week, with no further disturbances, no runaways and no rebellious acts, I accept. But first you must lay down your arms and surrender my house. It is outrageous that I am driven to impose on Mr Craig's hospitality here at Belmont. I require my home of you. Lay down your arms, release my wife and daughter and withdraw from my house, and I will grant your demands.

Frederick Wetherby.

'Why, this is wonderful!' cried Sophie, laying down the paper. 'Papa is extraordinary – he has seen what he must do. He has behaved with courage and imagination. I would never have believed it!'

The three men were silent for a moment, then Eli snorted.

'Mi not believe it fo' sure.' He scowled. 'Dis a trick, yuh know how buckra mind work, Julius.'

'Oh no!' cried Sophie. 'I'm sure father means this! It is the right thing to do. It is best for us all.'

Julius turned to her. 'You believe it because you want to believe it.'

'What do you mean?'

'If you was Massa, maybe we'd get our three days.'

'Of course you would!'

'Massa don't think like you.' Julius shook his head.

'Him nat a dog,' affirmed Lucas fiercely. 'Him snake. Him hide, him lie in de leaves, so yuh nat see him, den him strike.'

Sophie was convinced that her father's offer was a bold overture which could transform life at Mount Grace. She could not bear the thought that the slaves might lose the chance, though she understood their hesitations.

'Oh what can I do?' she cried. 'What can I do to help you? To convince you?'

'If he go back on his word, we all dead meat,' said Julius.

'Papa would never do that, I am sure.'

Julius looked at her. His face was still clouded with scepticism and uncertainty. 'You want to help us?'

'Of course!'

'You go to him. Go to yo' father. You know him. Ask him 'bout this. What he think. What he really think. You know him. You see his face. Look at his eyes when he speaks. You find out, come back to us.'

'Yuh crazy!' exploded Eli. 'Gib dis girl her freedom, she nat ever come back.'

'I would, Eli. On my honour. I have great sympathy with your cause. I would do anything –'

'Maybe yuh want come back, but yuh pappy say no.' Lucas looked at her tauntingly. 'What yuh do den? What can yuh do? Girl alone can't do nuttin'.'

Sophie knew this was true. Still the fire of her optimism blazed; she wanted to try, at least. 'I'll go. Let me try, Julius. I promise I'll come back.'

'Yuh goin' to give up yuh hostage, man? Give her up so easy, hand over de treasure, hand her back to Pappy, widout eben a murmur. Eh! Yuh sure a great fighter, show buckra we weak as shit,' sneered Eli.

Julius stuck out his lower lip and returned the glare. 'We still got Missus,' he declared. 'Massa knows that. What good is keepin' the girl, nat usin' her? She know how Massa t'ink; she clever girl, see into him mind.' He turned to Sophie. 'You go and see your pappy,' he said. 'Come back an' tell us what in his mind.'

Eli groaned, but Julius ignored him and took Sophie downstairs to the back door which was not barricaded, though it was guarded by a slim youth who looked no more than fourteen, cradling on his thin knees an enormous old musket. Julius summoned two men to escort her up to Belmont and gave them their orders. Sophie paused only to accept a drink and a piece of corn-bread, which she put in her pocket to eat on the way. For a moment Julius seized her hands. Despite the eyes of others, suddenly there was a moment of intense privacy between them. She could say nothing, paralysed by his sudden tenderness.

'Keep you safe, my beautiful woman,' he whispered, then kissed her brow. She cast a last glance at him and slipped out into the light.

He climbed back up to the armoury. A great heaviness was seizing his limbs: a dread of failure and humiliation worse than the dread of death. He had always trusted his instincts in the past, but now he found himself in a dilemma which confused his senses and puzzled his brain.

Eli and Lucas stopped talking as he entered the armoury. He knew they despised his decision and felt he was betraying the rebellion by letting Sophie go. Now they glared at him. He had expected solidarity in the greatest danger, but he had found instead dissent, contempt and vertigo.

'When yuh fuck dat girl,' commented Eli sourly, 'yuh leave yuh brain in de sand. De crabs have ate it.'

Sophie was nearing Belmont and longing for her father to appear to her as he had presented himself in the letter: a man of decency and fairness, committed to change. Hope and doubt battled in her breast all the way up the hill. Eventually Belmont appeared. Charles Craig came down the steps towards her, almost running, ignoring her armed guards.

'My dear Miss Wetherby!' he cried, 'You are safe! I cannot express –'

'I must see my father,' she said hurriedly. 'You must excuse me – where is he?'

'In my study – through the hall and to the right –'

Sophie hastened into the house and found herself confronted at first by Venus, whom she had last seen accepting Craig's sexual attentions that night which seemed so long ago. Her errand now was too important and urgent to permit much reflection on that matter – thank God. She heard men's voices, followed the sound and found herself in her father's presence.

'Great God!' cried Frederick Wetherby, leaping to his feet. 'What are you doing here, girl? Has he freed you? And your mother?'

'She is well, Papa – we are both safe. They have treated us well. Julius sent me to find out if you really meant it, Papa – if you really meant what you said in the letter. About granting the slaves' requests.' She spoke in a low, respectful voice and looked at the floor. She could not face his eyes yet. It was the first time she had seen him since her mother's revelations.

'The slaves' requests? Demands, you mean,' corrected her father. 'Look at me, child.'

Sophie raised her eyes. George was sprawling on a corner of Craig's desk and old Mr Greene was standing by the window. She could hear English voices in the next room. At last she met her father's gaze and blushed, for no matter how urgent the present business, she could not entirely expel from her mind the idea of his being the father of Julius and Flora.

'George, Mr Greene, if you would be good enough to leave us? I would like to talk to my daughter alone.' The door closed behind them and Frederick Wetherby opened his arms to her. 'Come,' he said. 'Do I not merit an embrace?' Sophie placed herself in his arms. 'It is a great relief to see you safe, my dear.'

'Oh, the slaves would not hurt me, Papa,' Sophie assured him. 'They simply want what they believe the King has promised. Are you really prepared to grant them their three days?'

Frederick Wetherby walked over to the window and looked out. His back was turned to Sophie, but she heard a convincing note of kindness in his voice.

'I'm a reasonable man, I hope,' he said. 'I regard the slaves in much the same way as I regard my children.' Sophie blushed again and was grateful not to be facing him. 'Wayward sometimes, ignorant certainly, needing help and guidance which it is my duty to provide. But I have come to feel that my slaves, like my children, may prove to be on the road to discretion. To enlightenment. A little judicious opportunity for them to organise their own affairs may be no bad thing.'

'You are in earnest, then?' Her voice sounded thin and small. She cursed the way she seemed to become a child again in her father's presence. 'It is important that I know, Papa. They – Julius – want me to go back and confirm that you will do what you promise.'

'Oh, yes, my dear. One does not stand obstinate against the tides of change. Remember King Canute. When one is faced with an irresistible force, one bows to it gracefully, retrieving what one can.'

'This is very good of you, Papa.'

'Not at all, my dear. Discretion is the better part of valour. I am merely acting rationally to avoid the shedding of blood. To be honest, I am in a way simply trying to take my enemy by surprise – by yielding to him just at the very moment he least expects it and thereby regaining my lost ground, and some initiative to boot.'

'But you really will grant what they ask?'

'Certainly, if they lay down my arms and remove themselves from my house.'

'Will –' She hesitated, hardly daring to say what she knew she must. 'Will you give me your word?'

He smiled and the smile was formal. He held out his hand. She took it. It was cold, which astonished her, the morning being so hot.

'I give you my word.'

'Oh, I'm so glad! They are not bad people, you know.' Sophie placed a kiss awkwardly on his cheek.

He turned amiably to her, and caressed her hair. 'You have a kind heart, my dear, which is a good thing in a woman. But you must behave with more decorum sometimes, you know.' Sophie held her breath. What was coming, now? A lecture? Instead, her father moved past her and rang the bell.

'And now I shall call Venus to give you some refreshment, for you will want to be going back to Mount Grace directly, I suspect.' Sophie assured him she would. He gave some orders, and now her urgent embassy was completed, she rendered him a more detailed account of her mother's health and spirits. Soon Venus brought a mixture of vegetables and prawns, cooked in a kind of pancake. Sophie devoured it – she had only eaten a hunk of corn-bread this morning and felt famished.

'You will find,' her father warned her as she prepared to leave, 'that the other planters do not think as I do. There are some here who consider me exceedingly foolish and see my course of action as leading to certain disaster. But take no notice of them. I am convinced that co-operation is the only way to make progress in this predicament.'

Sophie could not help thinking how pleased Aunt Sarah would be at this outcome. Her father's magnanimity had exceeded all her expectations. She reflected that she had not known him very long, after all, and hoped the discovery of his character would offer her many other pleasant surprises.

'I am sure you're right, Papa. I am proud of you – I am hardly able to express how much.' She kissed him effusively on both cheeks, and ran out.

As she left Belmont again with her guards, she heard laughter break out up in the house behind them. Her heart seemed to fill with sunlight at the sound, and she returned full of joy and hope.

31

Cleansing

Julius and Eli stood irresolutely in the armoury, with five or six of their comrades, considering Sophie's account of her interview with her father.

'Mi don't b'lieve it.' Eli curled his lip.

'I understand your doubts,' said Sophie. 'I would feel the same, in your situation. But my father gave me his solemn word. He says he will come at two o'clock, and if you will lay down your arms and leave the house he will give you what you want.'

Julius rubbed his nose sceptically. 'How we *know* that?'

'You must accept his word – my word, too. I was not sure, on the way there, that his offer was genuine. But he convinced me. His tone and his manner were very direct. And there were things he said which confirmed it, to my mind. He said the other planters did not agree with him. And he admitted that he had been forced to accept your demands against his will, not just by your action here, but because of what is happening all over the West Indies, and in America and France. So much . . .' Sophie struggled to express what was, in truth, considerable ignorance. 'So much turbulence. He feels . . .' She hesitated, aware now that she was expressing what she hoped her father felt rather than what she knew was in his heart. 'He feels there is a better hope of stability and security on Sabato, if he gives you your three days.'

'So you sure he's not lying?'

She did not hesitate. 'I would stake my life on it.'

Julius examined her face for a moment. He could not doubt *her* sincerity, at least. 'Go back to yo' mammy, then. We talk on it here.'

She went. There had been no tenderness in Julius's face, no intimate look or touch. He was completely absorbed by the perils of his dilemma. It was foolish of her to long for private, loving words with him, for a caress. Many lives were at stake, and many hopes hung on his decision. In any case, she knew she must stop longing for him in this way. It was not appropriate any more. She was grateful that the danger of their present situation, and the importance of her embassy to Belmont, had left her very little time to brood or grieve.

She found her mother tidying and folding her clothes in the linen press.

'I don't know why I am doing this,' she said, with a strange sound that was half a laugh, half a sob. 'It could not signify less, I suppose. The whole house may go up in flames within the hour. I may be dead by evening, and yet I feel I must make my clothes tidy. It is what women do whilst men occupy themselves with destruction.'

'Oh no, Mamma,' Sophie said eagerly. 'I have been to Belmont and seen Papa – he has accepted Julius's terms. He is coming here at two o'clock, the slaves are going to give up their arms to him and he will give them their three days. So nothing will be destroyed except what was vile and cruel. We shall have a new world here, and it will be fair and just.'

Her mother stared at her for a moment.

'You are a silly goose, Sophie,' she sighed. 'When your father comes back, they will all be hanged.'

'No, Mamma! Papa will give them their three days. He admits he must do it against his own inclinations, but it is for the sake of stability here.'

'Does that mean our house slaves will only work for three days? A diverting thought! Perhaps you can explain how we will manage?'

'Of course we'll manage! We can do more work ourselves instead of lazing about all day. I'll learn to cook.'

'You – cook?' Isabella Wetherby gave her daughter a withering look. 'And scrub the floors and sweep and wash and carry water as well, I suppose?'

'Why not? I'm young and strong, and I hate doing nothing.' Sophie was committed to her optimism. Since coming to Sabato she had often felt crushed and powerless. The chance to improve the slaves' lot by her own exertions filled her veins with energy. Her mother gave her a satirical look and shook her head doubtfully.

In the brief silence they became aware of a growing debate in the armoury above their heads. Voices were raised up there: they could hear Eli shouting and a high, piercing voice raised against him. So furious was the argument that it seemed there was something of a physical struggle: there was a slithering, bumping sound and the crash of some heavy object against the floor, and Sophie recognised Julius's deep voice echoing in rage above the noise, demanding order and solidarity.

'Well, if what you say is true, at least we shall have them out of the house.' Her mother sighed with relief. 'I can't stand all this shouting. And I can't bear the thought of that woman under my roof.'

'What woman?'

'That creature – Mimba Murphy.'

'Oh, Mimba isn't here, Mamma. She went to Demoiselle.'

'To Demoiselle?' Her mother cocked her head, alert.

Instantly Sophie regretted her words. She hoped that, if there was to be an agreement between masters and slaves, Mimba would be restored to favour, but nevertheless she should not have spoken. She had carelessly revealed the hiding place of the Maroons. She must learn to control her tongue. Her teachers had often said as much at school. 'Although she may not be there any longer.' She tried clumsily to repair the damage.

But her mother's curiosity was thoroughly aroused. 'What was she doing on Demoiselle? Was she hiding there?'

'They had to go there – to avoid the dogs. They must have left by now, I should think.'

'When you say "they" – are there many with her?'

'Not – I don't know. A few women and children only.' Sophie endured this interrogation in agony, cursing herself for her imprudence. 'Most of the runaways were these men, I believe Mamma – these ones who came here with Julius.'

'You are certainly well informed.'

'I – they told me their plans.'

'And you helped them, I suppose?'

'No – I told them I could not do anything which would endanger you and Papa.'

'And here we are, helpless in their hands. At their mercy. They could cut my throat at any moment. And do you still support them?'

'I did not –' Sophie trembled. 'I never wished – you must understand, Mamma, I would defend you with my life. I am torn between loving you and Papa, and sympathising with the slaves' cause. It is . . . quite dreadful, sometimes.' Tears began to well up. 'You cannot conceive of the agony of it.'

'I cannot conceive, indeed! My whole life has been an agony. Even when I was a girl, I was torn between Sarah and my mother: mother always wanting us to enjoy ourselves and dress finely, and Sarah always wanting me to be serious and help the poor. And then when I married Papa it was worse! The Wetherbys were so very grand and condescending, I was made to feel thoroughly ashamed of my own family. And yet I loved them still, I could not stop loving them, though I felt that was what the Wetherbys wanted. Especially Grandmamma Wetherby. She is a fine old tyrant!'

Sophie was astonished by this sudden bitter glimpse of her mother's history.

'Then, when Papa came out here, I was left behind at Hempshott. He was the reason I had married into their family; he was the only one of them I could love and he was never there. I was condemned to live among them and suffer their condescension, and accept his mother's criticism without a word. And then, when I found the courage to come here, defying all Grandmamma's deepest disapproval, I discovered – well, you know the rest. Don't tell me, Sophie, that I have never suffered. I have done little else.'

Sophie was silenced, but only for a moment. 'At least you had a sister who loved you dearly – Aunt Sarah is the best sister anyone could have, I think.'

'Ah, yes,' Isabella's mood softened. 'Dear Sarah. I will write to her, I think. I suppose it – perhaps for the last time.'

'No, Mamma. We will survive this. I am sure of it now. And the slaves will have their three days and be happy. I was writing to her myself – I shall finish the letter by telling her what has happened today.'

When their letters were finished, they felt hungry. Sophie undertook to visit the kitchen to see what she might find.

The house was full of clamour. People were bustling in and out, collecting things, as if packing up in preparation for an evacuation. There was a general sense of rising anticipation and everywhere voices were raised in argument. Insults were hurled, but strangely, not at her; the slaves were clearly in a state of turmoil and uncertainty. The ferocity of their debate revealed their desperation, for they certainly believed their lives were at stake. Sophie wished she could reassure them, though she understood how after decades, even centuries, of ill-treatment at white hands it was impossible for them to trust their masters. She thought it would be best to say nothing.

She found the kitchen in great disorder. Some damage had been done during the siege: fragments of torn wood were scattered over the floor. Food had been prepared and consumed, the dirty dishes and leftovers were lying about. There was no sign of Serafina, so after taking some corn-bread to her mother, Sophie set to herself, but had done no more than lift a broom, when the clock in the hall struck two.

Suddenly there was a shot from outside. Everyone paused; a prickling silence sprang up. She heard, in the distance, her father's voice.

'Come out, all of you, as agreed. Leave your weapons, come out and line up in the yard.'

Frenzied talk broke out throughout the house; there were a few scuffles, but gradually, one by one, the slaves moved towards the front door. Julius appeared. Eli was at his side, clutching at him, in a torrent of debate.

'Keep us weapon,' cried Eli, his eyes wide and white-rimmed. 'Talk wid he; get him signature on contract, proper legal piece of paper, promisin' we de t'ing. Get lawyer man up from Douglas-town, get 'im name down, get him signature, dat what buckra respect. De law.'

'How I do that now?' Julius was in an anguish of indecision. He went to the door; it was open a crack. 'Get us lawyer from Douglastown!' he called out. 'We want a contract, want it to be legal document.'

'Of course you shall have a lawyer!' came Frederick Wetherby's voice. 'We have drafted the agreement, here. See!'

Eli put his eye to the crack of daylight.

'Him got a piece of paper there,' said Julius.

'We nat know what it is,' hissed Eli. 'Could be nothin' – to fool us. Tell him we nat gib up us weapon till we see lawyer.'

'Bring the lawyer here!' called Julius. 'We want it legal!'

'Release my wife and daughter first!' came the reply.

Isabella had appeared in the hall. 'I shall go out to him,' she announced, with a sudden firmness of purpose and authority which astounded Sophie.

'No!' cried Eli, grabbing her arm.

Isabella Wetherby turned and glared at Eli. 'You will release me, Eli,' she ordered, 'as Massa requires.'

'Cut she t'roat!' came a voice from the shadow of the stairs. It seemed to infuriate Julius.

'Let Missus go!' he cried. 'Don't talk like we savages!' Eli's arm fell away; Isabella walked calmly to the door, opened it and strode out into the brilliant sunlight. The slaves manning the door seemed stunned for an instant. They stood back and watched her pass, then seized the door and slammed it shut again.

'What yuh done now?' groaned Eli. 'Yuh gib up yuh 'vantage, man. Keep de girl, keep de girl, she all we got nah.'

'Where is my daughter?' came Frederick Wetherby's distant voice. 'Let Miss Sophie go.'

Eli seized her arm.

'Don't hurt me, Eli! There is no need. You are going to get your three days, if only you give up your weapons and leave the house.'

'I nat b'lieve yuh!' Eli's eyes blazed.

Sophie turned to Julius. 'You believe me, don't you, Julius? You must!'

'Keep de house,' insisted Eli. 'Keep de weapon. Keep de girl, till we get de paper signed.'

'Let my daughter go and come out of the house!'

Julius's face began to shake: his lips trembled, his teeth chattered as if he were freezing to death, though sweat was trickling out of his hair. Sophie suddenly saw that he too was torn between two worlds, but his agony, now, was worse than anything she or her mother had known.

'I have your sister, Flora, here,' Sophie heard her father's voice. It sounded nearer. 'If you do not let my daughter go, she will be whipped.'

Julius lunged to the door and peered through the crack; Eli held fast to Sophie's arm.

Julius groaned, 'Him got me sister.'

The men at the door hissed in distress and added their own lament.

'Holdin' her so she hurt – buckra wid whip standin' by.'

'Look Massa cruel to him black daughter. Whip his own black daughter. Whip him own flesh! How he do dat?'

'Black daughter nat worth a cuss.'

'Tell him let Flora go, or we whip dis girl!' Eli jerked Sophie's arms backwards. She gasped with pain.

'Stop that!' Julius glared at Eli. 'Don't hurt me woman.'

'Yuh woman gib us nothin' but grief!' said Eli with venom. 'Since yuh go sniffin' roun' Miss, yuh lose yuh mind.'

'Nat so!'

'If you do not release Miss Wetherby and come forth, your sister will be hung up and whipped!' This was Ashton's voice, now; it had an edge of impatience.

'Tell 'im wi hang Missy up an' whip her so!' said one of the men at the door.

'Gib her a beatin'!'

'Mi want to do wid her what Julius do!'

'Knock her on de head!'

The voices rose behind them in the hall. There were many more men, now, than the eight who had first clambered into Sophie's room. She was stunned, paralysed with fear.

'Shut your mout'!' Julius suddenly recovered his authority, stung by the rising clamour for destruction. 'Yuh fools, nat know who yuh friends are. Dis a good woman. Brave. Love us slaves. Want us get us freedom. Help us. Risk it all for us. Would die for us, eh?' He turned abruptly to Sophie, who could only gasp and nod, so great was her terror. 'This girl a jewel, me people. Got a white skin but love us.'

'And got a fire in her tail fo' Julius!' came a taunting voice.

'Damn yuh!' Julius was roused, by this last remark, to a towering rage. 'She goes back, now. She go free.' He wrenched Sophie from Eli's grasp. Incandescent with a kind of holy rage, he obliterated all

251

dissent. 'We got to trust Massa 'cause the only other way is blood, blood, blood.' He took Sophie to the door, flung it open and pushed her out. She was dazzled, for a moment, and her legs almost crumpled beneath her. She saw a semicircle of planters, all holding muskets: her father in the middle, with her mother hanging back a little, behind him. Ashton's red-haired servant was holding Flora, her head twisted round beneath his arm. A slave-driver stood by with a whip.

'Let Flora go!' cried Sophie.

Her father raised his arm. 'Come here. And now –' He raised his voice to the slaves in the house. 'You will come out, all of you, and we will talk about your three days.'

A smile hovered for an instant about Ashton's face. A sudden shaft of dread crossed Sophie's heart. But she could do nothing.

'Come here, Sophie.' She went to her father's side, her heart racing in fear.

The door opened and Julius appeared. Slowly he walked down the steps. His bearing was wary and dignified, but he looked alone and helpless in the dust. He walked up to Frederick Wetherby and offered him his hand. It was accepted.

Other slaves came out, some reluctantly, all cautiously. Some emerged carrying guns and were instantly ordered to put them down. Seeing the superiority of the planters' firepower they obeyed and assembled in a silent group. The white men surrounded them, still holding their guns. Julius looked into Wetherby's face, searching for some signal of his intentions.

'Go and make sure the house is empty, George,' he said quietly, when it seemed all the slaves were gathered outside. George and Craig performed this task. 'Now,' said Frederick Wetherby, 'if you will all step this way, we shall accommodate you, gentlemen.' He gestured towards the works. 'To the manager's house, if you please. I will join you in an instant.'

The slaves shuffled off doubtfully, escorted by Ashton and his servant, Somerville, Dawson and Greene. A crawling sense of uncertainty hung in the air. Sophie held her breath until they had disappeared around the side of the building.

Frederick Wetherby turned to his womenfolk, embraced his wife and stroked his daughter's head. 'You have done well, my dear,' he said.

'You are going to give them their three days, aren't you, Father?' She could not dispel a deep agitation.

'All in good time,' he replied quietly. When the house was pronounced safe, he escorted his womenfolk inside.

'What is happening to the slaves?' persisted Sophie, but her father ignored her and, after surveying the damage, he went away again, outdoors – to the manager's house, Sophie supposed. Serafina appeared, looking distraught and frightened.

'Ah, Serafina,' said Isabella, 'make us some tea.'

'De fire gone out, Missus.'

'Then light it again.' Serafina obeyed. Isabella Wetherby walked to the parlour.

'How disgusting,' Sophie heard her say. 'Oh, my poor chairs! Tell Serafina to call some more girls up here. There's a lot to do.'

Sophie ran to the kitchen, where Serafina was blowing at a spark.

'Serafina!' Serafina looked up with an expression of anguish. Sophie was unnerved by the look. 'Mamma says we need more help. Can you get somebody else up to help? Ruth? Her friend – what's her name . . .?' The extraordinary whirl of events had disturbed Sophie's memory.

'Yes, Miss.'

Sophie hesitated. 'Can you tell me – do you know – what is happening to Julius and his men?'

Serafina opened her mouth, but Isabella Wetherby appeared in the doorway.

'Sophie, come and help me. Everything is in disorder! Bring a broom.'

For an hour work went on. Barricades were removed, making a splintering sound. The marks of naked muddy feet were steadily obliterated by bucketfuls of water and a great deal of effort. The chairs were soothed, the carpets comforted, the shattered bodies of the china dogs were swept up. Sophie saw her mother shed a tear over the decapitation of a porcelain shepherdess.

She worked alongside Serafina, but hardly knew what she did. All she could think of was the negotiation, taking place but a few yards away yet entirely inaccessible to her. George was admitted to their counsel. He could hear what her father was saying, even give an opinion. Her own thoughts and feelings were as nothing.

It seemed to Sophie that the men, closeted apart, exercised an effortless authority. But their counsel was fraught with difficulty. They had scarce sat down when a messenger arrived to inform Alexander Ashton that his eastern plantation was in flames, and probably, by now, one third of his income destroyed. He left for Pelican Bay at once, cursing the malice of his slaves, the incompetence of his manager, and the hostility of the gods, all thoughts of Mount Grace wiped from his mind.

There was shocking news, too, from the fort. The fever proved fatal to half the garrison, and the Governor had expired the previous Wednesday. Frederick Wetherby must punish his rebellious slaves himself. The moment of vengeance had arrived, but it was not sweet. Wetherby felt instead a terrible sinking dread.

George always irritated him: Julius was the son in whose intelligence he had taken a secret pride, the fruit of a passion so wild and delicious, it had possessed him utterly for almost two decades. Not a day passed, even now, but he longed for Mimba's touch. Banishing her for Isabella's sake was like closing the shutters for ever on the sun, and endeavouring to live by candlelight.

Ashton was gone; Dawson was drunk; Greene was asleep. He could not bear the sound of George's voice. Luckily, at the moment of his greatest need, Craig spoke.

'If you hang him, Fred, your own plantation will be in flames by midnight. By keeping him alive, you can prolong his punishment unbearably. Make them feel their only hope lies in your forgiveness. Otherwise we are at their mercy.'

Caught in this knot of terror, Frederick Wetherby found a reason not to execute his son, and clutched at it with relief.

32

Boiling Over

It was about half-past four when George ran in and picked up a sunhat. 'Julius is going to be flogged now, out in the yard,' he said. 'We've called the slaves out to watch – I must go.'

'Flogged!' cried Sophie in astonishment. 'But he – promised me! He promised me he would give them their three days!'

George looked at her tauntingly for a moment and shook his head in mock pity. 'What a child you are, Sophie.' He grinned.

Rage exploded in her heart. She ran to the back door, hurled herself down the steps and sped past the coral dripstone, the pump, the horse trough and into the yard. Here she paused for an instant, searching in a frenzy for her father's figure. She heard George's voice calling her, his steps behind her. A crowd of slaves was drawn up around the edge of the yard, their eyes full of fear and hate. They stared in incomprehension at her sudden dishevelled arrival. The planters and their servants surrounded the yard, armed with muskets. Julius stood in the middle of the dusty arena, staring straight ahead, his wrists bound behind him. Kendrick was ready, beside some trestles, holding a whip. He had a black eye and cuts on his face, evidence of the struggle in which he had been disarmed. No doubt his injuries would sharpen his desire for revenge.

But where was her father? Suddenly she saw him. He was standing on a small platform which was normally used for loading carts, mounting and dismounting. His back was to the sun and she could not see his features clearly. The brassy afternoon light flickered around his edges. He seemed wrapped in mystery like a pagan god. She ran across the space that was cleared, like a stage, for the flogging, reached up and seized his legs in supplication. His face floated huge above her, like an ogre or giant in a fairy tale.

'Go back inside!' he hissed ferociously. A drop of his saliva struck her face. She snatched a huge breath. She wanted her cry to be heard all over the island.

'You lied to me!' It came out in a howl, like the voice of an animal. 'You lied to me! You promised they would have their three days but it was a lie!'

A murmur ran through the crowd. Her father tried to shake her off, but she clung to his breeches.

'Get off, get off, damn you, you hussy!' he seethed. He kicked out at her. The toe of his boot struck her brow. It stunned her for an instant – she was seized from behind, recognised George's rough hands and as she struggled against them, her father slipped from her grasp.

'You lied to me!' she shrieked again. George was joined by another. Four hands wrestled with her; she could not resist their combined strength. They dragged her backwards, away from her father, but she would not be silenced. 'You lied to me! You gave me your word but it was a lie! A lie!'

Something seemed to tear in her throat. She tasted blood. The terrible shriek had hurt her; now words would not come. George twisted her body around, then thrust her downwards. Something struck her face as she plunged, then all sounds were dimmed as water thrashed about her head and flooded her ears, booming. They are ducking me, she thought, in the horse trough like a witch. Her lungs burned and she feared she would drown, but they hauled her up and her head was in daylight again, and she coughed and choked, reaching for the precious air with great rasping breaths. As she recovered, she became aware of a singing silence and found everybody's eyes upon her, and followed the silence to its cold centre, and found her father's face.

'You will be silent, Miss, or by God, I'll have you flogged as well, you damned insolent swine!'

The water streamed down her face. She glared through it at her father, defying him silently now. It was a kind of evil baptism; the water on her brow was not a promise of paradise, but a welcome to hell. Now she would stand still, not out of obedience but to show solidarity with Julius. She had to witness his punishment. Water flashed on her cheeks. She looked all tears. No, she would not speak again, not till the end of the world, she vowed.

Having satisfied himself that she was not going to move or utter a sound, her father turned back to his slaves, his temper newly lacerated by his daughter's ludicrous and dangerous intervention.

'Julius is to be flogged today.' His voice rang out across the silent yard, breaking and echoing against the corners of the buildings. 'You know why. Disobedience and ingratitude. Twenty lashes with the thong whip. And then the ebony switch. And then,' the words rolled on, washing around the edge of the yard like a flood that would rise and drown them all, 'we will rub the wounds with brine.' There was a sharp intake of breath among the slaves.

'Salt water,' whispered George with grim humour. 'That'll make the bugger sing.'

Sophie forced herself to look at Julius. His face was impassive. He stood with his weight on one leg, with a slightly relaxed angle of the hip. There was something subversive about his posture. It shrugged off the solemnity of the situation, suggested it was but a tedious interlude. Julius stared past his surroundings as if at some remote mountain top.

'You might ask me, why such a lenient punishment?' the master's voice went on. 'Why Massa so kind? Why do I only flog Julius, when for the same crime he could be burnt alive, or hung in a gibbet? I tell you. This is your last chance. Your last chance to be ruled by a kind master.

'And you know I'm kind. You get good houses. Rest on Sundays. Clothes. Medicine when you're sick. When Bacchus was ill, I sent my own daughter down with special medicine for him. Special medicine from England.' Sophie felt herself flare with new rage at this absurdity. 'So you know I'm a kind master. But if I hear the least whisper of any of that "three-days" nonsense, or there is any more running away, any more slacking or grumbling, I'll tell you what I'm going to do. I'm going to start treating you like Mr Aston treats his slaves over at Pelican Bay.

'I visited Mr Ashton recently. He'd had runaways. He'd caught them again five days later, no trouble. And he hanged them, there and then. I saw their bodies swing in the wind.'

The quietness deepened in the listening crowd.

257

'Some of you will remember Ananias. He was one of them. Ananias used to come here and sing. Well, I saw what was left of Ananias. The birds had pecked his eyes out. His jaw was hanging open and the wasps had made a nest in his throat. Wasps were flying in and out of his open mouth.'

A deep groan echoed among the people. 'Yes. Ananias's mouth was open, but he won't sing again.

'So this is your last chance. Julius gets a flogging today because I'm a kind master. But from now on, any more wrongdoing and you know what you'll get. Remember Ananias.'

Frederick Wetherby's speech was followed by a few seconds' tense silence. He looked around the assembled company, his eyes dwelling, it seemed, on every face. Then he gave a signal to Kendrick, who stepped forward and unfastened the rope binding Julius's hands. He led him forward a couple of steps to the trestle. Julius bowed his muscular body down across the wooden frame with the grace of a wave breaking; Kendrick bound his hands to the trestle's ends, then stood back and wiped his brow.

Kendrick raised his arm, and with a ferocious grunt, brought down all his sinewy strength on Julius's back. The thong bounced in the dirt afterwards like a wounded snake. Kendrick raised his arm again; Sophie closed her eyes. At the twentieth stroke, Sophie had to look. It seemed a betrayal otherwise. If he must bear it, she must see it. Kendrick's shirt was spattered with blood. Julius still had not made a sound, apart from an involuntary gasp as the air was forced from him.

'Now for the ebony switch,' said George with relish. 'It's covered with thorns. That'll make the devil sing.'

Sophie could not stay there any longer. She turned and walked across to the house which waited for her. She longed to escape into it, but it seemed an aching distance to walk in the sun and her legs were not working properly: it was as if her spine had snapped. Finally she reached the steps, as behind her the sharp scalding sound of the ebony switch broke out and at last a yelp of pain was forced from Julius's lips.

Back in her room at last, she closed the inner storm-shutters. She wanted to hear no sound from outdoors. Then, her head in her hands, she sank down on to the floor. A chair seemed too comfortable. A great flood of tears burst from her head. It seemed to her that she must have wept for an hour, for when at last she came to the end of it, the sun had moved and was warm on her feet, as if trying to comfort her. She raised her head and thought perhaps she should wash her face. Then she noticed that her loose floorboards had been repaired. New wood and shiny screws, made all secure. In vain she tugged at them, breaking her nails.

'Why not put me in my coffin, now?' she demanded aloud. 'And nail down the lid. Why not? You might as well!'

'Sophie?' Her mother had evidently been lingering outside her door. She hastened in and at the sight of Sophie crumpled on the floor, her face red and bloated from weeping, she shook her head. Now Sophie was the helpless one and her mother took charge, neat and purposeful in her movements.

'Come, this will never do. Here's some water – let me sponge this poor face – there.'

Sophie submitted. There was something soothing about it. 'I wish I were a child again, Mamma.'

'We all wish that, my dear.'

'Why is it so? When we're children we long to grow up, but we've no idea how horrible it's going to be.'

'Not all horrible. Now get up . . . that's right. Let's change your dress, shall we?' Change her dress? Must the day go on? For how many hours? 'It could have been even more horrible, Sophie. You've no idea.'

'What?' asked Sophie, dreading more but needing to know.

'George was all for hanging him, but Charles persuaded Papa against it.'

'Hanging – ?'

'George had almost persuaded Papa to hang Julius.'

Sophie's mind could only manage a feeble spasm, like an insect whose wings had been torn off. 'Hang . . . ? But Julius is our own flesh and blood, Mamma.'

'Yours, perhaps.' Isabella Wetherby shuddered fastidiously. 'I thank God, not mine.'

'But Julius is not to be hanged?'

'Thanks to Charles Craig. Now I must go. I must supervise the provisions for George's expedition.'

'What expedition?'

'He's off to Demoiselle tomorrow. To hunt down the last of them there. That woman must be stopped. She's a dangerous character.'

'Mimba?'

'Yes. We know she's the leader. Without her they will give up. If George catches her alive, she will have to be hanged. There can be no forgiveness for her, after what she has done.'

Sophie turned her face to the wall.

Next morning Sophie was summoned into her father's presence at eight o'clock. During the night her fury had cooled and hardened. She felt she had turned to stone. In the yard, in the dust, when she had screamed out her accusations, he had told her to be silent. She was determined to say nothing to him now.

He sat in his chair; she stood before him. For a moment he looked at her with distance and distaste, as one might look upon a thing that was inconveniently broken. Then he spoke.

'It is that aunt of yours I blame.' It was not what Sophie expected him to say. She felt a throb of indignation, but controlled herself. 'Sarah Sullivan should have married. There is mischief when a clever woman does not. She has nothing to occupy her time but deluding herself with mischievous ideas about matters she does not understand. She knows nothing of life here. You should never have been entrusted to her care.

'But you are also much at fault. You have indulged a foolish, hysterical temper. Your outburst yesterday could easily have destroyed us all. More than two hundred slaves there, assembled together, after a thwarted revolt – but a handful of us. Thank God we were so convincingly armed. Would you have liked to be the cause of your mother's death?' Sophie said nothing, but the idea affected her too much for her to bear his look and she turned her eyes to the floor.

He accepted this as acknowledgement enough, and continued: 'I am sending you home to England. We cannot have that kind of behaviour here. But you will not go back to her.' Sophie could not help flinching. 'No. You shall not be exposed to your aunt's fantastical notions. You shall go home and live at Hempshott with my mother.'

Grandmamma. Sophie heard the sentence with a deep, cold, sickening dismay.

'Unless I am convinced that your conduct will from henceforth be at all times quiet and civil, you shall be sent to England at the end of the month. You understand?' Sophie gave a slight bow. 'You may go.' She returned to her room.

George had already left for Demoiselle to hunt the Maroons. Frederick Wetherby, having satisfied himself that the atmosphere at Mount Grace was subdued and chastened, departed for Douglastown to report the restoration of order at Mount Grace and to discuss further augmentation of the militia. Kendrick was fully occupied in the sugar-mill. The harvest continued and the tempo of work was increased. Nothing more effectively reinforced the status quo or distracted the slaves more convincingly. Besides, the making of money had to go on. No domestic convulsion could interrupt that sacred ritual for long.

'I have asked Charles to be with us today,' Isabella informed her daughter at ten o'clock. 'Otherwise we are quite alone here, two helpless females, and after recent events I don't think we can trust anybody.'

Sophie shrugged. Helpless. Well, it was true.

'If we refused to breed,' she burst out, on a sudden thought, 'they'd soon take notice of what we want. We wouldn't be so helpless then.'

'What on earth are you talking about?' Isabella's teaspoon paused in mid-air, a few crystals of sugar scattering on to the table.

'Never mind.' Sophie got up. She recalled her father's threat to send her home to the chilly custody of Grandmamma Wetherby. She must be quiet. 'Nothing. Nothing, at all.'

'I tell you now, I will not have any discourteous behaviour to Charles,' said her mother. 'If you cannot be civil to him, you will please keep to your room.'

Sophie withdrew.

She could not read, write or, it seemed, even think. A complete fatigue possessed her. She lay on her bed, too tired to sleep, and stared first at the ceiling, then at the walls, for hours. Eventually her body reminded her that it had needs: despite the depth of her melancholy she felt hungry. She had heard the voices of her mother and Charles Craig murmuring out on the verandah for the past two hours, but now they had fallen silent. No doubt Mamma was dozing and perhaps Craig had gone for a walk. She might venture out and pick up a crumb or two – or ask Serafina for some fruit. She needed the refreshment of a change of room, at least.

Charles Craig was sitting on the verandah, alone. He looked surprised to see her and scrambled to his feet. It was the first time they had confronted one another alone and at leisure since she had seen him enjoying his mistress up at Belmont. Sophie remembered the distress and agitation it had caused her. It seemed a long time ago and fate had flayed and stung her so much since that the business with Craig now seemed faded, insignificant.

'Excuse me, Miss Wetherby,' he said, with a bow. 'Your mother is resting in her room. I will go and look around the yards.' And immediately he was half-way down the steps.

'Wait! Please don't go!' Sophie spoke on a strange impulse, of disappointment almost.

He paused, looking back up at her. 'I don't wish to intrude on your peace,' he insisted. 'And I really ought to walk around the yards and the works whilst your father and brother are away.'

'No! Please. Not yet. Come back.'

He looked surprised, indecisive, but he obeyed. They sat down, the cane chairs creaking in unison. Sophie had wanted to talk, but now could not find the words to begin.

'I thought you might prefer –' he began uneasily.

'Not at all . . .' She looked at her hands, shy of his eyes. 'I am too much alone these days. I'm bad company, I suppose.'

He opened his mouth, but hesitated. He had been on the brink of a gallantry: that he could not ever suppose her bad company, but he swallowed such foolishness, knowing that was not the way.

'You have had a lot to bear,' he said quietly, instead. She looked up with a soft hint of gratitude and nodded. They both turned away towards the garden. Someone was sweeping the path round the corner, out of sight. It sounded like slow breathing.

'What were you looking at? Before I came out?' asked Sophie, squinting into the glare of the sun.

'That humming-bird.' He nodded towards a heliconia bush. A tiny blue creature hung in the air beside it. 'I was thinking how it

manages to sustain itself on air. It just hangs there, on nothing.'
Sophie considered the bird. The delicacy of its long beak charmed
her. 'There will always be delight in birds,' he concluded.

'I suppose so.' The humming-bird sipped fastidiously at its
nectar. Somehow it made Sophie think of Alexander Ashton
guzzling his dasheen the night before the militia went out to hunt
the Maroons. 'Birds certainly have better manners than humans. I
wish I were a bird.'

'You –' He caught himself preparing another compliment. It was
not because she was Sophie Wetherby, about whom he had become
so twisted and tormented. He knew he would talk in this way
whoever she was, so long as she was a woman. His own deepest
habits began to irritate him. Deliberately he chose another path.
'You – are right. I would like to be one of those Magnificent Frigate
Birds that wheel about against the sun.' The ghost of a smile passed
across her face.

'You are ambitious,' she said. 'The brownest little sparrow would
answer my purpose.'

'You would like to be back in England, then?'

Sophie did not hesitate; the threat of a return there was more
horribly fresh than Craig could know. 'Oh no. I love Sabato. I hate
the cold. I hate that miserable greyness. The long winters when
everything seems dead. I would rather be a little bird in the forest
here.'

They both felt that this particular subject was exhausted and a
silence developed. Sophie did not find it uncomfortable, however.
She felt curiously free of embarrassment now. Perhaps she could be
more at ease with Craig, because all that courtship business was
over.

'What will they do with Julius?' she asked suddenly.

'He'll be put out to work with the field-gangs.'

'I suppose it could have been worse. Mamma told me that you
urged my father to spare him.'

'It seemed a waste.' He sighed, still looking out into the garden.
'George was all for hanging. But Julius is a talented fellow.' He
stroked his hair, as if comforting himself. 'Even flogging – in
another country, or more accurately, in another skin, he would
make his way in the world.'

'Do you mean you think his cause was just?'

There was a pause.

'I don't know. All I can say is, I think in his situation I would have done the same. And I can think of plenty of planters, out here, who deserve a flogging themselves – deserve it more than he does.'

Sophie was roused by his words. He had never spoken like this before. 'Who, for example?' she asked eagerly.

He turned his eyes on her suddenly, very sad and full. 'Myself, for a start.' She was silent. She could not imagine what was coming. 'Certainly. I deserve a flogging.'

'Why?'

His silence had dragged the question from her.

'I threw away – a chance I had – of great happiness, by my own beastly conduct,' he said quietly, looking away again. 'Your mother gave me to understand ... why you felt you had to end our engagement. It confirmed my intuitions. I shall regret it every day of my life.' Sophie no longer felt comfortable. He sensed it, and with an agile effort sprang to reassure her. 'But I will not speak of that again. I just wanted you to know that I regretted it more than anything, and that it has made me think – differently, and behave differently. I assure you –' he discovered, as he spoke, what he was feeling '– I mean to lead a very different life from now on. There is no going back to those foul old ways.'

She said nothing, wishing he would finish.

'Just one thing – how did you come to know of it? The girls told you, I suppose? The girls at Mount Grace?'

Sophie nodded. She could hardly tell him she had spied on him, out in the dark with Julius. The memory of his lewdness, that night, still had the power to disturb her. But now she had discovered her own sexual instinct, it disturbed her in many different ways at once.

'Well, it's all past, and I must endure the consequences,' he sighed. They shared a silence which seemed to draw a line under the matter.

'You must be quite confined indoors from now on, I suppose – your days of rambling about in the forest with Julius are over.'

'They are.' Sophie managed not to falter. 'Papa is very concerned for my safety.'

'Of course. Well, I was about to propose – would you care for a walk now? Nothing strenuous – just to and fro under the trees?'

'I would like that, indeed.' Sophie stood up, glad to be offered activity.

He rose and accompanied her down the steps. He did not offer her his arm. They strolled freely, but together. Sophie looked up at the nest of Golden Orupendulas hanging from the silk cotton trees.

'Julius is a great fellow when it comes to birds,' remarked Craig quietly. 'He knows, I confess, more than any of us could guess at. I suppose that is why you found him such a rewarding guide?' His look was sharp. There was anxiety in his eye; jealousy too, perhaps. She was determined to repudiate his curiosity and protect her memories.

'Oh yes,' she agreed lightly. 'And then, you know, he is my half-brother, of course.'

Craig bowed and blushed. He was not expecting this. The whole interview was yielding much that was surprising. And the most amazing thing of all was that she was so easily tolerating his company – in a fragile, bruised way to be sure, but she could not conceal it. He had expected, if he saw her at all, to be offered indifference or hostility, but had received more than civility. She had been open with him. It was pleasant. But he was determined not to let it unsettle him.

33

Quiet Days

George returned from Demoiselle at nightfall and sprawled on the verandah, dusty and sweaty. His mother and sister ran out to hear his news; his father was still away in Douglastown and would stay there a day or two more. Sophie was in the greatest agitation, expecting to learn of the death of Mimba and doubting whether she would be able to remain silent. Charles Craig offered her his chair and then drew back out of her sight. The dogs could be heard in the distance, growling and fretting as they settled beneath their tree. Serafina brought George a glass of claret and he watched her disappear back to the kitchen before beginning his story.

'It promised to be excellent sport at first,' he drawled, yawning and settling himself deeper in his chair. 'Those dogs are keen, you know, by Jove! I've never seen anything like it. They soon picked up a scent. We chased up through the dry scrub, right to the top and along the ridge, a good clear scent all the way but no sight of the prey. There's a sheer cliff up there, on the far side of the island – have you seen it, Craig? It's a stunning sight.'

Craig nodded. Sophie was in agony at this digression, desperate to know the outcome, but a suggestion of frustration in her brother's voice gave her a thread of hope.

'A stunning view,' Craig affirmed. 'About three hundred feet, I should say, the cliffs plunge down, and the frigate birds wheel about in the gulf there, and you can look down on them and watch them steal the tropic birds' catch.' He addressed himself to Sophie, but she was oblivious.

'But what happened, George?' she burst out.

'Well, damn me, but the trail went cold. All I can think is that they fell off the cliff, or perished somehow, but we found no trace of them, and no bodies either – which the dogs would have found directly, you know.' He sipped his wine meditatively. 'We found a couple of their boats, however, and we burnt them on the beach and grilled a few kingfish, to console ourselves for such a wretched day's sport. So if the damned blacks were concealed somewhere about the island they can't get off now, and since there's no water there they won't last long. I think we can assure father he's heard the last of that confounded woman.'

Then came the quiet days. Sophie sat still, trying to rest her bruised soul. She had become a shuttered house. Before, all her windows and doors had been wide open for the winds to blow through. Now, nobody on the outside could tell what was happening within. Most of the time a deep lethargy possessed her. She sat and sewed, or read, or stared. Tired by her low spirits, she slept a lot. But all this was part of a recovery, of the body at least. Youth and health restored her appetite, though she ate without relish.

They were not quiet days for the plantation, however. Frederick Wetherby returned from Douglastown with two new overseers, Jardine and Makepeace.

'Makepeace is aptly named, I observe, my dear,' Frederick informed his wife with satisfaction at the conclusion of the first week. 'The slaves only have to hear his step and they are all quite silent and craven. He is an even more terrifying presence than Kendrick I think.'

'I can quite believe it!' cried Isabella, 'for I assure you, Fred, I am nervous of the fellow myself. He looks like an old bulldog Mr Terence used to have over at Hempshott Bridge – do you remember?'

'What? – Old Snapper?' cried George. 'I remember him. Johnny Walsh dared me once to tie a rat-trap to his tail, but I could not get near. Damme! He was a vicious old beast. He foamed at the mouth at me, and I'll swear the foam was mad yellow.'

Sophie had watched Makepeace stalking about the yard. He was a thickset fellow, with great bags under his eyes and strange ears very close to his head. He had a way of hissing at the slaves and twitching his whip about as he paced up and down. His heavy tread, and the veins that stood out on the backs of his huge hands, suggested a weight of vindictiveness, a pressure to punish, which was an adornment in a man of his trade.

'I confess I'm delighted with him,' affirmed Frederick. 'And as Jardine is such a crack shot, if we ever get any trouble again I'm convinced we'll soon put it down.'

Sophie was embroidering a tablecloth. Her needle slipped and pricked her thumb, and the eager young blood rushed out and had stained her work almost before she was aware. Exclaiming in quiet annoyance, she sucked her thumb. Craig noticed this mishap and listened to the sound of her lips without any discomfort. He was pleased with himself. These were quiet days for him, too.

The harvest continued however, noisily and busily. Out in the fields, cutlasses and cane-bills flashed all day as the men cut the cane. They had been favoured with very dry weather, so the roads and tracks were good: donkeys and mules, harnessed and hampered with crooks for carrying the canes, were driven easily to and fro, and even the waggons and carts, drawn by heavy oxen, made good progress.

Confined as she was to the house, except when Charles Craig accompanied her on a walk about the grounds, Sophie followed the progress of the harvest mainly by listening to its sounds. At dawn the slaves were summoned to work by the blowing of conch-shells: a melancholy note which floated across the treetops with the first faint gleams of sunlight. Then the full orchestra gradually awoke: the rumbling of the mill-wheels, the cries and yells of slaves driving animals, the neighing of mules and braying of donkeys, the bellowing of cattle, the cracking of whips; Makepeace's deep gutteral bark and the higher, more searing oaths of Jardine and Kendrick. Above all, the sounds of the cane as it passed between the rollers went on and on, a crushing and splintering at the heart of things.

Sometimes a dull curiosity brought Sophie to the window at the south-western corner of the house, and through the slats of the jalousie she could glimpse carts arriving from the fields, loaded high with cane, looking like a huge untidy bird's nest on wheels, *Julius might have cut that cane*, she could not help thinking. *Julius could have touched that cart.* She had not seen him since his flogging. Though this was a torment, it made everyday life possible for her. Knowing Julius was far away and would not appear, she could compose her spirits, although she could never raise them. Her consciousness lay like a mist in a hollow, secret and opaque.

Her mother, of course, noticed all this and decided to be encouraged rather than perturbed by it. Anything was better than hysterics. This was not sulking. This was the quietness of healing, she was sure. George did not tease his sister so much as he used to; he was himself in subdued mood. The confinement and remorseless discipline of plantation life was beginning to irk him. He asked his father if he might make a trip to Barbados to examine the latest in weaponry, especially some German guns, but Fredereick forbade it.

'We need you here at present,' he objected. 'I don't know how you can suggest such a trip, having seen your sister and mother in the hands of rebellious slaves so recently. Until the harvest is over, and until we are convinced there are no more Maroons about, and that contagion of rebellion is quite cleared out of Sabato, you stay here, my boy.'

George submitted, and devoted his energies instead to a massive sulk, and eventually, when even the charms of sulking began to pall, to the project of clearing and repairing an overgrown road to Good Hope, about four miles distant, where the old ladies kept their school.

He found himself working quite hard at this task, partly because there was nothing else to do. Craig was not much fun these days, either. No bawdy evenings up at Belmont; nothing but reading and writing. George was denied his orgies and forced to take his sexual pleasure furtively at night in shadowy places behind the yards and offices, or in a glade he had found just above the river, half-way down the hill to the slaves' huts. It was a convenient place to meet the girls: half-way between their low huts and his lofty mansion. One did not wish to be too near the mansion, of course, when putting it about; one did not foul one's own nest.

Occasionally George dreamed he was living in London, intoxicated by the opportunity, the freedom, the anonymity of the great city, where there would be money to be made, deals to be struck and a sumptuous choice of coffee-houses and whorehouses for him to enjoy in effortless incognito. Here on Sabato he was watched everywhere he went, and it was always Massa George this and Massa George that.

Enjoying the role of experienced traveller, he had boasted to friends at home about the opportunities offered by Sabato, but now the weeks were beginning to stretch into months here, his restlessness returned and he planned, when his time came, to be an absentee planter, as his grandfather had been. George had an old schoolfriend, Robert Molyneux, with an estate near Tewkesbury in Gloucestershire, and he had often visited him, for the fishing there was extraordinarily good. Drenched with tropical heat, and watching his slave gang carting and tamping down basketfulls of stone, George recalled the soothing coolness of Tewkesbury's river, and also something Robert had said.

'What? Risk your neck and your health in going off to see to your plantations yourself, George? Madness, old boy! – Take our MP here, Sir William Codrington, he's got great estates in Antigua and Barbuda you know, and he's never been to the West Indies in his life. That's the way to do it. Get a fellow out there to collect the revenues for you and keep the blacks in order, and stay here fishing for salmon with me.'

'Bob, you are a lazy scoundrel!' George had retorted. 'If it were left to you, Britain would have no colonies at all. You're a disgrace to the race of Raleigh and old what's his name – that sailed around the world.'

'Francis Drake,' Bob had replied complacently. 'True, I have no desire to travel. To me, Bath lies at the remotest ends of the earth. But then, I am an angler. I like to lie in wait and let things come to me.' A couple of years later, George remembered hearing that Bob's MP, Sir William Codrington, had died, still without ever visiting his estates in the West Indies, and it gave him renewed food for thought now.

'Will Charles come down to dine with us tomorrow, George?' enquired his mother one sleepy morning. 'Or are you going up to Belmont one of these days? He promised me one of his first mangoes, he has the Julie Mango up there you know. I wondered if the first ones would be ripe about now. Sophie might fancy one.'

George tossed his newspaper aside. It was another irritation to have to read newspapers that were three months old. 'Oh, let's have him down here.' He yawned. 'I get so fagged out walking up his damned path, and he's really no fun any more – won't even drink, dammit.'

Isabella noticed that Sophie heard that remark with some interest. 'Charles is quite a reformed character, it seems,' she murmured approvingly, addressing her daughter. Sophie merely shrugged. Isabella said no more. But she had noticed that the only times when Sophie seemed to rouse herself, these days, was when Craig visited. Isabella was surprised, but held herself in suspense. She would not permit herself any conjecture. For once she would be innocent and wait, and watch, and keep her counsel.

Charles Craig did dine with them the following day, but brought no mangoes. They were not ripe yet.

'Ah well!' laughed Isabella. 'I was always such an impatient creature. I must learn from this. There is no rushing nature. Things will unfold in their own time.'

'But once something is ripe, it must be seized without delay,' said her husband. 'We must grind and boil the cane soon after it is cut, or much of the juice will be lost. And things go off so damned quick in this climate: what's ripe at noon will be rotten by dusk.'

'Fie, Fred, you talk of nothing but sugar!' cried his wife. 'You are an old bore.'

'The crop is still going along well, I trust?' enquired Craig.

'Ay, but it's a business. You are wiser to grow your spices, Craig, I think – the harvests are all at different times, and not so terribly demanding of labour and beasts. I lost one of my best oxen yesterday, carting two hogsheads down to the shore – a deep pothole that the driver didn't notice, a slip, a twist – a moment's carelessness and a fine beast lost. Broke its leg.'

'So will we have beef for dinner tomorrow, Papa?' enquired Sophie unexpectedly. She felt sorry for the ox, but she had always been fond of roast beef.

'No, my dear. A beast like the ox, that has worked, will be tough as hide. We let the slaves cut it up.'

'They call it tango,' added George, 'and by God, don't they scrap over it! It's a feast-day for them when we lose an ox.'

'It's a trouble, though,' sighed his father. 'We need five pair of oxen to draw two hogsheads, and the roads being so bad, and the heat so great, we are often losing them.'

'Not often enough for the blacks though,' smiled George. 'They'd like it to be tango every day.'

'It's true,' observed Craig, 'that the exertions required for the harvest of sugar are tremendous. I'm glad my own crops up at Belmont do not require so much suffering on the part of men and beasts.'

Sophie looked up. 'What are your crops?' she asked. 'Forgive me, I have forgotten – I know you showed us a coffee plantation . . .'

'Coffee, ginger, limes . . . I have a grove of mangoes, not ripening fast enough for your mother, I'm afraid, and then, let's see, tamarind, cinnamon, cloves . . . quite a variety.'

'I like the idea of your spices, Mr Craig,' said Sophie. 'For their beauty, and that they can be harvested with less cruelty than sugar.'

'Sugar is a beautiful sight too, you know,' said her father, 'when the canes are ripe for cutting. You must take your sister to see the fields, George, one morning early or after dinner when the worst heat is gone off. The flower is a lilac colour, Sophie, and hangs down round the silken floss at the top – you must have seen it – and this flower is so fine that once it's dry you can't preserve it: it simply crumbles away into nothing. Dust.'

'None of your pressed flowers, then, Sophie. Have you pressed any since you came?' asked her mother. 'It might be a sweet diversion.'

'It was Grandmamma who loved to press flowers, Mamma,' replied Sophie. 'I only ever did it for her.'

'Do you not like the practice, Miss Wetherby?' enquired Craig.

'I'd rather see them growing in the meadow. Or in the forest here. I like to smell them and touch them while they are alive.' At these words, a sad glitter crept into the corner of Sophie's eyes. Her mother was disappointed. Until this moment, her daughter had been more animated than for some time.

'Well, that was a fine guinea-fowl, Mother, and the kingfish, by heaven! The best I have tasted!' George leaned back expansively in his chair, patting his belly in appreciation of his dinner. Sophie noticed he was getting fat and she supposed she must be too, for lack of exercise. Suddenly there was a crack, and George seemed to jerk backwards, and tumbled over: the spine of his chair had split.

'George!' cried his mother. 'Have a care, don't be so rough –' He got up, dishevelled and a little shocked, and examined the chair-back.

'Good God,' he mused, 'quite shattered by my manly strength.'

'By your blubber, you mean,' scolded his mother. 'You are going to seed, my lad; you should get about more. Take him shooting, Charles, I beg, I don't like to see my son turning into a sucking-pig.'

'Never mind.' George gave up his attempt to reconcile the splintered pieces of wood. 'We'll have to get Julius up to fix it.' A sudden icy hole appeared in the conversation.

'Not Julius, dearest,' faltered Isabella. 'He is in the fields now, you know.'

'And damned inconvenient it is to have him there!' growled her husband, picking his teeth and scowling. 'Not a day passes but I feel the need for a good carpenter about the estate.'

'But you must not allow him back up here,' said his wife hastily, with a secret glance at her daughter. 'After his horrid crime, and nearly frightening me to death, and daring –'

'No, no, of course he can't go back to his old work, or retrieve any of his privileges,' agreed her husband. 'I've decided to get rid of him. He'd fetch a good price. A skilled man – and still very young.'

'None of the fellows hereabouts will want him. What! A notorious rebel?' cried George.

'I might get a good price for him farther off, however. He'd be safe enough on Barbados, for example. No mountains or forests there; they're not troubled with Maroons at all.'

'Would nobody like a little more pudding?' enquired Isabella after an awkward pause. Sophie's eyes were fixed impassively on the table.

'Yes,' her father concluded. 'I shall sell him. I am quite resolved upon it. As soon as the harvest is done – before, if the opportunity arises.'

Sophie's fingers found a lace panel in the tablecloth. Hands had made this lace, she thought. She must think about those hands and not her father's words. She could not help hearing them, but she must not let herself feel them. They must be stored in some remote archive, locked up there, to be examined much later; hours, days, months, years later, when their significance had faded.

So Sophie's third finger traced the whorls of intricate lace. This linen had come from England; had been her grandmamma's. It was a pattern of fernleaves. Perhaps it had been made in Nottingham. Old women with dry, nimble fingers, making webs like skilful spiders. As they worked, they might have exchanged jokes or gossip, rumours of long-lost loves and wars. They were all gone into their graves, now, the lace-makers, but these delicate webs they had spun remained; crisp and clean, giving pleasure.

But why were they crisp and clean? The efforts of Ruth and Mary in the laundry, with soap and starch and flat irons, were also invisibly present here. And beneath the cloth, through the lace, Sophie noticed the gleam of the polished mahogany. Somebody had made the table. Her heart increased its pace a little, but she did not allow herself to picture the carpenter.

Instead she followed the whorl of the grain, clearly visible through the lace inset, and stood suddenly under a great tree, its leaves flickering in the light, its branches full of birds' nests. What a cutting, hauling, fiddling, contriving animal man was! How many invisible hands had worked so that she could sit here and dine, grandly, like a paper cut-out princess. Her kind was cruel and ingenious; well, so were many other species. But she could think of no other animal that enslaved itself.

'I'll get another carpenter in to repair the chair and do a week or two's work, here,' her father was saying.

'I know of a fellow down in Douglastown who's a pretty fair carpenter,' Craig said. 'Amos, he's called. A free black. I'll get him up here for you if you like.'

'A free black?' Sophie was jolted from her reverie. 'How is that?'

'Slaves who have got their freedom,' explained Craig.

Sophie was instantly all attention. 'How do they do that?'

'They buy it, usually. Sometimes the owners grant them freedom as a reward, or in their will.'

'There's a place in Barbados', added George, 'called Sweet Bottom. It used to be Golden Ridge Plantation but when Francis Butcher, the owner, died – when was that, now, Father?'

'Some fifteen years ago, I believe. No! It must be more.'

'Well, when old Butcher died, he left instructions for his executors to pay for his slaves' manumission –'

'That's the legal method by which they are freed,' explained Craig.

'There were some twenty acres, as I recall.' Frederick Wetherby took up the tale. 'And they were divided up into five four-acre lots, for each of five freed slaves.'

'Yes,' affirmed George. 'It's a free village now. Sweet Bottom. That was Butcher's bequest.'

'Oh, how good of him!' exclaimed Sophie. 'What a fine thing, to leave behind a small corner of the world better than you found it, and your fellow-creatures happier!'

'Well, they were his children, as well as his slaves,' added George slyly.

A moment of embarrassment crystallised around the table. Sophie felt her face burn; she returned to her scrutiny of the lace.

'That's enough, George,' murmured his mother.

'Well,' Frederick Wetherby plunged on towards safer ground, 'if you can get Amos up here for me, Craig, I'll be very much obliged.'

'Mr Amos is his proper title, remember, Father,' grinned George. 'Must respect the fellow's dignity.'

After the occasionally dangerous passage of this dinner, having navigated across certain submerged reefs, Sophie found herself back in the harbour of her room with much to think of.

34

Comforting

Next day Sophie took her book out on to the verandah and sat and stared unseeing at the lines of print. Occasionally, following some obscure instinct, she turned a page, as the body in prolonged reverie refreshes itself with a sigh. But not a word entered her brain. Her mother arrived quietly behind her, having finished a letter to Aunt Sarah reassuring her that life at Mount Grace was once again peaceful and uneventful. Seeing Sophie's head bent over her book, Isabella felt a pang of tenderness. Thick, wild curls – so like her own. She stroked her daughter's hair. Sophie looked up. Her mother detected a faint twist of thought in the girl's expression.

'All well, my darling?' she sought to smooth away rather than confront anything uncomfortable.

'I've been thinking, Mamma.' Sophie closed her book with a snap.

Her mother's gentle face invited confidences, though the smile stiffened slightly at Sophie's words. 'Not sad thoughts, I hope?' said Isabella faintly.

'No, no – at least, not – I don't wish to upset you, Mamma, but I would like your advice.'

Isabella sat down carefully, as if surrounded by broken glass. 'Well?'

'What they were talking about last night – about how slaves can be freed.'

Her mother pressed her hand to her brow and sighed. 'I think, dearest, you had better leave such things to Papa. Do not bother yourself with estate matters. You will be happier, I'm sure.'

'I would happier if Julius were gone.'

Her mother flinched and looked away, as if struck. Then the

words seemed to grow into her understanding and present a way out of difficulty. 'You would rather not see him any more?'

'Not if I can't – talk to him, or even write, not share his thoughts at all. Just to see him pass in the yard, I – dread it.' Tears gathered in her eyes.

Her mother saw them, and took her daughter's hand. 'I suffer too, dearest, believe me. I can hardly turn my head any way but my heart is stabbed by the sight of one of his bastards.' Sophie wished her mother would not talk so, as if she were not addressing her daughter but another adult, a confidante. Her mother's fiery words seemed to scald Sophie's face. No tears would come, now, to soothe her; they had sunk back into her head as if afraid.

'Well if Flora and Julius offend you, send them away!' she cried. 'Free them. They'll go. Out of our sight. Why should you have to see them? I hate Papa for it.'

'Don't say that!' cried her mother, seizing Sophie's hand. 'Don't! I may say it myself, but I don't mean it. I love him, that's why I was patient at home in England for years, and then why at last, ignoring everybody's advice, I came here. And that's why it is such agony to think of him with somebody else. Even a slave.'

'If Julius and Flora were gone, would you feel better, Mamma?'

'And you, my dear.' Isabella grew reflective again, her own passion spent for the moment. 'Would you?'

Sophie closed her eyes and imagined her life going on here, year after year, decade after decade, if she were spared; saw herself go grey, the skin thicken and wrinkle, and always there would be Julius, a hundred yards away, his back turned, forbidden to speak. Her body would leap at the sight of him for years, she knew, until it began to grow cold and slow with age. And perhaps even then –

'Send him away,' she said quietly.

There was a pause.

'And supposing he were gone,' her mother's voice sounded careful. It tiptoed towards something it feared, but could not resist. 'You must believe me, Sophie: your heart would heal, I'm sure of it, and you might one day – learn to love somebody else.'

'No.'

'You feel that now, of course – you are a dear, passionate thing, but in time, perhaps . . .'

277

'I'd rather die.'

'Fie! Don't say such things, Sophie! You talk like a man sometimes – you were always such a tomboy. You are too fierce and bold.'

'I only say what I feel.'

'Young women's words should not be half so violent,' her mother chided gently.

'You spoke violently yourself just now.'

'Well, well . . . you are right. I feel the better for it. Sometimes, I confess, I have had to contain such terrible thoughts, it seemed as if they would poison my brain. Suffocate me.'

'Poor Mamma.' Sophie was not so overwhelmed at her own distress as to forget her mother's.

'Just remember, my dear, that this is not the end of your life. Only the beginning. Many girls have been disappointed in their first love. Others will come, when the heart has healed.' Sophie rejected this idea with an impatient frown. 'You may not believe me now, but just keep one thing in your mind: Nature can restore a broken heart.'

'Has it restored yours?'

There was a sickening pause. Isabella froze for a moment, like a cat that sees danger and decides to escape another way. She resolved to take refuge in jest.

'Oh, many times, my dear. Why, my poor old heart is as patched and mended as one of the Greek statues in Aunt Sarah's book. I had just such a little passion, when I was your age. I was at school, and how I longed to elope with my dancing-master, though he was an odd little scrap of a fellow with a face like a fox. My heart used to thrash about, on Thursday afternoons, to think that I might touch his hand! I very quickly forgot him, however, once I was out in the world.'

Sophie looked at her mother in dumb agony. This banter was unendurable. A passion for a dancing-master! She could never tell her that she had felt Julius moving inside her, under her heart. At last a tear burst from her eye. She felt it slide down and slip between her lips, saltily, as his tongue had done.

'Come.' Her mother wiped her face. 'No tears now, my darling. We have both confided in each other, we share our secrets. I feel my heart lighter already, don't you?'

Sophie sighed and nodded. She was beyond help, but glad to have helped her mother. Taking her hand, she stroked the fingers.

'This trouble here, about Papa . . . was why you started to bite your nails, I suppose,' she said. 'Wasn't it, Mamma?'

'Yes, I guess so. I was fretting, fretting all the time, you see. What a mess I have made of my poor hands! I shall stop it now, though. You have eased my heart and I know that if I feel fretful again, my dear girl will comfort me.'

Sophie put her arm around her mother and kissed her neck. The smell of violets still hung there, just as it had when she was a child. She rested her head on her mother's shoulder for a moment. It was the first time she had shared caresses since the night with Julius on the beach. She remembered what he had felt like, but curiously could not quite recall the exact detail of his face, though thinking of him occupied her every waking hour.

'Just one thing more,' said Isabella. 'I do want you to know, dearest, that I love Papa. He has given himself to another woman, but I can forgive that. It is not so significant in men. Their passions are both wilder and more transient than ours. Remember this, if a man ever causes you distress by his amours. They are very likely to be meaningless, a passing pleasure. Do not break your heart over it.'

Sophie stared in perplexity at her mother. A few moments before she had presented a convincing picture of a broken heart herself; now she rose, with an almost theatrical dignity, and straightened her dress, looking down on her daughter with a formal deliberation, as if to establish distance and authority again. Sophie was getting used to these abrupt transitions, but there was an odd quality to her mother's composure: she seemed to put it on boldly as if it were some extra garment she was now obliged to wear. It was odd that here, where the heat of the West Indies forced them into the lightest of dresses, so much more had to be hidden. Their bodies were half-naked, but their thoughts locked away.

'Papa has many fine qualities, as you know. He is a good husband. I would wish for no other.'

Sophie did not speak. Her mother placed her hand on Sophie's head, as if to bless. This scene, which had so relieved her heart, had begun with this gesture and would end with it.

'Dear Sophie! We must help each other always.'

'Help me now, then, Mamma!'

Isabella shuddered. So the scene was not over after all. She felt almost irritated by Sophie's persistence.

'What is it?'

'Ask Papa if he will free Julius and Flora.'

Her mother backed away, already picking at her fingers' ends again. 'You cannot ask it, my dear. I cannot do it. You must understand – I have spoken on this matter with Papa so many times, and our conversations have been so painful they have quite torn my heart to shreds. I cannot. The subject is too tender. Leave him to deal with it. You heard how he spoke last night. I am sure he means to send Julius away.'

'But what if he doesn't?' Sophie cried in frustration. 'I can't bear it going on like this, for weeks, or even years.'

'Then you must ask him yourself.' The verdict was crisp. A few shreds of pity still gleamed in her mother's face, but she had removed herself irrevocably from the arena. Sophie would have to step out into the glare of her father's attention and face alone whatever fury she might provoke.

'I will order us some tea,' murmured Isabella, smoothing her cheeks and straightening her ribbons before gliding away towards the kitchen. Sophie watched her go, admiring the light step, the billow of air in her muslin skirts. Her mother seemed to have recovered some of her youthful grace and elasticity: she almost floated away, like an Italian angel in a painting. Sophie herself felt huge and heavy, like an ancient statue carved out of stone, that had by some violent force been toppled over and now, pinned to the ground and overgrown by briars, could only stare helplessly at a world turned upside down.

35

Monkey

Despite her mother's discouragement, the small seed of hope in Sophie's breast refused to die. She returned to it constantly in her private hours. Slaves could become free. Why, then, Julius could. But how? She had learned, since coming to Sabato, how little women could do. She had no money of her own. But she had heard her father talk about the irritation of Julius's presence. Perhaps he would be sympathetic to the idea of freeing him, instead of selling him.

As her mother had refused to help, she must speak to Papa directly herself. For days she watched him come and go, observing his moods, trying to decide at what hour of the day he appeared most tractable. After supper seemed best, when a glass of port or madeira comforted his repose.

But at that time her mother was always there, and Sophie knew that to broach the subject in her mother's presence would be foolish. Much as she disliked Isabella's headaches, Sophie began to be irritated that none had occurred recently. Just a small headache was all she required – enough to send her mother to bed early. But then there was George, always lounging about and being satirical. Perhaps after supper was not such a good time after all.

Anxiety about speaking to her father in this way, compounded with an increasingly urgent desire to do so, began to make her feel ill. She was already lethargic; now a gnawing fretfulness ate into her stomach. She must speak. The tormenting business of choosing the right moment came to dominate her days – so much so that the purpose of her interview with him almost receded from the forefront of her mind, eclipsed by the practical difficulty of seeing him alone.

I will do it tomorrow, she said every night. Tomorrow. But when she had the courage, Papa was not there. If fate offered her a quiet moment with him, George would stroll in. And so it went on. Perhaps I shall never speak, she thought in despair one morning. The heat was increasing, it seemed – it was now early May – and the jug in her room was empty. She had poured it over her head an hour ago, to refresh her boiling brain.

Now she was thirsty – and restless. Instead of calling Flora or Serafina to bring more water or some juice, she decided to go out to the coral dripstone that stood behind the house, by the laundry, and sip some of the purified water from it. She put on her shoes and walked through the house. Nobody was about. Her mother was busy with a letter in her room; George was out supervising the construction of his road; her father was out, as usual. Sophie slipped down the back steps and walked along the path towards the dripstone.

Suddenly Julius came around the corner and was before her, a mere yard away. He was carrying one end of a washtub, another slave supporting the other end. Sophie's whole body flashed at the sight of him. Their eyes seized upon each other, he looked about to speak; Sophie began to shake, and sink, almost – and then there was the sharp crack of a whip.

'Git along there, you bugger, don't get in Missie's way, you clumsy devil, you dog, you!' Makepeace had been lurking in the deep shade of the lignum vitae tree and now came forth, flourishing his dreadful whip. Sophie wished she could hit him, but managed, with a heroic effort, to compose herself.

'They are not in my way at all, I assure you, Mr Makepeace. Please tell me, where is Father? I must speak with him.'

'He's over in the boilin'-house, Miss,' growled Makepeace, with a jerk of the head.

'Thank you.' Sophie departed without a backward look. Quickly she walked across to the mill area. The shock of seeing Julius had jolted her into action. It was unbearable to her to see him treated as a slave. She would rather not see him at all.

The terrible heat, and the overpowering sweet smell of the boiling-house, forced her to hesitate for a moment as she went in, but she soon spied her father's broad back at the furthest end. He was talking to one of the overseers. She went forward and touched his shoulder.

'Why, Sophie, my dear! What is it?'

'May I have a private word with you, Papa?'

'What, now? Is it urgent?'

Sophie hesitated. 'Only in that – it troubles my mind.'

Her father looked at her for a moment or two. She had been quiet, recently; so quiet, he had almost managed to forget about her existence, which was, in such busy and troubled times, what fathers required of their daughters. The hysterics were gone. Here was meekness, modesty, obedience. A sudden rush of remembered affection softened his heart. He took her hand and threaded it through his arm.

'Come,' he said. 'We will talk outside. This is a dreadful place for a young lady.' They walked out, across the yard, and under the silk cotton trees, where a rough seat had been set, made out of split timber, in rustic style.

'Well.' He handed her down. 'We will sit here for a moment. Now, how are you, my dear?' Looking closely at her for the first time for weeks, he noticed that her face looked pale and thin, though she was still comely in body. 'Are you well?'

'Oh yes, I thank you, Papa, perfectly.'

'Now, how can I help you?'

She hesitated. The dreadful moment had come. But it was not so very dreadful; they were sitting down, at least. Sophie was afraid the heat and anxiety might have made her faint. But she was comfortable; Papa was all attention and, it seemed, in a generous mood.

'Will I ever have any money of my own, Papa?'

This was not the question he had expected. 'Why do you ask, my dear?'

'Sometimes – well, there is a thing I would like to do, only I haven't any money.'

'What is it? A gown perhaps, that you've seen in the *Gazette*? Anything you fancy can be sent over from London, you know; your aunt will happily see to it.'

'No – not a gown, Papa. I am very easily contented on that score.'

'What then? – Ah, books! I should know you better, shouldn't I?

My Sophie is not a woman preoccupied with dress. Books not looks, eh?' He laughed in surprise at his own wit.

'Not books either, Papa – it isn't really something for me, at all, in a way.'

'Well, what the deuce is it, then?' cried her father, whacking his boot with a riding crop and beginning to feel impatient.

'We spoke – some time ago – of Mr Amos –'

'Ah, the carpenter fellow. He's coming tomorrow, as it happens. Craig has arranged it. He couldn't come at first, he was busy with some work in Douglastown, but he'll be with us tomorrow. Do you want him to make something for you whilst he's here, my dear?'

'No – it's not that. But when you were explaining to me how Mr Amos could come to be free, you talked about the village in Barbados, Mr Butcher's estate, which he left to his slaves, so they were freed when he died.'

Her father frowned slightly, sensing trouble. 'Well?'

'You said – or Mr Craig said, I can't remember – that slaves could be freed. They could buy their freedom.'

'Ah.' Her father watched her very carefully, now. His mood of expansive indulgence had shrunk and hardened. What was she about? He said nothing more; merely waited for her to complete her appeal. His silence unnerved her, but she floundered on.

'I just thought – if there was any money which one day might be mine – and if I could impose on your generosity so far as to ask for some of it now – I would like to buy Julius's freedom.'

Her father's eyes flared briefly, then narrowed. Still he said nothing. She gasped and writhed in his silence, but struggled on, suffocating.

'He is a man of – some talent, as you yourself said – wasted as a field slave – if he were free, he could go to England perhaps, be educated . . . make a life for himself.'

She faltered and finished her speech. No more could be said, however silent her father might continue. She had reached the end of her energy and felt a tremendous thirst. Of course, she had not drunk from the dripstone; she had been distracted by the sight of Julius. She sat still and wiped the sweat from her brow.

'It is out of the question,' said her father at length. 'A kind impulse of yours, but hearkee, Sophie, Julius betrayed the greatest trust I had placed in him – he ran away and returned to seize our house and challenge our authority. He could have been hanged for less. And am I now to reward him with freedom?'

Sophie was tempted to tell her father that the sight of his bastard son offended and wounded her mother, but the embarrassment of the subject forbade it. She was also keenly aware that any rebellious argument on her part would instantly revive the threat to send her home to Grandmamma. Once she had caught the tenor of her father's speech, she merely sat still and waited for him to finish.

'I could not do it; not in a thousand years, my dear. I'm sorry, but you must understand the way things are here. And now you must excuse me.' He got up and walked off to the boiling-house. He had not meant to leave so abruptly, but her appeal had carried them into areas fraught with embarrassment, and Frederick Wetherby was a man free to walk away from such things, thank God.

Sophie sat there for a moment feeling very dry and faint. A small girl passed nearby. Sophie called her over.

'Fetch me a drink from the dripstone, my dear.'

The child returned, bringing the dipper made of coconut shell and spilling most of it. More spilled on Sophie's dress as she drank, but she did not heed it. The child loitered.

'You may go, now.' Sophie got up wearily and walked back towards the house.

'Miss Sophie!' She looked up: it was Mary and Ruth, carrying the monkey.

'Here yuh monkey, Miss.'

They had tied a green ribbon round its neck. It had grown quite large, almost the size of a human baby.

'Where is your child, Ruth? Your little girl Sophie?'

Ruth's eyes filled with tears. For once she seemed unable to say much. 'She die, Miss.'

Sophie felt struck to the heart. 'Oh no! I'm so sorry! How . . . ?'

'She get sick and die. She get de flux.' Ruth wiped her eyes.

'I'm so very sorry . . .' Sophie laid her hand on Ruth's shoulder for a moment. Then she turned to Mary. 'What about your child?'

'He fine. He down wid Grandma 'cause I got to work. Here, take de monkey Miss. Him tame now. Him nat bite.' Warily Sophie accepted the creature. Mary gave her a small banana. 'Yuh give 'im dis fig nah. He love dat.'

Sophie peeled the banana and offered it. The creature grabbed it with enthusiasm and devoured it, then flung its hairy arms around her neck. She was alarmed, but amused. She laughed.

'Him love yuh, Miss. Him pleased 'cause he goin' to be white folks' monkey.'

'Ah – the monkey.' A voice sounded behind her; a shadow fell across her head. Charles Craig had come. Spent by her confrontation with her father, and perplexed by the embraces of the monkey, Sophie felt that his arrival brought some sense of rescue. He reached out and took the creature's hand. 'Good morning to you, Miss Wetherby, and good morning to your monkey. What is his name?'

'I don't know – I've only just acquired him. It's odd, but I had forgotten about his very existence.'

The monkey looked into their faces as they spoke, its eyes alert and curious.

'You've done well, girls,' said Craig to Mary and Ruth. 'Back to work, now.' He continued to play with the creature's hand. There was something disturbing about the similarity between the monkey's hand and his. It had fingers, joints, nails very similar, and its palm was bare. 'Strange . . .' he mused. 'Almost like a human hand.'

'I don't like it wearing this ribbon,' said Sophie. Now the girls had gone, she removed it.

'Where are you going to keep it? In the old birdcage?' Sophie had released the Tocoloros and the cage stood empty on the verandah. Julius would perhaps have dismantled it, if he had not been banished to the fields.

'Oh, dear. Not the cage. I hope not. I haven't thought about it. Couldn't I take it back to the forest and let it go?'

'It couldn't survive in the wild now,' said Craig. 'It's mother would have taught it how to look for food – now these girls have taught it that humans will bring food to it.'

'So,' sighed Sophie, 'it's neither one thing nor another.' Like Ruth's baby, she thought. Neither white nor black. Perhaps it's better that she died, poor creature.

And perhaps, Sophie pondered as they walked back to the house, the monkey was fidgeting in her arms because she was not enough of a monkey. But she did not feel herself to be a proper white woman either. She could not think like them, or feel like them. But there was nothing else she could be either. The monkey tugged at her bodice. It had been given the breast by Mary; Sophie now realised, with a flush of embarrassment, that it was looking for her nipple. Hastily she handed the creature to Craig, who placed it in the cage.

She looked away across the garden and saw a humming-bird hovering by a heliconia bush. That was it. She felt as if she were hanging in the air and only kept aloft by a desperate, an exhausted quivering.

36

Good Hope

Craig laid aside his book and walked to the window. The jalousie and hanging nets kept the worst of the night insects out. Tiny frogs had set up their chirruping concert. A breath of air reached his face; he savoured it for a few moments, then walked back to his desk, picked up the book and examined the title page again, as if unable quite to believe what he had been reading: *The Interesting Narrative of the Life of Olaudah Equiano*, London 1789.

It was an account, published but a few years previously, of an African slave, seized from his village at the age of twelve, transported in unspeakable filth across the ocean and sold on arrival in Barbados. 'On a signal given (the beat of a drum) the buyers rush at once into the yard where the slaves are confined, and make choice of that parcel they like best. The noise and the clamour with which this is attended and the eagerness visible in the countenances of the buyers serve not a little to increase the apprehensiveness of the terrified Africans . . . In this manner, without scruple, are relations and friends separated, most of them never to see each other again.'

When he had escorted Mrs Dodds and Miss Hambledon back to Good Hope after the engagement party, Charles had admired their library. Mrs Dodds, finding in him a receptive ear, had prevailed upon him, against all her expectations, to borrow the book. It had somehow intrigued him from the instant it came into his hands. For a start, it was striking that a slave might be able to write anything more than a crooked alphabet, let alone a book. And when he opened it, and gave his mind to it, a human character so intelligent and energetic had seized his attention, and a story so painful had begun to unfold before his eyes, that he could not help reading on and on, and feeling more and more disturbed.

Of course, the book had arrived in his hands at a propitious time. Sophie Wetherby's refusal of him, following so close upon her acceptance, had thrown him into despair and hatred. When he had deduced, from some hints of her mother's, that it was his behaviour with his mistresses which, coming somehow to Sophie's attention, had so fatally repelled her, his hatred had turned in on himself.

Cassie and Venus had been banished from his bed. Venus had fled gratefully; Cassie, feeling herself despised and her charms rejected, had sunk into a vicious patch of bad temper. Plates were banged down before him, doors slammed. But he steadfastly ignored it. He had departed on an inner journey and had withdrawn from his slaves as well as his neighbours into a contemplation of his life and habits.

The dog who has been beaten fears the stick, so Craig did not, these days, feel any sexual torment at the sight of Sophie Wetherby. He admired instead the delicate unfolding of her sensibility. Though he had not been indifferent, before, to her mind or her feelings, he had been blinded by the frenzy of his passion. But it had not stopped him pleasuring himself with his black girls. Sophie had been right to reject him. If his love had been worthy of her, he would have abandoned all his old lusts, no matter how comfortable, to sit in solitude at night and write poems to her.

He sat alone these nights, reading and even writing, though not poems. But it was all too late. He walked, now, to the looking-glass and stared into it. His face was in darkness, for candles burned in the room behind him. He looked almost black. For an instant he imagined himself a slave, waiting to be bought after a voyage whose dreadful details he now knew, thanks to Equiano's life story. He was waiting on a quay; white-faced men came, their faces flushed with eagerness, their light eyes glittering, their hands full of weapons, their pockets full of money. He shuddered.

Craig turned towards the candles and became white again. He went to the door and picked up a cane that leant against the wall. Then he opened the door and called to Cassie. There was a long pause, then he heard her slopping feet, her disgruntled cough and deep, aggravated sniff. She came in; bold, resentful but still obliged to obey. He handed her the cane.

'Whip me, Cassie,' he ordered and knelt down before her. She sighed, as if this was but one in a familiar catalogue of unreasonable requests and, without any appearance of enjoyment, set to.

'Something strange happened yesterday, my dear,' remarked Frederick Wetherby, getting undressed. 'I forgot to mention it to you last night; we were so preoccupied with that damned rats' nest under the house.'

'What happened?' Isabella, taking her hair down, looked at her husband in the glass. His face was twisted: turned back to front. She did not like his reflection. It was an imposter, like someone in a dream. Like him but not him.

'It was just – that Sophie asked me something odd.'

Isabella put down her hairbrush, alert and defensive. 'What?'

'She asked me if she would ever have any money of her own, and if so, whether she could have some now – enough to buy Julius's freedom.'

Isabella had been half-expecting this. She blushed and felt guilty, though Frederick, washing his neck, did not notice. She feared her husband's censure on the matter. Sophie's partiality for Julius should not have been allowed to develop. She should have prevented it. But it was hard to be a properly vigilant mother in this heat, with her constant headaches. She was sure Frederick would blame her. He would say she had neglected her duty.

But then a small rocket of indignation went off inside her. If Frederick had not neglected his duty, too, and so much more monstrously, Julius would not exist at all to distract poor Sophie. She clenched her teeth for a moment and tried to suppress her rage. Her recent conversation with her daughter had not altogether soothed her. Indeed, it had revived old resentments and set her off again on a treadmill of fury and pain.

'Well? And what do you intend to do about it, Frederick?'

'What do you think, my dear?'

'What do I think? What does that matter? When has it ever mattered?' She seethed.

Frederick was astonished at this sudden bitter tone.

'What is all this, Isabella? You know that your comfort and happiness are my first, my most serious care.'

'Had you really cared for me, had my feelings really mattered,

Julius and Flora would never have been here when I arrived.' She could not help it; this passion would flare out. 'I don't say they should never have been born; no, no, I understand men: that would have been too much to hope for, though God knows the agony it caused me –'

'We've spoken of this before –' But in vain did Frederick try to prevent his wife's righteous indignation. It flew at him and stuck to him like exploding cinders. He covered his head with a towel.

'Yes, hide your face! So you should! Well, so you got your bastards, very well, I accept it. But why did I have to face them when I came? You could have sold them before I arrived, or given them their freedom and sent them to Barbados, or even Douglastown, anywhere but here. Instead you leave it all exposed, to torture me and to betray Sophie into –'

She almost tripped and bit her tongue. She had scolded enough. He must not suspect Sophie's feelings for Julius were anything other than sisterly. That would set him off like a volcano and her own negligence would not escape a scalding. Carefully, she resumed. 'The fact is, and there is no point in concealing it from you, Sophie knows that Julius and Flora are your children.'

'How the deuce –!?'

'The same way I discovered it, I assume.' Isabella skated quickly over her own role in Sophie's enlightenment. 'Really Frederick, you are naive if you think that such interesting secrets can be kept, especially by slaves.'

Frederick Wetherby sat down heavily at his own dressing-table and shook some lavender water on to a handkerchief.

'So she feels a sympathy with him as her half-brother, I suppose?' he groaned.

'It would be natural. You know how warm-hearted she is.'

'What's to be done, then?' Frederick felt defeated. He wiped his neck, brows and jaws and then let his arm drop loosely to his side.

'Sell him. Now. You said you would. Don't wait till after the harvest. Send him to be sold at Barbados. He must be away from Sabato, altogether. Far off.'

'Yes, yes, I am about it. But you are ignorant of the difficulties, my dear.' Immense fatigue crept over Frederick's limbs: it was the heaviness of shame, that his daughter knew of his bastards. He wanted to do nothing; just to slump into bed. Above all he wanted this woman he had married to stop talking.

'What difficulties?' she demanded.

'I've tried to raise interest here, but my friends have laughed in my face. George was right, for once. I should have hanged him and that's the truth. I was weak. I spared him, when I should have struck.'

'What if you were to grant him his freedom? Wouldn't he go away then? Or would he linger about here making more trouble?'

'Give him his freedom, after all he has done?' exploded her husband, finding energy at last in contempt at this idea. 'And if I did, don't you realise that from that moment his conduct would be his own affair? He could stay anywhere he liked, and do anything he liked, and stir up whatever trouble he liked, if he were free – so long as he kept the right side of the law. Free men have certain rights, you know, Isabella. No, I'll send the fellow to Barbados by the next ship – his sister too, and have done with it.' He got up, heavily, removed the rest of his clothes and put on his nightshirt.

On the way to bed, he stopped by her dressing-table and caressed her hair clumsily. 'I would not hurt your feelings for anything, dearest,' he mumbled. 'I would not harm a hair on your lovely head.' Unfortunately, on removing his hand, the button on his sleeve caught in her hair and pulled a couple out by the roots. She winced, but the irony of it, following so close upon his words, could not help appealing to Isabella's satirical sense. After the hurt had abated she burst into a brief snort of bitter laughter. By the time they got to sleep they were friends again and Isabella, as the partner who had kept her dangerous secrets unsuspected, felt the talk had been a kind of triumph for her, in a small way. Julius would soon be gone.

Next day Charles Craig took tea with Sophie and her brother. George was in a mood of triumphant achievement.

'My road is quite through now, Craig. You can get right around through those coconut groves by the sea and across to Good Hope. We've had such dry weather, it's been far easier than I thought. I expect the whole thing will dissolve and fall to pieces when the rains come, but you ought to seize the moment and make a journey to Good Hope. Pay your respects to old Miss Hambledon.'

'Miss Hambledon?' cried Sophie. 'Might I go too? I should like to see her school.'

'That would be delightful,' Craig smiled. 'And as it happens, George, I was thinking of paying them a call. They've got the Baptists in.'

'What, are you going to be baptised?' George laughed. 'They plunge you head first into the river, you know, Craig. You'll end up more drowned than named.'

'No, I am quite adequately baptised already, I think,' said Craig. 'But Miss Hambledon and Mrs Dodds have invited the Baptists to build a small chapel at Good Hope.'

'What? For their slaves? But she cannot have more than thirty or so – less, probably, for Good Hope was never a great estate and I hear it has gone to pieces since old Dodds died.'

'Not just their slaves,' explained Craig. 'There's a few free blacks living there as well, fishermen, mostly. Some were freed when William Dodds died and have stayed on there, with the old ladies' blessing. Oh yes. There's quite a little settlement at Good Hope.'

'Well, I'd like to try out my new road, so let's go there tomorrow,' said George. 'I've got Amos looking at the old trap, patching it up somewhat, I'm sure it'll be roadworthy. We can leave early in the morning, get some dinner from the old dames, have a sleep on the shore, and be back by dusk.'

'What an excellent plan!' cried Sophie, her heart giving a skip for the first time for weeks. Here was an expedition to rouse her from the flat plains of her misery.

'Indeed!' George agreed. 'You can talk to the old dames whilst Craig and I go off for a swim and a look round. Then we won't have to bother with them for long. Capital! Perhaps sisters have their uses after all.'

'I would like to see the school,' agreed Sophie, putting her sewing away. 'But I suppose I must ask Mamma.'

Isabella readily agreed, of course. It was the very thing she most wished for: Sophie wanting to go out again, after her recent lethargy. And she herself had shamefully neglected to correspond with or visit Miss Hambledon and Mrs Dodds since their visit. Sending Sophie now to celebrate George's new road was a perfect plan. Sophie could take the dear old ladies one of Aunt Sarah's jars of greengage preserves and Isabella's very best wishes.

The excitement of getting the trap out, and harnessing a mule, called forth the inhabitants of Mount Grace just before dawn, and Isabella was grateful to her husband for his suggestion that Craig should drive the trap and George accompany them on horseback, so that in case there was any mishap they would have two mounts. She could not help admiring the pretty sight of her daughter, in sun bonnet and shawl, sitting next to Charles Craig in the trap. They made a handsome pair. It was sad that it could never be. But on that subject Isabella had quite given up all hope.

37

Learning

The conches were blowing to call the slaves to work as George's trap rattled down towards the sea through the acres of cane. The crop swayed in the morning breeze, looking like gigantic grass, far taller than the tallest man. Not that there were any men present to measure it by, yet.

'We are up even before the slaves,' remarked Craig. 'Whenever I see a beautiful dawn I vow always to rise early, but I can never manage it, somehow.'

'Nor can I.' Sophie smiled. 'George says I snore away till noon, sometimes, like a hog in a sty.'

'Most young ladies would not have repeated such a comparison.' Craig snatched a quick glance at her. The ribbons of her bonnet were streaming backwards in the wind. His buried passions knocked in their box, protesting that they were still alive, but he turned sternly back to the road.

'I can assure you, that's a compliment, coming from George,' said Sophie. 'And besides, I am very fond of hogs. We had a lovely old girl at Hempshott called Alice. She was a saddleback.'

'You are an agriculturalist as well as a naturalist, Miss Wetherby.'

'Well, I like animals.'

There was a pause. Sophie gathered her courage to overcome a small difficulty. 'I wish you would call me Sophie,' she burst out. 'As you did . . . before.'

'Have I earned the right?'

'I like my friends to call me Sophie.'

'Do you think of me as a friend, then?'

Sophie was wary. This kind of talk raked over the smouldering coals of their extinct engagement. But her revulsion at his orgy had dissipated over the weeks. Sunk in much deeper anguish, she had appreciated Craig's evident remorse, handsome apology and modest conduct. Moreover, he seemed to be the only person she could speak with openly, as a friend.

Most of all, she had noticed through one or two remarks he had let fall that not merely his conduct had changed but also his ideas. She was glad of his sober and attentive company these days; she had also begun to be interested in what was happening in his mind.

George, riding ahead, gestured to them to slow down. They were approaching a bend at the edge of the cane field. Skilfully Craig controlled the mule, gently they negotiated the corner and Sophie saw a glimmering vista open up: the early sun slanting into a large coconut grove running along the shore. George's road unrolled through it, smooth and flat; the jolting of the stony track through the cane field was over.

Sophie took off her bonnet. The sun was still low and the coconut palms overhead gave flickering shade. Her hair streamed back from her face. Craig stole a glance to his left. Her profile was beginning to glow in the morning light. Over the weeks, the sun had coaxed a patch of freckles to spring up on her nose. He knew they would be thought disfiguring in fashionable circles, but they reminded him of birds' eggs, and thrushes' breasts, and grains of dust floating in sunbeams.

'What are you thinking?' asked Sophie suddenly. He felt a slight physical shock. Why should she care what he was thinking? She had shown no interest in him or his thoughts for a long time.

'I was thinking of speckled birds' eggs, and thrushes' breasts, and motes of dust.'

There was a brief pause. Sophie was surprised at his reply. The words washed up to her like the lace of foam around a disintegrating wave. But she must not think of water, or the suck and fuss of foam about her toes. She could not go back to the beach at Marlidoun-doun. Julius would not ever be her lover again. Her mother had told her, quietly, the previous night, that Julius was to be sent to Barbados next Friday, to be sold.

She had felt a curious relief. She could not bear to see him as he lived now: despised, whipped, a thing. She would rather not see him at all. It left her life a blank, but a blank could be restful after so much torment, so many tears. Riding through this coconut grove, she discovered that she could take pleasure again in the dancing light on the waves, in the softness of the morning air, in the trade-winds on her brow. It was enjoyable riding in this trap, with a person at her side who would not offend or intrude. She needed another's thoughts to refresh her. But what did he mean by this talk of birds' eggs and thrushes' breasts?

'Why birds' eggs?'

'Something must have made me think of them.' He smiled to himself. Sophie had to be contented. A robin's nest came into her mind's eye. She had found it under a hedge at Aunt Sarah's. The eggs were deep turquoise.

'I used to love birds nesting back at home,' she sighed. 'But here I must be contented watching them flying about.'

Birds, startled by the sound of their approaching trap, flashed across their path now and again, or took off, clamouring, into the skies. Out to sea, Sophie could see the pelicans fishing: they looped up in flight, then dropped with a crash. It still made her smile. She felt she ought to smile as much as possible as if it would be good for her body. She looked down at her hands, folded in her lap. They seemed to be someone else's. Those hands had felt a lover's hand, a lover's skin, a lover's hair. But now they were empty. She felt sorry for them.

Sophie seemed to look down on herself from some remote height, as a bird wheeling against the sun sees its own shadow skim across the waves. Blankness, fathoms of air, an occasional sparkling arc of spray. The only important thing: not to remember. Pull the blankness across. Draw the blinds. Soon he would be gone and she need not cringe and flinch at every corner, in fear of seeing him. He would be a slave still, but in Barbados. Perhaps he would find a kinder master there.

Fishing boats appeared, bobbing beyond the breakwater, with pelicans perched on them. The road snaked inland, through a scrubby area.

'Old Dodds had a banana plantation here,' Craig pointed out the low trees, with bunches of bananas hanging from them. Flocks of small yellow birds were feasting on the fruit and flew off as they passed. As if taken by a sudden idea, Craig drew on the reins, cried whoa! and when the trap stopped, vaulted lightly down. Sophie wished she could move with such ease and strength. There was a grace in elastic young manhood which she found infinitely more admirable than the passive posing that was women's lot.

Craig reached up and picked several small bananas. George had dropped back to see what his friend was about.

'Small figs!' called Craig. 'For Sophie's breakfast!'

'I'll go on ahead,' cried George, 'and warn the old dames we are on our way!' He was gone.

Craig climbed back into the trap and presented Sophie with the smallest banana she had ever seen. 'Here,' he said. 'They call them figs, these small ones. The sweetest are no bigger than my thumb.' He laid his hand beside the fruit and Sophie had to smile, though she was remembering other hands: bigger, browner and roughened with hard work. All the same, Craig had good hands. She had noticed and admired them once, when she first came here. It seemed a long time ago.

They resumed their journey; she ate her banana and remembered the first one she had tasted, on her arrival at Mount Grace. Weary with travel, she had lain on the sofa and Mamma had fed her this fruit, saying it tasted all Garden of Eden. It still tasted good, but something had been lost. When she had first arrived at Mount Grace, she had been all eager anticipation and delight. The contrast with her feelings now was most painful.

Good Hope was a ramshackle old place, built almost on the beach, but standing back a little in a shady grove. There were several outbuildings, and a few slaves about: two boys sweeping with the branch of a tree; women carrying things on their heads; a youth approaching with George, to see to the mule. Craig handed Sophie down from the trap and George came up grinning.

'My, Sophie! Your bonnet is all cockeyed and your hair looks like a stork's nest! The old dames will think you a sight. They are up, by the way, and eager to see us. We are the first visitors these three months.' Dismayed, Sophie put a hand up to her hair, but George was already on the verandah and beckoning. Sophie felt a light touch on her shoulder-blade.

'It's nothing; you look perfectly charming; he is just being a brother,' murmured Craig. And the touch of his hand was gone.

Sophie felt grateful and followed her brother on to the verandah. The old ladies ran out to greet them; Sophie was fussed over and complimented, then it was Craig's turn.

'And how is your handsome fiancé? Looking happier than ever, I declare!' cried Mrs Dodds, falling upon Charles Craig in an ecstasy. The visiting party was thunderstruck. The old ladies had not heard about the broken engagement. Even George recognised that to disabuse them of their delusion would ruin the visit. They would never manage to recover from such a monumental, such a mortal, *faux pas*. Sophie blushed and boiled with embarrassment, George scratched his cheek, and under cover of his hand cast satirical glances at his companions. For him this would make a capital joke to laugh over afterwards. Craig stuttered for a moment, then recovered himself. Sophie prayed for him to rescue them.

'You cannot see many visitors at Mount Grace, I think?' he managed at last.

'No, no indeed not; we are quite cut off here, as you know. There used to be a sort of track over the mountain to Douglastown, when William was alive – do you recall it? No, it was in your uncle's time, I think – but now it is quite eaten up again by the jungle. No, the only way to Good Hope was by sea – until this fine new road of yours, George. What an engineer! I think he will make a name for himself, don't you, Mary?'

'Would you like to come and sit down?' asked Mary. 'And refreshment – I should think . . .'

'Ah! There I go! Prattling on and forgetting the first elements of hospitality!' cried little Mrs Dodds. 'I am obliged to you, Mary! Without Mary, you know, our visitors would have to stand on the verandah all night whilst I rattled away, and be eaten to death by mosquitoes. Come in, come in!'

They went into a dim drawing-room. Sophie was glad to sit on a chair that did not plunge about quite as much as George's trap.

'And now – what? Tea? Jezebel has just milked our house-cow. We have a house-cow, you know, Miss Wetherby – the most curious beast. Cattle here have great dewlaps, not like our dear Herefords. Do you remember those Herefords grazing under the elms at Much Dewchurch, Mary?' But Miss Hambledon was giving orders to a cross-eyed little slave-girl in a pink shift, with a bracelet of small shells about her brown arm. 'Our house-cow is called Dorcas – I do think all cows should be called Dorcas, though Mary thinks I am too fanciful in naming things.'

'Betsy might have been more . . .' commented her sister, smoothing down her strange moss-green dress.

'You must have a house-cow when you move up to Belmont.' Mrs Dodds beamed and Sophie cringed anew. 'Pray, when is the happy day?'

Sophie faltered. 'Nothing has been settled at all yet.' She strove like a creature caught in a net.

'But be sure we will tell you so soon as it is,' added Craig. Sophie gladly gave up the effort of conversation to him. 'Apart from the pleasure of seeing you both,' he went on, determined to direct the conversation along less painful paths, 'Sophie is most interested in your school – as indeed am I.'

'Ah! The school! Of course! That is Mary's especial care.'

All eyes turned to Miss Hambledon, who fiddled with her sleeves and looked hunted.

'Nothing really meriting the name,' she murmured. 'A few – one or two – of course when Mr Brown comes –'

'He is a Baptist, you know!' cried Mrs Dodds explosively. 'And a dear man, though he has red hair, which I always think must be so hot, you know. But I always say, what does the hair matter? For a man blessed with such eloquence!'

'When does he come, then?'

'Only once a week,' sighed Mrs Dodds. 'He cannot spare more time: they are starting up in quite a big way in Douglastown, you know. But Mary teaches them on the other days, and she is fearfully clever, she always was the clever one. I was the dunce. Ha ha!'

'No –' Mary twitched, shaking her head vigorously like a bird struggling with a worm. 'Not at all – merely a – I merely read, and . . .' She abandoned the attempt at speech. All her sentences seemed to melt away into nothing. Sophie noticed again how an unfinished air seemed to hang over her. Was she simply out of practice, since her sister's conversational powers were so robust? Was she afraid of saying something wrong?

'So you do have one regular visitor, at least,' remarked Craig.

'Oh yes, to be sure! But poor Mr Brown has no gossip, you know.

He is a serious fellow. He is not interested in love-affairs, at all, alas. Oh! You are such a handsome couple. I declare, aren't they, Mary?'

Sophie and Charles were spared further mortifying admiration by the arrival of refreshments. After some trivial news had been exchanged, and Sophie had tried to conceal her ignorance of the latest fashions in England, conversation turned to the attempted rebellion at Mount Grace, of which the ladies had heard something. Mr Brown, it seemed, was a more reliable informant about troubles with the slaves than about affairs of the heart.

George reassured the ladies that there had been very little in the way of trouble, the rebellious slaves had been punished, and that he and his father had a great store of guns and would be happy to lend them a fellow with a musket or two to defend them if need be.

'Oh, no, I assure you, we are not nervous, are we, Mary? There is nothing worse than being in a perpetual state of fear. If 'tis now, 'tis not to come as Hamlet said. We have lived to a ripe age, haven't we Mary?' Mary opened her mouth and closed it again. She did not look quite as ripe as her sister, somehow. The greenish tinge of her dress seemed reflected onto her face. 'And I shall say to myself, when my time comes, very well, Lord, for Thou hast granted me many years of pleasure, and now I thank Thee for reuniting me again with my beloved William – Mr Dodds, you know, dear.'

Sophie nodded sympathetically.

For a while, after this, Mrs Dodds grew maudlin with reminiscence.

Then, abruptly, Miss Hambledon got up. 'I usually go to teach at this . . .' she said, glancing at the clock. 'For it is too hot, you know, for the slaves to . . .'

'Oh, bless me, yes! How the time has flown!' cried her sister, shooting out of her chair like a billiard ball. 'Do go and see the school, by all means, I shall go and infuriate my dear cook with orders for a dinner – it will be very simple, of course, but it is a great, a very great delight for us to have you dine with us.'

'Do you . . .?' Her strange, halting sister hesitated. 'Would you care to . . .?'

'We would love to see your school, above all things!' cried Sophie.

'Very well.' Miss Hambledon addressed the floor. 'If you would like to . . . I must just get my . . .' She picked up a parasol and led them out into the glare of noon.

38

Parrots

'Good morning, children!'

'Goo' marni' Miss Am-boo-don!'

The school was a palm-thatched shelter on the shore: a rough roof, no more, against the sun, open on all sides to the winds.

'Today we have visitors from Mount Grace.' Miss Hambledon's voice was clear and strong. Now there was no fading away. The handful of small black children gazed up at her, open-mouthed. Sophie thought a peculiar contrast was presented between their black faces and white teeth and her white face and black teeth. The old dame smiled at her charges in pride at her visitors, and she smiled at her visitors in pride at her pupils.

'You may sit.'

The children sat cross-legged on the sand. Sophie noticed small ants crawling about everywhere; the children brushed them off their bare legs. Not far away a couple of pigs were nosing about and dogs barked occasionally. Fishermen were mending nets nearby in the shade of a sea grape tree; their desultory talk flared up from time to time. They had high, staccato voices and mad, skirling laughs. They were free blacks, she supposed. Their laughter had a different quality from that of the slaves. It had a crazy energy. Or was that just her imagination? She found the fisherman's talk a distraction, though she could not understand a word. The schoolchildren, who would understand it all, must find it even more distracting.

She had been provided with a stool to sit upon; George and Charles stood behind her. Most of the pupils stared at them. The children all had large, liquid eyes. Their hair shone with some sort of oil, but Sophie noticed many scars, scabs and insect bites on their skin. Miss Hambledon, a little flushed with excitement, demanded the attention of the class.

'Henry! Maria! Bathsheba! Eyes this way please. Now, tell our visitors: who is the greatest poet in the world? Hands up, please.'

'Shay-speeah, Miss!' A long-limbed boy at the back shouted the answer in a harsh voice, the breaking tone from child to man.

'Yes, Cuffy, well done. Now we will recite. O Romeo Romeo . . .' Miss Hambledon threw back her thin shoulders; the words rang out with intense feeling and punctilious elecution.

> 'O Romeo, Romeo! Wherefore art thou Romeo?
> Deny thy father, and refuse thy name;
> Or if thou wilt not, be but sworn my love,
> And I'll no longer be a Capulet.'

The children chanted the verse in a monotonous drone, their eyes now fixed on their schoolmistress's face, now wandering over Sophie's dress, now raised to examine the tall white men. Their lips mumbled over the alien words without understanding, or even attention. Sophie was troubled by the awkwardness of the situation. She could hardly understand a word of Shakespeare herself, though she did know, and love, these particular lines. The children obviously had no idea of their meaning, and without meaning the exercise was pointless. It insulted Shakespeare and the pupils as well. Sophie felt hot and uncomfortable.

Miss Hambledon looked almost inspired by the situation, however. The contrast between her rapt grin and her pupils' blank muttering could not have been more horrible. This was not education: this was a mockery. All the same, when the verse faltered to its close, the visitors clapped politely.

'Now, Miss Hambledon, you must excuse Mr Craig and myself,' said George, seizing the chance to escape. 'For we have formed a plan to swim out beyond the reef; we shall go around the headland into the next cove, not to distract your pupils.'

'Ah yes!' exclaimed Miss Hambledon. 'The water there is so very pure and clear. Quite turquoise, quite . . . Thank you.' She bowed gauchely. The men hesitated. Sophie ached to go with them, but it was out of the question. Craig looked at her with pity, George with gleeful triumph.

304

'My sister will stay for the rest of your lesson. She has been looking forward to this for weeks.' He grinned and was gone.

Dismally Sophie attended to the rest of Miss Hambledon's class. It went on and on in the same way: awkward gouts of Shakespeare, recited *en masse* without any explanation or enlightenment. Sophie endured it as best she could, admiring the faces of the children, living for the next sea-breeze, and trying not to be too obviously interested in the fishermen's work. It was an awful irony that the idea which had most enchanted her since she had arrived in Sabato – the possibility of a school for the slaves – had provided her with her most tedious hours on the island.

A flock of green parrots flew past: wak wak wak wak! The children all turned towards the bright flourish of green and red noise.

'Don't look at the parrots! Attend to me, Henry, please. Cuffy! Do you want a slapping?' The tall boy at the back shook his head; Sophie fidgeted; more recitation and then, at last, the lesson ended.

Accompanying Miss Hambledon back to the house, Sophie found it hard to express her feelings. 'You must be very tired,' she managed at length.

'Indeed – I always rest after class. I hope you will excuse . . . My sister will . . .' They gained the coolness of the house and Miss Hambledon faded off into a far room.

Mrs Dodds came forward and led Sophie into her own parlour. It was cheerful and full of ornaments, pictures and cushions, all cherished, but all bleached by the harsh tropical light.

'Here we will not disturb poor Mary,' she whispered. 'Do you like mango? Our first ones are ripe today. I have asked Sybil to prepare you one.'

Sophie sat down and gratefully devoured the mango, which refreshed her. Mrs Dodds watched her eat, whilst delivering a digression on tropical fruit which was infinitely more entertaining than anything Miss Hambledon had managed to produce for her African pupils.

'And what did you think of Mary's school?'

'She must – she is a most dedicated schoolmistress, I think.'

'Ah! But it is such a solace to her, my dear.'

'A solace?'

Mrs Dodds leaned close and modulated into a whisper again. 'Disappointed love!'

'Oh. I am so sorry,' Sophie faltered. Miss Hambledon was becoming more interesting.

'Yes. Alas! Poor Mary. It is all a long time ago now, but she has never properly got over it, poor thing. No husband to care for; no children. Here are my son and daughter, see? I was blest, Miss Wetherby.' Mrs Dodds produced two small miniatures: one of a solemn boy, the other of a pretty girl with ringlets.

'Where are they now?' asked Sophie, looking round.

'Oh, Julia is gone to Jamaica. She married Mr Henry Miles, you know, who has estates there. Very happy. They have three fine little daughters. I hope to see my grandaughters one day. Their mother keeps saying she will get their likeness taken for me, but it does not much signify, you know, when they are children. Children change so much; that is part of the joy of them.'

'And your son?'

'He is in the navy. At Antigua at present, I believe. It's possible he may call here on one of his trips. He too is married – his wife lives in Portsmouth, she had family there. He had a little daughter too. They lost several babies. I think his wife is not very strong. Of course I have not met her, but she does write me sweet letters. Emma is her name, and the child is Sarah Anne. They say she is like me.' Mrs Dodd's eyes creased into a twinkle. 'But I was such a hideous child, I hope the poor darling is not!'

'I am sure she is like you – and all the more handsome for that,' Sophie assured her. 'But tell me – if I do not presume – about your sister's engagement.'

'It was never an engagement.' Mrs Dodds shook her head and dropped her voice again. 'He was quite a dashing fellow, for a draper. Matthew Hartley was his name: a great tall fellow, with chestnut curls, you know, and he was quite smitten with Mary, believe me. She was not beautiful, but she had a strange charm, as a girl, a mysterious quality, quite wonderful eyes, Miss Wetherby.'

'But she did not like Mr Hartley?'

'Oh, indeed she did – too well, I believe, but they both had such tempers! I declare, I have had to walk away a dozens times – I often chaperoned them, you know, for I married first, though I am the younger. There was something not quite right about Mr Hartley, however. They quarrelled – very sad – I never quite got to the bottom of it. Mary would not tell me, but she was so cast down, would not see him, though he came several times and left without being granted an audience.

'In the end his patience was exhausted and he went off to Bristol. Imagine! Quite disappeared into that great bustling city. It was a shock. Mary did not expect it, I think. Her temper cooled, she looked about her, ready to forgive – and he was gone.'

'How dreadful! Poor Miss Hambledon!'

'Ah, my dear – the story is but half told. When her true love disappeared, Mary became quite inconsolable. Now father had at the time a new curate – a Mr Thornton. Not a tall man, inclining to the stout, perhaps, but tall enough. Not tremendously dashing either, it has to be said, though not as dull as some fellows are, quite a dry wit after dinner sometimes. Dear me! I was so lucky in my dear William! He was handsome, indeed, and kind. Though not really dashing – no, he entangled himself in his spurs to often for that. He was a clumsy fellow, to be honest, but you know, Miss Wetherby, that only made me love him the more, somehow.'

'And . . . Mr Thornton?' ventured Sophie, anxious not to lose the thread of the story.

'Ah yes! Well, being a sensitive young man he was interested in Mary, and her forlorn state appealed to his cherishing instincts. In truth, I believe he would have cherished her to death, if she had permitted it.'

'What? He loved in vain, then?'

'Mary was too distracted, my dear. Always going over the past. Over and over the same ground: round and round, like our oxen around the treadmill. Reading and rereading Matthew Hartley's letters; scanning the Bristol papers for any mention of his name – in vain. Dreaming of his past whispers, you know, when poor Mr Thornton was poised at her ear, ready at the drop of a hat to whisper fresh ones of his own. She would not listen.'

'Did he declare himself?'

'He did. Not quite understanding her state of mind, and hoping perhaps that her languor and melancholy might be a mere maidenly mood, he proposed, at a cricket match in Ledbury.'

'But she would not have him?'

'No. It was too soon after Mr Hartley's departure, she gave me to understand, though we all thought it was quite long enough after. Of course Mr Thornton did not cut such a fine figure as Mr Hartley, but he was honest, and decent, and kind. Mary went down to Weymouth to spend some weeks with our grandam; I repaired to London with William to prepare for the voyage out here. When Mary returned to Hereford, she found Mr Thornton married to Bessie Porter.'

'What! Married so soon?'

'Bessie consoled him for the loss of Mary, just as he could so easily have consoled Mary for the loss of Hartley. And he turned out a splendid fellow, you know. Got a parish near Bradford-on-Avon, a beautiful old place near Bath, and he and Bessie were blessed with – how many? Six or seven children, all survived, all flourishing. And poor dear Mary has none.' Mrs Dodd's lips quivered a little and she caressed the miniatures of her own children.

'Children, my dear, are such a blessing, I can't tell you. Mary came out to be with us after that – I contrived it, knowing what a confined life she would have led as an old maid in Hereford. Not that she was an old maid, quite, then, but it was inevitable after that, you know. Not many girls get more than two chances. It was known, you see, her partiality for Mr Hartley, it was an engagement daily expected, but which never came about, entirely through her unforgiving temper.

'And then Mr Thornton's addresses were very evident to all. No. No one would have wanted her after that. She began to be seen as awkward, you know.' Mrs Dodds sighed. Sophie felt unaccountably depressed. 'And I knew what a life she would have led with Papa, dear Papa! He was of a most severe temperament, I'm afraid. At least, I thought, dear Mary can have something of a life out here. She made but a sad aunt, however. With her own children, had she had any, things might have been different, but as it was – she does not seem quite to see or hear young people.'

Sophie thought of the schoolroom, and nodded quietly.

'She has not had much of a life, but there are things here which offer some consolation. There is such a tremendous contrast, you see, my dear, between the life of a married woman and the opportunities offered by spinsterhood, which are but lean indeed. Which is why,' here Mrs Dodds modulated into a major key and turned her face up to Sophie with a great smile of relief, 'it is so very delightful that you and Mr Craig are suited. Most of the planters are rough fellows, with no manners at all. But Mary and I have always loved Charles Craig.

'He is everything my William was: kind and handsome – and even dashing, which William was not, and though it is a worthless thing really, not a virtue at all, still it stirs one up, you know. One cannot help admiring it. So my dear, I think I can confidently predict, with Charles Craig at your side you are sure of a splendid marriage, and he adores you – that is plain. Oh, how wonderful it is to have such a cause for rejoicing!' And she took Sophie's hand and pressed it hard. Sophie managed a smile, but it was hard work, quite against the grain of a terrible knot that was gathering in her heart.

She was glad when the young men returned, refreshed from their swim. Miss Hambledon reappeared, looking if possible even more hauntingly mouldy than before. Sophie could not keep her eyes off her, searching for signs of the ruin of lost loves, and at dinner, watching Miss Hambledon chew her fish and peel her wrinkled passion fruit, Sophie felt her own appetite slip away under the pressure of a strange heaviness.

After dinner the sun was lower, and Sophie walked on the shore with her brother whilst Craig attended to some arithmetic for the old ladies.

'Take Sophie for a walk, George,' Craig had suggested, seeing her face clouded. 'It will refresh her, I am sure.'

Sophie gave him a grateful look and would rather have walked with him whilst George helped Mrs Dodds with her accounts, although she was not sure what she would have said. The details of Miss Hambledon's history hypnotised her and she hardly paid any heed to George's prattle, instead looking out across the waves and imagining a life through which love had scorched like a comet, leaving all burnt and spoilt. Until –

'Tedious old fool! But I suppose it keeps her occupied. I tell you, Sophie, I am bored to death with Sabato and as soon as the crop is over I shall go to Barbados, if Father will admit that the danger of rebellion is over – which is obvious to everybody but himself.' He kicked a stone into the sea. 'Craig is off, before then, probably. Bound for America.'

'What?' cried Sophie, as if she had received a physical blow.

'He's had enough; he's off. For a year or two, at least. He's going to Grenada first, he thinks, then Virginia. He wants to have a look at tobacco, it's a fine crop, you know.'

Sophie heard his words, but could not attend to them. Charles Craig was going; that was all she could comprehend.

'But when?'

'When's he off? I don't know. He's got no sugar to speak of to detain him. And Higgs, his manager, is a capable enough fellow; he's left him in charge before. He speaks of going at once; there's a boat bound for Barbados leaves next week, I believe. Bless me! I suppose that's the one Father means to send Julius on. Perhaps Craig could take him and sell him for us. Convenient, eh?'

The pelicans were still floating, stalling and crashing into the surf with ungainly grace, but Sophie did not smile to see them. Something caught her eye up ahead on the beach: something writhing. She ran ahead to see what it was, and found a small fish, cast up by the sea, drowning in agonies of air.

'Oh throw it back, George, throw it back!' she cried, curiously paralysed. George placed his toe under it and kicked it towards the incoming wave. It disappeared into the foam. 'Did we rescue it in time?' asked Sophie anxiously.

'Oh, who cares? You are so damned soft-hearted, Sophie. I declare, you'll start feeling sorry for sticks and stones next.'

George began to amuse himself by throwing stones into the ocean; Sophie sat at his side on the sand, transfixed by the image of a life cast up out of its cool green element, perishing in terrible sunlight.

39

Overturned

'So the day that was meant as a treat for you turned into a torment.'
They were riding home. The sun was low and mild. 'I'm very sorry. I
should have said something – tried to explain.'

'That would have been worse.'

'Yes, I suppose so.' Craig shook his head at the hopeless social
muddle they had found themselves in. 'Well, I promise I'll go and
see the old ladies by myself and assure them that there is no
engagement between us – that it was all a misunderstanding. But
that they are not to be embarrassed about it and that we are both
quite happy.'

'Oh yes!' said Sophie heavily. 'Be sure and tell them we are both
quite happy.'

He paused. Her evident irony seemed to be inviting him towards
a subject he would not dare approach by himself. Still, he could not
quite decide how to proceed. He dreaded offending her and could
not trust himself to avoid it.

'So you are going away!' she burst out suddenly. He was startled.

'I think perhaps I will.' Sophie felt herself sink at his answer. 'I
should have gone away weeks ago. Immediately after your . . . your
reply to me.'

'Why?'

'To be out of your sight. Not to embarrass or upset you by my
presence. But I was too stupid to see it.'

'You didn't upset me at all.'

'Oh, I did.'

'Not much, then.'

'A great deal.'

A pause. She found herself trembling. 'Well, I have forgotten it now.'

'I am glad.'

Sophie did not like to feel the conversation shrinking like this, around a false courtesy, when there was so much more to be said: such mountains heaved within her.

'I wonder if you will ever come back,' she said, launching herself recklessly into it. 'And if you do, what sort of creature you will find me. When will you come back? Ten years? Twenty? Thirty? Perhaps never.'

'Perhaps a year. Perhaps two. I'd like to see Virginia.'

'Oh, to be a man!' cried Sophie. 'You want to go, half-way around the world if it pleases you; very well, off you go. Come back in twenty years and find me a mad old woman.'

He was silenced by her bitter tone. Low orange light flickered on the smooth trunks of the coconut trees.

'Nonsense,' he murmured at length.

'I'm sorry,' said Sophie. 'I have seen and felt so much today – all unexpected things. I feel tired . . .' she faltered. A tear threatened to appear in the corner of her eye. She dashed it away. 'I felt sorry for Miss Hambledon.'

'Yes. But you will not turn into a Miss Hambledon, Sophie.'

'I might. She made a mistake and did not get the chance to put it right.'

He found himself on the edge of an abyss. He did not dare to move. The reins slackened in his hand. Suddenly the journey back to Mount Grace seemed ten times too short. But he was dumbstruck. Words would not come. A great pause opened; the clattering of the trap's wheels seemed self-importantly loud.

Sophie teetered also by the precipice. She hardly knew what she did, or said; some strange instinct had brought her to this point. It was as if all the pressure of the years ahead danced on the pin-prick of these few seconds.

'I just don't want you to go!' she burst out at last. He said nothing; he held the reins like an automaton, staring straight ahead. 'Whom can I talk to, when you are gone?' Still he said nothing, he was pale. His resistance now infuriated her. 'Say something!' she cried. 'What's the matter?' She was almost in tears.

He drew on the reins at last; the trap skidded to a stop in the dust. Suddenly they heard the sound of the sea. He turned to her. His eyes were full of broken light.

'I can't believe it,' he faltered.

'Can't believe what?'

'That you feel you can talk to me.'

'But you're the only person I can talk to! How can I talk to George? He's an idiot. If I try to be honest with Mamma she gets upset. I wanted to be friends with Flora but she wouldn't let me. I can only talk to you. You must realise that. It's obvious.'

'Forgive me.' He felt taut as a bow. 'I am extraordinarily stupid, it seems. But only out of a desire not to offend you or hurt you. I don't understand how we have come to this point – sitting here, in this trap – talking like this . . .' A flock of parrots flew by, their harsh cries echoing around the grove. 'I am only beginning now to learn how to please you, Sophie. Too late.'

'Not too late.'

The landscape seemed to freeze for an instant. Sophie's heart almost stopped. She was appalled at what she had said, but her words had been expelled from her as if forced by some dreadful blow.

Now she could see tears welling up in his eyes and his shirt twitching where his heart pumped.

'Only don't touch me,' she whispered. 'That was what I could not – '

'Of course not,' he breathed, drawing back slightly. They stared at each other for a few more seconds. He felt the mist was clearing to reveal some ravishing landscape, but he did not dare to look. 'Are you saying you forgive . . . ?'

'I have to forget the past,' said Sophie, with a sombre private emphasis. 'I have to begin again.'

'To begin . . .' The possibility of it caught his breath. A dawn was creeping up between them despite this late evening light. 'To begin to know you, and learn to please you.' It felt like a prayer in his mouth.

'If you want to please me,' stammered Sophie, 'will you please not go away.'

'How could I go away, now?' he asked softly.

'But a moment ago – '

'But now it is now.'

How he ached to touch her. The dying sun had glided her.

'What else can I do to please you?' he murmured, feeling joy flood into his heart and thinking *I must give thanks for this moment, somehow*. 'Something difficult. Anything. You know I would do anything for you.'

A sudden stillness possessed Sophie. She felt, creeping into every muscle, the first stirrings of a power. Through this man, who loved her, and whom she had learnt to trust, she could perhaps do things at last.

'Free Julius!' There: it was said.

Craig was taken aback. His eyes moved from her face for a moment, but that was a relief. 'Is that – is that what you most want? He means a great deal to you, that fellow?'

Sophie endured a sickening spasm, but held on to the edge of the trap, pressed her feet to the boards, and so survived it.

'He was a friend to me,' she said. 'He is my brother. If he were free, he could go to England, get an education, have a life.'

'You want . . .' Craig hesitated, venturing forth with the utmost delicacy and dread. 'You want him to go away?'

'What can his life be, here? I hate to see him here. And Flora. You would hate to see your brothers and sisters in slavery.'

'You are right.' Swiftly, he reached across and squeezed her hand. It was a purposeful act, a promise, and it was instantly over: nothing to offend her. He shook the reins. 'It shall be done.'

Sophie leaned back and closed her eyes. Great waves of feeling swept over her: relief, exhilaration, fear. She floundered in fathoms of space. She did not know whether she was lost or found. But Julius was safe. She followed him, in her imagination, to a quayside, not with him, but watching secretly from the shade of some trees; she saw his broad back disappear on deck, then watched the ship vanish into the sunrise.

Oh dear Aunt Sarah! she cried, in the privacy of her mind only, for want of paper, *what have I done? Have I done well? Julius is to be free – I pray you, take him to your heart, unfold to him all the treasures of your mind, give him wings, let him fly.*

Give him my blessing, for I must stay here, and a strange life is opening up for me, strange and awkward and frightening, and I don't know if I will curse or bless this day, but what else could I do? I speak in riddles, not to mystify you, but to conceal from myself what I have done until I am quite ready to face it.

On she went and on, talking to Aunt Sarah in her imagination, but frustrated for want of a reply. Suddenly, there was a sideways jolt, a curse from Craig, and she opened her eyes. His hand had flown across to protect her from the danger of a sudden stop – she felt its warmth against her bosom – now it was gone.

'The mule's gone lame,' said Craig. 'Are you all right? He stumbled on a stone, I think.' He leapt down to inspect the animal.

Sophie looked around her and saw, not twenty yards away, Julius's uplifted face.

They were in the cane field; Julius's gang were tidying up after the last cane-cart had left the field. He had been gathering the trimmed leaves and tossing them into a heap for fodder. Now he straightened up and their eyes met. Sophie felt his look drive into her, as if thrusting her back against a wall. Julius had seen her in the trap with Craig. She felt he somehow knew everything that had passed between them in the last two hours and hated her for it.

For weeks, now, she had had to endure not only physical separation from Julius, but any access to his mind. She had no idea what he was thinking. Deprived of his humanity and understanding, she had been driven recently to remember and repeat to herself all the words he had said to her. But the ones she recalled now gave her no pleasure. What had he said after they had seen Craig's orgy? 'You'll speak to him again, fo' sure. I think you'll marry him anyway.' Guilt and shame closed over her head like waters and she drowned.

'Back to work, you dog, you devil!' came Makepeace's guttural bark. The whip cracked. Sophie looked away. 'What's to do, sir?'

'He's lame – here, let's get him out of the shafts – What a shame Mr George has gone on ahead, I suppose he thought no mishap could befall us now.'

'How are you to get the young lady home, then? Damme, if our last cart ent just gone – no, wait, sir, I'll have you home in a trice – you idle dogs, you four! Come here! Yes, you, and Sam, Will, Julius, look sharp!'

Sophie stared at her hands again, her hands folded uselessly in her lap. She could do nothing, nor say nothing either: her tongue was folded uselessly in her head.

'Oh, but surely – ' She heard Craig hesitate.

'Don't you fret, sir, these devils will draw you home twice as quick as that old mule – or I'll have something to say about it.'

'I – if you are sure – '

Charles Craig climbed back into the cart. Sophie closed her eyes. Julius was to draw them home, like a beast of burden. She heard some noises, of harness perhaps.

'Now give 'em a little lick with yer whip, sir, just to get 'em in the right mood! Haw haw!'

Sophie wished she could shutter her ears as well as her eyes. Blindness and deafness would be a blessing, in this place.

'Of course not,' said Charles awkwardly. 'No need to – '

'Get along, you miserable beggars!' A whip cracked. Evidently Makepeace, despairing of Craig, had contributed a lash of his own. Sophie jerked backwards as the cart moved off. Her eyes were still closed. There was no sound of hooves any more. The slaves were barefoot, of course; their feet passed softly across the ruts and stones, though she could not help hearing their gasps of pain.

'I'm very sorry about this,' murmured Charles. 'It has quite spoilt your evening, I fear.' She said nothing, but wished it was only her evening it had spoilt.

She heard the panting of the slaves who drew her home; she smelt their sweat. Eventually she had to open her eyes. Julius's back was immediately before her: the back she had caressed. But it was not exactly the same skin she had stroked, loving its velvet bloom. Deep scars were etched into it: the scars of his flogging. Julius's back would feel different now.

Not that she would ever feel it. Now her task was to try to accustom herself to the idea of touching Craig. Not yet, not too soon, but eventually. She knew that she had given him grounds for hope. Yet his thin lips still disturbed her. In spite of all he had done and said in recent weeks to restore her good opinion of him, and even to enhance it, she recoiled at the idea of his dry, thin, white body. It was the very opposite of what she wanted.

She was indifferent to the master who held the reins – it was the beast of burden she longed for. And the final paradox was that though to all superficial appearances it was Craig who was of her own kind, she knew that it was Julius's flesh, his soft, dark, moist, exotic body, which shared her father's blood.

At least he is going away, she told herself. At least I have done that for him. Charles will arrange his freedom and he will go to England. He will never be whipped like a beast, never again. They arrived in the yard. The trap stopped. The slaves stood panting, trying to get their breath in great harsh gulps: the last few hundred yards had been a steep climb. His lungs must be bursting.

Craig vaulted lightly down and held up his hand for her to follow. The yard seemed full of noise: the clattering of the mill-wheels, the splintering of the cane being crushed. Clouds of hot air enveloped her from the boiling-house; people ran to and fro; dogs barked, beasts bellowed, asses brayed, and above it all echoed the brassy cries of the overseers. It was like an engine that could never be stopped, that was looming and would engulf her. She got up, unsteadily, held on to the side of the cart and stumbled slightly. Craig moved to catch her, and so did Julius, flinching with an instinct he could not prevent.

Her head rang with horrid noise: Julius's face, looking up, seemed suddenly to dwindle and spin.

'I'm sorry –' she gasped and, clawing at the air, fell forwards into blackness.

40

Germination

A candle appeared. She was in bed. A hand touched her. It did not smell like her mother's.

'Yuh a'right, Miss. Yuh a'right now.' Ruth's face appeared, leaned down and smiled at her. Then looked up at somebody beyond and behind. 'Go an' tell Missis she daughter awake nah.'

'Is that Flora?' Sophie tried to raise her head, but Ruth stroked her cheek gently back down on to the pillow.

'Dat Mary. Flora nat work in de house now. She wid de field-gang, she gwine to Barbados to be sold nex' week. Me t'ink it 'cause she offend Missus, Massa send her away, she sulky girl.'

Ruth's restless tongue was too much. Sophie groaned and longed for quietness. But she needed also to understand what had happened.

'Why am I in bed? Am I ill?'

'Yuh nat ill. Yuh faint in de yard, dat all. Mr Craig carry yuh in here. Yuh faint when yuh gettin' outa de cart, comin' home from Good Hope.'

Now she remembered: Julius's poor flayed back, the trip home from Good Hope, she recalled it stretching longer and longer backwards in the horizontal evening light. Parrots. Backwards to the school on the beach and the poor half-crazy old Englishwoman with the broken heart.

There was a soft step in the room, and the smell of violets. Mamma. A cool hand, softer than Ruth's.

'There's my darling. You fainted in the heat, that trip was too much, I have scolded George for keeping you there so long.'

'It's all right,' Sophie said.

'You stay in bed now, dearest. The girls will wash you and bring

318

you some food. Then sleep. Tomorrow you will be better. I must go and reassure Charles. He is fearfully worried.'

Sophie sighed and turned over on to her back. Her mother kissed her brow and left the room.

'Come, Miss. Take yuh dress off.' It was Mary's deeper voice. Sophie sat up obediently. Ruth and Mary deftly unfastened the bodice and coaxed the fine dress off. Then they both looked at her body and exchanged a glance.

'Did I hurt myself when I fell?' asked Sophie, wondering if there was some bruise, some injury.

'No – Mr Craig, him catch yuh – we see it happen, we in de laundry workin', we come out in de – '

'Hush, please, Ruth!' exclaimed Sophie. The girl fell immediately silent. 'My head aches a little. I am not used to fainting. I never fainted in England. But since I came here, I have been near to swooning quite often.' Ruth hesitated. Mary poured water into the basin. 'I'm very dirty . . .' pondered Sophie, discovering she was wearing a breastplate of dust. 'Why, I am covered with dead flies. How disgusting!'

'Yuh lie back, nah,' said Mary, who had a more soothing presence. 'We wash yuh.'

Sophie obeyed. Their black hands moved gently about her; the sponges, caressing her body, left her clean and quiet. A perfect stillness seemed to steal over her. Julius was saved. He would go to England, have a life. Flora also, perhaps. With him. She thought of their life there, hoping people would be kind. Aunt Sarah was her main hope. She did not have the courage or the strength to think of her own future.

'I feel so tired.' She noticed the girls exchange another glance. She felt a communication between them. 'You don't think it's anything serious, do you?' Ruth stopped washing, looked at Sophie's body again.

'Can I feel yuh, Miss?'

Sophie nodded, becoming anxious. Gently Ruth felt her breasts, then her belly.

'Mi think you got pickny in yuh.'

'Got what? Pick – what?'

'Pickny.'

'Baby,' added Mary, reproving Ruth with a glance. 'How long since yuh saw yuh blood? Long time?'

Sophie sat up, horror rushing to every pore. She could not remember when she had last seen her blood. Twice only, since she came to Sabato, she was almost sure. Terror drained her face.

'Yuh feel tired?' asked Mary. 'Sick?'

'Very tired,' breathed Sophie, her voice no more than a flutter. 'Very tired for weeks now. Like lead.'

'Look yuh breasts, Miss. Look the blue rivers here.' Sophie looked. Her breasts were indeed swollen and tender, the veins enlarged against the milk-white skin. She grasped the girls' hands.

'She goin' to faint again,' said Ruth. 'Oh my! Get de water – '

'No, no – lay me down only a moment – ' Sophie lay down and her head cleared. It was the shock. A child – Julius's child – inside her.

'You're sure, aren't you?' Ruth nodded. 'You've had children yourself, you know the signs.' She stared at the slave girl for a moment, suddenly gaining a slanting glimpse into her life. 'I envy you, Ruth, do you know that? You lost your baby and that was terribly sad. But you can have a child any time, nobody tells you not to. Nobody even asks who the father is.'

'Well, they ask,' Ruth smiled slyly, 'but mi don' have to tell.'

'I can't believe it!' marvelled Sophie. 'You're a slave, but in some ways you're more free than I am.' She did not ponder for long over this paradox, however. The horror of her situation overwhelmed her. 'However can I tell my mother?'

She squeezed her eyes shut, but it only made the imagined tableau more vivid – her mother screaming about monsters, her father . . . what would her father do? Her blood ran cold at the possibilities. Again she remembered something Julius had said: that if she took a slave as her sweetheart, her father would hang the man.

'Yuh want stop the baby?' asked Ruth softly. 'Eli got a herb. Mi ax him make a drug for yuh.'

'No!' Sophie did not hesitate for a moment. This child was all she had of Julius. She would never part with it. She would part with her own life first. Even if it was a monster she would love it. 'How long will it be before it shows?'

Ruth cocked her head on one side. 'Maybe two month. Maybe three. Yuh got good dresses, hide plenty under dere.'

Long enough for Julius to be freed, to leap away into his new life, certainly. But what then? Charles Craig had some rights, too.

Sadly she laid her head down. She could not encourage him, knowing she expected another man's child. Even though delaying telling Craig could give Julius and Flora their chance of freedom, she could not bear to deceive and wound him so much a second time. She felt the beginnings of tenderness towards him now. And there was her own self-respect. To rescue Julius, must she abuse and perjure herself? Encourage Craig, knowing she must devastate him all too soon? She could not do it. She would have to speak to him in the morning.

Craig walked home immensely relieved. Though Sophie had fainted, her mother had assured him it was nothing serious. Isabella Wetherby had offered him the hospitality of Mount Grace for the night, but he wanted time on his own. He did not want to be talking. He needed solitude to admire the prospects unfolding before him.

First there had been sensuality. Black girls with their firm breasts, their springy arses, their strong legs, their obedient tongues. Then his erotic enslavement at the sight of Sophie – all that foolishness. The constant erections, the feverish masturbations, the rage and thirst for female flesh – any flesh – to touch whilst she burned in his brain.

Then her rejection of him. Hate, torment and finally austerity. It had been a revelation: that austerity could be sensual, too. Sending Cassie away. Emptiness. Opening books Mrs Dodds had lent him, reading by candlelight until his eyes ached. His sexual instinct had plunged underground, like a river in limestone, gushing forth only in the dark caverns of his dreams.

But now – he paused at a bend in the track and looked back, across the ocean, beyond Demoiselle, dark in a sea gleaming like mercury – now something was beginning which promised the most delicate, the most divine satisfaction of all. This time it was his soul which soared up, quivering with expectation, longing to be caressed.

He reached his house. He would not dare to think of the day when he might welcome her here as his own. Now he did not need to thrash around in fantasies about the future. The present had acquired a blessed quality. He smiled at Cassie, who returned his radiance with a glare. Did he want chicken? It was already cooked, waiting long time. Yes. He would like some. On the verandah, thank you.

He walked out there; the wood of the walls and floorboards ticked, still warm from the day. The creamy trumpets of the datura sent forth their perfume. The tiny frogs had launched into a throbbing chorale; the air seemed silken and the mass of the forest canopy, tumbling below him to the sea, was robed in moonlight. Every living moment sang with joy. He fell to his knees, and looked up to the stars.

'Thank you!' he whispered.

Cassie arrived, carrying a tray; saw him kneeling. 'Yuh want me thrash you?' she asked contemptuously. Craig sprang to his feet with unusual energy.

'No thank you, Cassie. We are past all that now. Redemption.' Cassie did not know the meaning of the word and would never feel its grace in her heart. She put down the plate and shuffled off.

Cassie's gloom could not spoil anything, not a jot. The dinner, though not one of her best, tasted ambrosial; his bed welcomed him like his mother's lap. He did not expect to sleep at all, but suddenly awoke and found it was already light. There was a split second before he remembered his great good fortune, then it spread all over him like the dawn air: cool, delectable.

He got up, bathed and dressed, called for a cup of chocolate and then set off down the track to Mount Grace. His whole mood was morning. He felt light and trim and new, as he had done when he was a boy. A sudden impulse made him stop, pluck flowers – white orchids and cream datura – and weave them into a coronet. The datura was poisonous, he knew – but not to the touch – and its scent overpowering. The flowers would soon flag, but not before he had arrived and crowned her.

She was sitting on the verandah; waiting for him, it seemed. As he drew near, she rose and dropped her gaze. He liked this modesty; he would admire her every delicate hesitation. He seemed to float up the steps; now she was near enough for the faint sweetness and warmth of her skin to wreathe his face. He placed his coronet on her head and stood back to admire the effect. But she would not raise her eyes.

Slowly Sophie reached up and removed her crown. She looked at the flowers, smelt them, fingered them.

'Beautiful,' she said. 'But aren't they poisonous?'

Instantly he regretted having included the datura. 'Not unless you eat them I believe.' He smiled. 'Which I hope I can trust you not to do.'

She looked grave. 'Sit down,' she said. He obeyed. He began to feel a tremor of misgiving. No, he told himself. I have vowed to admire all her hesitations.

Sophie could not speak for a while. She watched Serafina bring coffee and passion fruit juice. Craig took the merest sip, looking around him at the glorious morning and occasionally, with brimming eyes, stealing a glance at her. He had never looked so happy. She fiddled with the flowers in her lap. Sweet, but poisonous. Happiness was a mistake. Hope was a curse. Below the flowers, below the folds of her fine lawn gown, life was doubling and redoubling with a venomous energy, destined to destroy Craig's fragile delight and plunge her from equilibrium into the abyss.

For a moment she allowed herself to recognise the man she might have had: the man changing, learning, drawing towards the ideas and passions she herself cherished. Gentleness was in his eyes now. It would have taken a long time, but with Julius gone, perhaps, she could eventually have accepted Craig's crown and acknowledged the congratulations of the old ladies at Good Hope. But now, all that was impossible. She was not going to marry anybody. Perhaps she was not even going to live very much longer.

'I have to tell you,' she broke at last into speech, with a suddenness that startled him. 'I have to . . . disappoint you.' She bit her lip; tears welled; she held them back; he blenched.

'What is it?'

'That understanding we reached – '

'Last night? On the way back?'

'It's no good.' She forced herself to look him in the eye. She had to watch his hopes shrivel. She could not leave him to suffer it alone. 'I can't tell you how much I regret it. How it wounds me to have to say it.'

323

'But why?' he breathed, almost suffocating. 'Have your feelings changed since last night?' There was an edge of exasperation, as well as bewilderment, in his voice.

'Those feelings I had, I still have.' She stared at him in anguish, unable to pluck out the dreadful truth by the root. 'It's what I have discovered since then.'

'Discovered, since then?' She nodded. 'What, about me?' Madly he raked through his conduct. A hundred foul crimes rose to reproach him. No redemption, then. A refined cruelty was what heaven had planned. 'Ye gods! I am full of sins, Sophie.' He leaned towards her with desperate intensity. 'I cannot undo them, but I thought you understood – thought you forgave me. You cannot forgive me, then?'

Sophie threw herself towards this foothold. 'It's you who would not be able to forgive.'

He shook his head in amazement, groping emptily at her riddles. 'But I could forgive you anything – anything. What is it, in God's name?'

'I am going to have a child.'

He froze. She could say no more. They seemed locked there together for an eternity.

George strolled out of the house, rumpling his hair sleepily. He grinned at Craig. 'Up early, Charles, what?'

Sophie prayed, not knowing whether she prayed for him to stay or go, just that the hideous moment should be brought to an end. George yawned and stretched. His bones cracked. 'We might go shooting today. I must just attend to something in the yard.' He sauntered down the steps, whistling and singing as he went off round the side of the house: 'Over the hills and far away . . . over the hills and a great way off . . .'

They sat still until the whistling died. Then came a space which had to be filled.

'Julius?' asked Craig, the word coming out broken and crooked, like a peculiar bark.

She nodded. It was said now. This moment, though dreadful, was more restful than the agony that had hurtled about in her before she had spoken. Craig was blinded and sat for a moment contemplating his inner wreckage. Then he looked up, sensing her infinitely worse predicament.

'What will you do?'

Yesterday she had begged him for help and support when her needs were but modest. Now, in direst extremity, she knew she must dismiss him absolutely, and at once.

'People have survived worse.' She got up with a curt shrug and he also scrambled to his feet. 'I think you should go now. I'm sure you should go, before George comes back.'

'Yes – yes . . .' He fumbled, slow, numbed, confused by her brisk initiatives. 'I must – I cannot – what will you tell George?' He could only manage to speak of the merest details.

'I'll tell him you are gone to prepare for your voyage.' He felt dizzy. 'You will want to go now, immediately, I think.' She spoke swiftly, and with amazing composure, finding a strength in his dazed state.

'Yes, I suppose I will.' He hardly knew what he was saying.

'I would be glad if you would go, now.'

He looked up, faltering towards a double sense. 'What – go home to Belmont, now, or go – ?'

'Go altogether.'

He nerved himself up at last. He held out his hand. She took it.

'Goodbye, then.'

'Goodbye.' Her voice only broke on the last syllable, but she turned immediately and went into the house. He saw nothing now: he heard nothing, but walked off into the sound of crushing and splintering.

41

Kindling

Sophie spent the rest of that day in her room. It was easy, after her fainting fit of the day before, to demand a day's rest and solitude. The scene with Craig had exhausted her and she needed to recoup her energies before confronting her family. She knew she had committed the worst sin an English daughter could inflict on her parents. To bear a child outside wedlock was the ultimate disgrace. And for the father of her child to be a servant would be bad enough, but a slave – a half-breed – and the bastard son of her own father . . . The bizarre family dimensions of her condition suddenly appeared to her in all their agonising coincidence.

'I am to present you with a grandchild, Father, and there is no other grandfather to rival you for its affections.' It was economical, at any rate to have but one grandfather instead of the usual two. Hysterical laughter seized her for a few moments and she snorted into her pillow, hauling her breath in with great racking gasps, whining with helplessness.

Eventually the tyrant hysteria ebbed, leaving her flat and exhausted, hiccuping wanly. Now more sober reflections flooded in. Her memory suddenly began to offer examples of girls in her condition who had drowned themselves, thrown themselves off cliffs, whose bodies had been found in ditches or under hedges. She remembered a cottage in Hempshott that held a dreadful secret. It was the home of an old dame, who cared for a young woman who had had a child out of wedlock.

Eliza Mustoe had been Hempshott's dark secret. She had worked as a dairymaid up at the Manor, left abruptly and retreated into total seclusion with her aged aunt, who kept bees in the orchard and never once mentioned to anybody the existence of her niece's child.

326

Their cottage was set back from the lane, with thick hedges shielding the front garden as if the house itself cringed away from public view.

Occasionally Sophie had heard a child's voice behind the hedge, but Mother had always hurried her along, as if they were passing the cage of a dangerous animal.

'Who is the child who lives there, Mamma?' she had asked.

'There is no child there, my darling.'

'But I heard one!'

'It must have been visiting, then, perhaps.'

Even then Sophie had asked herself: does my mother think I am stupid? But she had also sensed a disgrace, something too shameful to mention, which upset her mother, and therefore she lapsed into obedient silence. In the end one of the maids dropped a hint, and by listening acutely to Mamma's conversations with Aunt Sarah she had realised what Eliza Mustoe's situation was.

Aunt Sarah was her only hope. If she could somehow get to England, Sophie felt almost certain of her aunt's support. But there was a grain of uncertainty even so. She knew her approaching confinement would bring a powerful social shame. Perhaps it would prove beyond even Aunt Sarah's tolerance. Would it perhaps be better to go to France, where she would be completely unknown? She had heard much talk of *Liberté*, *Egalité* and *Fraternité*, and they were principles which appealed to her ardent soul. But English society, which considered itself in all ways superior to its blood-soaked neighbour, had so far offered her very little in the way of liberty, equality or brotherliness.

What had she experienced, after all, in that travesty of adult life she had lived since coming to Sabato? She had been lied to and locked away; forbidden to associate with the man she loved, who was treated not as an equal but as a chattel by her father. As for brotherliness, she shuddered. George's was a model of conduct for which she had nothing but contempt. She had come to feel that his high spirits and loud gaiety concealed a heart that was utterly indifferent to anyone else's welfare, especially her own. He always told her what he wanted, what irked him, what he planned to do. Never once did he ask her how she fared.

Even the morning after her fainting fit, when she and Craig had been on the verandah and George had appeared, he had simply yawned and thought of shooting, and wandered off about his own business. Not a word of concern for her. She had not considered it properly at the time, being at the worst pitch of her conversation with Craig, but it struck her now. Brotherliness? A mockery.

As for his conduct with his slave mistresses ... the flame of indignation sprang up again.

'Miss . . . ?' The door opened and Ruth came in. She was carrying a coconut shell covered with a scrap of cloth. She set it on the table. Sophie roused herself.

'What's that, Ruth?'

'That cassava. Strong root. That make yuh blood come again, if yuh want. That send de baby away.'

A stiletto of horror passed through Sophie.

'Thank you,' she said. 'I don't think – but thank you.'

'One more t'ing.' Ruth hesitated.

'What?'

Ruth looked around her: she had shut the door quietly. There was no sound of anybody near. All the same, she dropped her voice to a low whisper. 'Julius want to see yuh. Dis afternoon, when yuh Mammy asleep.'

'But how will he get away from Makepeace and the other overseers?'

'We got an hour fo' us nyam.'

'Nyam?'

'Food for we – mi come, when Julius ready. He wait in de mango grove. Mi go wid yuh, look better yuh walkin' wid me – Missy takin' exercise, after yuh a bit sick.'

'Does Julius know about the baby?' Ruth nodded. 'Does he want us to escape together?' Ruth shrugged, but looked very doubtful.

Sophie lay back on her pillow, her heart beating violently. She almost could not bear any more agitation. If only she could lie here on her bed for the rest of her life and nothing more happen. Nothing at all. Then she realised this was in some measure a longing for death and, horrified by her own cowardice, got quickly out of bed, dismissed Ruth, washed her face and looked out through her barred window.

She saw leaves, the great fronds of one of the cabbage palms on the terrace, flying sideways in the wind. Shutters banged. There was a storm coming, perhaps. Down below in the dirt, three women were working in the vegetable garden: one hoeing, two weeding and watering. A baby belonging to one of them was crawling about. It found an interesting stick, and heaved itself into a sitting position to examine it.

The roundness of its dark head roused a wave of tender feeling in Sophie, as did the fumbling little hands, their pink palms wrestling with the bark, already acting out some creative idea. The stick was to become a flute, perhaps, a sword, a drumstick, a magic wand. She longed to feel the weight of the child in her arms, to smell its head, to touch its rough hair. Hypnotised for a moment by this desire, she felt her breasts tingle in a peculiar way.

Looking inside her dress, she found a pale droplet of moisture at each nipple. This was a message from her child. The monster, as she thought of it. The word monster was not hideous any more. It had acquired a tenderness. She tried to imagine Julius's child. Most half-caste children she had seen seemed to manifest the negro hair and full profile. She hoped Julius's would. She would not want a child of hers to have the thin lips and cruel noses of her own kind.

She turned away from the window, picked up the coconut shell containing the cassava, walked swiftly from her room to the kitchen and, finding Serafina's back turned, she threw it on to the fire.

'Could I have some fruit and corn-bread, please Serafina?' Her belly cried out for food. The monster was hungry. It must be fed, not expelled with poisons. She was ready to defend it and nurture it – to the end.

The hour came when she must dine with her mother and George. Papa was out in the fields, supervising the cane harvest. George drank too much at dinner and then carried the bottle away to his own room.

'George is so restless,' sighed Mamma. 'He needs society, I think – needs companions. Charles is really too quiet for his taste. He was hoping Charles would shoot with him today, but though he was here early, when George was ready, he found he had slunk off back up to Belmont.' She gave Sophie an enquiring look. Sophie shrugged.

'He came to see if I was recovered, and having satisfied himself, went home, not feeling quite well.' She kept her voice steady and casual. 'And he has to prepare for his journey, you know, Mamma.'

Isabella looked keenly at her daughter. 'You will miss him, I am sure,' she said.

'We all will.'

Sophie put aside her napkin with a curious, deadly calm. It was easy to talk about Craig with composure because she knew that soon, within the hour, she would be seeing Julius. No matter how short their interview, no matter what was said, whether painful or sweet, the anticipation of it blotted out everything else.

'I shall go and rest now,' she declared, getting up. 'And perhaps take a little turn about the garden later, with Ruth to give me an arm, you know, Mamma.'

Her mother nodded, not really listening. 'I am sure George is drinking alone in his room,' she fretted, half to herself. 'I wish Papa would come in. When this wretched crop is in, he will have more time for us all.'

Sophie slipped away, glad that George had drawn upon himself their mother's anxiety. In the privacy of her room she washed, dressed her hair and examined her face with some agitation. She had seen older cousins getting ready for balls and levees, and thought their preoccupation with their own faces ludicrous. Why stare into a mirror when you could read a book or play cricket or go birds' nesting?

But now Sophie gazed into her own looking-glass with perplexity. Her face was so horribly pale; her hair stuck out unbecomingly. She could not like herself. How could Julius like her? Compared to the slave girls, she looked half-finished, brittle, quaint, unhealthy. She walked up and down. Would Ruth never come? She peered through the bars of her window, hoping to catch sight of Julius's figure in the far depths of the garden, but there was nothing.

Then Ruth came. Sophie's heart leapt; she took the girl's arm and, without speaking, they walked quietly out of the house. Racking snores came from George's room and passing across the verandah they could see Sophie's mother asleep in her favourite chair, her face crooked and crushed against her shoulder, her mouth open.

330

'Don' walk too fast, now,' whispered Ruth. 'Look like we strollin'.'

Sophie leaned on her and tried to dissemble, though every muscle yearned to fly to Julius as fast as possible. Round the side of the house now; past the edge of the yard.

They walked through the grove of mangoes, which shielded them from the house, and then a patch of shade moved. It was Julius. Sophie's heart rose like a rocket. Ruth melted away. Sophie did not hear or see anything except him. She stood hypnotised for a moment; she could not move. She had not spoken to him since the moment during the rebellion, that last moment, when a clamour had risen among the slaves to beat her, rape her, perhaps even murder her, and Julius had turned on them in a fury and let her go.

She had assured him that her father would keep his word to them, being convinced of it herself, and Julius, against his more accurate instincts perhaps, had set her free. He had wished her to be safe from his own kind. Giving up his last hostage was a betrayal too – of his fellows, which must have cost him dear. Seeing his face now, full of despair and pain, she understood that she had been fatal to his cause, and that he must, many times since, have cursed his tender hesitation on her behalf. Worst of all, there now flashed into her mind the possibility, despite her outburst at the flogging, that Julius might believe she had betrayed him; had known that her father did not intend any amelioration of the slaves' condition, only victory and punishment.

Julius looked at her without pleasure. His face was sour, his eyes hard and proud.

'Papa betrayed me too!' she burst out. 'He gave me his word that he would help you and then broke it. Oh, don't be angry with me, Julius! I can't bear it!'

He said nothing, only stood back, in the shadows. She did not dare move close, though every instinct urged it. The sun lay on her head like a great weight.

'I've thought about you, every day,' she whispered. 'Every hour.' Her mouth was dry. Her knees were weak. 'And I feel so much joy, because there is a child coming.' She searched his face for any sign of gladness, but his expression was veiled in a profound mystery. He was still silent. An edge of fear began to intrude on her. Up till now,

331

she had still cherished the hope that he loved her. But he would not speak. 'You asked me to come,' she concluded weakly, with a helpless shrug. 'What for?'

'Listen.' He spoke at last. 'I'm goin' to tell you what to do.' She became very still, poised between dread and hope. 'You got to tell your father that I rape you.'

'What?'

'Tell him I forced you, that time we were in the forest.'

'But that's not true! I loved you and I wanted you. Why must I lie about it?'

'Then he'll forgive you. Take care of you.'

'But he'd hang you.'

Julius shrugged. 'I don't want to live.'

'Why not? Don't you want to see our child?'

'I'm going to Barbados to be sold. So I won't see you anyway. And if I stay here, that worse. I see you riding with Massa Craig in the trap, he carries you into the house, he got his hands on you – they kick me out of the way.'

'I've told Charles Craig I won't marry him,' said Sophie, feeling tears come. She had longed to see Julius for so many weeks, but this was almost worse than separation.

'You'll marry him for sure,' said Julius. 'That's a'right, so long as I gone and don't have to see it.'

'But he won't want to marry me now – if I have the baby. Nobody will. And in any case, I don't want anyone else.'

'He loves you like mad. I see it in his eye.'

'But I don't want him, Julius! I want you!'

'You can't have me. I'm going to be sold or hanged. I don't care which. Hangin' is a quicker way to get peace.'

'But don't you want to see your child?'

'Better you take the herb Eli send. Better no child at all.'

'How can you say that? I've thrown the cassava on the fire and I won't take it! I was longing to see you and all you do is tell me to kill our child, or tell Father you raped me so he can kill you. What's wrong with you, for God's sake?'

'I'm a slave, that's what's wrong.' She was silenced. 'And you're a white woman. We both Massa's things.'

'I won't be a thing.' The flame of indignation in Sophie's breast flared into a blaze. 'We've done nothing that Father hasn't done himself. No, he did worse, because he was married to Mamma when he took Mimba as his mistress. He betrayed Mamma when he fathered you.'

'He's not my father.' Julius looked indignant.

Sophie's anger stalled. 'What?'

'He's not my father. My father a half-caste man, Jeremiah Murphy. Used to work for Mr Dodds down at Good Hope.'

'But Julius – ' a strange incandescent hope was rushing through Sophie's body. 'Are you sure? My mother told me – '

'Your mammy was deceive by that old story.' Julius shook his head. 'My mammy told Massa Fred he was my father, so he come to love me a bit. Give me books, teach me to read.'

'But he's not your father really, at all? But this is wonderful, don't you see?' she whispered. 'Oh Julius! If only Papa could be persuaded to free you, we could marry. And why not, in heaven's name?' Her voice, squeezed by intense longing and indignation, soared up to a shriek; it echoed among the mangoes, which hung blushing and swollen between their leaves. Blushing, swollen, ripe, fruitful – and ready to be devoured.

The wind had dropped; the air was still. Far away, in fathoms of sleep, her mother heard her daughter's cry, and woke.

'Sophie . . . ?' her voice came feebly on the sultry air.

'See, now you wake your mammy. You crazy.' He backed away. The conches sounded, calling the slaves back to work. Their melancholy cries hung on the air. But Sophie would not succumb to the atmosphere of defeat. She had smelt an escape.

'I may be crazy,' she promised him fiercely, 'but I will not give in! The injustice of it – I won't creep about any more like a criminal. You're not my brother; you're my sweetheart, and if I can't have you, I won't have anyone. I'll tell them tonight. Come to the house.' Julius still backed away, shaking his head in foreboding.

'Julius! Stand still a minute! Will you marry me?'

He raised his hands and eyes to heaven, and rubbed his head in eloquent despair at her insanity.

'I said will you marry me?'

'Sophie . . . ?' Her mother's voice rang out in the distance again, stronger now.

'If you were free, if you were a white man, would you marry me? Or don't you love me very much after all?'

He scowled. 'I love you terrible bad.'

'Then come to the house tonight and ask for my hand.'

'Crazy . . .' He looked lost, hopeless, spent.

'Sophie . . . ? Are you there?'

'Come! Come tonight? Or I won't think you love me at all.'

He stopped for a moment, and appeared to come to a decision. Perhaps he felt it was better to run into the cannon's mouth than die slowly of wounds in a ditch somewhere. At last Sophie saw something kindle in his eyes. 'I come.' He nodded, and disappeared through the trees.

Sophie turned on her heel and walked calmly back towards the house. Ruth appeared and glided up to her. 'Take my arm,' she whispered. 'Look like yuh weak, like yuh ill.'

Sophie shook her off. 'No,' she snapped. 'I'm not weak or ill, Ruth. I'm strong.'

They came upon the baby she had admired through her window. Sophie bent to pick up the creature. Its mother, hoeing nearby, smiled shyly across. The child was light in her arms; it whimpered anxiously at the closeness of her white face.

Sophie's own mother appeared, clattering down the verandah steps in some agitation. 'Sophie! Didn't you hear me call? Are you all right? I heard you shout.'

'I was only singing, Mother.' Sophie handed the child abruptly to her mother and walked past her into the house. Springing up the steps, she burst into song indeed, as soldiers terrified of the approaching battle whistle in the darkness before the dawn:

> 'All creatures that on earth do dwell
> Sing to the Lord with cheerful voice;
> Him serve with fear, His praise forth tell,
> Come ye before him, and rejoice.'

42

The Last Supper

By the time night fell, all Sophie's courage had ebbed away. Her father had come in from the cane fields in a rare temper: a cart had overturned, he had lost two more oxen, the driver was at fault; and the sugar-mill was not operating properly either: one of the cogs kept jamming. Sophie heard him shouting in his room, throwing things about, and her mother trying to pacify him.

'Give me a glass of claret!' he cried. 'And don't preach at me, woman; I've had enough today!'

'Don't call me woman – you sound like a labouring man sometimes, Frederick.'

'I am a labouring man, for God's sake! – And worn out by it. This damned climate will be the death of me. I've had an ache in my shoulder all day bad enough to make a fellow howl with pain. Get me some claret, I say, and a decent supper on the table within the half-hour, and leave me alone till then.'

'Well, I hope you soon recover your manners,' Sophie heard her mother say. 'George needs a better example. No wonder he's turning to the bottle, and as for poor Sophie, she is more and more eccentric these days. I wish I had never brought her here – I wish I'd never come myself. To be sitting about in this heat all day, with no one to talk to, no society, is enough to drive the most rational person quite out of their wits. And if I had never come, I would never have heard and seen those things that have quite broken my heart!'

Sophie heard her mother storm out of the room and close the door with a bang. Her father groaned. She could hardly have chosen a worse time to reveal her condition and for Julius to arrive and ask for her hand. But it was too late. Julius was coming.

Or was he? He had seemed most reluctant to accept the idea,

335

hanging back and shaking his head as though she were mad. At the moment of farewell in the garden he had remained ambiguous, untouched. The more she thought about it, the more she felt he might have been humouring her. What she had asked him to do was preposterous. What? Ask her father for her hand in marriage? Even if they could convince her father that Julius was not his child, and had he been the most trusted, the most accomplished slave, the fact that he was a slave was enough to forbid the match. But Julius was in deep disgrace, had led a rebellion. Other masters would have hanged him long ago.

She slumped on her bed, crushed by her own thoughts. Julius would not come. She was sure of it now. She had best conceal her state from her parents for a few days, if only to give herself time to recover from the tumult of seeing him. Once her spirits were composed, she might best discover what to do. For the time being, she must keep very still and quiet. For the monster's sake as well as her own. Her body was the child's citadel. It must not be damaged or shaken by any rough shocks.

I shall begin, thought Sophie, by sitting quite still here until supper, and making sure my heart beats softly and evenly, and that every muscle in my body is relaxed, and my eyes closed, and my brain at rest . . . There was a tap at the door. Her eyes flew open again. What now?

'Come in!'

It could not be Mamma, she always knocked and entered straight away.

Ruth crept in, her face full of concern and care: so different from Flora. There had always been something forbidding about Flora, something defended. But Ruth was affectionate, loyal, conspiratorial. Even now, without speaking, by her looks alone she conveyed the most eloquent sympathy to her young mistress. Swiftly she brought something out of her ragged pocket – a letter. Sophie's heart leapt.

In the instant it took Ruth to hand the paper across, for the space of a heartbeat, as it hung in the air between them, Sophie anticipated the worst, prepared herself for disaster. It was some dreadful confession, she was sure: Julius would not come tonight. He thought the project hopeless. He begged her to abort their child. He was running away. He was hanging himself – to save his master the trouble.

'Go – go, thank you, Ruth,' she gasped, unable to bear the presence of anyone whilst she read his words. Ruth vanished and Sophie's trembling fingers tore open the letter. But it was not from Julius at all.

Belmont, half-past five.

My dear Sophie,

Since we spoke this morning I have been in the greatest tumult of mind, as you may imagine. To hear that you are with child dealt me a painful blow. I confess that since our journey back from visiting the old ladies – only last night, it seems an age ago – I had formed a hope, much too hasty no doubt, that we might develop an understanding which could ripen into something which might give you pleasure as well as comfort.

Though the shock of your news, and your dismissal of me, is a wound from which I still bleed, I beg leave to share a few thoughts with you. You spoke as if you wished me gone, and gone directly. But if you thought I might stay to reproach you you are wrong. You have done nothing I have not done – indeed, if you were a man, this association of yours with Julius would appear as a solitary indiscretion, in comparison with which my own sins are a plague of locusts that could blot out the sun.

I do not address you therefore from any position of imagined moral authority, only as one poor struggling sinner to another. Nor do I reproach you for yielding to your passion, for though the thought of it racks me with jealousy I am well aware I have no claim on you. This morning you sent me away, but I do not wish to be gone. You said last night I was the only person you could talk to. Now more than ever you must need a sympathetic friend to help you bear what will be a severe trial.

I hate to think of you facing this alone. Having to confront your parents with it – your defencelessness. I shudder at the thought of it. I would spare you it if it were possible. Could I do so? Dear Sophie, let me renew my offer of marriage. We could be married immediately and go away – my notion of travelling to Virginia could be revived – you could accompany me, before any outward sign of pregnancy were visible. You could bear your child in America, in secret. Your parents need never know. We could find a home for it, a loving home, in America, I am sure.

But if your instinct were to love and cherish it, I would accept it as my child too. I know it will be a half-caste, but I would not be the only planter to have a mulatto child. I promise I would be a good father to it and delight in educating it as you, without knowing it, have educated me. It will be half yours, and for that reason alone, very dear to me. And there is something I have never told anybody – over the years I have become convinced that I will never have a child of my own.

So if you wish to escape, I am ready. If you cannot endure the thought of marriage to me, but would like to go away, I would travel with you as your brother. Believe me, I would never insult you with those attentions which so distressed you in the past. I imagine in your present state such things would be most unwelcome in any case.

If you want to stay on Sabato, tell me what I can do to help you. My heart, mind and possessions are at your disposal.
　　　Your most devoted,
　　　Charles Craig.

Sophie leapt up as if scalded. She could not comprehend such generosity. A moment ago she had been alone and trapped; now she could depart with a trusted companion. He offered a solution which did not assume any acceptance of him as a suitor at all. All the vastness of America to hide in. Her parents need never know she had had a child. Her parents' approval of Craig's proposal was certain. In an instant, Sophie's prospects shifted from disaster to complete, immaculate escape.

But though reason might recommend Craig's proposal, every instinct rebelled against it. Passion, not reason, must have impelled him to make such a reckless offer. She understood extreme passion, having felt herself seized and shaken only a few hours earlier, when a patch of shade moved and became Julius. Every breath in her gathered itself up for Julius. They would confront her father. She was tormented, though, by the memory of Julius backing away.

What if he did not come? Or if he came, what if he was punished, banished, lost to her for ever? It was madness. Julius backed away; Craig came forward. Julius urged poison; Craig offered education. In rejecting Craig, was she acting in her baby's best interests? Yet how could she go away with Craig knowing his feelings for her, unable to return them, but taking advantage of his protection?

A gong sounded through the house. Supper was ready.

Her father, washed and changed, received her dutiful kiss almost without looking at her. His attention was fixed on his wife, whose eyes glittered restlessly over the table. She straightened a knife here; fiddled with the napkin; brushed a speck of dust from the table. George had not yet appeared.

'Go and knock on Master George's door, Serafina,' she ordered. Serafina obeyed.

Sophie saw her mother throw a look at her husband: a look at once offended and anxious. Frederick sipped his claret and stared into the flames of the candles. Sophie felt that, at that moment, he was entirely unaware of her existence. He raised his head at the approach of his son, however.

George shambled to the table, looking dishevelled. He had obviously been drinking all afternoon.

'George, you have not shaved or combed your hair,' objected his mother.

'Had a plaguey headache all afternoon,' growled her son, sitting down heavily.

'An apology to your mother and sister might be in order,' observed his father coldly.

'I apologise.' George scowled at his mother and sister. 'Shall I go off and lie under the house? You can throw me a bone.'

'Don't talk like that, sir! If you can't be civil, you can return to your room.'

'Not – not in front – ' Isabella fluttered about the conversation, struggling to prevent a scene in front of the slaves. Serafina and

Viola were poised to serve the supper. 'George will feel better so soon as he has some food. I know those headaches. He has got them off me, Frederick.'

'He has got them off his damned bottle,' commented her husband sourly, unfolding his napkin. 'Well, come on, girl, let's have the soup. What is it? Pumpkin?'

'Turtle.' At last his wife found reason for a smile. 'Your favourite.'

Sophie was also fond of turtle soup, but the weight of her hidden secrets dragged at her innards most horribly. She managed to sip a few spoonfuls by staring at a picture on the wall, behind her father's head: a painting of a racehorse against an English sky.

'That is one good thing about Sabato,' acknowledged Isabella. 'The turtle soup.'

'We sell the shell of the Hawksbill, too.' Her husband was always ready to talk about business. 'Though the Green turtle's shell is not worth anything.'

'How do they catch them?' asked Sophie, drawn into the conversation against her expectations by the mention of natural history.

'They come up on to the beach at this time of year,' explained her father, 'at night, to lay their eggs, and so we turn them over and kill them there.'

A sudden horror filled Sophie's soul. The female turtle, impelled by maternal instinct to abandon her safe element, comes ashore to help her babies into the world and meets with the cutlass and the knife.

Tears fled down her cheeks; streaked down her neck; sank into and stained her dress. They were silent tears. It was a few moments before anyone noticed them.

'Why, Sophie, dearest, what is the matter?' asked her mother. 'Serafina, Viola, you may go. I will ring for the next course.'

The girls departed. Sophie covered her face with her napkin and sobbed silently to the bottom of her lungs. A strange sound, like the shriek of hinges, escaped her. She felt her mother's hand on her shoulder. Mamma had got up and come round to comfort her. 'My darling, what is it?'

Sophie lifted her head, struggled to recover breath. Suddenly there was a creak; the shutters stirred; they all looked towards the dark side of the room.

'What's that?' hissed Isabella.

'Only the wind,' said George. 'Cursed storm blowing up.' Indeed, there was the sound of sighing outside, as the fronds of the tall cabbage palms began to stir.

But the jalousie still rattled in an impatient, meddlesome way; suddenly it burst open and a small dark figure leapt into their midst. Isabella gave a shrill cry; her husband struggled to his feet.

'What the deuce – ?'

'It's Sophie's damned monkey!' cried George. 'Here's sport! Tally-ho!'

'Oh, it's got free!' cried Sophie, half in triumph, for she had hated to see it trapped and miserable in its cage. The monkey scrambled up nimbly on to the sideboard, scattering the dishes, which cascaded on to the floor, smashing and shattering the fine Worcester bone china and Venetian glass.

'Oh! Stop it! Stop it!' screamed Isabella. 'It will destroy everything!'

'I'll get my gun!' George lurched to his feet.

'No!' cried Sophie, also leaping up. 'You mustn't hurt it!' Alarmed by the noise and confusion, the creature sprang from the sideboard on to the table, scuttled across it, sending more glasses and spoons flying and knocking over the claret bottle. A great red stain fled across the immaculate cloth; the monkey leapt into Sophie's arms.

There was a sudden silence and stillness. The bottle gave a last few spent gushes. The monkey hid its face in her shoulder.

'I am going to have a child,' said Sophie.

Her mother's pale face opened like a painting of a scream, but no scream came. Her father's face froze; something like a grunt escaped from George's lips. He staggered, and caught hold of the back of his chair.

'By Jove,' he snorted, struggling to hold back his glee, 'Craig's tupped her after all!'

Frederick Wetherby turned to his son with murder in his eye. 'Get out of my sight, you ruffian!' he snarled, fetching George a stinging blow across the mouth. George looked astonished, staggered backwards noisily amongst the broken china and collapsed on to a chair.

Isabella faltered towards Sophie, holding out a shaking hand. 'Is it Charles, my dear?' she stammered. 'If it is, though we are deeply –'

'Julius is the father,' said Sophie, strengthened somehow by the warmth of the monkey's body in her arms.

'Julius?' Her father's face seemed to explode.

'Oh Frederick – be –' But her mother's faint protests were swept aside by a volcano.

'How dare you?' thundered Frederick Wetherby, spewing out the bile which had been gathering inside him for the past hour, finding release in this last epic insult to his authority. 'A daughter of mine, play the strumpet with a slave? I'll have the fellow hanged and you flogged, Miss – and sent away, so help me! Yes, you shall rot in a damned cottage in a bog somewhere, and never offend me again with your insolence!'

'Frederick!' cried his wife, 'do not be so –'

'What crime have I committed?' cried Sophie, finding her fury again at last. 'How dare you dismiss me from your sight? You who have done as you pleased since you came here – although you were already married to Mamma.'

'Get out! Get out!' Her father quivered; a vein writhed like a snake on his brow. 'Don't you dare speak to me in that way! Go away!'

'I will not! I will speak, and you will hear me. Since I came here I have seen nothing but injustice and cruelty. You treat your beasts better than your slaves – even though some of them are your own children.'

'Madness!' roared her father, clutching at the stained tablecloth, so that a fork shook against a fallen glass, a strange vibrating sound, like the clatter of a cracked bell. 'Madness! Take her away!'

'No!' she went on, her voice ringing loud above the rattling of the shutters in the wind, her heart flooding with exhilaration. 'You'll hear this. Your slaves are free to love whom they like; your son, following your example, is free to love whom he likes; only I am a prisoner. Well, I won't be your daughter any more. It's all a mockery, all of it, all. Hang me, or make me your slave, for my part I'd as soon be dead as be your daughter.'

Her father frowned, but a strange expression crept over his face, as if a thought had struck him from far away and long ago. He sat down, his eyes still fixed on her, and staring. Suddenly the jalousie, loosened by the monkey, banged open again in a gust of wind; the monkey, startled, jumped from Sophie's arms and out into the night. Her mother cringed as it passed as if it were the devil. George gazed at Sophie in a fumbling, unfocused way, as if he had just noticed her existence for the first time.

Sophie felt her anger mysteriously depart with the monkey's warmth: she stood now empty, awaiting her fate, unable to defend herself any more. Her father could, if he had chosen, have brushed her away at this moment like a breadcrumb; but still he said nothing, only seemed to stare out from a kind of boggling stupor.

There was a sudden growl of air and a roll of thunder behind the mountain.

'Oh, there's a storm coming!' gasped Isabella. 'Serafina! Viola! Fasten the shutters! – Oh! What's that?'

George was too drunk, and his father seemed too stupefied, to hear it, but Sophie's ears had caught the strange popping, cracking, devouring sound, and she ran to the window – her mother was instantly there also. Orange flashes sprang up through the trees, in the direction of the mill yard. Sophie could smell smoke.

'Frederick!' her mother screamed. 'We are on fire!'

Wetherby lurched to his feet, and ran out of the room; his wife and daughter followed.

'Devils!' he cried. 'Devils!'

The whole works yard was catching ablaze: the offices, the boiling-house, the smithy. A weird booming sound came from all directions, floating over the tops of the trees.

'They're blowing their damned conches,' gasped Wetherby. 'Trying to scare us to death. But they won't succeed! Bring me my gun – I'll take a few with me!' He leaned against the balustrade in a peculiar way, clutching his shoulder. George appeared on the verandah behind them and stared at the tableau in complete paralysis. 'Fetch me my damn gun, I say!'

Two flames detached themselves from the fire and began to run towards them. For a moment Sophie felt a shiver of superstitious fear. Then she saw it was Julius and Eli, carrying flaming brands.

'You dog, you swine!' cried her father at Julius, staggering down the steps to them, hugging the balustrade. 'Destroy me, would you? I made you, sir; and now you destroy me, ruin my daughter. Go on; set fire to the house! Kill us all where we stand! Kill us and be done with it!' Julius and Eli stood before them, panting, but hypnotised by their Master's speech.

Suddenly Wetherby's body sagged. His wife rushed to support him and Sophie, filled with a strange tenderness as he crumpled, ran to help.

'Squeezing me – ' he gasped. 'Squeezing me to death, here – ' he tugged at his choking collar; she ripped it apart. His eyes closed.

'Fetch some water – fetch him some water!' cried Isabella. But nobody moved. They all watched as Frederick Wetherby keeled over sideways on to the earth at the foot of the steps, in a crazy, half-comical angle.

'Papa! Papa!' Sophie felt for his pulse; there was none. His brow was clammy. Great flakes of ash spiralled down around them: the scene was lit up by the blaze, as bright as day.

'Frederick! Oh, Frederick!' sobbed her mother, chafing his dead hands, searching desperately for signs of life.

'I think he is gone, Mamma,' said Sophie.

Her mother uttered a harsh sound, leaned forward for a moment and rested her brow on his breast, shuddering. Then she seemed to recollect something, and reached imploringly towards Julius and Eli. 'Spare us!' she begged. 'Let us go!' They were armed with cutlasses; their torches flared; they towered over her pathetic, crawling figure. 'George!' she crowed weakly. Sobered by the moment, George slithered down the steps. 'Oh let us go, Julius!' she cried. 'Have mercy. Get the trap, George – spare us, Julius! We'll go to Good Hope – and get a boat round to Douglastown, and go! You can have it all! You can have your freedom! Only give us our lives!'

Julius simply stared. George staggered off towards the stables. Isabella seized her daughter's wrist, but Sophie shook her off.

'I am staying, Mamma!' she said fiercely. 'Sabato is my home. My child belongs here.'

'But they will kill you!' Her mother gave a great hooting call: 'Kill you, Sophie!'

344

Sophie looked at Julius and Eli, then down at her father's folded corpse. 'So be it,' she said and fell to her knees before them.

With a last fearful, frantic look, and a cry of horror, Isabella picked up her skirts and ran off after George into the darkness.

The fire was too bright now to see Julius's face, but she reached out both hands to him in supplication. A supernatural calm had leapt into her breast. For a moment she did not care if she lived or died. She closed her eyes and felt not a cutlass blade, but a human hand: Julius's palm beneath her fingertips. He raised her to her feet.

Something hit her on the brow. A raindrop. Eli looked up. Thunder sounded, rolling and echoing over the island. The men ran under the house to shelter. Though Mount Grace was open and empty, its master dead, its mistress fled, the sense of trespass still lingered strongly enough in their imagination for the slaves' first instincts to be to avoid entering. Sophie followed them, and together they watched the percussion of raindrops, at first small and scattered, then thick and fast, until great sheets, torrents of water sluiced down. The flames hissed and hesitated, faltered and flickered lower. In less than half an hour there was nothing left but pools and ashes.

43

Behind the Curtain

When it was over, they ventured out. The body of Frederick Wetherby still lay where it had fallen, but the folds of his saturated coat gleamed in the moonlight. Sophie could not see his face. It lay in a shadow. She was glad.

'We must take him inside,' she murmured. 'Lay him out – I don't know how – ' she faltered.

Julius stilled her anxiety with a raised hand. 'Eli will call the women,' he said. 'Juno laid out Massa William from Good Hope when he die, Juno knows how the buckra do it.'

'Where must we bury him?' wondered Sophie. 'Where is the nearest church? Must we take him to Douglastown?'

'We bury him behind the house,' said Julius. 'It's too far to Douglastown, he'd stink. Eli will get some men, we'll dig him a grave in the mango grove.'

Sophie stared at her father's corpse, hardly believing he would not stir, get to his feet and take control again. The disbelief was stronger than any sense of grief or loss as yet. He lay at her feet, finished; her mother and brother were fled. With the disintegration of her family, all authority over her had evaporated. She could do what she liked.

She raised her eyes from her father's body to what was left of his inheritance: the smoking mill, the boiling-house, its roof quite gone, ashes spiralling from the offices and the smithy. All destroyed. The house had survived, however. It awaited her first step, her first decision: with freedom came responsibility.

Everything felt new: it was as if she had just arrived. Ashes blew about her ankles. She stared around, avoiding Julius's eye. She did not want to open herself to him whilst Eli was standing by.

'So much destroyed.' She shook her head. 'But I understand why you started it.'

'We nat start it!' cried Eli indignantly.

'What? How then?'

'Yo' brother George. Him in de office this afternoon, burnin' papers an' drinkin'. Him drinkin' brandy, terrible drunk, knock over glasses o' de stuff. We was runnin' to warn Massa, help put de fire out.'

Sophie was embarrassed. She had thought she was forgiving the slaves for a crime which, though horrible, was understandable: in fact she had insulted them with her suspicions. Much later, it occurred to her to wonder if Eli's words had been a tale, to divert blame. But it did not seem to matter. She was sure, if she had been a slave, she would have wanted to burn down the place of her enslavement. In any case, the thought of George burning papers to disguise some vice or folly of his own was all too likely, and she had herself seen him lurch about, careless in his cups. It was a shame her father had died blaming Julius for his ruin, but she hoped that if there was another life beyond this one, he would find enlightenment there.

'I'm sorry,' she said humbly. 'Thank you.' Eli nodded stiffly, accepting her apology. She sighed; ran her fingers through her hair. She was dirty and sticky with the heat, the ashes and smuts. She wiped her face and looked at her fingers. They were black with grime. 'I must wash myself.' She looked towards the house. But somehow she felt shy of entering it as its mistress. She recoiled from the first order she must give.

Julius noticed her hesitation. 'Come,' he said. 'We go to the waterfall first, wash there.'

Leaving Eli to prepare for his master's burial, Sophie and Julius walked to the edge of the forest. Still he did not touch her and Sophie began to fear that he never would again. Perhaps he had never loved her. Her passion for him had certainly pitched him into disaster. Perhaps, in this private place, he would satisfy some mysterious demand of Fate and take her life. The thought struck her dumb.

Julius went on ahead. He did not turn back to help her, but she hardly needed help. The shape of the path was familiar to her: its twists and turns, the fallen log, the swags of hanging vine glimmering in the broken shafts of moonlight. She felt she was walking home. This was where they had met. This was where she had so often felt that turbulent longing for him. If he must kill her, let it be here.

The waterfall's sound came first. How many thousands of years had it been making that noise? Before any human beings had come to Sabato, animals had come here to drink and bathe. Moonbeams played around its sluicing freshness. Without removing either shoes or clothes, she set foot in the pool, but Julius caught hold of her arm and motioned her to wait for a moment. He went in first, but strangely not as one washing himself: fully clothed, he walked into the waterfall and disappeared beyond it.

Sophie watched, astounded. The curtain of water fell as before, bouncing off rocks, cascading over ledges, but Julius had gone. For one foolish moment she wondered if he had disappeared, if this was all a dream and any moment she would wake and find herself back at Mount Grace, with Mamma and Papa in their places.

But she did not wake; the splashes of cool water were sharp and clear on her skin, and suddenly a shape appeared through the cascade. It was not Julius. Sophie's heart missed a beat. It was a plump figure, female, dignified, moving slowly, her bulk briefly outlined with white foam as she passed through the waterfall.

'Mimba!' gasped Sophie.

Mimba's sharp cheekbones creased into a grin. 'You thought I dead, darlin'? Mimba got plenty o' fight in her yet.'

'But you disappeared – George went to Demoiselle with the dogs and he said you must have . . . it's like a dream.'

'You nat dreamin', darlin'. I nat a jumbie. Feel me!' She stepped from the pool, taking Sophie's hand in her strong fist. She was hot, wet and alive.

'How did you escape from Demoiselle?'

'We lay a trail. No place to hide there, so we lay a false trail for de damn Cuban dogs. Then we come here. No dog smell us through de waterfall. Safe from Massa here. Big cave in behind here, plenty room fo' people sleep.'

'Are there more of you in there?' asked Sophie.

'No. Since dogs went back to Douglastown, only me. Sleepin' on de rocks. It hurt but it safe.'

Julius appeared carrying a small bundle: his mother's possessions.

'Well, my father is dead, now,' said Sophie. 'And my mother is gone, with George. Mount Grace is ours, I think, so you must come home with us and get dry clothes and food, and sleep in a soft bed. You can choose whichever bed you like.'

'I know which bed I like,' said Mimba with a wry grin. 'Dat used to be my bed, I know dat bed well, but dat yours now, children.'

Sophie blushed. But the embarrassment brought her to a question she burned to ask. 'Did Julius tell you I am going to have a child?'

Mimba's eyebrows shot up and her eyes flared white in the darkness. She turned to her son. 'What? Yo' nat tell me de girl got pickny comin'. I got buckra grandchile comin'!' She gave a whoop of joy, and taking Sophie in her arms, lifted her off her feet for a moment in her delight.

'And I'm proud that my child will have African blood!' gasped Sophie.

'Yo' give him a good chile,' said Mimba with a cunning grin, 'maybe I let him marry you.'

Sophie turned to Julius. Love seemed to pour out of his eyes. She saw at last that he was not going to kill her, but cherish her.

'I go now,' said Mimba. 'You stay here, wash, nat worry 'bout me. I goin' to find a little bed in me old home. I see yo' in de marnin'.' She raised her bundle, secured it on top of her head and strode off.

Free now at last from human enemies and from all taboos, Sophie turned her face up to her lover's. For a moment he hovered above her. She could feel the warmth of his skin on her cheeks and his breath in her nostrils. Then their lips touched and a delicate thrill danced down through her body. Pregnancy seemed to have brought an intensity of sensation: as she felt his tongue enter her mouth, tingling rivers rushed down across her breasts and belly.

He caressed her cheeks and ears and neck; her breasts, her belly where his child lay, her hips, her buttocks, then his fingers moved between her legs, eased them apart, lifted her up. She wound her legs around his body; he carried her into the waterfall. Gently he set her down; the water drummed on her head. His breeches, a mere rag, were soon gone and she felt his cock already stiff and hard, yearning for her, like a muscular animal eating from her hand.

He eased her dress down her shoulders, though it was wet and clung to her skin; eased it down till her breasts appeared, swollen by pregnancy. He groaned and she felt his body jump eagerly at the sight of her nakedness. The dress fell into the pool; he turned her around. Looking down. Sophie saw how dark his hands looked and how white her breasts glimmered within them.

'Bend over,' he whispered, his breath hot on her neck. Supporting herself on a rock, Sophie bowed forward as Julius had bowed down to receive her father's lash: and so she received her lover's body, which she had thought never to feel again. She gave a shrill cry of exultation when he entered her, a cry that was instantly mimicked by a bird somewhere above their heads in the canopy. She wondered how many hidden creatures were watching and hoped they were, witnesses to a tender ceremony they would all understand.

Afterwards they washed. She lifted up her face and laughed as the water pummelled her; she laughed and choked and spluttered. She felt Julius's hands combing through her hair, sliding over her shoulders, gently stroking her breasts clean. It seemed to her that he washed off her fear and sufferings, and as she stroked his head she wished that this ceremony could cleanse him of the filth of slavery for ever, not just his scarred body, but his soul also, though she knew that such a wrong could never be washed away.

His hair was stiff and crisp even under the torrent. She drew his face down for a quiet kiss: all tenderness, no urgency, a blessing. His breath was still sweet, like a creature of the forest canopy who slept among the leaves and clouds, ate only seeds and fruit, and never touched the ground where things died and rotted.

She left the pool, squeezed the water out of her dress and then was suddenly caught by the sight of him under the waterfall, still washing himself, quietly now, self-absorbed, his penis hanging slack as he massaged his thighs and loins. She had never seen him at ease before. There would be many moments like this, she supposed, when he turned away from her to give his attention to something else. She must not mind too much, or she would become a slave herself.

*

Up at Belmont, Charles Craig was woken by a smell. It was violent in his nostrils. Smoke! He leapt up and ran downstairs, naked, and out on to the verandah. Belmont, the estate, the outbuildings were all safe and quiet, slumbering in the heavy tropical night. The smell of smoke was everywhere, though. A dog barked from one of the distant slave huts.

As his eyes adjusted to the darkness, he realised that the smoke was blowing up from Mount Grace. He could hear nothing, see no flames, not even a glow. But his heart hammered with anxiety. He ran back indoors and pulled his clothes on, fumbling with buttons and laces, his mind reeling. Once dressed, he pulled on his boots, armed himself with a pair of pistols and plunged off down the track.

Half-way down, his haste made him slip, tumble and crack his head against a tree-trunk. A brief faintness forced him to sit still for a few minutes, quite against his desperate urge to find Sophie, make sure she was safe.

'Damn it! Damn it!' he muttered, massaging his tender skull. Then for a second he looked up at the stars. 'What game are you playing?' he cried, furious with the gods. 'There are worse sinners than me to be punished, sleeping sound tonight.'

But perhaps the gods had some final resolution in mind, he thought, standing up and waiting for his head to clear. He had bloodied both legs, tearing the knees out of his breeches. The wounds bled and stung, but nothing seemed broken. Perhaps the fall was just a warning. More haste, less speed. That had certainly been true of his courtship. Only when he had stopped trying altogether had he discovered he had endeared himself to her.

And now? Who knows what was happening down there. Last night she must have had his letter, offering to take her away. She knew he longed to rescue her, come what may. He resumed his anxious descent, holding on to trees and branches as he went. The path was slippery. It must have rained while he slept. A branch broke; he slipped again, landing this time on his buttocks. Absurd, ludicrous, comical. The gods were laughing at him. Climbing back to his feet again, he paused for a moment. He was quite close to Mount Grace now. He could hear voices, people running about. Something had happened.

Looking down through the trees, he could see a strange oblong glow. The smell of burnt sugar filled the air, but more than that: wood, metal, perhaps even animals had perished. Perhaps even – but he would not dare to think it. And now he could see the roof of Mount Grace. The great house still stood. He murmured a prayer of thanks and stepped out of the forest.

It was plain that the mill yard had almost burnt down. The glowing oblong he had seen from above was the remains of the boiling-house. The rafters had collapsed in, dragging the upper parts of the walls with them, but the rain had evidently dampened down the conflagration and now only embers remained. But he did not have time to inspect the damage. A figure danced towards him: a thin young man he recognised as Lucas, the blacksmith's assistant. He was holding a bottle, twirling round and round in the moonlight, laughing and shouting.

'Hey Massa Charles!' he cried. 'Good marnin' – sah!' His greeting had a satirical emphasis which Craig ignored.

'What's happened down here?' he demanded. Lucas's high spirits were muted slightly by the sight of Craig's pistols.

'It de slaves!' cried Lucas. 'We people hab ris' – like in St Domingue – we goin' to be free! All de overseers run away! Massa nat goin' to flog me no more! Julius hab kill him, burn de place down, buckra all gone, all dead.'

'All dead – what, Miss Sophie and her mother?' Craig caught at the man's arm and in his anguish almost broke it.

'Dead, gone, I don' know. Garamighty! Don't break me bone!'

Craig hurled Lucas away and ran towards the house. The door was open. He hesitated for a moment, made his pistol ready and sped up the verandah steps. No sentries were posted – he stepped inside. No sound. A candle burning in a hurricane glass in the hall. The door to Sophie's room was closed.

Suddenly he heard a wail. It came from the Massa's bedchamber. A female voice: a cry of grief. It came again. He knocked, his heart hammering. Was it Sophie? There was no reply, only the wailing. He pushed the door open.

The body of Frederick Wetherby lay on the bed before him, stark naked. Two black women were washing it and another sat beside the corpse wailing and ululating. At the sight of Craig, they paused.

'Miss Sophie!' he whispered. 'Is she here?'

One of the women pointed behind him. 'Sleepin',' she said.

Craig went out, and paused for a moment outside Sophie's door. He had never been inside her room, never seen it, but often tried, in vain, to imagine it.

'Sophie!' he called softly, and knocked. 'Sophie! It's Charles!' There was a soft rustle within, and a sleepy summons.

Charles opened the door. All was dark. The bed was not where he had expected it to be. But there was a movement within the mosquito nets.

'Sophie!' he whispered urgently. 'Are you all right?'

A strange sound came from behind the nets: a high-pitched squeal that broke into grunting laughter. His blood froze. Had Sophie been transformed somehow into a monster? Was he still dreaming? The mosquito net twitched. He dared not move, or speak any more. He kept his pistol levelled at the bed, though his hand was shaking so much he could hardly hold the gun.

The curtains were thrust aside and a black face looked out. Craig jerked in astonishment.

'Massa Charles Craig!' came a voice, a little croaky with sleep, but jaunty and immediately recognisable.

'Mimba!' Craig had known Mimba well. For years before Isabella Wetherby had joined her husband on Sabato, Mimba had played hostess at Mount Grace. 'What's happened? Where is Sophie? Is her mother dead?'

'Massa only die.' Mimba yawned. 'Missus and Massa George, they gone along Good Hope in de cart. They goin' home to Englan' in de marnin'.'

'Lucas told me they were all dead.'

'Lucas talk kackaw,' snorted Mimba, rubbing her face. 'Fire start, Massa die, him heart stop when he see de fire. Missus and George run away, them gone to Good Hope.'

'But what about Sophie?'

'She's a'right,' grinned Mimba, jerking her head to the left. 'Try nex' door.'

Craig withdrew. Sophie must be in George's room then. He wondered why Mimba was occupying Sophie's little bed.

Knowing that Sophie was still alive did not calm him. It only intensified his longing to hold her in his arms, to assure her she was safe, to rescue her, carry her up to Belmont and cherish her there for ever. Perhaps this scare would have convinced her that only he could keep her safe. He shook his head for a moment. The fall and the blow had left him disorientated. This was the right door though, and Sophie was behind it. Forgetting his manners in his desperate longing to see her he entered, and saw Sophie and a black man, embracing on George's big bed.

Craig's head almost burst. The black man turned, indignant at the interruption. It was Julius. Sophie sat up, naked; he saw her naked at last, and her breasts were like two great eyes, staring in alarm at him.

'What! Charles!' she cried.

'He's goin' to shoot me,' growled Julius. 'Go on! Shoot! I know you want to kill me, long time. I know you want her. Well, I been her man for two whole hours, that too much happiness for a slave, so shoot!' He spread his arms wide, like a crucifixion. In the still moment, Craig's gun trembled in his hand. He was horribly hypnotised by the invitation. Every word Julius said was true. He could shoot him now, with perfect justification, and satisfy the jealousy that gnawed his heart.

'Of course he won't shoot,' said Sophie calmly, drawing the bedcovers up around her with peculiar dignity. 'Charles is a generous man. He will be happy for us. Julius is not my brother after all, Charles. We are to be married as soon as we can get a priest. You must congratulate us.'

Charles Craig let his gun fall to his side. Julius stared. Sophie smiled.

'You are pleased for us, aren't you?' she whispered.

He hung his head, ashamed of her praise, knowing how close he had come to an act of brutality. Beside the door was a small table. Some needlework, a sampler of hers, was set aside there. Gently he laid his gun down beside it, then looked up.

'I wish you joy,' he murmured. 'But – are you sure you're safe?' Part of him still yearned to save her, to do something.

'Oh, quite safe, thank you, Charles. There is no rebellion here. The fire was an accident. Tomorrow we shall start to rebuild the works.' Her face seemed full of mysterious light.

'You look different,' he puzzled.

A shimmering smile broke across her face. He had wished her joy; this, alone of all his wishes, had been granted. He understood, bowed and withdrew.

44

A Blessing

Charles Craig accepted at last that he could not have her. This brought an unexpected sense of relief. His instincts had warned him from the first and in some remote part of his mind he was prepared for rejection. But his magnanimity, once aroused, proved enduring, and beyond the pain of losing her there was a curious pleasure in being generous, quite against the grain of his education and his experience as a planter.

Sophie soon had further need of his help. She married Julius in a Baptist ceremony at Good Hope, at which Craig attended her, and through his eloquent advocacy Mrs Dodds and Miss Hambledon were persuaded to accept the shocking truth that Sophie had lost her heart not to the dashing Craig, but to a slave. Julius's dignity and grace upon the occasion impressed the sisters deeply; their ideas were far less conventional than any of the other planters' on Sabato and Sophie rejoiced to have such neighbours.

Afterwards, she had intended to be mistress of Mount Grace with Julius at her side: to give her slaves their three days, if not free them altogether. Charles Craig was endeavouring to explain the dangers of such a course, when George returned from Barbados and Sophie's aspirations for the estate were immediately crushed.

Having seen his mother safely embarked for England, he came back to claim his inheritance, to discard his sister for her impurity and revile her for her presumption. The estate was his in law – she, as a woman, was nothing; Julius, even less. Strenuous argument on the part of Charles Craig, however, mitigated the worst of George's fury and he was persuaded to settle a meagre sum on his sister, and to accept the manumission of Julius, Mimba and Flora.

As a free man, Julius could get a living with his skill, and together with Sophie's small annuity they were confident of being able to support themselves in the world. But where to live was the first question. George had taken possession of Mount Grace and his hostility would have driven them forth, if the memory of his vices and cruelties and the threat of worse to come had not already made the place unpleasing to his sister.

Just at this time there was sad and unexpected news from Good Hope. Miss Hambledon had died of a fever and Mrs Dodds, suddenly alone and hearing how things stood at Mount Grace, invited Sophie and Julius to live with her in the ramshackle old house on the beach. Sophie was grateful and delighted. It was the very thing she would have wished for, and Julius's misgivings were soon dispelled by the excellent old lady, who was always careful not to intrude on their privacy, but ever ready to be of service. She proved a great solace to Sophie during and after her confinement.

The baby was a healthy boy. They named him Harry and he was doted on by a brace of grandmothers, for Mrs Dodds and Mimba were forever contending who should rock the cradle. Mimba settled nearby with Flora, who soon married a fisherman, produced her own baby and seemed slowly to learn from her infant how to smile.

Having seen Sophie safely delivered and happily, if precariously established, Charles Craig decided to take his leave. The following year saw the American Declaration of Independence. Tempted by the opportunities of a new country, he went to Virginia, found a wife and devoted his energies to education. He sold his estate at Belmont to Alexander Ashton, who, growing wealthier all the time, became a kind of monarch of the north-western side of Sabato, absorbing into his empire the smaller neighbouring estates as they faltered and failed.

The restoration of Mount Grace proved too great a challenge for George. The removal of his parents' influence paved the way for a wholesale decline into debauchery. He neglected everything and, tiring at last of the responsibilities of estate management, decamped to Havana, where he captivated a pock-marked Cuban heiress and devoted the rest of his days to dissipating her fortune.

The land at Mount Grace duly fell into Ashton's grasp and the great house, though at first used by a manager, eventually fell into decay. The forest pulled it down: within ten years nothing remained

357

of Mount Grace but a few charred walls and the great water-wheel rusting among the undergrowth. Sophie was not sad to witness this disintegration of her former home. Understanding the barbarism which had been its foundation, she wished the forest to obliterate it for ever.

Sophie was grateful that she had been able to detach herself from the business of slavery and begin a new life in what seemed to her almost like a new world. Her annuity, though small, disturbed her, for it was derived from the system she so abhorred, but as Julius's work flourished, she was able to use her own income to improve the school at Good Hope, where in the intervals between her six babies she joyfully presided.

When, after five years or so, Mrs Dodds died, Sophie received a visitor who turned all her grief into joy. Aunt Sarah had waited only to persuade her sister to forgive Sophie, and though the idea of a black son-in-law was at first repugnant and terrifying to Isabella, Sarah's arguments were so formidable, and Isabella's temper so volatile and tender, that eventually the desired tolerance was achieved.

By the time of Sophie's second confinement, Isabella awaited news of her new half-caste grandchild with all the impatience of a fond grandmother. She was, however, grateful that Sophie's unusual domestic establishment remained on Sabato and was therefore, from an English point of view, invisible. By the time of Sophie's third confinement, Isabella had remarried, finding a second, more devoted husband in a local gentleman farmer – a match much urged by her sister Sarah, who now felt free to take up her niece's oft-repeated invitation to join them at Good Hope.

Active in mind and body, burning with energy and still not forty-five, Sarah Sullivan considered she had much to contribute both to Sophie's household and to her school. The family gained a loving and resourceful member; the school, a vivid and captivating teacher, and Sarah, living to the astonishing age of eighty-nine, at last in 1838 saw the loathsome state of slavery abolished and died a happy woman.

Though the elegant mansion at Mount Grace disintegrated, the ramshackle old house on the shore at Good Hope survived, as carpenters' houses generally do. Even the occasional hurricane seemed to leave no more than slight damage. Lying below a hill on the leeward side of the island, it was sheltered from the blustering Atlantic gales, and the people of Sabato often observed that when the Lord sent a storm, the free fishermen of Good Hope were spared, whilst the elements tore furiously into the great houses of the planters, confounding their detestable luxury.

Mrs Dodds had left the house at Good Hope to Sophie and Julius, with the acquiescence of her distant heirs, who were too busily engaged in their lives to trouble about their mother's few possessions. Apart from repairing and improving the house, Julius became an accomplished cabinet maker. His furniture, in Jamaican satinwood and Honduras mahogany, was highly prized not only on Sabato but on the neighbouring islands. He loved to decorate his work with carved friezes of breadfruit and acorns, to celebrate his marriage, the union of the Old World with the New. One such piece, a six-drawer mahogany press, can still be seen today, at Sunbury Plantation house, on Barbados.

Though her brother never ceased to think of her and refer to her as a fallen woman, to Sophie it seemed that she had not fallen from grace but flown up out of hell into a dazzling place, where their lives had been miraculously preserved and their happiness had taken root and grown riotously, like some voluptuous tropical vine. Behind her house, the mountains of Sabato were almost always veiled in mist. Every day she looked up at them in admiration, but she knew now that she would never be able to climb up there, or write her Natural History of the place. Too many duties required her attention at Good Hope. But she met the chores of her relative poverty with cheerfulness, refreshed and sustained by the love of her husband, children and aunt.

Theirs was an establishment on the fringes of society, however: a disgrace in the eyes of the white planter class, but also, Sophie sensed, unpleasing to the slaves. Only the few free blacks and halfbreeds who gathered at Good Hope seemed to offer her the acceptance she craved, forgiving her her white skin as they recognised her courage and good nature. The outcasts shared the freedom which she and Julius had claimed, and compared to this delectable quality all sense of dispossession vanished.

Besides, Sophie could not feel that her own culture at least could offer many benefits worth having. The more she learned of life, the more she was dismayed at the organised savagery of much of human society, especially that part which prided itself most on its elegance and refinement. But watching the fishermen drawing in their nets in the pearly morning light, with pelicans crashing into the waves and a dusky babe at her breast, it seemed to Sophie that she had been especially blessed to pass her days in a place as near to paradise as it was possible to find on earth.